ECHO OF DECEIT

Echo Series
Book 2

SOPHIA ST. GERMAIN

ISBN: PB: 978-91-531-0557-2, HB: 978-91-531-0558-9, eBook: 9789153105558

*To anyone who's ever been
told to stay grounded — keep flying.*

Kian

He couldn't stop looking at her.

As Lillian slowly approached him with eyes locked on his, a shudder skittered down his spine.

She was the most beautiful creature he'd ever seen.

He'd thought so even before, but with the long black hair, steely gray eyes, and glittering dark wings, she was magnificent.

Terrifying but magnificent.

Lillian placed a hand on his chest, and a jolt shot through him.

From the moment he'd seen her in that market, he'd suspected he was her mate. His heart had almost stopped when she'd stormed through the crowd, white hair billowing behind her and eyes narrowed on his father's sentries.

Since that day, he hadn't been able to stop thinking about the wild woman with the wicked temper, who, without hesitation, would risk her life for what she believed in.

He'd wanted to push her away, had wanted her to leave the trials, get her out of his mind. But he hadn't been able to stay away. Not when he could feel every emotion flowing through her, the determination and desperation, and the unwavering belief that she could make Orios a better place.

He didn't deserve her.

But he would spend the rest of his life trying to become worthy.

"Please don't kill me for interrupting whatever is happening, but we have company."

Finn spoke behind Lillian, but Kian couldn't tear his eyes from his mate. When she whirled around and snarled at Finn, a shocked laugh escaped him.

For her to be so protective of him when she'd only yesterday broken—*shattered*—his heart made his soul sing.

Kian knew when he told her how he felt that she'd turn him down, but he hadn't been able to squash the small hope that she'd see—see the bond between them.

Still, he hadn't told her what he suspected when she asked how he could find her when she was in danger, how he sensed it. He'd thought about it, but he didn't want to make the choice harder for her, use the bond to sway her from Eli.

As memories of their conversation in the cave flashed through Kian's mind, the warmth in his chest turned ice-cold. What Eli had done—what he'd forced Lillian to do...

Kian tensed, his hands clenching. He couldn't believe she was still standing. Shock was perhaps masking it now, but Lillian had loved Eli deeply.

How would she recover from that? Recover from killing the man that she'd loved?

Deep in thought Kian barely noticed the three winged women approaching them. Only when they dropped to their knees before Lillian, their black wings flaring behind them, did he avert his gaze from his mate.

"We've been looking for you, Your Majesty." The dark-haired Valkyrie was still bowing in the sand, her eyes locked on Lillian as she spoke.

The two blonds' eyes darted between himself, Finn, and Sam. Apprehension whispered over his skin at their narrowed gaze and sharp eyes, and Kian's hands twitched toward his sword.

He glanced at Lillian. She stood unnaturally still, staring at the three Valkyries with her mouth hanging slightly open.

His eyes followed her parted lips, how her bottom lip trembled slightly as she drew a breath, and a deep ache, a near blinding need, filled him.

He'd been so close to kissing her in that cave. Would have if she hadn't pushed him away.

Agony tore through his chest at the memory. Her rejection had twisted through his heart like a knife—had hurt more than anything he'd ever felt in his twenty-six years. Worse even than when he'd found his mother lifeless on the floor, his father sitting in a chair swirling a glass of liquor beside her.

The thought of his father was enough to break Kian's trance. Clearing his mind, he shifted his gaze to Finn, who grinned at the blond Valkyrie twins from his spot next to Lillian.

Kian shook his head; nothing would stop Finn from flirting, not even the threat that hung heavy in the air as the twins surveyed their group with their hostile blue eyes.

As if he heard him, Finn winked at him, then turned to face Lillian, and from the way she met Finn's eyes, he guessed a silent exchange passed between them.

"Please stand." Lillian's voice was strong, as if breaking the curse had somehow made every part of her stronger.

The power that radiated off her vibrated across his skin, his own magic humming along to the darkness that had twirled around her wrists back on the Skandi.

The Valkyries rose as one, standing tall, their wings casting long shadows on the beach behind them and the golden bands over their brows glinting in the moonlight.

"How did you find us, Majesty?" The brunette spoke again, her gaze leaving Lillian to sweep over the group.

When Kian met her stare, her eyes widened slightly before she snapped them to the twins.

Lillian turned to him, and another jolt slammed into him, nearly leaving him breathless as their eyes collided. He had to stop himself from stepping forward, rifting her somewhere they could be alone. He needed to speak to her, needed to feel her touch again. Needed to know what was going on in that beautiful mind of hers.

Lillian's eyes flared as if she was thinking the same thing, but when Finn cleared his throat beside her and raised a brow, Kian blinked, forcing his mind out of the daze.

He was the one who had gambled when he rifted them here from Echo and hoped that the old man on Hindra, who claimed that the Valkyries were living on Seigard, one of the forgotten islands in the Eastern Sea, was indeed not just another drunk.

His gaze remained locked on Lillian as he said quietly, "I met a pirate in a port on Hindra who mentioned that he had seen ravens flying east over the sea. He claimed the Valkyries were hiding in the forgotten islands, that ships avoided this area because of the large shadows that flew over them when they sailed by."

A clang of metal had him rip his eyes from Lillian's. The Valkyries all drew their swords, baring their sharp teeth. Kian unsheathed his own, his guard instincts taking over, keeping his pulse steady as he flitted his eyes between the three of them, waiting to see who would charge first.

"This is a trap." The brunette glared at Lillian while the other two watched Kian with glacial eyes. "He's the Crown Prince. Alek must have found out where we are, using you to draw us out."

Darkness surrounded them, blocking the cliffs ahead and silencing the crashing waves behind. Only because he could still taste the salt on the wind softly breezing through Lillian's magic did Kian know the world around them still existed.

Blinking, he tried to make his eyes adjust, but he couldn't even make out the sword in his hand. He forced himself to stand still, ears trained, not sure how much control Lillian had over her newfound power.

Lillian let out a low snarl, "Drop your swords right now. Or I will kill you without another thought. I don't care who or what you are, I won't hesitate."

Her voice dripped with ice, and the authority in it made the magic in his veins purr. Despite everything, a smile played on his lips.

Lillian would get used to this queen business quickly.

"As you wish, Majesty."

The shadows slowly slipped away. When Kian could see again, Lillian still had darkness swirling around her hands, unyielding as the night sky hovering above the beach, ready as she glared at the women. Her eyes were nearly black, shadows flickering behind the gray as if her entire being was filled with it.

She took a step forward, placing herself between him and the three Valkyries. "Prince Kian brought us here as the king was about to attack us." Lillian's voice was still commanding, a low growl rumbling in her chest. "You will not hurt him or the other men here."

Kian sliced his gaze to Finn, who met his eyes with a tight smile, and then to Sam, who studied the Valkyries with a tilted head.

The Valkyrie nodded. "I think it is foolish to trust him, Majesty. But we will not harm him without your permission."

Even as the brunette spoke, the twins still held on to their swords, so Kian kept his own readied as well, tightening his grip on its hilt.

Lillian hissed softly, "Foolish would be to trust the women I've just met. It seems you know who I am and who Kian is. But you haven't told us your names or who you are."

The dark-haired Valkyrie bowed her head. "I apologize, Your Majesty. I'm Madick, and this is Else and Elya."

The twins waved, their postures loosening slightly as they finally sheathed their swords.

Reaching out a hand, Madick took a step back. "We have been looking for you for so long that we forgot our manners. Please follow us. We'll take you to the castle so you can meet the Elders."

A small wrinkle formed over Lillian's brow, but she nodded. "You lead the way."

When the Valkyries turned toward the dark cliffs, Lillian stepped up behind them, casting a glance at Kian, and the ground beneath him seemed to pulse with each beat of his heart when she offered him a small smile.

She was so beautiful, even bloodied and dirty from the final trial.

As he smiled back at her, trailing his eyes over her midnight hair and those dark eyes, a pang of pain shot through his heart. He'd thought that first smile she offered him, when the sword glinted over her neck, would be the last one he'd ever see grace her face.

Kian shifted as cold rage danced across his skin at the memory, more chilling than the sea breeze sifting through his uniform, and he promised himself he'd spend every day for the rest of his life making sure Lillian smiled more often.

But her smile fell when her hands brushed her thighs, where her daggers usually were sheathed, and raw pain flashed across her face as she tore her eyes away and fixed them on the cliffs before them.

He'd always been able to read her so easily. Kian wasn't sure if it was the mating bond, but he could see the red-hot agony in her hunched shoulders, even in her gait, as she followed the Valkyries up a narrow path weaving its way between towering black rocks. It broke his heart to see her head dipping forward, her once so assured steps hesitant in the sand.

At only eighteen, she was too young to shoulder the burden her father and Eli had placed on her—and the weight she'd have to carry as she embraced her destiny.

But she wasn't alone, and he'd carry as much of it as she let him.

The beach he'd spoken about in that cave felt long gone.

He'd follow this woman wherever she would go. Even shadows and death would not pry him from her side.

Finn stepped up behind her, hand on his sword. A set jaw replaced his usual mischievous smile, and hardness lined his eyes.

Glancing over his shoulder toward the wild eastern sea and the moon that hung above it, its reflection playing in the crashing waves, Kian prayed he'd made the right decision in bringing her here.

Then he fell in step next to Finn as Sam took up the flank.

$$\rule{3cm}{0.4pt}$$

2

Lillian

Kian's eyes burned into her back when they walked through the narrow passage between two rocky cliffs. The smell of saltwater faded as they reached a dense forest, the moonlight streaming through the tall trees casting silvery shadows on the mossy ground. Lillian took a deep breath, allowing the night around her to dull the heightened emotions brimming under her skin, easing the darkness threatening to consume her.

She'd lost control back on the beach.

When the Valkyries threatened Kian, darkness ripped from her without her calling it forth. Lillian swallowed—it had been the same way on the mountain, where she'd killed those two men without a second thought.

She made herself draw shaky breaths as cold dread roiled in her gut. For a second, she hadn't been sure if she'd killed them all, but then she'd sensed Kian and Finn through their bonds. Turning her head, she stole a glance at Kian, noting his narrowed eyes and the scowl that overtook his features when his eyes snapped between her and the Valkyries leading them.

It was strange how different the mating bond felt. Her bond with Finn was easy, a low humming in the back of her mind. With Kian, it was like fire burning under her skin, a need to be close—to feel him. The sensation was so strong it made it difficult to breathe. She yearned to touch him again. Needed to speak to him alone.

Had he known she was his mate when she'd turned him down?

A crushing weight settled on her chest as she remembered their conversation in the cave. Kian had begged her to choose him, had stood on his knees with hope burning in his eyes. And while deep down, in the dark place inside her, she'd known there was something connecting them, she'd chosen Eli.

Lillian clutched at her chest when Eli's desperate face flashed in front of her eyes.

He'd never loved her, at least not in the way she'd loved him, but he'd still sacrificed his life for hers.

She'd been a mission.

His final mission.

A sob lodged in her throat, and she wrapped her arms around herself.

She was the reason her father and Eli were dead.

Lillian, we've got you. You are all right. Breathe, silver girl.

Glancing over her shoulder, she caught Finn's worried gaze.

Lillian drew a trembling breath.

Once she was alone, she could break apart—could submit to the pain—but she needed to make sure her friends were safe first. Straightening her shoulders, Lillian forced air down her lungs and focused her eyes on the Valkyries before her, leading the way through the dark forest.

One of the blond twins—Lillian thought she might be the one called Elya—slowed her steps and curiously studied her, her head cocked to the side while her black wings carelessly moved with the wind.

Lillian narrowed her eyes, but Elya only winked and continued staring.

She was about to snarl at the blonde when the world went dark, a shadow blocking the moon.

Whipping her head up, she sucked in a breath.

It was too big to be a raven, its wings spanning over forty yards. A shriek pierced the air as it dove, then spread its massive wings and flew out over the sea, and Lillian gasped when she met familiar icy-blue eyes just before the shape disappeared over the dark cliffs.

"*Dragon*," Finn whispered in awe.

"They fly over here sometimes." Elya still stared at Lillian, her blue eyes piercing as if they saw through Lillian's very soul. "They aren't loyal to us anymore, but they like to keep track of our movements."

"Elya!" Madick hissed at the blond Valkyrie.

"What?" Elya glared at her. "It's true. But maybe now that our queen has come back, the dragons will too. I never got the chance to bond with one, and I should like to."

Madick's hand lashed out, and she slapped Elya so fast that Lillian almost didn't catch it. Tears welled in the blonde's eyes, and without another word, she spread her wings and took off through the trees. After throwing Madick a murderous stare, her twin followed, the wind from her wings whipping Lillian's black hair around her face.

"Why aren't they loyal to you anymore?" Lillian bit her cheek to stop herself from snarling at Madick.

She knew Valkyries were ruthless, but the slap hadn't been to hurt Elya, only to humiliate her.

It made her feel sick.

"It doesn't matter." Shaking her head, Madick spun around. "We're almost there."

She gestured ahead through the thinning tree line, where soft, flickering light broke through the cloak of darkness.

Lillian opened her mouth to argue, but upon glancing in the direction Madick pointed, she snapped it shut.

A massive castle made of shiny black stone appeared

before them. It was embedded far up into the side of a mountain, the night sky caressing its walls.

Hundreds of Valkyries flew around the many tall towers, the light from the lanterns lining the impossibly high walls reflecting in their black wings.

When wonder flowed through the bonds, she turned her head to her friends. They'd all stopped in their tracks, their heads tilted up to stare at the beautiful but intimidating castle.

Warmth trailed over her face, and her cheeks heated when she met Kian's green eyes, and a smile lit up his face. A smile slowly spread across her own face and she quickly turned around before she did something stupid.

Like, throw herself at him right here.

But the heat spread through her body, and images of Kian's tattooed chest from the day at the lake filled her mind. She sucked in a breath; his swirling tattoos were twin to the shadows that now lurked under her skin. Dark plumes that danced across his broad, muscular chest.

It wasn't until Finn loudly cleared his throat that she snapped out of it.

His laugh echoed through the trees when she glared at him.

We need to figure out a way for you to keep those thoughts to yourself. You're making me hot for Kian. And while I am not opposed to men, I don't expect you would like to share.

Her blush deepened, and she shifted her eyes to Kian, who tilted his head as he studied them. Lillian thought her face might melt right off when he raised a questioning brow. Shaking her head, she quickly turned back to the castle.

"Welcome to Volantis." Madick offered them a tight smile. "As you can see, it's not possible to enter from the ground, so you'll need to fly up. I can carry one of the men."

Lillian stared at her blankly. She could barely walk with the wings, and this woman expected her to *fly*?

Madick eyed her when she noticed her hesitation. "It will come naturally. Feel the wings and how they're connected to

your mind. You're in control. They're part of you, Majesty."
She slowly approached her. "May I touch them?"

Lillian furrowed her brow but nodded.

"Our wings are sensitive, as you'll find out." Madick's face softened—becoming beautiful as the hardness drained from her features. "We don't touch another Valkyrie's wings without permission. And that goes for humans, too." She threw a pointed glare at Kian.

When she reached out and cautiously stroked her wings, Lillian shuddered as the newborn nerves in her back responded to Madick's touch.

"Feel them here." She placed her hand in the middle of Lillian's back. "They're an extension of you. Like your arms, you can reach out with them."

Lillian tried to feel them, stumbling as they unfolded.

"Good," Madick nodded. "Now, close your eyes. Let go of your thoughts. Just feel the wind and let your wings react to it. They'll know what to do."

Lillian huffed a shocked laugh when her wings whipped the air, lifting her a few inches from the mossy ground. The wind wrapped around her body, taking her higher, and she smiled at the new sensation.

Glancing down, she found Kian watching her with dark eyes and a proud smile playing on his lips. Her body reacted instantly, heat burning through her limbs causing her wings to flare, and she tumbled down, landing on her side with a soft thud.

Wincing, Lillian got to her feet, smacking Finn who shook from laughter. But she couldn't help a small giggle escaping her own lips.

That hadn't been very graceful.

Madick frowned as her eyes flitted between them. "It's supposed to be easy. We learn when we're only three."

Lillian's smile fell, her shoulders hunching at the Valkyrie's disappointment.

"Don't you dare speak to my queen that way."

Kian stalked up to Madick, his face inches from hers as he snarled, "Apologize right now. Or I will make you do it. And I promise you, I'll enjoy every single moment of it."

There was nothing gentle in the hard lines of his face, nothing but ruthlessness in his eyes and in the slight curl of his lip as he stared the Valkyrie down.

Madick's hand twitched toward her sword, but after meeting Lillian's narrowed gaze, she clenched her hand. "I'm sorry, Majesty," she mumbled.

"I'll rift myself, Lillian, and Sam up. Tell me where to go." Kian's voice remained cold as he continued to glare at Madick, not backing down an inch.

Nodding slowly, Madick instructed him to rift them to the left tower, then spread her wings and took off, shooting for the balcony jutting out from it.

Finn shifted into his golden-brown owl, and with a soft hoot, he followed her into the air.

When Kian gently gripped her hand to rift them, a current danced over her skin, and Lillian couldn't stop herself from leaning into his broad chest. Wrapping his arm around her, Kian released a soft breath before he rifted them away.

____

3

Finn

____

Volantis was incredible.

Spreading his wings, Finn let the wind carry him up to the tall towers. Peering into the softly lit windows that lined the walls and studying the many balconies jutting out over the forest, a sense of wonder washed over him.

Elya and Else circled the left tower, their large wings casting long shadows on the polished stone walls. Finn soared on the wind until he flew next to them, letting one of his wings playfully graze Elya's as he passed her.

When she hissed, he winked with an amber eye and carefully steered toward a large balcony, where light from open glass doors spilled onto the shiny stone.

Swiftly shifting, Finn leaned against the railing and took a deep breath of salty air while gazing at the vast ocean that lay in the distance beyond the forest.

The twins landed gracefully next to him, and without missing a beat, Elya glared at him and hissed, "We typically wear clothes in Volantis, shifter."

Finn threw his head back and laughed. "Does my body fluster you?"

He couldn't stop himself from wiggling his brows when a

hint of red tinted Elya's cheeks. "I guess you do spend a significant time around only women."

Elya stepped forward, a sneer twisting her features, but Else grabbed her arm. "Leave it, sister," she whispered.

Finn eyed them curiously.

Elya seemed like fun. He was already getting under her skin.

The other one kept her distance though, her body tense as she hovered beside her sister. As her gaze cautiously met his, he offered her a coy smile.

Else quickly averted her eyes, a hint of a blush creeping up her slender neck and headed through the two large glass doors at a near sprint.

When she returned a few moments later, she threw him a purple robe.

Laughing, Finn slipped his arms into it.

This was going to be great.

Beautiful, strong women with wings?

Finn's grin widened. This was going to be more than great.

Kian appeared before he could offer the twins another suggestive comment, and Finn snapped his attention to the green-looking Lillian and Sam who stumbled as Kian let go of their arms.

Finn winced when Lillian ran to the balcony railing to empty her stomach over it, and he quickly made his way over to shift her long, dark hair out of the way.

As she continued retching, he stared at the black strands in his hands.

She still looked like Lillian, like the friend he loved. But she also didn't. She was still small, with that wicked temper he thoroughly enjoyed, but the darkness now cloaking her wasn't just in her hair.

When Lillian gratefully glanced at him as she wiped her mouth with her sleeve, shadows danced behind her eyes.

Squeezing his best friend's hand, he promised himself that he'd be there to see them light up again.

Turning around, he swept his gaze over the group.

Kian's eyes were fixed on Lillian as she stepped back from the railing, trailing with her when she approached Madick as the Valkyrie landed. Kian's entire body curled and turned toward Lillian, inching closer when she hesitantly came to a halt before the dark-haired Valkyrie.

Another grin spread across Finn's face.

He couldn't wait to see what would happen once those two finally got together.

"The Elders—our leaders—are in a meeting. We will show you to your rooms, and they will get you once they're done." Madick offered. "You must be tired, so I'd suggest using the time to rest."

Finn frowned. Their queen had just returned, and the Elders were *too busy?*

Kian also studied Madick with narrowed eyes. Stepping closer to Lillian, Kian brushed his fingers against hers, eliciting a shiver not visible to anyone but that vibrated along the bond Finn shared with Lillian.

Lillian only nodded, and when a wave of despair rolled down their bond, his heart clenched.

She needed to be alone. Mourn the boy she loved, even if he had deceived her so viciously.

Finn balled his fists. He couldn't believe Eli had made her choose between them—how he had fooled them all.

But a part of him also hurt for the young man.

If he'd been in Eli's place, he might have made the same decision.

4

Lillian

Madick showed them all to individual rooms in a softly lit corridor, with walls made from the same shiny dark stone as the castle itself.

Finn and Kian had initially protested, arguing they should stay together, or at least two and two, but Lillian convinced them it was fine. The rooms were next to each other; it wasn't like anyone could attack them without the others hearing.

Lillian softly closed the white-tinted door and sank to the floor with her back against it, not bothering to take in the details of the room she'd been given. Sensing Finn tense at the agony that flitted down the bond, she searched her mind, now so much clearer after the curse had been broken.

For the first time, she could see how the silver and golden twirls connected them, how it would always connect them, but that door she'd been able to open to let him in could also keep him out.

Cautiously nudging it shut, her mind became fully her own, her thoughts and feelings bouncing against the door but not through it. When she was certain she wouldn't force Finn with her into the deep pit of darkness that threatened to consume her, Lillian covered her face with her hands and wept, her sobs racking her body as she tried to stay silent.

Hot tears streamed down her cheeks and dripped onto her torn leathers as her mind replayed the moment she'd killed Eli, then viciously flashed to her father's apology as he was murdered before her eyes.

She slammed her hands against the wooden floor.

They were wrong.

She wasn't strong enough for this.

Her chest cracked wide open, and her lips parted in a silent cry when other memories surfaced, now tainted by the echo of their deceit.

How her father meticulously trained her but was so unwilling to let her join the rebellion. How Eli closed her off to all others, taking the place of her best friend and lover, assuring her that they were all each other needed.

They'd done it out of loyalty and love.

Deep down, she knew that, but it did nothing to soothe the pain from their sacrifices.

A soft knock interrupted her mourning, and Lillian shot to her feet.

Clearing her throat, she got out, "One moment."

She wiped furiously at her face with the sleeves of her dirty tunic before she called out with a hoarse voice, "Come in."

Kian slipped into the room, closing the door behind him before snapping his eyes to hers.

The sight of him nearly took her breath away.

Unlike her, he'd taken the time to bathe and change. Dressed in black trousers paired with a simple white tunic, snug to his muscular arms, and his thick black hair still damp, he was unfairly handsome.

Glancing at her own bloodied and dirty clothing, she sniffed the air cautiously.

Lillian winced at the coppery tang, the harsh stench of

sweat, and as Kian approached, she took a step back, closer to the floor-to-ceiling windows lining the back of the room.

When his face tightened, she mumbled, "I… I didn't have time to take a bath."

Kian rolled his eyes and closed the distance between them with three assured steps, pulling her into his strong arms, careful not to touch her wings as he held her tight against his chest. She couldn't help it—her body relaxed against his, moved with his chest as he blew out a deep breath.

"Lillian, there is nothing that will keep me away from you." His hands tangled in her hair as he gently pulled back to look into her eyes. "I don't care what you smell like or what state you're in. You're the most beautiful creature that has ever walked this realm. If you'll have me, I will be at your side forever, in this world and the next, and whatever else comes after that, regardless of what you *look* like."

A lump formed in her throat, and Lillian's voice shook when she asked, "Did you know?"

He brushed her cheek with his thumb, trailing his eyes across her face. "I suspected. I could sense when you were in danger. Could just think of you when I rifted, and I'd get to you. And I can't get you out of my head. Awake and asleep, you are the only thing on my mind."

She nodded slowly, listening to the strong heartbeat hammering against Kian's chest, her own falling into rhythm with the steady thumps.

"I know you're hurting, my beautiful queen. We can take this slow; give it as much time as you need. But I will never leave you, Lillian. If I had to choose between you and the whole world going to hell, I'd still choose you. I never had a purpose before, but I do now. *You* are my purpose, Lillian. It was always you."

She leaned into his warmth, wrapping her arms tight around him. The smell of forest at night filled her, settling over her like a calming blanket and forming a protective barrier around the broken pieces that were her body and her mind—perhaps the only thing holding her together at this point.

Lillian's head barely reached the top of his chest, but when she peeked at him through her lashes, his mesmerizing tattoos twirled right above the collar of the soft tunic. Using her fingers, she mindlessly trailed the swirling pattern.

They were so similar to her own darkness.

When she let them follow every curve, every beautiful arc and bend, Kian's breath hitched. He stood frozen, but his face was so close, bent down, the tip of their noses almost touching.

With a soft sigh, he closed the final distance, resting his forehead on her own, his eyes locked on hers. As his warm breaths blew strands of her hair out of her face, Lillian's heart thundered, heat crackling in her veins and a pull tugging at her gut.

Slowly, she trailed her fingers up, across his cheeks and lingering by his full lips.

A shudder rippled through him, an echo of it vibrating through Lillian's own body, and her fingers trembled as she stroked his dark brows and high cheekbones down toward his jaw.

Kian closed his eyes, a smile pulling at his lips. "If you keep doing that, I'll be breaking my promise of going slow in the next second."

"Kian." Lillian's voice was hoarse, and the trembling was no longer contained to her fingers but racking her entire body.

Her mind went blank, consumed by the desire flooding her veins.

His green eyes darkened as he opened them, and his grip on her hair tightened. A low moan escaped her when his fingers brushed her neck.

Kian laughed softly and the sound sent another wave of warmth through her.

Something snapped inside her then, and she saw the same resolve mirrored in Kian's blazing eyes.

They reached for each other, fingers digging into soft skin, desperate to get closer.

A loud tap on the window had them both freeze, and a snarl involuntarily left Lillian's throat.

Whirling around, Lillian bared her teeth at the two ravens perched on the small balcony outside her room, narrowing her eyes as the smaller one impatiently tapped its beak on the glass.

Stalking forward, she threw open the glass doors. "You two have the worst timing."

But she couldn't shake the small part of relief that settled in her stomach, a faint blush tinting her cheeks as she realized what she'd almost done.

She'd lost control again.

Perhaps in a more dangerous situation than that at the beach.

The ravens let out an amused caw. *Hello, Majesty.*

She stared at them, gaping.

Finally. The larger raven tilted its head. *It was ever so frustrating trying to communicate with you on that mountain. We thought you would go and die on us in that avalanche with your royal stubbornness.*

Kian moved to stand beside her, lacing his fingers with hers. The heat inside her burned hotter, her wings flaring at his touch, and she was careful not to let her gaze slip to his, determined to keep some ounce of control.

He eyed the ravens. "Are they speaking to you?"

"It seems so." Lillian shook her head. "Who are you?"

The smaller raven scoffed. *We're your guardians, of course. Do you know nothing of your heritage?*

Lillian shook her head again.

I'm Hanin, and this old brute is Munion.

Munion let out a gruff caw. *Hanin, manners, please. I apologize, Your Majesty. Hanin is young, but I promise she's had the best training. Your aunt oversaw it herself.*

Her eyes widened. "M-my aunt?" she stuttered, and Kian's grip on her hand tightened.

Oh dear, she doesn't even know of Grete. Hanin waved her wings impatiently.

Hanin! Munion shook his large head, his beak snapping at her. *Your Majesty, your aunt is on her way now. If I may offer a suggestion, I'd recommend you take a bath. You're to meet the entire Elder Council, and it might be prudent not to show up muddy and bloodied.*

Lillian stared at them while a million thoughts ran through her head.

She had an aunt?

All the Valkyrie leaders were coming here?

What would she even say to them?

Nerves, all too similar to those she'd felt during the trials, made the hair on the back of her neck stand. Only Kian's strong grip on her hand and the gentle squeeze of her fingers kept her anchored.

Finally, she nodded, even if her voice shook more than she liked. "Yes, you're right."

A bath would be nice if only to provide her with a bit of reprieve from receiving more information she hadn't been privy to. And if she were to meet all of the Elders, she needed to gather herself. Breathe to calm the tangling emotions inside —like her father and Eli always taught her.

The ravens cocked their heads before taking off.

See you at training tomorrow, Hanin shouted as she dove.

Lillian turned to Kian, and upon meeting his blazing gaze, pain stabbed at her chest—yet again making it difficult to breathe.

What had she been thinking, almost kissing him?

Eli's body wasn't even cold. It hadn't even been a full day since she… She swallowed, trying to squash the memory of his broken body in the snow.

But as his crazed eyes continued to flash in her mind, Lillian bit her cheek so hard copper filled her mouth and whispered, "I should take a bath. The Elders are supposedly arriving soon."

When Kian's eyes flitted between hers, she averted them

and walked toward the bathing chamber adjoining her room, where a huge tub already filled with water stood upon four golden legs.

"Will you find me later?" Kian asked as he walked toward the door.

Without turning around, Lillian nodded.

She continued staring at the bath until she heard the door close softly behind her, guilt swimming in her gut, sloshing like the water in the bath before her.

And even as she scrubbed every inch of her body, she couldn't shake the dirty feeling of shame that layered across her skin.

5

Lillian

Lillian studied the leathers she'd pulled from the small closet in her room. They were beautiful, soft, skin-tight, and adapted for her wings. Small golden wings adorned each shoulder, and they were lined with some type of material that withstood the chilling wind that blew into the room from the balcony doors she'd left open. She'd never seen anything like them and couldn't recall if it was what the Valkyries that escorted them here had been wearing.

Shrugging, she pulled them on.

It wasn't like she had any other clothes. Her satchel was still on the Skandi.

The thought of Eli's body, which she'd also left behind on the horrible mountain, made her chest constrict once more. But there were no tears left, even as her chest cracked with each beat of her heart at the thought of him.

As she drew a deep breath, there was a firm knock on the door, but before she even had a chance to respond it slammed open and a beautiful blond Valkyrie stalked inside, flanked by Madick and another Valkyrie. The two hovered closely behind the blonde as their sharp eyes swept across the room.

When a huge man tailed them through the door, Lillian's eyes widened.

The man had wings!

Flashing a row of perfect white teeth, he offered her a wave with one of his large hands as he leaned against the fireplace. He was beautiful—tall and blond, his features resembling the fair Valkyrie in the front—and he wore leathers identical to the ones Lillian was dressed in.

"Hello, Lillian." The blond female stepped forward without offering a handshake or other type of greeting, her piercing eyes only dragging slowly over Lillian's body and face. "My name is Grete. I am the leader of the Valkyries and of the Elder Council. I am also your mother's sister."

Lillian cleared her throat. "Hello."

She didn't know what else to say, but Grete clearly already knew who she was. Letting her own eyes sweep over the blonde's features, she wondered if this was what her mother had looked like. Sharp, lethal beauty, with an aura of authority that made Lillian want to take a step back.

"I wanted to welcome you to Volantis personally. I'm sure this is all overwhelming, and your ravens told me about the horrors on the Skandi, but we do hope you will soon feel at home here."

Nodding, Lillian glanced between Grete and the man who peeked over Grete's shoulder.

"This is Aaron." Grete waved her hand in the direction of the man. "He is a distant relative of yours. Well, all Valkyries are related, of course. I've asked him to take care of you and your company in the first weeks."

Lillian frowned. "But… but he is a man?"

"That I am." Aaron grinned at her, his blue eyes raking over her appreciatively. "It's very rare for the offspring between a Valkyrie and their mate to result in a male, but it does happen. I am the only one alive I know of, though."

Grete waved her hand again, impatiently this time. "Well, Lillian, I'm sure you must have many questions. I asked the

Elders to come to this wing instead of our usual meeting room. I heard you haven't mastered flying yet, although I'm sure you will quickly. I suggest we go meet them."

Lillian narrowed her eyes. She'd only broken the curse a few hours ago—it's not like she'd had much time to practice. "What of my friends?"

Grete smiled tightly, though there was no warmth in her eyes. "We don't allow humans or shifters in our meetings. Your friends are well taken care of, I assure you. They'll be provided with food and clothing to ensure a pleasant stay."

Lillian wanted to protest, but she had so many questions, and the Elders would hopefully have the answers she was looking for, so she held the retort on her tongue.

Quietly, she followed Grete and Aaron out of the room. The two other Valkyries walked behind her, their stares burning into her back.

When she glanced over her shoulder, they both gripped the pommels of their swords tightly, their eyes trained on her.

6

Lillian

Grete led them through a white marble hallway, lit by lanterns with sparkling silver flames that cast steely light on Grete's blond hair. Lillian blinked, but the fire within the lanterns was still silver.

"It's one of the Elder's magic. She is a dragon fire wielder. It's quite rare." Aaron sidled up next to her. "She is old, a couple of hundred years, but she is still strong."

Lillian furrowed her brow. "Hundreds?"

Aaron nodded, flashing her that grin again. "You didn't know we're almost immortal? Of course, most of us die in battle, but some of the lucky ones have been around for a long time. Grete is well over seven hundred by now; she was significantly older than your mother."

Lillian swallowed. She'd never heard that Valkyries were immortal, and her mind immediately snapped to Kian.

He was human.

And humans were definitely not immortal.

"I can't believe you're finally here." Aaron's gaze flickered over her. "Did you know we shared a nursemaid, and that we were born on the same day? Apparently, we wouldn't calm unless we lay in the same bassinet. Well, at least that's what the Elders told me. My parents died protecting yours."

Lillian halted, stumbling as the weight of her wings threw her off. "We did?"

"Yes. Our mothers were best friends. My mother was the Queen's Hand. Apparently, we were betrothed from birth. A Valkyrie Queen and a winged male consort would have been quite the pairing, I think." Aaron laughed softly. "Even believing you were lost forever, I still had hope."

"I will not be *marrying* you," Lillian snarled, the unease she'd felt giving way to anger.

Aaron raised his hands, his blue eyes wide. "I wasn't saying that. We don't know each other, Your Majesty. I was merely trying to fill you in. Since you broke the curse, I'm guessing a lot of information was withheld from you. I mean, unless you killed the man you loved on purpose?"

Lillian sucked in a breath as grief and anger wrestled for dominance within her. She settled for glaring at him, trailing her eyes over his black leathers and perfectly combed hair, then hurried her gait to fall in step with Grete instead.

"If you're my aunt, why did you not look for me?"

Grete barely spared her a glance, her steps quickening as she motioned for Lillian to follow her down another long hallway, this one with floor-to-ceiling windows that let the silvery moonlight in, mirroring the light from the lanterns. "I looked for you every day, Lillian. We had ravens and spies out for eighteen years."

Lillian raised her brows. If Kian had figured it out, how could her family not have? Especially since they'd known her parents when the curse affected their appearance. Although it wasn't uncommon to be blond with light eyes in Orios, she'd never come across anyone with hair as fair as her own or with the same pale, almost shimmering skin.

"We're here." Grete pointed to two large wooden doors, each adorned with a golden Valkyrie wing that met in the middle.

When Grete opened the doors, Lillian blew out a deep breath, trying to settle the pulse thrumming in her ears.

Ten Valkyries, dressed in identical leathers, were seated at a large marble table on wooden chairs that had been adapted not to constrict their wings. They all rose when Lillian stepped inside, bowing deep, and she gawked at the wave of black feathers, at the beauty of each and every one of the Valkyries in the room.

"Welcome home, Your Majesty." A small woman with gray hair falling down to her waist spoke from the far end of the table. "We cannot express how pleased we are to have you back."

"Thank you." Lillian tried to smile at the woman as she met her cloud-gray eyes.

"Please, take a seat." Grete pointed to a chair at the end of the table as she slipped into the one at the head, and Aaron took the one next to her.

Sitting down, Lillian curiously eyed the Valkyries.

They were of all ages, a few with graying hair like the small woman who'd spoken when she entered, but there were also two who could pass for Lillian's age.

Although she wasn't sure how the Valkyrie aging worked.

Perhaps they were much older.

"Well." Grete clasped her hands atop the white table. "We have our queen amongst us at last."

Unease pricked her skin, and Lillian frowned as she realized it was the first time Grete had referred to her as something other than Lillian.

"As the leader of the Valkyries and the Elder Council, I suggest we let Lillian ask the questions tonight. Then, she can attend our next meetings to learn more about her Queendom." Grete stared expectantly at Lillian.

Her mind went blank, not a single question she'd burned to ask filling it as a sea of eyes burned into hers.

"Maybe we can introduce ourselves to the poor girl," the gray-haired Valkyrie said gently. "I haven't heard her story.

But we are all aware of how the curse had to be broken, and I'm sure our queen has much on her mind."

She smiled gratefully at the old Valkyrie, her bottom lip trembling slightly as blue eyes flashed in her mind. *I am giving up everything, everything for this, Lillian. I have to.*

"Yes, I only broke the curse..." she swallowed, "a few hours ago. I do have many questions, but I'd like to know who is in this room."

It would also give her a moment to collect herself, to stop the tears that yet again burned behind her eyes.

"Well, I am Tild. I am the oldest of the living Valkyries, and I knew your parents very well, Your Majesty." Tild smiled at her, her eyes soft as she continued in a lower voice. "You look so much like them both, Lillian Volantis. It's eerie how much of Liv there is in you."

The others in the room introduced themselves as well. Lillian struggled to remember all the names—too overwhelmed by the eyes that roved over her—but there was another older woman who studied her with kind eyes, Anick, and the two young ones were Valeria and Breit.

"Your Majesty, perhaps you can begin by sharing your story?" Tild smiled at her again, and something like warmth tried to claw its way into Lillian's chest at the motherly look on her face.

Lillian nodded and quietly explained how her father and Eli had kept her identity a secret her whole life and how Eli had sacrificed his life to let her live.

But as the Valkyries began pressing her with clarifying questions—intimate questions about how her father and Eli had fooled her, how they'd managed to get her to fall in love, despair made her stutter.

When she couldn't bear saying another word about her father and Eli, couldn't stand the raw pain crackling in her chest and her heart and her mind, she forced it down, allowing anger to gain a foothold.

Licks of heat rose on her neck, and Lillian interrupted the

onslaught of questions. "So how come so many humans figured out who I was and how to break the curse, but you all did nothing?"

She winced inwardly when the Valkyries around her raised their brows; the words had come out harsher than she'd meant.

But she was angry, *so angry*, at the sacrifice her father and Eli endured on her behalf, and this interrogation did nothing to soothe her heightening emotions.

"As I've already told you, Lillian, we searched for you day and night for eighteen years. We couldn't go ourselves, not with King Alek hellbent on eradicating our race. I'm sure you wouldn't expect your people to die for you as they would have if they showed themselves on Hindra or Echo," Grete snarled.

A growl left Lillian's throat before she could squash it, and she leaned forward in her chair, glaring at Grete. "My people *did* die for me. People I loved."

"Take a breath." Grete waved dismissively at her. "It's not fitting for a queen to lose her temper in this way, as you shall learn."

Lillian rose so quickly that her chair fell backward with a loud thud.

Snarling and with wings whipping behind her, she stalked up to Grete.

Madick and the other Valkyrie, who'd escorted Lillian to the room, slipped in between them and readied their swords, nothing in their gazes but fierce determination as they stared her down. Brushing her hands against her thighs, Lillian cursed silently when she realized she didn't have any daggers.

She needed to find weapons quickly.

"Everyone, let's calm down." Tild rose as well.

Walking up to Lillian, she gently grabbed her elbow, her bony hand squeezing softly. "She's not lying. We did look for you, Your Majesty. Grete's ravens were out every week. Please, she didn't mean any harm. Let's sit down and continue talking."

Lillian took a deep breath but didn't move, unable to control the emotions now that she'd let them out.

What did it matter if they liked her, anyway?

Eli was dead. Atli was dead. Astrid was dead. And she was sure many, many rebels had died tonight. More souls on her conscience. More people who'd died for her, who'd died for her to get revenge on King Alek.

For her to get even.

She didn't need the Valkyries to like her; she needed them to fight for her.

Lillian bore her eyes into Grete again. "Why are you hiding on this island? Alek is capturing children on Hindra and Echo, then doing Orios knows what with them. Why won't you work with the rebels?"

The room went silent, and Lillian's nostrils flared as she flitted her eyes around. Only a handful of the Valkyries met her stare, the rest mumbling to each other, their gazes cast down.

"We cannot risk our people, Lillian."

She ground her teeth—she was getting *really* tired of Grete's voice.

"So many of us died when your parents were overthrown. And the humans did nothing. Why should we risk our lives for them?"

Lillian didn't even try to stop the next growl. "So you will just leave them in Alek's claws? I thought you were warriors."

Tild gripped her elbow more firmly. "Your Majesty, while we disagree with the curse Adeon placed on your parents, he supports Alek. If we turned on the king, we'd turn on Adeon. And we're not strong enough to take him on."

Lillian narrowed her eyes. "But I am. That's why he was scared of my parents, wasn't it? Because they were strong enough to take him on?"

"We don't know that you are. While you're likely very power-ful, given who your parents were, you have had your powers for a few hours, Lillian. From what we've heard here today, you've done enough for Orios the last few years to last a lifetime. Why don't you take some time to rest? You are safe here. You don't have to fight anymore." Grete glared at her behind the two Valkyrie guards, and several of the Valkyries nodded in agreement, a chorus of concurring mumbles echoing through the room.

"We will train you to master your wings and your power and to take your place as queen. Your people need stability, Lillian. You've only just returned to us; you need to spend time with them."

"Grete is right, Your Majesty," Tild said softly.

Lillian bit her cheek when her father's voice rumbled in her mind. *You cannot act on emotion alone, Lillian.*

He'd trained her for *this*.

He'd known what she'd have to face, what would happen if she broke the curse. Drawing a shaking breath and flexing her fingers, she forced herself to listen to him, to not fly at Grete.

"What about my friends?"

Grete waved for Madick and the other Valkyrie to return to their post by the door. "They may stay. While we're not exactly thrilled to host Crown Prince Kian, I've understood he is your friend."

Lillian cleared her throat. "He's my mate."

Gasps erupted around the room, and Aaron stared at her with wide eyes, his mouth falling open.

"What?" Lillian narrowed her eyes again.

Tild stepped back, her blue eyes sad as they met hers. "Your Majesty, your people will never accept him as your consort. His father murdered their queen. Your mother."

A chill snaked down Lillian's spine.

"Have you established the bond?" Grete rose and took a step toward her.

Lillian blinked.

"Have you bedded him, completed the blood sharing?"

Lillian's face heated. "No," she whispered, wishing she could fall through the marble floor.

Grete blew out a breath. "Then it's settled. You will reject the bond. It's rare, but you'll survive. There are eligible men around here. I'm sure we'll find someone to keep your mind off him." She shared a look with Aaron.

Lillian's ears buzzed, and when her shadows began twirling around her wrists, seeking permission to strangle the woman before her, she stormed out of the room before she lost control again, perhaps killing the entire Elder Council.

It probably wouldn't be the best first move as queen.

Her pulse pounded behind her eyes with each step, and her vision remained red-tinted as she sprinted down several long hallways before she found her way back to her room.

Sitting down on the bed, she slammed her hand against the wooden frame, wincing when a splinter lodged in her hand.

She hadn't expected it to be easy, but she hadn't expected the open hostility, even if she'd lost her temper.

She would have to figure out a way to get them on her side —and quickly.

She couldn't risk her father and Eli's efforts to have been in vain.

7

Kian

Kian couldn't sleep. After tossing and turning for what felt like hours, he rose from the bed and walked out onto the small balcony connected to his room. The dark sky was clear, the night quiet, with no Valkyries flying around the tower, only thousands of stars and the big moon looking back at him from where it hung over the dark sea.

He sighed as he placed his hands on the cold stone railing. Somewhere in the east, his father was surely seething, planning his revenge. He hadn't missed the cold smile that grazed his father's face when he rifted them all away, a lethal promise playing on his lips.

He'd never had any affection for his father—even before Alek killed his mother. There had been nothing warm or caring about him; his idea of father–son bonding consisted of involving Kian in his scheming for world domination.

Kian gripped the railing until his knuckles blanched. He wouldn't let his father get anywhere near Lillian, even if he had to kill the man himself.

He wasn't a young boy anymore, not like he had been when he'd found his mother on the floor with blood pooling beneath her thin body. He couldn't protect her, but he could protect Lillian now.

Tilting his head toward the sky, he wished the bond would allow him to speak within Lillian's mind as she did with Finn. He hadn't seen her since he'd left her room, and he worried for her. Kian couldn't put his finger on it, but there was something about this place that made him uneasy.

He'd shared a somber meal with Finn and Sam earlier that evening. It had been mostly quiet, apart from Finn taunting the poor twins that stood guard by the door.

Kian shook his head. Elya had been stealing glances at the shifter the whole evening. Finn was definitely about to get himself into heaps of trouble.

"No! Please! *Please, you don't have to do this!*"

Kian sprinted out of the room upon hearing Lillian's desperate cries, his sword ready in his hand. Finn already stood outside her door, his face pale as turned to Kian.

"She's having a nightmare. It's quite vivid." Finn worriedly shifted his gaze to the door. "I think it might be best if you go in. I'm not sure she'll want to see me. Not now."

Silver lined Finn's eyes when Kian searched his face. "It wasn't your fault, Finn." Kian reached out and clasped his shoulder. "He was going to kill you."

Finn glanced at his feet, his hair falling into his eyes and shoulders hunching. "She is filled with regret, Kian. What if she believes she chose wrong?"

Another scream rang from her room, and Kian set his jaw as claws of anger dug into his gut.

She had hurt enough—he refused to allow more pain to consume her. Even if they were only dreams, he would make sure she never hurt like that again.

"She doesn't. It's a dream, Finn." Squeezing Finn's shoulder once more, Kian kicked the door open and stalked into the room, his muscles locked as if to fight her nightmares themselves.

The moonlight streaming in from the windows illuminated

the tears that streamed down Lillian's beautiful face as she tangled in the bedsheets, and the beads of sweat that rolled down her exposed neck soaked her white nightgown.

His heart ached for the young queen, tangling with anger at seeing her in pain yet again. He hadn't accepted it during the trials, and he wouldn't accept it now.

"Lillian," he whispered.

When she kept thrashing, Kian didn't hesitate. Climbing into her bed, he pulled her into his arms and stroked her hair, whispering soothing words until she quieted.

Her eyelids fluttered, and as she opened them, dark shadows swirled behind the gray like a brewing storm raging inside her. When he glanced down, her shadows caressed his entire body, filling the bed and snaking across the floor. He shuddered when his own magic buzzed over his skin, welcoming the darkness.

Cupping her chin, he tipped her face up. "Hi, beautiful."

"Hi." Her voice was hoarse from crying.

He pulled her closer so her face nestled into his neck and her body was flush with his. Tensing, he realized just how thin her nightgown was; he could see every outline of her body, the four jagged scars from the Garm that stretched over her stomach. Heat exploded within him, but he pushed the thoughts away.

This was definitely not the time.

Still, Kian had to fight his body's reaction with everything in him when her scent invaded the space. She smelled like the evening sky, darkening after a beautiful day. It was intoxicating, nothing like he'd ever experienced before, and he couldn't help it—he lowered his head so it rested on top of hers and drew a deep breath.

"Are you smelling me?" Lillian glanced at him, a small wrinkle forming over her nose.

Kian grinned at her. "I just wanted to make sure that you'd really taken a bath."

She swatted at him, but her face softened, and when a

smile tugged at her lips, his heart swelled and beat so hard he imagined Finn could hear it from outside the room.

Orios, when this woman smiled, the whole realm stopped.

Kian gently brushed his thumb over her flushed cheeks. He wasn't sure if he could keep his promise of going slow. His whole body hardened when this beautiful, wild creature stared back at him with those searching, dark eyes—the most beautiful eyes he'd ever seen, even while shrouded in darkness.

He'd never wanted anything so much in his entire life.

Lillian closed her eyes, and his heart sank, unwilling to go another moment without staring into those dark clouds.

"Kian," she whispered and placed a hand on his chest, right on top of his thundering heart. "We need to talk."

His heart stopped.

Pulling back, Kian's eyes darted between hers. His muscles locked when more tears filled her eyes, making her lashes heavy as the drops clung to them before falling down her flushed cheeks. Breathing through his nose, he forced the anger down. There wasn't anyone he could kill for hurting her —at least not yet.

"I met with the Elders this evening." Lillian glanced at the hand that rested on his chest. "They... they don't approve. Of us, I mean."

Rage burned hotter inside him. He couldn't believe the Elders had known Lillian for a few hours, and they'd already informed her that they disapproved of her mate. A familiar feeling made his vision pulse, and he couldn't stop the growl rumbling in his chest.

His father had a penchant for controlling every aspect of his life and had tried to mold Kian into a mirror of himself. Perhaps he would have succeeded if he hadn't made the mistake of leaving Kian on Hindra, where he'd met people with love in their hearts and learned there was another way.

"Lillian. My queen. Do you approve of us? If so, I don't give one shit about what these *Elders* think." He brushed her tears away with his thumb, aching to lean in to kiss them away, to kiss her until she forgot everything else. "If you'll have me, I'll stand by you forever. Yours is the only opinion I care about."

Lillian stared at him thoughtfully, her storming eyes searching his face, leaving a trail of warmth in their wake. When she leaned in, his heart stopped again. Heat coursed through his body as she came close enough for them to share air, her scent fully enveloping him.

Stars exploded in his mind, his skin burning like wildfire when she softly brushed her full lips against his, a current running through him as if lightning itself had been shared between them in that kiss.

He went to pull her closer and deepen the kiss, but with unnatural speed, Lillian slipped out of his arms and rose from the bed, shivering in the breeze from the cracked balcony door.

"You should go." She wouldn't meet his eyes.

Kian frowned, the heat quickly leaving his body as ice-cold apprehension replaced it. "Go?"

He rose from the bed and stalked up to her. Lillian backed up against the wall, but Kian followed, placing his palms on the wall on each side of her, trying to keep his eyes on her face and not on the alluring lines of her body that were clearly visible through the sheer nightgown.

"Kian, *please*," she whispered, still not meeting his eyes.

He shook his head, "No. I backed down once, but I am not making the same mistake again. Not when it's not something *you* want. What was that kiss, Lillian? A goodbye?"

She remained quiet, staring down at her bare feet. Orios, even her feet turned him on. He tore his eyes away from them and used his finger to lift her chin. Shadows once again darkened her eyes, like plumes of inky black fire burning in them.

Good, she was getting angry.

Hopefully, she would snap out of this and yell at him. Hell, he'd even take her throwing a dagger at him instead of this helpless version. He could handle another scar on his cheek. But not another on his heart.

Not if it wasn't because *she* wanted him to leave, because *she* didn't want him. But he could feel it—could feel that she ached for him the same way he did for her. And he would not give up, not as he nearly had on Echo.

She was his.

And he was hers.

"Since when do you listen to anyone? The Lillian I know would have killed them on the spot for even trying to suggest she do something she didn't want to."

A snarl vibrated in her throat in response, and when she narrowed her eyes, Kian grinned, which only made her snarl louder.

His chest tightened upon seeing the smoke dancing behind her eyes. No one had loved anyone as much as he loved this insane, vicious creature.

He'd fallen so hard when she hissed and spitted at the other novices, never once backing down. And when she'd stalked into his room, daggers in hand, ready to take him down, he hadn't been able to breathe from how hard his heart pumped.

There was definitely something wrong with him.

"Do I need to *make* you leave?" she hissed.

"I didn't realize you were into violence. But I should have figured," he winked, and a smile pulled at his lips when her face turned bright crimson.

"Don't worry; I will leave. But don't think for one second that this is me backing down. You're turning me down again? I am not going to make it easy for you, my dark queen."

When she blinked at him, he leaned forward, his lips brushing her ear, and whispered, "Trust me, I am going to make it *very* difficult."

Kian laughed softly when her breath hitched in her throat.

He would win her over, even if it would take the rest of his life.

With a final look at her, he turned to walk out of the room, lingering in the door frame, but when she didn't call for him, he softly closed the door.

He meant what he said.

He wouldn't back down, not until she told him it was what she wanted—what she needed.

Stalking into his room, he lay down on the bed, but it took a long time for sleep to come, his mind still buzzing from thinking about Lillian's lips against his.

When it finally did, his dreams were filled with fire and shadows and wings.

8

Finn

Lillian was awful at flying.

The two ravens had been trying to teach her all morning, cawing their amusement as she miserably failed to heed their instructions. Finn gasped for air in between fits of laughter as she once again crashed onto the stones that lined the large balcony they stood upon.

A small ember of worry filled him when she remained on the ground—that looked like it hurt. But when he reached out through the bond, the only thing that was hurt was her pride, so he continued laughing.

They'd been out here since dawn when one of the ravens had knocked on his window until he got out of bed and went out to find his friends yawning, dressed in black Valkyrie fighting gear to shield them against the wind that whipped around the dark castle.

Apparently, the Valkyries were expected to partake in fight training every day, and Finn and the rest weren't trusted to be alone in the castle, so they'd have to follow the Valkyrie schedules.

Not that it bothered him. He was always up for honing his fighting skills, so he'd been happy to find a set of leathers waiting for him on a chair outside his room. The black trousers and jacket fit him perfectly, and he'd caught Elya giving him an approving once over when Kian rifted them all down to the training ground. Although, she'd quickly looked away when he winked at her.

He glanced around the fighting ring that had been built upon a large balcony about halfway down the castle and found Elya staring at him again with impenetrable but curious ocean-blue eyes. When he grinned at her, she flashed her teeth at him, but the corners of her mouth curled ever so slightly.

His smile widened—this was definitely going to be fun.

Kian trained with Else on the other side of the ring, keeping far from where Lillian kept tumbling onto the ground.

Finn frowned. He hadn't seen them talk at all today. Something must have happened when he left her room last night, even if he hadn't felt that deep despair from her anymore.

But he wasn't about to risk his neck and ask Lillian, not when she growled and slammed her fist so hard against the ground she'd, yet again, fallen onto that clouds of dust whirled around her. His eyes trailed her as she rose, snarling at the ravens that she needed a break.

"Are you just going to stand there and flex your muscles, or are you actually going to train?" Sam sidled up next to him, flicking his hair out of his face.

Finn grinned at his friend. He'd been quiet, mostly observing since they arrived. It was good to see his spirits lift.

"Let's show the ladies how it's done." Finn wiggled his brows. "Elya, will you do me the honors?"

Elya stalked up to him with a sly smile on her face. "I'm pretty sure I'll make you wet your pants, boy."

A tiny ember of amusement flickered down the bond, and Finn snorted. Of course, this wild woman would amuse Lillian; they were both equally insane. Orios help them all if they ever become close; the two forces of nature would probably burn the whole realm down.

Why am I not surprised you're enjoying this?

But the question only whispered within his own mind.

Lillian had yet again shut the connection between them—something new he wished she hadn't learned how to do. He'd discovered it this morning when his greeting had echoed back to him, across a dark void where the silver and gold twirls should be.

He shifted his gaze to where she stood, eyes vacantly staring across the balcony, and sighed. He'd felt the nearly unbearable pain from her nightmare yesterday.

She probably needed more time.

Shaking it off, he turned to Elya again, forcing a grin. "Boy? I'm a twenty-five-year-old man, and nothing scares me."

Elya threw her head back and laughed. "I have a century on you, *boy*. And even I have fears."

Lillian's worry vibrated inside him, so strong it broke through the barrier she'd carefully shaped around her mind.

Finn tilted his head. "So, how do you age then? You don't look a day over twenty."

Thank you.

He winked at Lillian when she met his gaze.

"We remain pretty much the same from the age of eighteen until we reach a few centuries or so. Once we pass that, we begin aging more quickly. But some of the Elders are almost as old as Adeon, and they still only look to be in their fifties in human years."

Elya glanced at Lillian, who was pretending hard like she wasn't listening. "And if we find our mate, we can tie his or her life to ours." Elya swallowed. "In most cases, at least. They'll age the same way we do. Otherwise, it would be quite problematic, I would think."

Lillian's shoulders loosed, a breath of release rushing down the bond. Finn tilted his head; even if she and Kian didn't seem on speaking terms today, she clearly cared enough to worry about living without him.

Hopefully, they'd get over whatever was happening between them quickly. She needed Kian, even though she'd never admit it. He'd known already during the trials Kian had fallen for her, and even though she'd fought it, Finn had seen her reluctantly break down her walls as well.

He tried to catch her eye, but when she kept her gaze down, Finn turned back to Elya and winked at the blond Valkyrie. "Thank you for the history lesson, that was very insightful. How about we switch to a lesson in fighting? I've heard a legend that you women are the best fighters in Orios."

Elya laughed again and waved him forward, a smirk playing on her lips. "First of all, we're not women."

Laughing, he tilted his head. "And second?"

He didn't have time to react before Elya charged him, and he fell hard on his back, his head smacking into the stone.

Blinking, he tried to focus his eyes on the blonde laughing down at him, offering him her hand. "Second of all, it's not just a legend."

Finn grinned as he stood on shaky legs, readying himself as Elya circled him.

He'd known this was going to be fun.

9

Lillian

Lillian stared with wide eyes as Elya flew around Finn with impossible speed, whipping her wooden practice sword and hitting her intended mark every single time.

She'd never seen anything like it. She'd thought *she* was skilled; but if Elya that easily had Finn on his back, Lillian knew she'd be no match for the Valkyrie.

No jealousy stirred in her at the thought, though, only determination, and she promised herself she would rival the Valkyrie one day.

Everyone on the balcony paused their training to watch the golden-haired man and the blond Valkyrie charge each other—two gilded forces to reckon with.

Finn's soft groans as Elya's sword hit him again and again —quite hard from the jerks he let slip—were the only sounds apart from the whistling wind blowing across the large balcony. When Elya once again had Finn on his back, her wooden sword at his throat, Finn chuckled, his amber eyes glittering.

Lillian studied her friend, still lying in the dust on the balcony, and suddenly wished he could share his carefree nature with her like he could his shifter abilities.

Even just a little bit to help counter the darkness threatening to drown her.

Wincing at the tightness constricting her chest, she watched Finn and Elya grin at each other as the Valkyrie offered him a hand to get up.

When eyes burned into the side of her face, she tore her eyes away, and immediately wished she hadn't.

Kian's eyes darkened when their gaze collided, and Lillian flipped back around so quickly that she nearly lost her balance again and had to brace herself against the stone railing while glaring at Hanin, who cawed a laugh at her.

Clenching her fists not to slam them into the stone, she drew a deep breath.

She hated that she had to push him away, every fiber within her burning to reach out to him, to be back in his arms. An almost feverish warmth whispered across her skin as she stole another glance at him, seeing his muscles play beneath the Valkyrie leathers, his black hair glistening in the morning sun.

But a wave of glacial guilt quickly washed the heat away, and she had to brace herself against the railing once more to remain standing.

She'd killed the last man she loved, and even if she could find a way to forgive herself, she couldn't risk being with Kian.

She needed the Valkyries on her side—and if staying away from him was the answer, she had to be strong enough.

Her parents had risked everything for love.

She couldn't afford to make the same mistake.

"Kian. Why don't you show us how a prince fights?" Elya strolled up to Kian's side, playfully twisting a strand of her blond hair.

He nodded, not once glancing in Lillian's direction, and unfastened his jacket. In only black leathers, his ripped chest glistening from sweat and his tattoos twirling in the soft sunlight, Kian stepped into the ring.

Lillian couldn't tear her eyes away from all that bare, tan

skin, and a yearning to take him and fly off somewhere far away coursed through her.

With a soft whistle, Elya followed him into the ring. "What is in the water on Hindra?"

Tensing, Lillian took a step toward the Valkyrie, her eyes narrowing.

Calm down, silver girl.

Finn reached out as if to sling his arm around her shoulder, but when Lillian flinched, he lowered it again.

Hurt flashed across his face, hardening those beautiful, soft features, and Lillian eyed him pleadingly, begging him to understand.

When sorrow rolled down their bond, bitter shame tore through her and she tried to force herself to reach out, but her hands wouldn't leave her side.

She couldn't be normal with him.

Couldn't be Lillian and Finn—the best friends.

Not now.

Not yet.

Not when Eli's face flashed before her eyes every time she looked into Finn's amber ones.

Swallowing, she made herself to turn back to the fighting ring where Kian and Elya circled each other, and when Elya threw her head back and laughed at something Kian said, there was nothing left inside her to stop the shadows that ripped from her hands. Shaking, she tried to reign them in, tried to get control of the magic roaring in her veins.

She didn't truly want to hurt Elya, but she wasn't sure if she could subdue the shadows.

When Elya's mouth lifted into a vicious smile, a warning snarl left Lillian's throat before she could squash it, and her shadows whipped the air, pressing to be released upon the Valkyrie.

Elya needed to step away from her mate.

Right now.

"Your Majesty, I didn't realize you'd begin training so

early." Aaron landed on the ground next to her and Finn, gracefully folding his wings. "I went by your room, but it was empty."

Lillian tore her eyes from Kian. "Why did you go by my room?"

"As Grete mentioned, I'm meant to keep you company, to teach you about our ways." Aaron smiled at her. "I volunteered for it, of course. And I'm happy for it. The fighting gear suits you, Your Majesty." His gaze raked approvingly down her form, leaving goosebumps of unease in its wake.

Lillian glared at him, her shadows reaching for Aaron instead, and when he merely regarded them with a flicker of curiosity she swore a soft snarl reverberated within them—as if her magic couldn't stand his eyes on them either.

"Thank you, but that's not necessary. I can handle myself."

Aaron, unwisely, took a step toward her. "Of course you can, Your Majesty."

When he placed a hand on her arm, Lillian fought a grimace, and the darkness around her thickened.

"You should probably take a step back," Finn warned beside her. "Those shadows of hers are not just for show."

Aaron ignored him, his eyes still fixed on hers as he inched closer. "I only wish to make it easier for you. I'm sure you haven't heard much about our history or culture—Valkyries are not known for keeping many records. And without sounding too full of myself, I'm also one of our best fliers. I could help teach you if you'd like. I watched you before, and it seems you might need a few pointers."

She could barely hold on as rage swirled in her gut. Her vision clouded, a red tint lining at the edge of her gaze as Aaron's grip tightened around her arm.

"Get your hands off my queen. Now." Kian appeared between them, and while his voice was quiet, there was no mistaking the threat in it.

Her darkness purred with happiness in response, and she drew a deep breath when the pressure finally relieved.

Aaron lifted his hands and backed up. "Take it easy, friend. I am only trying to help her."

"I'm not your friend. If you touch her without her permission again, I will kill you," Kian's voice was like ice as he glared at Aaron.

"No need for that. I'm confident I'll get her permission." Aaron winked at Lillian before unfolding his wings and taking off, whipping the air around them as he headed for a higher part of the black castle.

Lillian narrowed her eyes as she stared at Kian. "I can take care of myself," she hissed.

But her shadows betrayed her, softly caressing one of his biceps, tracing the pattern of his tattoo. She tried to force them back, groaning when they resisted.

"I told you; I am not backing down. Not until you, and you alone, give me a direct order that that's what you want. And regardless of my feelings for you, he made you uncomfortable, and I will not allow anyone to make you feel that way." With that, Kian stalked off back into the ring.

"Are you ever going to put the poor man out of his misery?"

Lillian glared at Finn before stomping toward the ravens again.

She needed to learn how to fly—quickly—so she could leave these stupid, stubborn men behind.

10

Lillian

Her entire body still ached from relentlessly crashing onto the balcony as she tried to make her wings cooperate—as she tried to stay airborne for more than a few precious seconds.

With sore limbs, Lillian pushed off the bed and opened the glass doors out to the balcony. Drawing a deep breath of crisp and tangy air, she looked up at the clear night sky and the large moon looming over the island.

The feathers in her wings blew softly in the ocean breeze, and she gently brushed her fingers through the bottom of them, her wings stretching out behind her in response.

She sighed as she leaned her arms on the railing.

How could it be so difficult to fly?

Madick said it should come naturally, but it definitely didn't come naturally to Lillian—quite the opposite. As soon as she lifted a few inches from the ground, she'd tried to focus, tried to let the wind bring her up, but her mind was elsewhere, and she'd become distracted, causing her to tumble onto the hard stone without fail.

Shame slammed into her so strongly that she could taste its sharp bitterness. If she couldn't even master her wings, how was she going to save all of Orios?

A lump formed in her throat as she thought of how Eli, Atli, and Astrid had sacrificed their lives for her to get here, how they had believed in her so much that they'd gladly left this world behind.

And she couldn't even master the basics of being a Valkyrie.

Yet again, her magic pressed to be released upon the emotions stirring inside her, and she shuddered as she repressed it, forcing the darkness deep down until no whisper of shadow remained.

She could not lose control again.

Lillian clenched her fists as the darkness seemed to rip open a deep hole within her, filled with burning guilt and regret.

Their deaths were useless—as useless as she was.

It should have been her who died. She hadn't killed Alek, the Valkyries wouldn't side with her, she couldn't fly, and was barely mastering her magic.

"Well, this is a pity party if I've ever seen one."

Lillian snarled, unable to control the darkness bursting out and surrounding her, forming a protective shield.

Spinning around, she found Elya smirking at her, leaning against the marble fireplace in her room, where silver fire crackled. She forced herself to take controlled breaths until her darkness unwillingly retreated—very unwillingly, upon remembering Elya sparring with Kian.

"What are you doing here?" she asked when she'd caught her breath.

Elya slowly approached her, her long legs gracefully stepping over the white rug lining the floor. Joining Lillian on the small balcony, she didn't spare Lillian's shadows a glance as she rested against the stone railing while flicking her blond hair out of her face.

"I saw you struggling today, and I thought you could use some practice without an audience. If you're not too busy wallowing in guilt and shame that is?"

A growl built in Lillian's throat, but she swallowed it, swallowed the anger that lurked so close to the surface.

Clutching to pride wouldn't serve her, would be as useless as she was.

"Why would you help me?" She studied the Valkyrie, a hint of envy stirring at how she easily furled her wings against the wind and gracefully handled her body.

Elya's blue eyes reflected the moonlight as she eyed her. "I know what you're going through," she said quietly.

When Lillian frowned, Elya continued in barely a whisper. "I, too, have lost people I love. My parents, my friends, my—"

The Valkyrie blew out a soft breath. "I know the guilt that consumes you. The hopelessness you can't shake. The belief that it should have been you in their place. But it shouldn't have been you, Lillian. They made their own choice. Like you can make your own choice now. I don't know you, but you don't seem like someone who gives up easily."

Lillian nodded, shifting her gaze to the moon again.

"It just hurts so much," she whispered, surprised at her own words.

But there was something in Elya's gaze that made her believe she truly understood.

Elya placed a small hand on her shoulder, and they stayed silent for a few moments, the wind roaring and the distant crashing of waves the only sound in the night.

After a while, Lillian cleared her throat. "I'd like for you to teach me if you're still willing."

Elya nodded, "Get up on the railing."

Lillian stared at her with wide eyes. "What?"

Elya grinned at her, but the smile didn't comfort Lillian at all—there was a wild edge to the Valkyrie's curled lips. "I think you need some more motivation."

Lillian shook her head, backing up a step. "I'll die if I fall from here."

Elya winked, "Exactly. As I said, motivation. But if you're too scared…"

Lillian shook her head again, but when Elya laughed softly, she groaned and stepped up onto the railing, wobbling slightly as the strong wind blew through her wings.

Shuddering, she glanced out over the forest, over the vast sea in the distance, and the ground far, far beneath her.

Lillian turned her head over her shoulder. "Now, what?"

Elya stepped up beside her, offering Lillian her hand. "Now we'll step off. Trust your wings, Lillian. I saw you today. You're in your head. It is natural for us, and it will be for you as well when you stop thinking. You need to have an empty mind and allow your instincts to take over. You're a Valkyrie now. Unlike humans, we can actually trust our instincts to lead us. It's part of who—what—we are."

Pushing the guilt, the sorrow, and the pain away as best she could, Lillian drew a deep breath, trying to clear her mind. Her wings spread, and she smiled slightly when she felt the connection to them, how they were truly a part of her.

"Good. Continue like that. Trust your wings, and trust yourself. Keep ahold of my hand, and keep your head clear. Now we step off." Elya squeezed her hand, gently pulling Lillian with her as she stepped off the railing into the dark night.

"It's working!" Lillian gasped as her wings kept her in the air.

Elya laughed softly, still holding on tight to her hand.

Glancing down, Lillian stared at the many balconies lining the black castle walls and the forest beneath them, and her stomach dropped when she realized just how high up they were. She sucked in a breath when her wings flared, and she dropped a few inches closer to the unforgiving ground.

"Lillian!" Elya raised her voice as they quickly began losing height. "Clear your mind. Trust your instincts."

"I'm trying," she got out through gritted teeth, but when waves of guilt washed through her and her loved ones' faces flashed in her mind, they began falling more rapidly, the trees below growing larger and larger.

"Shit, shit, shit," Lillian hissed.

Elya's wings whipped the air forcefully, but the Valkyrie was smaller than her, so she did little more than slow down the free fall. "Seriously, Lillian, clear your mind! We are going to die in a minute otherwise," she growled.

Lillian drew deep breaths, but Eli's face, those last moments of his life, was etched into her mind.

We made her strong.

She whimpered as she thought of how wrong he was. She wasn't strong enough for this. Her chest constricted as her father's and Astrid's faces filled her mind. *I know you will make me proud.*

They were wrong.

She couldn't do this.

"Lillian! Shit. I can't kill our queen." Elya desperately tried to reach her. "Seriously, clear your mind now!"

When they kept tumbling down, whistling past softly lit windows, Elya softened her voice. "Lillian. Think of Kian, Finn, and Sam. They need you. You will break two bonds, and you might very well take them with you."

Lillian sucked in a breath when Kian and Finn's smiles replaced the images in her head.

She couldn't risk their lives.

She closed her eyes.

She could do this. She *would* do this.

Her mind went blank as she let the night embrace her.

She would do this. She repeated the sentence in her head until her stomach didn't feel like it was falling out of her body.

"You can open your eyes now," Elya said gently.

Lillian slowly pried her eyes open.

A shocked laugh escaped her when the castle was now far beneath them, the dark night sky surrounding them in all directions and the stars winking at her—so close it felt as if she could reach out and touch them.

Elya sighed shakily. "I thought you would kill us both for a second there. I swear the Elders would have found me in the afterlife and killed me again if something happened to you."

Lillian glared at her. "It was your idea, you know."

Elya laughed, a raspy but genuine laugh. "I know. I'm known for being a little bit reckless." She grinned at Lillian. "But you're doing it. I had a feeling."

Elya lifted both of her hands in the air. "See, you've got this."

Lillian pushed away the fear that threatened to consume her upon realizing that Elya had let go of her hand, forcing her mind to go blank again. "So, where do we go now?"

Elya motioned for her to follow, and even if she was a little wobbly, Lillian did not fall through the air as the Valkyrie had her fly laps around the tall castle.

When Elya pointed out the different parts of the beautiful castle—the ballrooms, the living quarters, and the different training balconies—it distracted Lillian enough to keep her mind off the guilt and pain.

Still, when Elya directed her back to the balcony connected to her room and bid her goodnight, Lillian's knees nearly buckled from the feelings that surfaced as she blew out a breath of relief at standing on solid ground.

On shaky legs, she headed to bed, not bothering to remove her clothing as she collapsed on top of the blankets, praying her dreams wouldn't be haunted by her dead loved ones.

But she didn't have much hope.

11

Kian

Kian's heart nearly stopped when he watched Lillian step off the balcony and then proceeded to fall hundreds of yards toward the tree-filled ground. He'd prepared to rift and save her, but thankfully, it seemed Elya managed to help her as she quickly appeared again, flying on her own, her dark hair whipping around her face as she sped toward the shining moon.

Even as pride filled him, he promised himself he would have a word with the grouchy Valkyrie tomorrow. She had risked his queen's—his mate's—life tonight. And that was not something he would ever approve of.

A knock interrupted his internal rumbling. Before he could respond, the door flew open, and Kian reached for his sword. But it was Finn's sorrow-lined face that popped through the crack.

"Can I come in? Or are you planning on fighting me?" Finn glanced at his hand, gripping his sword tightly.

Letting go of the hilt, Kian shook his head. "Sorry, I think I'm a bit on edge."

Finn offered him a crooked smile, a ghost of his old,

57

mischievous ones. "Yes, I heard mumbling and was worried you had gone mad."

Kian rolled his eyes. "Lillian just stepped off the balcony with that Elya."

Finn nodded, his golden hair limp as it fell into his eyes. "I saw her tumbling down—nearly gave me a heart attack. But seems like she got a grip on it. Those two are made of the same stuff. I don't envy anyone who dares go up against them." Finn gestured to the small couch by the crackling fireplace. "May I sit?"

"Of course." Kian pulled up a chair to face the leather couch.

There was no way he and Finn would both fit on there. All the furniture in this castle was so small. He guessed it was a consequence of it mainly consisting of women, even if some were quite tall.

"What's on your mind, Finn?"

Finn shrugged, a shadow crossing his face. "I'm just lonely, I think. I went to Sam's room, but he wasn't there, so I thought I'd try you. I thought you might be lonely as well. Seems like Lillian is avoiding us both."

Kian's stomach churned at the emptiness in his friend's eyes and at his hunched shoulders as he leaned back on the couch.

Finn and Lillian had been so close during the trials, especially once they bonded. But he hadn't missed how Lillian stayed away from Finn, shied away from his touch, his company.

He dragged a hand through his hair. "She'll reach out to you again, Finn."

When he met the shifter's amber eyes, doubt shone in them.

"She will, Finn. It's only been two days. We need to give her time. We can't possibly understand what she's been through—what she is still going through. She killed the man she loved. She had to choose between him and her best friend.

Then she broke the curse and found out I'm her mate, and then the Elders—her people—are hesitant about her. I should think that would cause the most resilient to waver. But it's Lillian. She will get through this."

Finn stared into the fireplace, and not even the flames flickering in his eyes made them seem more alive. "I hope you're right."

They remained quiet, lost in their own thoughts until a scream broke the silence. Shooting to their feet, Kian and Finn stormed out of the room, both gripping the hilts of their swords tightly.

But as Kian tried to open the door to Lillian's room, he found it locked. When he banged on it, the screaming quieted, but the door remained closed.

He stared at Finn, certain that the wild look in Finn's eyes was mirrored in his own. "Should I break down the door?"

Before Finn could respond, Lillian's voice sounded on the other side.

"Please, don't break the door." Her broken voice was quiet, raspy from screaming, and thick from emotion. "Just go to bed. I'm fine."

Kian sighed. "Lillian, you're not fine. Please, let us in."

He loved her stubbornness, but right now it was becoming increasingly frustrating.

She needed them, and if she'd just let them in, not just inside her room, but into her mind, they could help her. *He* could help her, relieve some of that weight he was sure was crushing her chest.

"No. Please, just leave." Lillian sounded exhausted from the other side, her voice so different from the strong, assertive one Kian was used to.

"Finn, please stop trying to reach out through the bond. I'm fine."

Tears welled in Finn's eyes, and before Kian could stop him, the shifter stormed off down the dark hallway behind him.

Shit. He hesitated for a moment, debating whether he should follow Finn, but Lillian took precedence, so he forced his feet to remain still.

"Lillian," Kian softened his voice, sitting down with his back against the door. "Please, let us in. I promise neither of us will push you in any way. We just want to be there for you."

He could swear he heard her sit down on the other side, that he could feel the heat from her body through the white wood.

"Please, Lillian," he whispered, sensing there was no point in trying to make her angry—he could almost smell the despair rolling off her.

"I can't, Kian. I'm sorry," her broken voice whispered.

The sniff that followed nearly had him break down the door after all. He ached to hold her, to see those beautiful gray eyes light up again, to see one of those rare smiles grace her face again.

But the door didn't open, and he doubted his barging in would help.

"Then I will stay here tonight. I'm right outside if you need me."

Kian settled against the door when Lillian didn't respond, assuming her silence as confirmation. Closing his eyes, he listened to her soft breaths and the low thumping of her heart through the wood.

He'd stay here forever if she needed him to.

12

Lillian

She woke, still leaning against the door, to whispers.

Lillian's face was dry from the salt in the many tears she'd shed last night, and her body ached, either from flying or from her sleeping position. Perhaps both.

But she hadn't had any more nightmares as she slept against the door, listening to Kian's deep breaths and his steady heartbeat as he fell asleep.

She snapped up her head at a soft knock on the door.

"I brought you breakfast since we all know you can't cook."

Lillian shook her head at Finn's attempt at a joke, even as no smile pulled at her lips. Forcing her aching limbs to straighten, she unlocked the door.

She didn't want to push Finn away, but she didn't know how to look into his amber eyes and not see the choice she'd made—Eli's bloodied face, her dagger in his chest.

I am giving up everything, everything for this, Lillian.

She nearly choked on the dry sob that lodged in her throat.

When Finn gently opened the door with a plate of food in his hands, she glanced down at her feet, blinking to rid herself of the tears that welled in her eyes. Guilt nearly paralyzed her when she glimpsed the worried expression on his face through her lashes.

"Where do you want it?" Finn asked, trying to catch her eye as he stepped into the room.

Lillian shrugged. "You can put it anywhere. Thank you."

She couldn't make herself meet his heavy-hearted stare as he bent his head and placed the plate on her small wooden nightstand.

Finn cleared his throat. "Well, I'll get out of your way."

Lillian nodded, but when he walked by her to leave the room, she reached out to grip his hand.

"I'm…" she swallowed. "I'm sorry, Finn. I just… I need time. But please, it's not your fault. I don't regret saving you. And I love you. But…" Her voice broke, and fresh tears burned behind her eyes.

Finn squeezed her hand. "I know, silver girl. I love you, too. When you're ready, I'll… We'll be here."

When Lillian glanced at him, Finn offered her a small smile before walking out the door.

Closing her eyes, she drew a deep breath.

She didn't think she'd be hungry, but as the smell of meat and boiled vegetables wafted through the room, Lillian almost sprinted to the plate of food. In minutes, she'd gobbled down the whole thing, burning her fingers in the process.

She guessed flying had drained all her energy reserves.

As she licked her fingers, rolling her eyes as Finn had forgotten to bring anything to eat the food with, another knock—harder this time—interrupted her.

"If you're bringing a fork, it's too late," she called out.

When the door opened, and Aaron appeared, dressed in a soft silver tunic and black trousers, not a strand of blond hair out of place, she threw her head back and groaned before she could stop herself.

He laughed quietly, "I guess I deserve that."

Aaron strode into the room but didn't close the door.

"I apologize if I upset you yesterday. It wasn't my intent, Your Majesty. But we are to start lessons on our culture and traditions today, and I thought a good place to start would be the library. There will be other Valkyries around so that you won't be alone with me. I've gathered that I might have made you uncomfortable so far."

Lillian narrowed her eyes. Aaron being considerate appeared to be a complete turnaround from how he'd approached her so far.

Tilting her head, she studied him as he glanced around the room, taking in the messy bed and the blanket on the floor before his eyes settled on her again.

"I understand that you might not trust me. But I promise you, I will not touch you unless you ask me to or say anything you might deem inappropriate, Your Majesty." Aaron gave her a crooked smile, nervously pulling at his tunic.

Lillian sighed through her nose. She'd promised herself not to let her pride get in the way, and she needed to learn more about her people—about herself—so finally, she nodded. "Only if you call me Lillian."

Aaron winked and gestured for her to follow him, "As you wish. Lillian."

He quietly told her about the castle as they walked through the long halls, still lit with the silvery fire, and down several winding black marble stairways.

Her mother built Volantis after she bonded her dragon. She wanted a place close to the dragons, where only the Valkyries and their mates would be welcome.

Because of the long war between Hindra and Echo—a result of the War of Gods—where humans and shifters had taken one side and the Valkyries and Adeon another, Liv wanted a sanctuary where pregnant Valkyries or those too old or too young to fight could live in peace.

Lillian frowned. "So if humans were against Adeon, how come he supports Alek now?"

"Humans seem to always turn to where they think they'll

gain the most power…" Aaron sighed. "And I guess gods do, too. When Liv and Ivar finally brought peace to Orios, Adeon must have realized how dangerous they were. If humans, shifters, Valkyries, and the dragons stood together against him… There was a chance they could overpower him. So he went to the power-hungry Alek and his angry, weak magic wielders and offered them more power if they took Liv and Ivar down."

Lillian shook her head. "So Adeon gave Alek his powers?"

"Yes and no. Alek was a fire wielder already, but as you know, magic has a price. He could only do small things. Like lighting a fireplace or a candle. Maybe set a tree or two on fire. But not the kind of magic he has now. Adeon removed the barrier for his magic, allowing him an endless well to tap into. Even Valkyries can't do that. Magic tires you out; it draws on your energy. You must have felt it when you used it the first time—the tiredness?"

When Aaron glanced at her, she nodded. She'd felt ready to faint after she'd killed those two guards, a strange emptiness in her body as if she'd used up every reserve inside her.

Lillian winced at the memory, the lives she'd taken without a thought. How easy it had been for her to kill two men she knew nothing of.

"Alek doesn't have that. He doesn't get tired." Aaron shook his head. "Since I'm male, I don't have magic, but I can't even imagine being able to go on without a price. It's unnatural. Even your parents—the strongest magic wielders Orios had seen in a long time, if not ever—couldn't go on and on."

Cold fear swept through Lillian. If Alek was that powerful, how would she even take him on? She'd thought they'd at least be evenly matched, but if Alek's power rivaled that of a deity, was given to him by Adeon himself…

She gritted her teeth—she'd find a way.

She had to.

"I'm looking forward to seeing what your shadows can do, though. I heard your father's magic was a sight to behold.

Wielding the sun, molding it to his will, even turning night into day—he rivaled the gods. And your mother, while her earth powers weren't offensive, she made Hindra thrive like it hadn't in centuries."

When she eyed him, Aaron's brows snapped together. "You didn't know? They were truly extraordinary, Lillian. And I'm sure you will be as well once you take the throne."

She wasn't so sure of that, so instead of responding, she studied the paintings lining the walls, the maps of Orios mixed with depictions of wars and Valkyries.

When they passed yet another set of open doors, fire sparkled under her skin, and before she could stop herself, Lillian sliced her gaze to the side.

Kian, Finn, and Sam sat in a room to her left, the floor-to-ceiling windows letting in the late summer sun and bathing the room in bright light. She jerked when Kian's head whipped up, and when their eyes met, a chill danced down her spine.

"Come on, one more floor, and we're in the library." Aaron gently tugged her by the hand, and Lillian let him drag her away from the room, but not before seeing the flash of hurt that crossed Kian's face.

13

Lillian

Guilt still made her cringe when Aaron led them into the extensive library. Everything inside her wanted to go back to that room, take Kian by the hand, and tell him they should be together—that they belonged together.

But the thought of Eli and Atli wouldn't let her.

She couldn't risk what they'd begun, the mission that now lay heavy upon her shoulders.

Lillian trailed her eyes around the room, trying to push away the thoughts as she studied the glass shelves lining every wall of the square room and the large crystal chandelier glittering in the middle, shining its soft light on the two purple velvet chairs Aaron guided her to.

A few other Valkyries hovered in the back of the room, stealing glances at her as they browsed the shelves, but as soon as she met their eyes, they looked away.

"So I'm guessing, even though you don't know much about your parents, you know a little bit of your ancestry?" Aaron asked gently as he picked a few leather-bound books off a shelf and sat in the chair beside her.

Lillian nodded, carefully drawing her wings in, trying to

mimic Aaron's graceful folding to ensure they didn't rasp against the chair.

"I've read some. I know Adeon created the original Valkyries and that Eir is our original mother. I know about the… mate bonds. But I don't know much else."

Aaron studied her, his head tilted and his blond hair reflecting in the candlelight from the chandelier. "I'm sorry, Lillian. I can't imagine how overwhelming this all must be."

She narrowed her eyes. "What game are you playing?"

Aaron shook his head. "I'm not playing a game, Lillian. I realize I came on too strong. And I'm not a bad male. It's just… When you've been told stories about the mighty heir that your parents, who died before you were one, betrothed you to, I got a bit too excited. But I realize Kian being your mate complicates things."

When a growl reverberated in Lillian's throat, Aaron lifted his hands. "I meant no disrespect. But you haven't consummated the bond, so can you fault me for having hope?" Aaron offered her a weak smile.

Lillian sighed. "Aaron, you realize I killed the man I loved." She swallowed the lump that formed in her throat. "Even if the Elders accepted Kian, I am nowhere near ready to be with anyone. I can't even think about it. Not now. Probably not for a long time."

But her treacherous heart constricted when Kian's name left her lips, hammering against her ribcage at the thought of his eyes, his thick black hair, and strong shoulders.

Lillian clenched her fists. How heartless was she? It had been days—days!—since she killed Eli. The man she supposedly loved.

No, the man she loved. She had loved him and still did, and she didn't know what that said about her.

Aaron glanced at her white knuckles. "The mating bond is the strongest bond we have, stronger than even the familiar bonds. Don't fault yourself for your feelings. It's nature. It's a gift. The feelings, the need, won't go away unless you reject him. And I'm not certain they'll ever fully go away, even then. But even if it's rare, people do reject their mate. Grete did."

When Lillian eyed him to continue, Aaron's lips curled, his sharp teeth glinting beneath.

"He was evil. Power hungry. A killer. He betrayed her during the War of Gods, even as all the other mates stayed on our side. He couldn't handle Grete being more powerful than him, so he turned against her—against the Valkyries."

"Is that why she is so bitter?" Lillian raised her brows, struggling to feel any empathy for her aunt, not after the way she'd treated her and had spoken about Kian.

Aaron stretched his arms over his head, the silver tunic shimmering as he placed his hands behind his neck.

Glancing down, he responded quietly, "She did what she had to do for our people. She couldn't be with someone who betrayed us. Mate or not. But yes, I think it changed her."

A small shiver of unease ran down Lillian's neck.

But Kian hadn't betrayed them. His only fault was his father. And he'd done more for the rebels than Grete or the Elders ever had.

She quickly changed the subject. "You haven't found your mate?"

A shadow crossed Aaron's face. "I don't think I have one. The few other male Valkyries that existed at least never found theirs before they died. From what I've been able to gather, they all mated other Valkyries who either lost or never found their mates."

Lillian nodded, picking at her black leather tunic.

Aaron continued. "But some of them seemed happy, even if a chosen mate will never have the same bond as a fated one. The fated bond has some similarities to your bond with Finn —you're able to speak without words and feel the other at all times. But unlike the familiar bonds, you can't share magic, and it can also weaken you. Since you tie your mate's life to yours, if you die… Well, so does your mate. And if your mate perishes, the pain might very well bring you to the brink of death as well. Many Valkyries fade away not long after their mate passes as most are unwilling to live without them."

Strange, Lillian thought. But perhaps it made sense. The mating bonds were for reproduction, not for fighting like the familiar bonds.

She cleared her throat. "So how do you consummate the bond? I mean, apart from what my aunt mentioned."

When her face heated, Aaron laughed softly. "You'll really need to get over the modesty, Your Majesty."

She cast him a narrowed glance.

"Sorry—Lillian. As you'll learn, Valkyries can be quite direct, and we're definitely not shy about what we take pleasure in. We fight in the open, we love in the open, and sometimes we seek pleasure in the open," he winked. "But it's quite simple. You consummate the bond, and similar to what I guess you did with Finn, you seal it in blood. Breaking a consummate bond is not possible—not by ourselves. We need the gods —Adeon—to do it. He did it for Grete, and of course, I wasn't born then, but I heard it was brutal. She nearly died."

Lillian shuddered. She couldn't imagine the pain if it was this difficult to keep her distance from Kian, and they hadn't even consummated the bond. She didn't even want to think about a world in which she rejected him or Adeon somehow came in between them.

"Thank you, Aaron. Maybe we can talk about something else? Like how many Valkyries are here, and what do you all do?" *Since you're not helping the rebellion*, she wanted to add, but she didn't want to risk Aaron stopping being so open.

Aaron nodded and spent the rest of the day explaining how Volantis' society worked.

There were a few hundred Valkyries on Seigard—Lillian winced at how many must have died that day eighteen years ago—and about half of them were mated. When Aaron explained they all lived in the castle, Lillian's eyes widened.

She hadn't realized just how big Volantis was.

No children had been born in the past eighteen years—

and not for lack of trying—making Aaron and Lillian the youngest Valkyries alive. No one knew why, but there were hushed rumors that Adeon had something to do with it, that something happened the day her parents were murdered.

The Valkyries spent the days training for battle—as they were bred to—while the mates handled everything else. Since they were humans or shifters, they could travel to Hindra and Echo to trade, and they also managed the dining hall where most of the Valkyries ate common meals.

When the moonlight streamed in through the small window behind them, Aaron motioned for Lillian to follow him back to her room. None of her friends remained in the glass room when they passed it, and relief and loneliness battled within her as she glanced down at the soft carpet lining the hallway.

Finn

Finn knocked softly on Lillian's door, but there was no answer when he called out that it was dinner. Leaning his forehead against the wood, he could hear her even breathing through it and realized she must be sleeping.

He sighed. She probably needed rest, but Lillian hadn't joined them for a single meal since they arrived, and she was looking thinner by the day. Knocking one more time, he held his breath. When the soft snores continued, Finn walked with heavy steps back to the dining room.

Kian and Sam were already seated at the large oval table, covered with a white tablecloth and several plates of food. The smell of fish and potatoes washed over him, joined by the woody smell of wine that a human man, dressed in the simple purple tunics the mates favored, poured into golden cups.

His friends looked up when Finn entered the double doors, and a pang of pain seared through him at the worry crossing Kian's face when he didn't find Lillian behind him.

"She's sleeping." Finn slipped onto a hard wooden chair, keeping his gaze on the golden curtains sparkling in the moonlight streaming in through the large windows behind the table.

"I tried waking her, but she must be exhausted."

When he shifted his gaze to Kian, emotions flashed across his features, but finally, he nodded and reached for a goblet of wine.

Even if Finn didn't share a familiar bond with him, it was clear he debated whether to force her to the table—feed her if he had to—like Finn himself had considered. But they both knew better; Lillian didn't do anything she didn't want to do. And if they pushed her; she'd push back twice as hard.

Sam cleared his throat. "She just needs time. But she'll come back to us. She was the same during the trials, wasn't she? Trying to do it all herself, never asking for help."

Finn wasn't so sure about that, but before he could respond, Elya and Else swept into the room and took the two seats next to him while neatly folding their black wings behind them.

"Such gloom. I didn't realize everyone in this court was so prone to self-pity." Elya rolled her eyes while brushing some dust off her black jacket. "I took the queen for a flight yesterday, and she almost had us both killed with her moping."

Kian growled, "She did great. She is hurting, but she still participates in all training and does everything you ask of her. *You* risked her life, Elya, and you will not do it again."

Finn narrowed his eyes at the blonde as Sam asked, "What does he mean?"

Even if Finn was intrigued by the Valkyrie, he'd seen Lillian fall yesterday, and he wasn't about to have her risk Lillian's life, especially when she was in such a vulnerable state.

Worried, he reached out through the bond, but it was quiet—a black, empty silence. Finn ground his teeth—he really wished Lillian wasn't so skilled at shutting it off.

Elya rolled her eyes again. "She needed a bit more encouragement. I gave it to her, and she flew. I think it was successful, myself." She lowered her voice, glaring at Kian. "And don't tell me what to do, human. I was only trying to help her, and as you saw, it worked."

Kian glared back at her, his green eyes nearly black.

Finn raised his hands before a full-on fistfight broke out. "Calm down everyone. I agree with Kian. No more risking our queen's life—she is not herself right now. Now, I suggest we eat before this gets cold."

Kian muttered something under his breath—too quiet for even Finn to pick up, but began shoveling food onto his plate.

Sam curiously studied Elya and Else while sipping wine from his golden cup—the only one who seemed the slightest bit relaxed, exactly like he'd been during the trials. The calm anchor to their group.

Finn cleared his throat, trying to break through the thick silence that lay heavy over the table. "So what is there to do here except train?"

He would never admit it, but every muscle in his body ached from Elya kicking his ass again in the training ring today. The Valkyrie had slammed him down so hard he'd lost his breath, and large bruises had bloomed across his abdomen where she'd whipped him with her wooden sword.

Elya grinned. "Not much. Unless you want to join the mates in the kitchen? Otherwise, we train every day." She lowered her voice, but even so, Finn didn't miss the sharp edge to it as she added, "Even if Grete never has us do anything with said training."

Finn nodded. "I guess I might need an hour or two more before I can take you."

When Elya threw her head back and let out a raspy laugh, he mock-frowned. "I don't give up easily, Valkyrie."

"I'm sure you don't, boy." Elya leaned back in her chair, flicking her gaze between Finn and Kian while swirling the wine in her cup. Actually, his cup, Finn realized as he glanced at the table.

Elya raised her brows in challenge, but Finn just threw her a lazy smile. "If you're so eager to get my lips on you, you could just ask."

As color stained Elya's cheeks, a wide grin overtook his face, growing bigger when Elya glared at him.

Sam finally interrupted their stare down. "So, what are the Elders doing, seeing as they're leaving Lillian's training to their foot soldiers?"

Both Elya and Else snapped their heads in his direction, and Finn couldn't stop a small giggle from escaping when Else responded quietly. "You humans truly need a lecture in manners. Perhaps we should ask Aaron to have lessons with you as well? While we might have an Elder Council, we are a free people. We are all skilled in fighting, and we all make decisions for ourselves. Our queen may command us, but we have the right to object. We're not *foot soldiers*—we're not barbarians like you humans."

Elya slung her arm over her sister's shoulder. "Hear, hear, sister. We volunteered to train with you and Lillian. But we shall stop if we wish."

A knife could cut the tension in the room, Sam now glowering at the twins, rivaling Kian's narrowed gaze.

Glancing at the many swords leaning against the table, Finn quickly said, "We appreciate the training. We're just curious. Since Lillian isn't gracing us with her company, we have no way of understanding what's happening within this castle outside of the training ring and the meals. Although I will say both the training and the food have been superior to anything I experienced on Hindra or Echo."

When he elbowed Kian, his friend inclined his head and grudgingly admitted, "He might be just the tiniest bit right. I'm glad Lillian has you to help her, even if I'd prefer not to see her tumble toward the ground again. And we do appreciate your hospitality."

Elya's face softened, and Finn sucked in a breath at the genuine, albeit small, smile that played on her lips. "Mates. Always so protective. And you're not even bonded."

She met Kian's eyes, and something passed between them

at that moment. "I don't think you're such a bad match for our queen," she said softly, almost as if to herself.

Kian bowed his head to the Valkyrie, offering her a small smile in return.

Clasping his hands together, Finn grinned at the table. "All right, is there any more of that wine anywhere? I wouldn't say no to another glass or ten."

Laughter bubbled across the table as the charged atmosphere began to fade, and even Kian smiled when Elya declared that she knew where they kept the good wine, ordering one of the mates to bring them a few bottles.

Leaning back in his chair, Finn blew out a soft breath.

If they could only get Lillian to join them next time, everything might very well work out.

15

Lillian

She flew out of bed at the hard bang on the balcony door.

Hanin waved her wings eagerly until Lillian threw open the glass doors, letting the cool morning air drift into the room.

Shivering, she reached for a soft white robe to pull over her nightgown, grateful that the Valkyries had stocked up her closet with anything she might need.

It's way past dawn, Your Majesty. And I heard you flew! Some of the other guardians spotted you. I can't believe you did it without us.

She didn't miss the sour undertone in the young raven's caw.

Before Lillian could respond, Munion joined Hanin on the balcony, his large frame balancing on the stone railing.

Great work, Your Majesty! You shall learn to fly as well as any Valkyrie—better—in no time. We're so proud of you and even prouder to have the honor of being your guardians.

Lillian snorted. "I doubt it. I was barely able to stay up last night. And what do you mean by other guardians?"

Hanin rolled her eyes. *All Valkyries have two guardians. They're not as great as we are, of course.* The raven winked at her while offering a mock bow. *We were assigned to you because we're the best of the best.*

Munion smacked the smaller raven over the head with his wing. *Modest as always, young guardian. But she's right, Majesty. We were handpicked by the Elders when Tyr, the dragon king, informed us you were alive. We are the best fliers, so we had the best chance of following him to Echo to try to find you. However, since you hadn't broken the curse, we weren't exactly certain how to handle you. You were quite frightened of us.*

Lillian shook her head. "Can you blame me? You blinded someone the first time I met you. And I'd only just found out I wasn't human. I didn't know if you actually could tell it was me."

Hanin sighed, but after a stern glare from Munion, she kept her beak shut.

No, Majesty. That's why we didn't just pluck you off the mountain, which Hanin initially insisted on. And even if the price you paid was too high, I'm glad we didn't. Or we might not have had you back at all.

Lillian bit her cheek, the dull ache in her chest sharpening at the mention of Eli.

The sorrow will pass, Majesty. Munion tilted his head, his dark eyes filling with empathy. *The brave man made an even braver choice—a choice you cannot fault him for or blame yourself for. One is only responsible for the actions one has control over. And you were not in control, but you can be now.*

Tears filled Lillian's eyes. "But it was my choice to kill him. How is my life worth more than his?"

It isn't.

Munion lifted his wing to smack Hanin again.

Wait. The younger raven narrowed her eyes. *I'm not saying her life isn't worth anything. But he didn't force our queen to make that choice because her life meant more than his. He did it because her life is tied to so many more. It wasn't just about you, Majesty. It was about Orios, the Valkyries, the dragons, and the many other creatures who fled under Alek's rule.*

Lillian nodded slowly, but guilt still pressed on her chest, making it difficult to breathe.

She wasn't so sure she would be the one to actually save all of those people, even if Eli and her father had believed it. She hadn't made any progress in convincing the Valkyries to help and hadn't seen a whisper of the dragons since that first night.

Munion tilted his head. *How about we train a little? Physical activity seems to help most species when they need to get their minds off something.*

Lillian nodded again. "Let me just get dressed."

Turning around, Lillian went to the bunched-up pile of leathers she'd left on the floor yesterday—too tired to fold into the small closet in her room. When she glanced at the balcony, the two ravens stared at her expectantly.

"A little privacy, please?"

The ravens cawed as they turned their backs, but not before Hanin rolled her eyes again. *Valkyries know little modesty, Majesty.*

Lillian grumbled internally. Aaron had said the same thing.

16

Lillian

"I don't know if this is the best idea."

Lillian shook her head, peering out over the balconies and the grassy ground far below—somehow more intimidating in the bright sunlight. At least in the dark, she couldn't see the many ways she could die if she fell.

A brisk wind blew through her unbound hair, the salt in it sticking to her face. "Maybe we should start from the ground?"

You did it last night, Majesty. You can do this. Munion glanced at her while whipping his head encouragingly, his black eyes kind as they swept over her.

And if you fall, we'll catch you. We're stronger than Elya, and we can carry you. Hanin winked and spread her wings wide, the black feathers sparkling in the sunlight as she easily took flight with the help of the soft sea breeze.

Lillian drew a deep breath.

She had done it yesterday. She could do it today.

With shaking legs, she stepped onto the wide stone railing, holding out her arms to keep her balance as her wings unfurled. Nerves and dread tangled in her stomach, small knots knitting themselves together as she cast a glance down again.

"You've got this!"

Lillian growled as she almost fell off the balcony when Elya's voice rumbled above her. She whipped her head up, finding the blond Valkyrie in the air, waving at her. "Come on! It's a beautiful day. We'll show you all of Seigard."

Yes! I want to show you our home! Hanin soared next to Elya. *Come on! We can't have a queen who's afraid of flying.*

Lillian frowned when Hanin and Elya let the wind take them further and further up in the clear sky, all the while gesturing for her to follow.

As if it were that easy.

Munion cawed softly. *Don't mind them, Majesty. Hanin was terrified for months when she learned how to fly and then again when she learned how to fight. She likes to pretend that she's not scared; it helps her. But she fears being a poor guardian. You should know her father was your mother's guardian. And while he couldn't stop Alek, he put up enough of a fight to get you and several others to safety. She has a large wingspan to fill.*

An ember of guilt settled in Lillian's stomach. So many had died for her and her parents—not just Valkyries and mates but guardians and perhaps many other creatures she hadn't learned of yet.

Munion clicked his beak. *It's our duty, Majesty. Do not feel sorry for him. He was proud to go down defending your family, as we would be to do for you, as would any guardian properly protecting their Valkyrie.*

"Do you have a choice in becoming guardians?" Lillian tilted her head, some of the unease leaving her as curiosity about the ravens and Valkyries' relationships took over.

Of course, we have a choice. Munion shook his head. *Valkyries might be known for their temper and for being ruthless, but you are a free people. You do not demand service—not in the way humans do. You protect us and are loyal to us as well. It's the same way with the dragons. They only bond with you because you can offer them something in return.*

Lillian frowned. "What could we possibly offer dragons?"

Magic, of course. Dragons have fire, but if you bond with them, they can channel your magic as well. Just as the little owl can.

Little owl.

She wasn't sure if Finn would like that name too much.

Lillian straightened. She had used so many of Finn's abilities, but she hadn't even thought about him channeling her power. Shame burned across her skin.

She hadn't even thought to offer.

When Munion eyed her, Lillian nodded thoughtfully. "Grete has not offered to train me in wielding my magic yet. Maybe you can teach me?"

We cannot teach magic, Majesty. We do not possess any magic of our own, so it would be unwise for us even to try. Since guardians only belong to one Valkyrie in their lifetime, neither of us is too familiar with how you control your gifts. I'm afraid it would be a disaster if we tried. But flying, we can teach.

She swore Munion grinned at her.

Look down.

Lillian glanced down, realizing she was far above the castle. Whipping her head to the side there were soft, white clouds floating past them in the gentle breeze, clear blue sky surrounding them. She reached out to touch them, her lips curling at the moisture sifting through her fingers.

"How did I even get here?" Lillian tried to feel for her wings, and her stomach surged as she dropped several feet.

Don't think, Majesty.

It was easy for him to say. He was a bird; flying was in his nature. She'd been human for eighteen years, and humans didn't fly.

Lillian squeaked as she dropped another few feet, faster now.

Majesty—

Lillian didn't hear the rest as she fell free through the air, screaming as she tumbled toward the dark stone castle. Desperately, she tried to get her wings to cooperate, but they only flapped against the strong wind surging through them.

A flash of black appeared, and Kian's strong arms wrapped around her before rifting them back to her balcony.

His arms tightened around her for a moment before he gently set her down, and emptiness immediately washed over her without the warmth from his body.

Even if it had only been a few seconds, her entire being craved that touch. Trembling, she forced herself to remain still instead of slipping back into those strong arms and resting against his broad chest.

"I apologize if I intervened too early. I saw how well you were doing. But when you screamed..." Kian scratched his stubble.

It was longer than she'd ever seen it, and her breath caught in her throat when the shadows on his jaw somehow made him look even more handsome.

Lillian took several deep breaths to calm her pounding heart before quietly responding, "It wasn't too early. I had no control."

She glanced down at the stone balcony, grateful for the solid ground beneath her boots.

"I..." she started but trailed off as she met Kian's eyes, the worry lining them.

Everything in her wanted to reach out and touch his face, smooth out the hard lines she knew she was causing. But instead, she averted her eyes and whispered, "Thank you."

Kian offered her a small smile. "I'll always be here to catch you when you fall if you let me."

Lillian thought he might reach out for her, but he remained still, casually leaning against the railing as if he hadn't just saved her life—again.

She couldn't help but sweep her gaze over him, appreciating how the Valkyrie leathers snugly fit over his broad chest and arms. As she met his eyes again, his lips curled further, and she nearly groaned when a blush threatened to creep up her neck.

"Well, I should probably…" She pointed to the glass doors to her balcony.

When Kian nodded, she turned and walked away from him, feeling his eyes burn into her back and clenching her fists not to turn back around and fall right into his arms.

Fall right into him and never look back.

17

Kian

Kian gripped the railing so hard he thought he might rip part of the stone off. To let her leave with those hunched shoulders and that haunted look in her usual steely eyes took every ounce of self-control he had.

He knew she needed time, that she needed to figure this out for herself, and he had little doubt she would. Her unwavering strength was one of the reasons he'd fallen so hard in the first place. He'd watched her firsthand during the trials, how she'd stood up to his father not once but twice on that mountain. But he wished she'd let him help her. Or at least let him stand beside her as she took this realm for herself.

Not that it surprised him that she pushed them away, tried to shoulder all that weight and pain and sorrow by herself.

She'd been the same way when she thought she was sick.

Kian sighed and slowly followed Lillian into the castle. Heading into his own room, smaller than Lillian's but comfortable, he dropped down on the bed.

Someone had lit a fire in the marble fireplace to help warm the room, and the flames danced on the small couch before it. Deep in thought, he barely noticed when Sam and Finn slipped through the door.

84

"We're heading out to explore the castle," Finn said softly, his usual upbeat tone absent. "Are you planning on staring into that fire all day, or would you like to join us?"

Kian slowly looked up, forcing himself to hold back a wince at Finn's pale face and blank stare, at the dark half-moons lining his eyes.

Straightening his shoulders, he flashed his friend a smile.

They couldn't fall apart.

Lillian needed them, even though she wouldn't admit it, and they would be of no help to her if they also walked around this castle as ghosts.

He nodded. "Sure, why not? I think we all could use something else to think about."

Sam offered him a crooked grin. "That we could. I, for one, am excited to see something other than the dining room and the fighting ring."

A gravelly laugh had Kian snap his head to the door.

"Men who don't only care about weapons and food. Now that's new." Elya winked at them. "Come on. Grete probably won't be too happy if she finds you outside the east wing, so we should go before she somehow appears. She likes to sneak up on you, especially if you're up to no good."

Elya instructed Kian to rift to the south side of the castle; there was a large balcony he should be able to land on. When Kian nodded, Elya and Else, her constant silent shadow, took to the skies.

Kian glanced at Finn. "No flying today?"

If Finn wasn't training, he'd mostly been in the skies, flying laps around the island, a golden shape letting the wind take him wherever it blew.

Finn shook his head, a ghost of a smile gracing his face. "I should probably wear clothes if we are to meet other Valkyries and humans."

Kian snorted, "You're probably right," and gripped Sam and Finn to rift them away.

Elya and Else waited for them on a wide balcony, facing

the vast forest to the left and the mountain the castle was built into on the right.

When he glanced up, snow already sprinkled the top of the mountain and the wind that blew through his hair made him shiver.

Summer was definitely making way for fall.

"Come on. We'll show you where most of the Valkyries and their mates spend their time." Elya impatiently waved for them as Finn and Sam drew deep breaths against the nausea from the short rift.

When their stomachs calmed, they followed the twins into the castle, and Kian's mouth fell open at the many Valkyries walking through the softly lit hallways.

Normal fire burned in the lanterns lining the walls in this part of the castle, and the floors were covered in black carpet, embroidered with silver Valkyrie and raven wings in an intricate pattern.

Else pointed to an extensive training room to their right. "This is where most Valkyries train. Only the Elders use the training ring you've seen so far."

Kian stared at the Valkyries sparring with each other, flying and running at impossible speeds. A few mates also practiced hand-to-hand combat on a raised platform in the back of the room, their movements unbelievably slow compared to those of the winged women.

Elya followed Kian's eyes. "Mates are also expected to keep up with their training. Although, we're not the best at training them since we have different ways of fighting. They tend to prefer to train with each other."

"Wouldn't it be better if they learned your ways?" Finn tilted his head when one of the men stumbled, falling off the fighting ring. "They don't seem very skilled, even to human standards."

Elya shrugged, but her voice was edged as she responded, "Since we haven't been fighting for a long time, Grete doesn't seem to prioritize it. I'm surprised she even has us keep up at this point. She's made it very clear she doesn't see a need for us to go to war anymore. Since we no longer protect Adeon and we're not partaking in the human world, our main occupation seems to be hiding. Let's move on."

Elya guided them through a long corridor, showing them the communal dining room, where fifteen or so mates were cooking and gossiping.

When Sam's stomach rumbled at the delicious smells that wafted through the halls, Elya rolled her eyes. "Let's get some food."

The humans curiously eyed them as they walked up to the tables lined with food but averted their eyes when Kian stared back at them.

"They've been instructed not to interact with you yet, not until Lillian has been introduced. Although it's impossible to keep secrets here, everyone knows their queen is back and that she brought the Crown Prince with her," Else mumbled beside him.

Kian nodded as one of the mates offered him a plate filled with vegetable stew and potatoes.

"Thank you," he said, giving him a small smile.

The man's eyes widened, and he quickly scurried back into the kitchen. Kian overheard him excitedly whisper that he'd seen the prince to the group of men in there.

As they ate, Elya explained that the south tower was the largest, and each Valkyrie had their own quarters in here. Depending on their status—defined by their fighting skill—and whether they had a mate, they had a one—or two-bedroom apartment.

At the bottom, there was a large balcony, where they grew food, managed by Valkyries with earth magic and some of the mates interested in farming. Then there was the training ring and a few rooms for socializing, including a ballroom.

"You really have everything you need. I understand why Grete prefers to keep you here," Sam nodded.

Elya studied him, a frown forming between her brows. "I

guess. If you think being locked up in a castle is everything you need."

When Kian met her eyes, understanding filled him.

He'd also spent most of his life locked up in a castle under his father's rule.

18

Lillian

After her awful attempt at flying, Lillian declined to try again when Hanin and Munion tried to convince her, arguing she needed to rest. But as she lay on her bed staring up at the beams lining the ceiling, restlessness set in, and even though she risked running into her friends, she spent the rest of the morning strolling through the long halls of the tower.

After a few hours, she stumbled upon a brightly lit hallway, with large windows lining the entire right side and painting after painting of Valkyries on the other. Lillian slowly surveyed each one, sucking in a breath when a pair of light gray eyes stared back at her, the same raven-black hair as her own tumbling down the beautiful Valkyrie's shoulders.

"That's Liv. Your mother."

Lillian jerked when Grete's voice interrupted her thoughts.

Keeping her eyes on the painting, on her mother's somewhat sullen expression—so similar to Lillian's own frown, she asked quietly, "What was she like?"

Grete sidled up next to her, and when Lillian cast a glance to the side, Grete's blue eyes lovingly trailed her mother's features, her expression so different from her usual hard, unforgiving one.

"She was wonderful. As soon as Liv walked into a room, it lit up, and no male or female could stay away from her. She had so much love to give, and she gave it freely without expecting anything in return."

Tracing her finger over the small wrinkle between her mother's brows, Grete continued. "It wasn't a surprise to anyone when my mother named her queen, even though I was older. But she was restless and impulsive as well, and she believed she could do anything—survive anything—as long as she had love in her heart. It was her downfall in the end. She couldn't let go of your father, not for Orios, not even for you."

Heart aching, Lillian thought of how she very well might stand before the same decision as her mother—not because Adeon told her so, but because of the legacy her parents left behind—the mess they'd left behind.

Grete offered her a sad smile. "She hated that painting. She could barely sit still as it was, and she had to spend hours sitting for it."

Lillian glanced at Grete, raising her brows. "Why did she have to do it then?"

For the first time since she'd met her, Grete's face softened as she trailed her sky-blue eyes over Lillian. "Because we all have to do things we don't want to do. Especially when you're a leader, Lillian. And besides, it's tradition to have a painting of each queen that ascends the throne."

"Is your painting here somewhere?" She swept her gaze across the many frames on the wall.

Grete shook her head, her features hardening again. "I'm not queen, Lillian. I merely led in your absence, and I shall continue to do so until you're ready. However long it may take."

Lillian narrowed her eyes at her. "So, when will you deem me ready?"

Not that she particularly yearned to be queen nor felt ready to take on the responsibilities, but something stirred in her at Grete's dismissive tone. She couldn't put her finger on it —but there was something calculating, cold in Grete's voice.

"When you've learned what's needed to be queen. I hear you're making progress with flying and that you've joined Aaron to learn our history. Once you've mastered those, we'll train you on your abilities." Grete raised a brow when Lillian ground her teeth. "Any issues with that?"

Drawing a deep breath, she shifted her gaze down. "No," she said quietly.

Even if Grete got under her skin, she could see that the older Valkyrie was right. She was nowhere near ready. It was time she took flying and learning about the Valkyrie customs truly seriously.

She couldn't disappoint any more people. Including herself.

"Good," Grete flexed her wings. "I've asked Aaron to meet you in the library; I suggest you head on over there now instead of sulking around the halls of this tower."

When Grete spun around without another word, Lillian nodded to herself and slowly made her way down the spiraling staircases to the library, where Aaron was already waiting with a large stack of books in front of the two chairs by the window.

"Hello," Lillian waved half-heartedly.

"Hi, Lillian," Aaron grinned at her. "I thought a history lesson could be a good start today. What do you know of the War of Gods?"

Lillian sat down in the soft chair. "I know that the gods considered it an act of war when Adeon created the Valkyries… us, I guess. And the rest of the gods turned on him, with the humans and shifters on their side and the Valkyries and dragons on Adeon's."

Aaron nodded. "Almost correct. We make Adeon stronger; we were created to protect him. But dragon fire is the only thing that can actually kill, or at least harm, a god. So, while they didn't necessarily mind Adeon creating us, when the first

Valkyrie bonded with a dragon, the gods began to fear us. They worried Adeon would have too much power, that he could take them all down. So they convinced the humans and shifters—and any other magical beings they could—to go to war and take him down."

Nodding, Lillian picked at a book on the gods. "How did they convince the humans and shifters to join their side? When I lived as a human, very few still honored the gods, if any, outside of Alek's court."

"They promised to leave Orios, stop meddling in human and shifter business, and allow them to take care of the lands without any interference from the gods. But as you know, they failed in taking on Adeon, and there were severe losses on both sides. In the end, the gods and all other creatures struck a deal to end the bloodshed. The gods would all leave Orios and retreat to Vaelia, their homeland. Adeon wasn't welcome to join, though—the wounds from the war were too deep—-so he was to remain with his Valkyries on Hindra but leave the rest of Orios be."

Lillian hummed, vaguely remembering parts of the story from her father's history lessons growing up. She hadn't been particularly interested—was more focused on training and learning as much as possible about Alek so she'd be able to help the rebels.

"So where did Adeon go after what happened with my parents? If he's not in Vaelia, he must be somewhere in our realm."

Aaron shrugged. "He came and went after the war, mostly to check in on us and make sure we were ready should he be attacked again. But we don't know where he actually lives. Perhaps he created a new world just for himself. No one has seen him since he cursed your family and cut ties with all Valkyries for disobeying his orders."

Lillian frowned; for such a power-hungry god to live alone in a new world seemed quite unlikely, especially since he now supported Alek.

"So, he could be anywhere? What does he look like? Could he be on Echo with the king?"

Shaking his head, Aaron closed the book he'd been looking at. "Unlikely. We don't think he truly liked Alek. Alek was just a means to stop your parents from uniting Orios and risk turning all creatures against Adeon. As for what he looks like, he is fond of changing appearances. Of course, I've never met him, but I've heard him described in different ways. He does have a scar, though, a burn mark over his left eye from a dragon he slayed."

Aaron leaned forward in his chair. "I think it's good we haven't seen him, Lillian. He must know by now who and what you are, and he hasn't come after you. Perhaps he will leave you be."

A shiver snaked down her spine.

Adeon was the cause of so much destruction—for so many lives lost during the war and its aftermath, from her parents' attempt for peace and from Alek crowning himself king. And she very much doubted he would leave her be.

Suddenly cold, Lillian wrapped her arms around herself.

If it came to that, how would she take on both Alek and Adeon?

19

Finn

There were no stars as Finn flew around the castle, only dark clouds roaming the sky.

Grateful for the night sight his owl provided, Finn steered toward the forest surrounding Seigard, letting the wind dictate the speed at which he flew. Circling the dark forest, then steering out over the dark cliffs towering over the beach, he tried to clear his mind, but it proved difficult as Lillian's haunted face flashed before his eyes.

If he could sigh in owl form, he would have.

He'd been naive in thinking everything would work itself out here, that Lillian would overcome that awful night on the Skandi and still lead with her unwavering strength.

She was a ghost of herself, and not just because of the weight and color she'd lost; there was nothing of the determination and insolence she'd had in the trials when he watched her endure the Valkyrie training. She quietly followed the orders she was given, eyes down and jaw clenched, as if even looking into another pair of eyes pained her.

And her nightly dreams—when she wasn't aware enough to shut him out—were filled with so much guilt and shame, so strong that Finn himself often woke up drenched in sweat with his heart pounding against his ribcage.

Shuddering, Finn glanced toward the west, where his family still lived their life on Hindra, and wondered if he'd ever see it—and them—again. But even though he missed them, even missed the mundane life they'd led, there was nothing that could make him leave his familiar's side.

No, he would stand by Lillian until his dying breath, even if she forever remained this shadow of herself.

He knew Kian and Sam were adamant she'd snap out of it, but they didn't feel her—feel the despair that opened inside her like a dark pit—like he did. Even if Kian could feel whispers of her emotions from time to time, they hadn't fully bonded yet, and Finn was certain that the steadfast belief Kian harbored would waver if they had.

Letting out a soft hoot, he steered toward a balcony in the east tower—not his own, not yet. He couldn't stand being alone in that small room, couldn't stand hearing Lillian's desperate cries as soon as she went to bed.

Upon landing, he quickly shifted and drew a deep breath of salty air as he stared out over the dark island.

"Don't you ever wear clothes?" Elya joined him on the balcony, shamelessly letting her eyes sweep over his body.

Finn tried for a smile, tried to muster up a flirtatious comment, but failed when a distant scream reached his sensitive ears.

Clenching his fists against the wave of anguish that rolled through him, he mumbled, "I didn't feel like going back to my room."

Elya's sharp eyes locked with his. "It won't always be like this, Finn. It's been a few days. Give her time."

Nodding, he shifted his gaze out toward the sea again.

"So, what's the deal with your group? I understand Kian is our queen's mate, and Sam is her friend, but what about you and Lillian? Are you friends? Lovers?"

Finn snapped his gaze to hers, noting the hint of color in

her cheeks, and despite himself, he grinned. "Are you asking me if I am spoken for, Elya?"

The Valkyrie's brows snapped together, and she shook her head violently as a blush crept up her neck.

Chuckling, he turned toward her, leaning his elbow on the railing. "You are! The lethal Valkyrie warrior wants to know if I am available."

"I do not," she growled. "I am merely trying to understand the dynamics in our queen's court. It might be problematic if the queen has a lover if she ever decides to accept the mate bond."

Laughing louder, Finn took a step forward, so close he nearly brushed up against the leathers she wore. But Elya didn't back down, only tilted her head so that she could keep his gaze.

Still, the deep blush painting her cheeks betrayed her resolve, and when her eyes darted down, lingering for a moment, electricity crackled over Finn's skin.

Elya's eyes slowly lifted until they met his again, and he didn't miss the ember of heat that sparked in her deep blue eyes.

Leaning forward until he could smell her sweet, flowery scent, he whispered, "Well, if anyone else is interested, please tell them I am very much available. Lillian is my best friend and we have never been, nor will we ever be lovers."

His lips brushed her ear as he pulled back, and a shiver ran through the Valkyrie, her wings flaring slightly.

Taking a step back and clearing her throat, Elya said quietly, "That's good to know. I'll be sure to inform anyone who asks. And if you keep walking around here without clothes, I'm sure you'll have many offers. There are already whispers of the golden shifter all over Volantis."

Finn winked at her. "Perhaps I don't want many offers. Just the one."

Lips twitching, she spun around, and as she walked off, she

glanced at him from over her shoulder with that sweet blush still staining her cheeks. "Good night, Finn."

As he made his way back to his room, some of the weight that lay on his chest had lifted, and he found himself smiling as he lay down in the small bed.

That night, his dreams weren't filled with Lillian's despair but with blond hair and rosy cheeks.

20

Lillian

The following weeks, she trained every day.

Since Grete informed her that before she was introduced to the people, the Elders wanted her to master both flying and her newfound power, she poured every ounce of her energy into training and the lessons in the library with Aaron. Most nights she was so tired she tumbled into bed, barely remembering to remove her leathers before falling into deep, often nightmare-filled, sleep.

And while Lillian wanted to smack Grete over her head for her condescending tone every time she checked in on Lillian's progress, she hadn't pushed her for when she believed she would be ready again.

She had yet to come to terms with her new title herself, and the thought of being introduced to a mass of people as their unknown queen made her want to vomit. The Elders had been hesitant enough about her during that first meeting, and she didn't want to think about what the rest of the Valkyries would say.

Two weeks ago, she'd finally stopped crashing into the ground, even if she was far from as skilled as Elya and Aaron, who often accompanied her during her flight training.

Aaron, true to his words, had quit his flirtatious comments and was actually a pretty good teacher, Lillian grudgingly admitted.

He was also quite helpful in getting her up to speed with the many strange Valkyrie traditions, even if she could have gone without knowing about the mating rites they held several times a year to try to further the bloodlines.

She blushed just thinking about it.

She didn't mind Elya's company either—the Valkyrie didn't push her, and they mostly flew beside each other in silence. Although she could sense Elya casting glances at her when she thought Lillian wasn't looking.

Hanin and Munion joined them most days, and while Munion offered helpful advice, Hanin didn't shy away from voicing sarcastic comments whenever Lillian lost focus. Even so, she'd grown close to the ravens, who had become her constant companions while she avoided Kian and Finn.

While Kian seemed to understand, Finn still tried to reach out to her through their bond daily. But she'd become quite skilled in shutting him out, spare him the turmoil that roiled inside her.

She still needed space.

The grief of Eli, Astrid, and Atli continued to wake her up at night, and learning the Valkyrie ways was overwhelming enough without a possessive mate and worried best friends hovering over her.

Lillian swallowed hard as a knot of loneliness formed in her throat at the thought of her friends. Shaking her head, she dressed in the leathers she wore daily and quickly brushed her hair.

Today, she was finally to practice wielding her shadows and she needed to focus.

Grete had come by her room last night and told her to prepare. She'd be training under the supervision of herself and Tild.

Tild's fire magic was close enough to her own power that

she should be able to give her some pointers. And close enough to the king's magic, Lillian thought.

Every day, she woke with more urgency, feeling as if she was running out of time to convince the Valkyries to help her take him down, and she needed to show she was strong enough to take on Alek before she made her next attempt.

When she left her room, she immediately caught Kian's searing gaze from where he was leaning against his door in those damn leathers that showed off the swell of his muscles.

Lillian groaned quietly. Why did the man have to be so gorgeous?

She'd managed to avoid him the past few weeks, eating alone in her room and flying off from her small balcony when she left to avoid the hallways in the tower. But as she met his eyes, the pull of the bond nearly made her breathless, and she just stared at him, frozen.

"Hello, Lillian." Kian offered her tight smile. "It seems you've been avoiding us."

Lillian glanced behind him.

"No. You are not running away. Not this time." Kian stepped away from the door to block her path.

She glared at him. "I am on my way to training."

When she took a step forward, Kian evaporated and then appeared right in front of her, his body flush with hers.

"You can spare a few minutes," he purred.

A shiver went down Lillian's spine, and her hands twitched toward him. The urge to run her hands down his broad chest was so intense they began shaking. She clenched them into fists, trying to lock down the treacherous emotions churning within her.

She was so close now.

She couldn't afford to give the Elders any reason not to help her.

"Step back," she growled.

Kian reached out and gripped her hands, lacing his fingers

with hers, pulling her closer. "No. You've avoided us long enough. It's time to come back to us, Lillian."

He stared at her defiantly, his green eyes burning into hers.

The heat from his body distracted her, and the bond crackled and sparked between them until she could almost see the connection that pulled them together.

Through gritted teeth, she snarled, "Kian. Step. Back."

Kian leaned in closer, trailing his gaze over her face, his soft breaths caressing her cheeks. "Is that an order, my queen?"

"It's a warning." Lillian narrowed her eyes.

Chuckling, he tilted his head, his eyes glittering in the silvery light from the lanterns behind him. "There may be more darkness inside you now, but like I've said before, you won't hurt me."

Lillian ripped her hands away and raised them, her shadows twirling around her fingers. "Try me."

"As you wish."

Without a moment's hesitation, Kian gently gripped her hands again, and she groaned when the darkness only caressed his hands, swirling down his arms and torso playfully.

Not that she was really trying to hurt him but could they at least pretend?

He leaned in so that his forehead rested on hers, and her heart began pounding so hard they both looked down at her chest.

Kian laughed softly, "Even your shadows know what they want, Lillian. When will you?"

Closing her eyes, she drew a deep breath through her nose.

The gaping hole within her spread, ice-cold despair filling her veins, and when she glanced up at him again, a lonely tear snaked its way down her cheek.

"When I finish what the people who sacrificed their lives for me started."

She shoved him and stormed off before he could respond.

21

Kian

He'd pushed her too far.

Kian stared at Lillian's dark hair streaming behind her as she ran away from him, her wings unfolding as she threw her too-thin body off the stone balcony and slammed his fist into the wall.

He'd tried to make her angry, had needed to see that fire within her that had burned so bright during the trials.

But there was only an empty shell where his fierce and unyielding mate stood.

Even as she stayed away, he didn't miss every time her shoulders hunched, or how her face tightened, or how she drew deep breaths to school her features back into neutrality.

He wished she would let him in, in whatever way she could—he didn't care if it was only as a friend.

Or at least that she would let Finn in. The guilt that now permanently lined Finn's grin was almost as unbearable to watch.

Their group was broken.

He cursed Eli and Atli then, even if he knew that without them she wouldn't be alive.

She hadn't been given a choice, and he was beginning to fear the choice that had been made for her had broken her beyond repair.

Sighing, he walked to Finn's door and knocked softly.

"Come in."

Finn and Sam sat on the balcony, enjoying the sunny fall day, with Else and Elya hovering by the back wall of the room.

He nodded to the Valkyries, rolling his eyes at the many weapons strapped to their backs and the fighting gear they were clad in. "The past weeks haven't proven that we can be trusted?"

Elya's lips curled into a sneer. "Trust me, we'd rather be anywhere but here."

But he didn't miss her glance toward Finn as she spoke.

"I'm pretty sure you have very good reasons for being here," Kian mumbled as he walked out on the balcony.

"Did you find her?" Finn cautiously eyed him.

Kian nodded grimly. "I'm beginning to wonder if it was a mistake bringing her here. She is their queen, for Orios sake, and they haven't even announced her arrival to her people."

"It's because of Grete." Elya slipped up beside him.

"Elya!" Else hissed as she followed her sister. "We shall not speak of this."

"Sister, is she not our queen? Are they not her court?" Elya threw out her hands. "You're not the only one hurting from seeing our queen wither away. She was supposed to make it better, create a new world for our people."

"What do you mean?" Kian frowned, eyeing the blond Valkyrie as heat crept up her neck.

Her nostrils flared as she glared at her sister when she tried to pull her off the balcony.

Shaking off her sister's hand, Elya took a deep breath. "When Queen Liv was murdered, those of us who survived fled here. It was awful. We lost so many to King Alek's flame. The Valkyries needed stability, and Grete stepped up. But she was supposed to find our rightful queen, not continue as regent. I'm not sure, but I have a feeling she wasn't looking especially hard for Lillian. And the dragons left this island, and us, seventeen years ago because of her. Their leader, Tyr, couldn't stand her and wouldn't submit to her rule as she was not the rightful heir. I always wanted to bond with one." Her voice became wistful at the end of the sentence.

Else fidgeted behind her, hovering like a restless shadow. "Elya, we really shouldn't."

Elya ignored her. "She is set on Lillian marrying Aaron. She has Aaron eating out of the palm of her hand, and if Lillian marries him, Grete will be able to rule behind them. She will never have to step down."

Kian snarled—he knew that woman was bad news. "She is not marrying him."

"We need to make Lillian see it. Make her fight back again." Finn rose and stalked over to Elya, towering over the Valkyrie. "Will you help us?"

Her cheeks flushed at Finn's intense stare, but she nodded. Else bit her lip behind her, but she also inclined her head after a nervous glance at her sister.

Sam flitted his eyes between them while leaning back in his chair. "Shouldn't we allow Lillian the time to grieve? It's only been a few weeks, and I can't be the only one who hears her at night. She has fought so hard and lost so many. It seems to me Grete is trying to give her some space to recover. Perhaps we need to give her that as well?"

Kian and Finn shared a look.

Sam was the more peaceful one in the group, but Kian couldn't side with him on this, even if a small voice inside him agreed that Lillian shouldn't have to continue fighting, shouldn't have to shoulder such a heavy burden at her young age. But she was withering away more each day, and he didn't think space would reverse it.

Not anymore.

When Sam caught their exchange, he shrugged, "It was

just a thought. If you prefer to try to awaken the dark queen, I will help."

Kian leaned against the railing and glanced at the vast ocean ahead of them.

He prayed it wasn't too late.

22

Lillian

Even if her flying needed more practice, a flicker of thrill filled her upon finding she was more of a natural wielding her shadows. She tuned out the small voice questioning her excitement of mastering something so deadly.

She could finally do something useful.

The darkness was an extension of herself, as if she had always known it. And perhaps she had. Even as a human, that dark hole inside her had opened at a moment's notice, her emotions widening the gap, driving her to rash and sometimes dark actions.

Lillian found it easy to will the whispering plumes out and could sense the switch inside her head that would turn them deadly. Tild and Grete had her practice lifting branches, and a smile played on her lips when she figured out how to solidify the shadows and rip large, rotten ones off the trees. Even a large boulder hadn't been any trouble to throw over a hundred feet into the ocean.

But when Grete asked her to do it again, exhaustion swept through Lillian, and the shadows merely caressed the boulder before evaporating. She panted as she tried to will them out again, but only wisps twirled around her hands.

She turned to the Valkyries behind her. "How do I get them back?"

Grete sighed. "Practice, sleep, food. It takes years for us to reach our full power." Her gaze flickered over Lillian, eyes lined with disapproval. "You wield your magic so carelessly. You're not feeling how much energy you need to draw; you're just wielding to your full extent immediately. So… you run out."

Lillian was about to snarkily respond that she could have mentioned that when they started practicing but was interrupted by a soft voice.

"Your Majesty, would you allow me to touch them?"

Another of the Elders had gracefully landed by them while Lillian practiced. She introduced herself as Stine, and the same midnight hair as Lillian's cascaded down her back. Her eyes were brown, though, and her complexion darker than Lillian's. Stine smiled shyly when she introduced herself, but her eyes never really met Lillian's.

Lillian took a step toward the Elder. "Of course."

It took all her strength to will the darkness to leave her hands, her body shaking from exhaustion and a consuming emptiness filling her veins.

Her magic shifted in the light breeze from the sea as the plumes reached out toward Stine. The Elders had brought her to a cliff towering over the beach—far from Volantis. She guessed they had little trust in her ability not to hurt anyone.

"Oh!" Stine exclaimed as she gently shifted the shadows between her fingers. "You're not a shadow wielder."

A wrinkle formed between Lillian's brows. "What am I then?"

Stine offered her a small smile. "You're wielding the night sky itself." Her smile broadened. "I've never felt anything like it. But with a father who could wield the sun, it does make sense."

Grete shot her a sharp glance. "A sky wielder." Her mouth tightened into a thin line. "Only the gods should be able to wield the sky and the sun. Make no mistake; Adeon will come after you once he finds out you're alive. He won't accept this."

Lillian shuddered but forced her voice to remain steady as she met Grete's glare. "He can get in line."

They all snapped their heads up when a screech rang above them. A huge black dragon flew over them, slowing its speed as it studied Lillian with icy-blue eyes that glimmered in the moonlight, and she sucked in a breath when she recognized it as the one from her meadow and from the Skandi.

A knot tightened in her chest.

It felt like a lifetime ago she'd been kneeling at her father's grave on her way to the capital. So much and so little had changed since then—her mission was still the same, but her outlook was so very different.

Her magic pressed to reach out to the dragon, and without a thought, she allowed a plume of darkness to shoot toward it. The dragon inhaled the piece of night she'd sent with one of its large nostrils before whipping its head toward her once more.

Good to see you alive, young queen.

Lillian gaped as the dragon spread its wings and disappeared behind a cloud bank.

"What happened to the dragons?" Lillian turned to Grete. "Why don't they protect you anymore?"

When Grete only pursed her lips, Tild answered. "The dragons are fickle creatures. They always come and go, as they have done for millennia, depending on how they perceive the reigning Valkyrie. Your mother loved them, and they loved her. But after Adeon turned on us, they didn't want to risk the association."

Lillian stared at her, a million questions at the tip of her tongue.

"There is no point in seeking them out." Grete interrupted. "They're laying low, as shall the Valkyries."

"I think I've proven my strength today." Lillian glared at the blond Valkyrie. "With more training, I could fill this whole damn island with darkness if I want. Kill anyone on it. I can take down the king. And Adeon, if I must."

"Lillian, the Valkyries will not rise against King Alek. We lost too many, and we need to protect our own." Grete curled her lips into a sneer. "And you have a great deal of training to do before you become that strong. You should rest. Get to know your people. Become the queen we believe you can be. Do you really want to subject your people to the horrors a war would bring as your first act as regent?"

"Am I not queen already?" Lillian snarled. "I will tell my people of the horrors King Alek upends on his people. And I'm sure they will rise with me." She lifted her chin in challenge.

Grete and Tild shared a glance.

"Your Majesty. Since your mother passed, we've decided as a council that while the royal line is inherited, the Elders need to vote to ensure its leader is fit to take the throne. We cannot risk angering Adeon and endanger our people again."

Tild slowly approached her, pity shining in her eyes. "And while your strength is truly impressive for just beginning to grasp your power, you don't have more than three votes as it stands."

"My mother was *murdered*. Your queen was murdered," Lillian hissed, ignoring the news of a vote. "By the very same man, you refuse to confront. Are you all cowards?"

Grete raised a hand. "Little girl, you've been here a few weeks. You don't know us or your people. You're asking strangers to fight a war that's not theirs to fight."

Little girl.

Lillian bristled, a red haze covering her eyes. Her darkness ripped out of her, and she shoved it down Grete's big mouth. Grete grasped at her throat, her eyes bulging from the lack of air, and Lillian smiled when the darkness purred at the free rein.

"Majesty! Stop this right now." Tild gripped her shoulder

tightly. "We do not kill our own, no matter how strong our emotions might be."

When she sliced her gaze to Tild, her gray eyes were hard, and silver flickered behind them as if the Elder was readying her own magic.

Forcing herself to draw a deep breath, Lillian willed the darkness to return to her. It reluctantly retreated, like a rubber band that was about to bounce back at any moment, lingering around her hands.

Still, she smiled slightly.

She'd found another way to draw up more power.

Falling to her knees, Grete gasped for air while shooting Lillian a murderous glare. Lillian bared her teeth back, a warning growl vibrating in her throat.

"Enough! Both of you." Tild's voice was commanding as she stared at them. "Your Majesty, you will need to win the council over. I support you; I think these men should pay for what they've done. But you need to be clever if you want all of us on your side. No queen has ruled the Valkyrie with fear. And no queen ever shall."

Lillian winced at the ancient Valkyrie's words. She knew her temper wasn't proper for a queen.

But Grete had a way of *really* getting under her skin.

23

Lillian

Lillian glanced out over the wild sea, watching as the waves crashed onto the beach, their licks nearly reaching the black cliff she stood upon. Grete had flown off as soon as she caught her breath, not sparing Lillian another look.

Her shoulders slumped, and tears burned behind her eyes as she fixed them on the dark horizon.

But not from guilt.

No, Grete deserved what she got.

But from the weight of her father's and friends' sacrifice. Three people she loved had died for her. So that she could live and save Orios. And she couldn't even keep her temper long enough to convince the Valkyries to help.

"Your mother struggled with being queen in the beginning as well." Tild stepped onto the cliff beside her.

The gray-haired Valkyrie conjured small embers of silver fire, like fiery raindrops, letting them light up the darkening night around them. "She was young, barely a century in human years."

Lillian threw her a look, and Tild smiled. "It's young for a Valkyrie, Lillian. You're practically still a child in our eyes. That's why it's important you get the Elders on your side.

They need to see that you're fit to rule, even if we all can appreciate you've experienced much in your young life. It was the same for your mother. She had all these new ideas, many of which the Elders didn't agree with. Like when she decided to try to seek peace and found your father."

Tears filled the older Valkyries eyes, but she smiled through them. "The Elders didn't approve then either, but your mother fought hard and got them on her side."

A few of the small droplets of fire floated toward Lillian, and she trailed them with her eyes as they flickered in the air before her. "How did she do it?"

"Patience and understanding of our politics, but she also brought back the dragons. It was the first time in a century one of us bonded with a dragon, and it's only happened a handful of times before that. As you know it's what started the War of Gods. But what many don't know is that Adeon never meant for us to bond with them. It's the one creature he is truly afraid of. Many of us don't even try. It's too dangerous, and even if we succeeded, we'd be openly challenging Adeon. Especially now that he's rejected us as his children."

Lillian frowned. "But what about *your* magic? Aaron told me you're a dragon fire wielder."

Tild laughed softly. "They like to say that, don't they? I don't wield actual dragon fire, not the kind that could harm a god. My fire just mirrors the dragons' silver flames, and though I'm powerful, I could not take on Adeon."

Nodding, Lillian asked quietly, "How did my mother bond with a dragon? And why didn't they help her when Alek attacked?"

"She was quite reckless when she was young. A force of nature that wouldn't take no for an answer," Tild winked at her, and Lillian's face heated.

"She went to Seigard—back when the dragons lived here —wanting to see one for herself, and when she came back, she'd bonded with their leader Tyr's consort. Mind you, she was half-dead when she returned, but she refused to speak to what had happened. As for why they didn't help, we cannot know for sure. The dragons only spoke to your mother and wanted little to do with the rest of us. But perhaps Alek had something on them that kept them from coming to provide aid that day. He always tried to find ways to make them bow to him."

Realization dawned on Lillian when she remembered what Kian had said about the silver dragon: how his father kept her as security.

But she'd set her free.

"If he doesn't have anything on them, do you think they would rise up against him?"

Before Tild could respond, Aaron landed beside them on the cliff, and they both turned to face him. A chill snaked down Lillian's spine at the haunted expression on his face.

Tild stalked up to him with her cloak billowing behind her. "What happened?"

"Our spies found where Alek keeps the children. And what he plans to do with them. There is an Elder meeting being called right now. Tild, you're wanted immediately." Aaron didn't meet Lillian's eyes.

She squashed a growl threatening to leave her throat. "I will be coming as well."

Aaron started to argue but quieted when Tild raised her hand. "Our queen will join the meeting. She needs to learn, and this is her fight."

Nodding slowly, Aaron motioned for them to follow when he took to the skies once more.

24

Lillian

The Elders milled about in small groups, hushed voices swirling through the oval room and unease crackling in the air. Madick and another Valkyrie guard were posted by the door, their postures tense as they kept one hand on the swords hanging at their waists.

Grete's face hardened when Lillian walked through the double doors, but she didn't say anything; she only pursed her lips and averted her gaze.

Forcing herself to leisurely stroll to the other end of the room, Lillian took deep breaths. She would control her temper this time, and she would get these damn Valkyries to listen to her.

"Elders, please sit." Grete motioned toward the table. "One of our spies returned this evening and he brought the news we've been waiting for."

The room quieted, the only sound the Valkyries' wings brushing the chairs as they all took their seats.

Grete glanced around the room. "As you all know, we've been trying to find out what the king does with the children he takes. Our belief was that he was looking for our queen, which he initially was, but he has also been collecting children with specific gifts. And he is using them to create an army as we feared. But it's worse than that. Alek has found a vessel."

The Valkyries gasped collectively around the table, but Lillian frowned. "A vessel?"

Grete's eyes flew to Lillian. "Yes. He has someone who can channel magic from others and share it with whoever is around. Alek can now access the gifts of every person in his army and guard, and the vessel can also make every person in the army a fire wielder or whatever other magic the king prefers. He could take over the whole realm."

Lillian went cold, ice coursing through her veins and the hair on the back of her neck rising. She might have had a small chance to take on Alek himself, but an army of fire wielders?

Leaning forward, she braced her hands on the marble table to steady herself. "We need to stop him, now. Alek won't stop with Hindra and Echo; he'll come here as well. I promise you, he will not leave these islands alone."

Grete studied her for a moment before shifting her gaze to the rest of the Valkyries in the room. "We'll decide as a council what we'll do. Our spies have not heard anything about Alek coming here. There has been no indication he is inclined to. But we'll put it to a vote. In two days from now, we'll gather and decide if we should act."

Lillian shook her head violently, clenching her jaw not to snarl at the Elder. "We should act now. We don't know what he's planning. What if it's too late?"

A few Valkyries nodded, mumbling their agreement, and a flutter of hope spread in Lillian's stomach.

"I agree with—" Tild started.

Grete slammed her hand on the table, interrupting Tild and quieting the murmurs. "We'll decide in two days. Our traditions dictate that we allow the Elders to make informed decisions, and we shall do so now as well."

"But—"

When Grete snapped her head toward Valeria, the Valkyrie closed her mouth and threw Lillian a look.

Grinding her teeth, Lillian squashed the growl pressing to leave her throat. She needed to keep her head this time. Some of the Valkyries seemed inclined to help, and she couldn't risk losing their favor because of her dislike for Grete.

Hopefully, it wouldn't be too late.

25

Finn

Finn grinned to himself. Tonight, he'd finally get to do something other than train and share meals with a brooding Kian and quiet Sam. The Valkyries were throwing a party in honor of the fall harvest, a festivity he'd loved back home on Hindra.

He had very fond memories of rolling around in the hay with a few men and women in the late hours of the night.

His smile widened when he donned the soft white tunic and matching white trousers laid out for him on the bed. The Valkyries had style; he had to give them that. His heart beat harder as he imagined what Elya would wear, her small but enticing body clad in pure white.

He shook his head when desire slammed into his chest. It had been a while since a woman had entranced him in this way, but he couldn't stop thinking about the blonde and the sneer she usually gave him when he flashed her a smile.

Not that it bothered him. Her violence and grouchiness did little to deter him. On the contrary, heat flared inside him when she yet again challenged him. And he didn't miss the times she glanced at him, believing he wasn't paying attention, the glimmer of heat in her own eyes.

Well, that's an image I wish to burn from my mind.

A wave of warmth washed over him at Lillian's words, at the flicker of amusement he sensed from her. While she had stopped completely shutting him out, allowing him to sense her emotions more frequently, she hadn't spoken to him in weeks, and he missed it.

I missed you too. I'm sorry, Finn.

He laughed softly.

Tonight was going to be perfect.

Kian and Sam waited outside his room, and without a word, Kian rifted them to the south tower where the festivities would take place. It was full of Valkyries, all dressed in white with beautiful golden bands over their brows, some adorned with sparkling gemstones. Their black wings, starkly contrasting with all the white, glittered in the light from the several gilded chandeliers hanging from the tall ceiling.

Finn spotted Elya immediately. She was leaning against one of the shiny black walls in the rounded ballroom, drinking from a goblet filled with golden liquor while smiling at something her sister whispered in her ear. She was as beautiful as Finn had expected, dressed in a floor-length white gown, simple and without adornments but hugging every curve on her body.

"Well, I'm off," he winked at Kian and Sam, the former shaking his head as Finn gestured toward the twins.

When Elya noticed them, she flashed her teeth as he grinned at her.

"Good luck," Kian snickered, and Finn laughed—a genuine laugh—as he began to make his way over.

"Good evening, ladies. You look ravishing tonight." Finn bowed deep. "May I join you for a drink?"

Else offered him a small smile while Elya rolled her eyes. "If you must."

Finn grabbed a goblet from one of the glass tables lining the walls and clinked it against each of theirs. "To the most beautiful women in this room. And the most beautiful man." He winked and drained his glass.

The corners of Elya's mouth twitched. "You don't think much of yourself, do you?"

Finn threw his head back and laughed. "Why should I be humble? I know I'm gorgeous, and so do you. Let's celebrate being young and beautiful."

Elya snorted and shook her head but tensed when Finn stepped closer. He leaned in close enough to be enveloped by her flowery scent, but she didn't back down as he whispered against her ear, "So what do you do during these festivities anyway?"

He glanced around the room. Hundreds of Valkyries huddled in groups by the walls, but there were also humans, primarily men, mingling among them, all with golden flutes in their hands as they socialized.

"I don't know if you can handle it, boy." A sly smile spread across Elya's face.

Finn tilted his head. "Try me."

There was very little he couldn't handle, and damn was he going to let Elya intimidate him. She kicked his ass enough in the fighting ring.

"The fall festivities are meant to bring prosperity to our people. When we lived amongst humans, it was an opportunity for us to find our mates and continue our bloodline. While most of us won't find our mate tonight since we don't have enough new men and women, we're still expected to pair up if we can. No children have been born in the past eighteen years, and we're all required to do our duty to change that."

Finn grinned. "Sounds like an excellent party. I will definitely be enjoying myself."

He let his eyes trail over Elya's body suggestively, his grin widening when her face heated. "So, will there be any dancing, or will everyone just be standing around trying to find someone to take to bed?"

"The music will start once the Elders arrive and welcome

everyone." She pointed to a small balcony jutting out above the dance floor. "They should be here any moment now. I'm guessing they might also be introducing our queen since they allowed you to partake."

Finally.

They'd been here for weeks, and while he'd heard the gossip when they ventured outside their designated tower and when he flew laps around Seigard—making it clear the Valkyries and mates knew exactly who resided in the room beside him—Lillian hadn't been introduced to anyone outside the Elders. He'd wondered if they were to stay locked up in that tower forever.

When drums started, he quickly snatched another flute and downed it, winking when Elya rolled her eyes and moved closer to the balcony.

26

Kian

He sensed her before the drums started.

The bond pulled Kian away from Sam, toward a marble balcony jutting out over the rounded ballroom. Below it, Finn already stood, and Kian joined him and the Valkyrie twins as the room fell silent.

Humans carrying drums entered from two large side doors and positioned themselves in the middle of the room, thrumming a steady beat that silenced everyone in it. Anticipation crackled in the air as everyone fixed their gazes on the balcony above.

When fear slithered along the bond, Kian's body tensed, every nerve inside him charging, ready to rift to save her. But then Lillian stepped onto the balcony together with Grete and Aaron, and he sucked in a breath, hearing Finn do the same beside him.

She was magnificent.

Lillian wore a floor-length white and gold dress, open on the sides, showing off her long legs and leaving her entire back open to display her wings. A thin golden band was wrapped around her waist, accentuating her shape—and the only thing keeping the dress from parting.

But it was the band over her brow that made him straighten his back. It was pure gold, two Valkyrie wings woven together over her forehead, beautiful against the straight black hair that fell down to her waist.

She was Queen.

His Queen.

Heat ignited inside him, burning across his skin, mingling with pride and awe as he beheld her. When she shyly glanced around the room, their eyes met, and she jerked as if the electricity between them physically shot through her. Lillian kept her eyes on his for a moment longer before she drew a deep breath and averted her eyes.

But no cold filled Kian at her rejection.

Not anymore.

He would not give up until she ordered him to do so. But even if she did, he would not leave her side. No, even if it would kill him to stand next to her without truly being with her, he'd do it. He'd made a vow that he would never leave her, and he would keep it.

Even if she took another consort.

He wouldn't be like his father—selfish and evil. He'd put his feelings aside if Lillian chose another, for her, but also for Orios. His family had caused enough destruction, and it lay upon his shoulders to rectify it. So, regardless of what happened between the two of them, he'd stand by Lillian's side as she created a new—a better—world.

"Welcome, Valkyries, mates, shifters, and humans." Grete approached the railing, with Lillian and Aaron following close behind her. "We are honored to be together for another fall festivity, where we will do our duty in furthering the Valkyrie bloodline."

The Valkyries cheered, their wings whipping the air so hard that the glasses on the tables lining the room shook as they shot glances around. When Kian felt eyes trail him as he shifted his weight, he frowned and glanced at Finn, who grinned and wiggled his eyebrows.

Kian sighed; he'd apparently already been informed.

"Tonight is a special night indeed. Not only is it the fall festivity, but we finally have our late queen's daughter amongst us. Everyone, please join me in welcoming Lillian Volantis back to the Valkyries."

The cheers were deafening when Lillian stepped forward and awkwardly waved to the filled room. A smile graced her face, but there was fear in her eyes as she stared at the large crowd.

Kian ached to rift up and take her hand, get her out of there. But he squashed the urge—she needed to find the way out of darkness herself, regardless of how much he wanted to help. He'd always be there to catch her when she fell, but she'd already learned how to fly. Hopefully, it wasn't long until she knew it herself.

But when he shifted his gaze to Grete, he ground his teeth. She was responsible for this, if not fully, at least partly. For instilling doubt and fear in his queen.

Glancing at Finn, he found him frowning. "She wasn't even introduced as their queen," he whispered.

Kian nodded.

He'd noticed that as well.

27

Lillian

There were so many eyes on her.

Lillian struggled to breathe as she plastered a smile on her face and looked out over the group of Valkyries and humans who cheered below. A sea of white, of black wings, of unfamiliar faces. Except her small group of friends to the right, where Kian's stare burned, and Finn's gaze whispered over her skin. She couldn't allow herself to look at them for long, worried her mask would crack if she met their friendly eyes.

A hand brushed hers, and she snapped her head to the side, locking eyes with Aaron's blue ones.

"You'll get used to it," he whispered. "You're doing great. Now we only have to fly down, and the festivities will begin. They'll all be too preoccupied with flirting and dancing to stare at you."

Lillian raised her brows.

"No one told you about fall festivities?" When she shook her head, he continued. "I apologize. I should have informed you. As we've discussed, we're all meant to do our duty in producing offspring, so anyone who can is expected to pair up tonight, even if they haven't found their mate."

Lillian's face heated, and she flinched back when his hand

brushed hers again.

Aaron pursued his lips to stop the smile that threatened to spread across his face and quickly clasped his hands in front of him. "No one will fault you if you don't participate, Lillian. You're not used to our traditions."

"But you will join us for the first dance," Grete hissed at her. "It's time to fly down. Please make sure you land gracefully, as all eyes will be on us. Then I expect you two to kick off the dancing."

The blush on her cheek burned, but she swallowed and nodded. She needed to do everything right so that the Valkyries would vote in favor of going against Alek tomorrow.

Aaron reached out his hand again, letting her make the decision. "We can fly down together. I'll make sure you won't fall."

Lillian began to shake her head, but when Grete arched a brow, she made herself take Aaron's hand. He squeezed hers quickly before stepping up onto the railing and pulling her with him.

The drums silenced the moment they stepped off, and Lillian's heart flew up into her throat, pounding so hard that her entire body vibrated.

Thankfully, her wings and mind cooperated, and they flew a single lap around the room while the Valkyries below clapped and whistled before landing in the middle of the dance floor.

She couldn't stop herself from glancing toward where both her bonds were pulling her and met Kian's eyes, sparks crackling between them the longer their gazes stayed locked. But when his brows furrowed, his jaw ticking, she realized she was still holding onto Aaron's hand.

Lillian quickly released her grip, watching Kian's shoulders lower and the hardness in his face softening. He offered her a blinding smile, and she almost smiled back before catching herself and tearing her eyes away.

Music began flowing through the room, a soft, gentle

melody that echoed between the curved walls.

"Shall we?" Aaron gently gripped her hand again.

Sighing, she nodded. She could do one dance. She *would* do one dance.

Aaron's arm circled her waist, and he placed her hand on his chest—right over the golden Valkyrie wings sewn onto his black jacket. "Just follow me."

Aaron was a good dancer; he confidently led her through the steps, and she blew out a breath of release when the dance floor filled with other Valkyries and humans.

"How are you feeling?" Aaron asked while slowly guiding her across the dance floor.

She cleared her throat as he spun her, slightly worried that the revealing dress Grete had ordered her to wear would expose more than she wished. "A little overwhelmed."

He nodded, "As is expected. But you're doing great. Even Grete won't find anything to complain about your behavior the past few weeks. That's why they finally introduced you today."

Lillian almost snorted. Grete definitely hadn't been too happy when Lillian almost strangled her yesterday, but if Aaron wasn't aware, she wasn't about to bring it up.

Aaron squeezed her hand. "I'm grateful you're giving me a chance, Your Majesty. I know I might have come on strong, but I was so happy to see you alive. And you're so beautiful, it's difficult to stay away."

Lillian's face heated. "Aaron, I—"

"May I step in?" Kian stared at her intently, and her heart skipped a beat at the raw emotion burning his eyes as he took her in.

"We're having a conversation." Aaron glared at Kian.

They both ignored him.

Lillian couldn't look away. Kian was dressed in pure white, and she thought she might like it even better than the black he usually favored. It made his tan skin shimmer and accentuated his muscular arms and chest as the soft fabric clung to them.

She groaned when her magic left her hands on its own accord, caressing Kian's exposed neck and arms.

Aaron cleared his throat, and Lillian jerked. "Your Majesty, shall we continue?"

She flitted her gaze from him to Kian.

She shouldn't.

But when she met Kian's eyes and hope shone brightly there, her chest constricted, and she shook her head, "I will dance with Kian."

Aaron held her for a moment longer before blowing out a soft breath. "Very well. Take care of our queen."

And as Lillian met his eyes, she realized Aaron didn't just mean during this dance.

He gracefully stepped back, offered her a deep bow, and quickly found another partner amongst the many Valkyries eyeing him.

Lillian and Kian stared at each other, and her heart thundered against her ribs when he reached out and pulled her flush to him. Her whole body relaxed against his, and Kian blew out a breath when he leaned his head on top of hers, strands of his black hair tickling her cheeks.

"I'm sorry I danced with him," she whispered.

Kian tensed for a moment before holding her tighter, his own heart hammering in harmony with hers. "Never apologize to me, Lillian. I am sorry I pushed you so hard. I made a vow that I'd never leave you, and I won't. Even if you choose Aaron or someone else instead of me, I'll be by your side. I understand your obligations as queen, and I won't stand in the way of them."

Tears burned behind her eyes, and Lillian wished for nothing more than to tell him there was only him. That she was his, as she was meant to be, as she would always be.

But she couldn't promise him that, not when she was so close to getting the Valkyries on her side. So she nestled her face into his chest, pretending for a moment, while his strong arms protected her from the outside world.

28

Lillian

After a few dances, during which they both remained quiet but held on to each other as if the other would disappear if they softened their grip, Sam tapped her shoulder. She offered him a small smile when Kian finally let go, shifting her into Sam's arms. With a final long look, Kian told her he'd be by the drink tables.

Lillian nodded—she'd find him after.

"I'm glad you're not shutting us out anymore." Sam smiled at her, his brown eyes kind, while slowly spinning her in a circle.

She glanced at her feet. "I'm sorry. I know I haven't been the best friend while we've been here."

"Lillian." Sam searched her face. "No one faults you. What you've had to deal with would have broken any other person I know, including me, Finn and Kian. You're doing amazing."

She nodded slowly. "But I shouldn't have shut you all out. I know I hurt Finn; he barely meets my eyes these days."

"He feels guilty, Lillian." Sam's eyes filled with sorrow when she met them. "You had to choose between him and Eli."

She winced at the agony stabbing at her heart as the memory from that night, forever burned into her mind, flashed before her eyes. *I have given up everything, everything, for this.*

"I'm sorry, I'm sure you don't want to think about it. But you must know it wasn't your fault. You didn't choose this. You only tried to save your friend."

Tears welled in her eyes. "I killed him, Sam," she whispered.

"And Finn would be dead if you hadn't. It was an impossible choice." Sam squeezed her waist. "I know you're working hard to save Orios, but it's all right if you want some time to heal, Lillian. You have fought so hard for so long. We're safe here. It's not all on your shoulders."

Lillian frowned. "But what about your brother? And Finn's family? And all of those children? I'm the only one that can help them. It *is* on my shoulders."

Sam held her tighter. "You cannot do it alone, Lillian. We would come with you, of course. But you have to be prepared for the risk that we all could die because of it. You don't think Alek will have mercy on his traitor son, do you?"

Lillian froze. She hadn't even considered that Alek had seen Kian rift them away. "I'd make them stay back."

Sam shook his head, pity filling his eyes. "You know as well as I do that they never would, Lillian. And neither would I, for that matter."

A chill skittered down her spine. No. No more of her friends would die because of her. Lillian glanced around the room for her friends when her eyes snagged on a familiar face.

Sucking in a breath, she pulled out of Sam's hold, ignoring him as he asked what was happening. The man's eyes widened when they locked with hers, and when he quickly exited the room, she didn't care that she bumped into dancing couples or about the Valkyries that snarled at her when she accidentally brushed their wings as she followed him.

"Wait!"

She rushed her steps, sprinting out of the double doors to the ballroom. Lillian followed him down a dark corridor with no lanterns lining the path, panting as she pushed herself to run faster.

"I said wait!"

When the man reached a dead end, he flipped around, his breathing labored.

"Mr. Florian?" Lillian slowed her strides, her heart beating out of her chest. "What are you doing here? *How* are you here?"

The flower monger slowly lifted his eyes to meet hers, guilt lining his face. "Hello, Lillian. It's good to see you again."

A chill spread throughout her body, her darkness responding immediately and wrapping itself around her arms, ready to lash out.

"What are you doing here?" Her voice was glacial as she studied his face, waiting for a reaction.

He cleared his throat, "It's not what you think."

"Don't tell me what I *think*. Tell me why—how—you are here."

Red clouded her vision, and she drew a deep breath to try to steady herself.

Florian sighed, a flicker of sorrow shadowing his eyes. "I've been a spy for the Elders for the past eighteen years. Anick is my mate, and it's been difficult being apart, but they needed eyes on Echo, and I volunteered."

"And *what* were you spying on?" Each word she forced out felt like a shard of ice, laced with barely contained rage.

Florian wrung his hands, shifting uncomfortably before her. "Lillian, I couldn't be sure you were her. I told Grete of my suspicions, but we decided to wait and see."

Lillian snarled, "You *knew*."

Her darkness shot out, and Florian let out a small yelp when it whipped him, leaving an angry red line across his bare arm. Biting her cheek, she readied another lash. But when the smell of forest filled her nostrils, she stilled.

"What's happening here?" Kian wrapped his arm around her shoulders while eyeing the man before them with a blank face.

Lillian searched his eyes, but when he only gave her a small smile, she relaxed into his hold, grateful her outburst didn't faze him.

"They knew about me. He is one of their spies, and he lived right next door to me all my life." The words came out clipped, Lillian panting as she held on to her darkness as it threatened to lash out again, retribution for the deceit.

Kian's face hardened, his body tensing beside her as he snarled, "Get the hell out of here right now because if my queen doesn't kill you, I surely will."

The lethal edge in his tone did nothing to soothe her own rage, her magic roiling inside her, purring at the threat.

Florian didn't waste a second, stumbling down the hallway as he tried to get away as fast as possible.

Not sparing the man another glance, Kian turned and pulled Lillian into his arms, whispering against her hair, "I'm sorry. I know you can handle yourself, but I thought he might need a warning before I ripped his head off."

Lillian snorted, "It's fine. It was probably for the best. He was kind to me growing up. He used to make me the most beautiful flower crowns for the summer solstice. But Grete and I have a few things to discuss, I think."

Slipping out of Kian's arms, she motioned for him to join her as she followed Florian down the corridor. Lillian didn't bother trying to squash the fury coiling in her gut.

She'd had enough of Grete, and it was time to let her dear aunt know.

29

Kian

Kian smiled at the wildfire burning in Lillian's eyes, the eerie flames of darkness behind them.

Finally.

Her darkness trailed her like a royal cape when she stormed down the hallway, her steps assured as she approached the ballroom. She paused before entering the double glass doors and turned to him, her jaw set as she yet again burned her stare into his.

"Will you go with me?"

His heart swelled at her words, and he could only nod as thickness clogged his throat. Pride and love and need tangled within him upon seeing her alive again, upon seeing that shell of a person fight back to life.

Lillian reached out a hand and gripped one of his tight before dragging him with her into the packed room. Without hesitation, she stalked up to Grete, where she danced with a tall, gray-haired man.

"Hello, aunt." Lillian's voice was like velvet, but the underlying sharpness was unmistakable. "I'd like to have some words with the Elders. Right now."

Grete stilled and excused herself to the man. He bowed

deep before casting a curious glance at Lillian, then quickly walked off.

Grete turned to them. "Lillian. I do not see—"

Kian growled, "You will address her as Your Majesty."

He was done with this arrogant Valkyrie talking to his mate like she did. She needed to show Lillian the respect she had earned, in addition to what had been given to her as a birthright.

Lillian winked at him before closing the final distance to her aunt, invading her space. Small embers of darkness whirled around the Valkyries, as if her magic couldn't wait another moment either.

She bore her storming eyes into Grete's. "You heard my mate."

Kian nearly stumbled when his heart began beating out of his chest, but when Lillian squeezed his hand, he steadied himself.

Orios, he loved this woman.

And when she called him her mate…

"You will gather the Elders now. Or I will unleash hell upon this ballroom. I don't think my people will be able to *further the bloodline* if they're all dead, do you?" Lillian smiled sweetly, displaying those sharp canines he couldn't wait to feel rasp against his skin.

Finn and Sam slinked up behind them, both with their hands on their swords, eyes wide, and Kian grinned when he met Finn's amber ones.

"She's back?" Finn whispered.

Kian inclined his head, and Finn's grin finally resembled the ones Kian had gotten so used to on Echo. He gripped his friend's shoulder as tears flooded Finn's eyes when he sliced them between Lillian and himself.

"I'm waiting."

They all turned their heads to Lillian when she snarled at Grete, and Kian's grin widened when the blond Valkyrie cowered under Lillian's authority, shying away from the veil of darkness that surrounded her.

Grete seemed like she was about to say something else, but after Lillian threw her a murderous stare that even had Finn shudder, she turned around to follow her queen's orders.

"We'll be in the meeting room." Lillian spun on her heel, still with a tight grip on Kian's hand. "Sam, Finn, please join us."

Quietly, she led them to a large oval room where Madick and another Valkyrie Kian didn't know were posted outside.

"Bring three more chairs, normal chairs, as these men don't have wings."

After casting one glance at Lillian's face, neither of them argued. They only bowed their heads to their queen and walked off.

"My *aunt*," Lillian's lips curled, "has apparently known about me for a long time."

Finn stiffened beside Kian. "How?"

"One of her spies was my neighbor growing up." Lillian shook her head and released Kian's hand to pull at her dress.

Kian straightened his back, trying to keep his eyes on Lillian's, not on all the soft skin she had on display. "What do you want to do?"

Lillian stared at each one of them. "I want to kill her."

When they blinked at her, her mouth lifted into a small smile. Kian couldn't help himself; he grinned back at his queen, and she winked at him.

"But I won't. I will try to convince them to help us. And if they disagree, we will leave. Find a way to take on Alek ourselves."

Lillian quickly told them what she'd learned about his father and what he was planning with the children.

Kian clenched his fists when anger crackled over his skin. He wasn't sure if it was possible to hate his father more than he already did, but there seemed to be some room within him now that he knew exactly what he intended to do.

"I won't insult you and ask you to stay behind," Lillian glanced at Sam. "But I'm not sure what we will walk into if we take on Alek. Your father." She met his eyes briefly, and Kian nodded. "It might mean certain death for all of us, so don't make this decision lightly."

An icy hand gripped Kian's heart then, upon imaging a world where Lillian didn't exist, where the wild woman before him didn't breathe, didn't shake him to his core every time she fixed her piercing gaze on him.

But that's not what she needed to hear and damn him if he would hold her back because he wanted her safe. She was his, but he loved every part of her, even the reckless ones that tended to get her into all kinds of trouble.

Kian's voice was strong when he responded. "I made you a promise that I will never leave your side. I just have one ask."

Lillian eyed him, inclining her head.

"When it's time, I want to be the one who kills my father. I may not have supported him, but I stood idly by for years. I don't intend to do that again."

Lillian was quiet for a moment, but then she reached out a hand and touched his cheek. "As you wish."

"I'm always in, silver girl." Finn pulled her into a long hug, both of their eyes shimmering with tears as they held a silent conversation. Kian had to look away when tears burned behind his own eyes watching them.

When Finn finally let go, Lillian cleared her throat and glanced at Sam. He dragged a hand through his hair, staring at his shoes.

"Sam, you don't have to come. We'll all understand. I know your brother is sick, and you've been away from him for too long." Lillian reached out for his hand.

Sam took it, his eyes darting between Kian and Finn before he responded. "I will come as well. My brother is safe for now. But we should take the time to plan, Lillian. After what you've told us about Alek and his vessel… I'm worried we'll walk straight into a death trap."

Lillian smiled at him. "You're always our voice of reason, Sam. But I'm not suggesting we take him on. Not yet. We get the vessel out of his hands first."

Kian eyed his friends, the resolve in their faces, the light behind their eyes, and winked at them. "I, for one, am excited to utilize all that training we've been doing."

"Well, we're all here now." They spun around at Grete's voice. "What's so urgent it couldn't wait until after the festivities?"

Squaring her shoulders, Lillian said quietly, "Please, have a seat."

30

Lillian

A flush crept up her neck, and her magic begged to be released when Grete took the seat at the head of the table without another glance at Lillian.

Her aunt had known about her, perhaps her entire life, and had done nothing.

Grete wanted the throne for herself; Lillian understood this now. But hurting Grete wouldn't get the Valkyries on her side—wouldn't do anything but put her in an even weaker position. So she remained standing as the rest of the Elders took their seats, her friends slipping onto the chairs that Madick and the other guard had brought in.

"Lillian."

She narrowed her eyes when Grete began speaking.

"I apologize—*Your Majesty.* We don't allow humans in these meetings. You know this."

Lillian's nostrils flared at her tone, but she kept her voice even. "*Aunt,* these are new times. These men are part of my court, and they will be allowed wherever I am. And given the old friend I stumbled into this evening, I suggest you're very careful with what you say next."

When Grete's face drained of color, Lillian had to hold back a smirk.

Tild leaned forward. "Majesty, we'll allow it. May I ask why you called this meeting?"

"We've waited long enough. I am calling the vote for whether you will stand against Alek."

She paused to glance at Kian, and Lillian had to suppress a smile at the pride that glittered in his eyes.

"I ask you, as the heir to the throne but also as one of you, to join me in taking him on. Alek will try to take over this whole realm. I'm certain of it. And it's time someone took him down."

She met the eyes of every Valkyrie in the room, a few of them inclining their heads. Valeria and Breit, the youngest Valkyries, even offered small smiles when she got to them.

When no one spoke, Lillian glanced at her friends, and Kian met her eyes, a question in them. She nodded, and Kian rose from his seat.

"I know you don't trust me, given who my father is. But your queen is right. Alek will not stop, and I promise you he will come. He hates your kind, and he hates the dragons even more. He won't stop until you're all dead." He took his seat again, but several of the Valkyries studied him closely, whispering to each other before they averted their eyes.

"Elders, our queen has spoken. Let's put it to a vote." Tild rose from her seat, brushing strands of her gray hair out of her face as her gaze swept across the room. "All in favor of standing with our queen, please raise your hand."

Lillian held her breath when the Valkyries glanced at each other, and her stomach dropped when only three hands shot into the air.

Valeria, Breit, and Tild were the only ones in favor.

A smug smile spread across Grete's face. "Well, it's settled then. The humans will stand alone."

Lillian ground her teeth, but she'd been prepared for this, hadn't had much hope they'd come around—that they'd leave this comfortable castle. "They won't stand alone. I will stand with them."

Finn and Kian rose to stand next to Lillian, Sam following a moment later.

"We will stand with our queen." Kian gripped her hand, and Lillian gratefully squeezed it as his strength and conviction flowed into her, grounded her.

"So will we."

The room turned as one to the door where Elya and Else hovered, the latter barely visible behind her sister, her face ashen as her eyes warily darted around the room.

"That's not a decision for you to make." Grete slammed her hands against the table, her face heating. "You are not part of the council, nor do you have a say in whether the Valkyries stand with her."

Elya's smile was more of a teeth showing. "I didn't say the Valkyries would stand with her. I said we will. Or are we prisoners here? I thought we were free to go as we please."

Grete pursed her lips but remained quiet.

Stepping up to the two blond sisters, Lillian eyed them both gratefully. "Thank you."

She hadn't dared hope that the Valkyries she'd begun to consider her friends would dare go against their Elders, but when Elya spoke, a small ember of hope sparked in her chest. Perhaps she wasn't insane. Perhaps there was a chance that they could succeed.

However small that chance may be.

The twins bowed low, and Elya winked at her when she straightened. "We only wish to follow our real queen."

Lillian turned back to the room, her voice clear as she addressed the Valkyries. "We will leave tonight. I hope this is not the last time we see each other. But if it is, thank you for letting us stay and for letting me learn your customs. Regardless of what happened here today, I promise I will always stand with you if you need it."

Not a single one of them met her eyes, not even Tild.

But it didn't matter.
She had her friends.
She wasn't alone.

31

Lillian

The Valkyries quickly vacated the room after the vote, and Lillian asked her friends to meet her in her chambers as soon as they'd packed their belongings. When she found herself alone in her room, she blew out a breath and steadied herself against the door.

I promise I will try to make you proud.

Not just Atli, but Eli and Astrid and everyone else that helped her get here. She braced herself for the excruciating pain to sear through her at the thought of her lost loved ones, but only burning determination filled her.

All decisions so far in her life had been made by someone else.

It was time she made some of her own.

And she would start tonight.

A hard tap on the window made her snap her head up. Slowly walking up to the small balcony, she opened the glass doors to find Munion and Hanin resting on the railing outside.

You weren't going to leave us behind, were you? Hanin glared at her, and Lillian smiled at the two ravens.

"You're free to stay, but I'd love for you to join us if you'd like."

Hanin huffed, and Munion smacked her with his wing. *We're your guardians, Majesty. We will follow you wherever you go.*

Warmth filled Lillian, and she walked up and wrapped her arms around the large bird and then stroked Hanin's beak, even as the raven huffed louder at the touch. "Thank you."

Something warm settled in her stomach as she met the ravens' black eyes.

They'd come quite far from that terrifying first encounter on the mountain.

The door opened behind her, and another wave of warmth washed over her at the sight of her friends, flanked by the two Valkyries walking through the door.

Finn grinned and ran up to her, lifting her up and swinging her around. She swatted at him when he set her down but didn't shrug off the arm he slung around her shoulder.

I missed you so much, Finn. I'm sorry for everything.

He squeezed her shoulder tighter and cleared his throat.

Kian beamed at her as he approached, and Finn nudged her forward right into his waiting arms.

"That was incredible. You are incredible," he whispered into her ear, too low for anyone other than Finn to hear.

Lillian blinked furiously as tears filled her eyes and she pulled out of Kian's arms but kept a hold of his hand.

"All right, enough with this. I've cried enough for a lifetime already, I should think."

The thick tension in the room lifted when they all erupted into giggles at her words.

When they finally quieted, the group stared at Lillian expectantly.

Bile rose in her throat as she stared back at them.

She was responsible for them now, and they were looking to her to make decisions. And if she made the wrong one…

Shaking her head, she didn't let herself finish the thought.

"Thank you for trusting me enough to follow me into this. I can't say I'm not scared because I am. I'm terrified."

She glanced at the group and caught Elya's eyes. When the blonde winked at her, Lillian offered her a small smile in return.

"But people I loved died because they believed that I could do this. That we could do this."

Kian squeezed her hand, and she shot him a grateful look. "Even if I die trying. I want to do just that. Try. But I might be leading you to death, too. And I am not sure if I can handle more people dying because of me." Lillian swallowed.

"We wouldn't die because of you, Lillian." Kian shifted to stand before her. "We would die for something we all believe in. We believe in you, but we also believe in what you're trying to do. We're all making this decision for ourselves."

Finn nodded, "He's right."

"We barely know you, and we'll stand by you because what you're doing is right." Elya glanced at Finn as she said it, and Lillian grinned when the Valkyrie's cheeks reddened.

You're in so much trouble, friend.

Finn winked at her. *I know.*

Lillian straightened her shoulders. "All right. As long as everyone knows you're free to leave whenever, for whatever reason, without explanation, I say let's do this."

And what is it exactly that we're doing? Hanin tilted her head.

Lillian paused and glanced around the room. "We're going to get that vessel out of Alek's hands."

32

Kian

Kian blew out a breath when he finally sat down after rifting them all back to Echo. Exhaustion lay heavy on his limbs, his magic not used to bringing so many along at once.

They had to leave the ravens behind as he couldn't rift them along with the rest of the group, so the guardians would fly as fast as they could and catch up with the group in a few days.

Kian looked out over the tall, snow-covered mountains surrounding them. Cold seeped into his bones; not from the snow that piled outside the small cave they were staying in for the night, but from the memories of when they'd last been here.

He could still smell the smoke on the wind, feel the panic that surged through him when he hadn't been able to find or sense Lillian in the chaos. Kian shuddered as he remembered his father's fire dancing over his palms as he found her on the mountainside, the lethal smile he'd given Kian when he rifted Lillian and the others away.

"Do you want to go inside? I can take the next shift." Lillian joined him in the small crevice outside the opening.

Kian shook his head. The small cave was full of people

and Valkyries, and he needed some time to get his strength back.

Understanding glimmered in her eyes. "Then I'll stay with you if you'd like?"

Kian shifted so there was space for her to sit down in the crevice beside him, and the cold left him as soon as her body touched his. When she rested her head on his shoulder, he shuddered for a different reason.

"I'm sorry that I pushed you away. Again." Her words were barely a whisper.

His heart ached for his queen; even if her rejection had pained him, he knew it was so much worse for the woman he loved. Yet again, decisions had been made for her, not taking her own opinions or feelings into account.

"I told you never to apologize—not to me. I understand, Lillian. You forget I was a prince. I didn't have much say in anything growing up." Kian wrapped his arm around her and pulled her closer. "We're here now. That's all that matters."

Lillian blew out a breath, her voice still low but full of clarity. "I do want you. I've wanted you for a long time, Kian. But I'm scared. I've lost so many, and I don't think I'll survive if I lose you as well."

With his heart pounding in his chest, the beats echoing in his ears, Kian couldn't stop the smile that spread across his face.

He shifted to face her. The wind blew her black hair around her face, and her cheeks and nose were red from the cold. Small snowflakes stuck to her long lashes and hair, sparkling in the dim light that shone from the fire inside the cave.

She was so beautiful, and it shook him to his core when he realized this woman was his. This wild, insane, loyal, loving woman was his mate.

"You will not lose me." He cupped her face with his hands, rubbing his thumbs over her cold cheeks. "I love you. I will follow you to the end of this earth, to the afterlife, or wherever else this life may take us. There is nothing that can keep me away from you. Wherever you go, Lillian, I will be right next to you."

His smile widened when her breath hitched in her throat.

"Kian," she whispered.

"Yes, my dark queen." Kian eyed her flushed cheeks, his jaw clenching as he remembered what had followed his name the last time they were this close.

"Will you kiss me?"

His heart stopped.

When she leaned forward, her cheeks burning under his hands, his heart started beating again, harder than it had done before in his life. Her eyes searched his face, heat filling her gaze, and he blew out a breath.

"I thought you'd never ask."

Then he kissed his mate.

33

Lillian

When Kian's lips touched hers, a growl rumbled in his chest. Lillian's body responded immediately, heat coursing through her in waves as Kian wove his fingers into her hair to deepen the kiss. She wrapped her arms around his neck, fire igniting in her core when he pulled her head back, his mouth hungrily exploring hers until her mind went blank.

She might have moaned; she might have said his name. But all was forgotten when stars exploded between them, and everything around her faded away.

There was only him.

Kian pulled her onto his lap, and she wrapped her legs around him, her hands tangling in his black hair, desperate to get closer. His lips were so soft, and he was confident when he kissed her.

He wasn't holding anything back.

His body hardened beneath her, and when she nipped his bottom lip, his grip on her hair tightened, and his tongue slid across her lips, seeking permission. She opened for him, giving him full access.

When their tongues met, a low moan escaped her. Lillian

pulled at his jacket, needing more, needing to feel his skin against hers, but when he laughed softly, she froze, uncertain.

Kian met her eyes, only love shining in his green ones, and nipped at her bottom lip until she offered him a small smile.

"Lillian, if we continue like this, I will take you against this damn mountain. And while I'd be the happiest man alive, I doubt you want an audience for our first time."

Seriously, I'm trying my best not to listen, but you're both really loud.

Lillian laughed hoarsely. "You're right. Finn's hoping for a show."

Laughter boomed down the bond. *I'm truly not. I might have little inhibitions, but you're my sister, Lillian. As much as I love you, this is making me a bit nauseous.*

She shut him out as she leaned in again, kissing Kian softly, heat coiling inside her yet again. When he pulled her closer, she stilled, and Kian searched her eyes questioningly.

She hesitated, willing her nerves away, but her voice still trembled when she whispered, "It wouldn't just be *our* first time, Kian."

He froze for a moment, then untangled his hands from her hair and cupped her face.

"Lillian." He closed his eyes, emotions racing across his features. "And you almost let me do this right here." Kian shook his head. "This cold, awful mountain is not where your first time will happen. You deserve the world, and while I'll be by your side as you take it for yourself, I will give you something better than ice-cold stone and snow."

Lillian's whole body tingled under his intense gaze, but she nodded. "You better find that place soon."

The smile that overtook his face made her breathless.

"I promise."

34

Lillian

When her heart rate finally lowered enough that her entire body wasn't shaking, Lillian dragged Kian with her into the cave. The others snickered when they entered, but after Lillian narrowed her eyes, albeit with a blood-red face, they quieted.

Even if Finn still shook where he was seated next to Elya and Sam by the fire they'd built. Finn's eyes sought hers, but she refused to meet them, especially when another chuckle escaped him.

Lillian stared at the wall behind her friends as she cleared her throat. "We'll stay here tonight. Tomorrow, we'll scout while we wait for Hanin and Munion. From Grete's spies, we know that Alek is keeping his army somewhere below the Skandi. We'll figure out where and who the vessel is, and then we'll plan."

"I don't understand why we didn't go to the dragons first." Elya rose to her feet, brushing off some dust from her leathers and impatiently stretching her neck as she bore her eyes into Lillian's. "They could have burned these damned mountains to the ground."

Lillian glared at her. "Because we don't know if they'd even help us. Tild told me my mother was half-dead after she bonded with one, and I'd prefer to have some strength left to take on Alek should I even succeed."

When Elya opened her mouth again, Lillian raised her hand, and thankfully, the Valkyrie quickly shut it.

"These mountains are dangerous. We will need to keep an eye out, not just for Alek and his army, but for the animals that roam here. I was almost eaten by a Mungan when we were here last, and I believe Sam encountered a few other creatures."

Sam shuddered. "Yes, I ran into the Fenrirs. I'd love to avoid them this time if possible. They nearly ripped my legs off."

Lillian winced. "We'll have to take watch in shifts. I don't want anything or anyone sneaking up on us. I'd prefer it if we did it two and two."

"Oh, I'm sure you do." Finn threw his head back and laughed while the rest of the group giggled.

Lillian's face heated, but she ignored him. "Finn, I suggest you and Elya take the first one."

When Finn grinned, Elya sighed loudly.

You're welcome.

Finn winked at Lillian, while he sent a soft *thank you* down the bond.

35

Finn

The Valkyrie paced back and forth outside the small cave as large snowflakes began falling, sticking to her black wings. Her posture was tense, and at the smallest rush of wind, she stilled, the feathers in her wings shifting the only movement.

"You could sit down, you know. There's space, even with your wings. I promise Lillian and Kian didn't actually do it right here." Finn patted the ground.

Elya snorted, a flicker of amusement reflecting in her eyes, but shook her head. "I prefer to be on my feet if some wild creature charges us."

"Ah, come on, I'll hear them from miles away. That's how I got away unscathed last time. I heard them and ran in a different direction."

Elya sighed, but when she shivered from yet another strong gust of wind, she finally made her way over.

Finn gestured to the spot beside him. "I've kept it warm for you."

She narrowed her eyes as she sat down, her arm nearly touching his, close enough that he could feel the heat radiating from her. "You better keep those hands to yourself, boy."

Finn laughed quietly. "I thought you dreamed of these hands and what they can do."

When Elya only glared at him, he lifted his hands in the air. "I promise, these won't go anywhere near you. Unless you ask, that is."

They sat quietly for a while, listening to the wind howling between the mountains and watching the mountainside whiten as the snow stuck.

"How was it growing up on Seigard?" Finn eyed the blond female.

Her face was always so tense, her jaw set, her expression hard. He ached to smooth out those strong lines and see her smile—one of those genuine smiles he'd caught her offering her sister.

And he'd also like to do a lot of other things to that beautiful mouth.

Elya snapped her eyes to his. "I didn't grow up on Seigard. It's only been my home for the past nineteen years. But it was fine. I had Else, so I wasn't completely alone."

"What happened to the rest of your family?"

Elya sighed, but to his surprise, she responded. "My parents died defending Lillian's mother. They were so loyal to Liv, they believed in the new world she was trying to build—a better world. But when Adeon cursed Liv and Ivar, they sent us to Seigard with most of the younger Valkyries. And since my—" She averted her eyes and whispered, "Never mind."

Finn gently clasped her shoulder. "You can tell me, you know. It might seem like I don't take many things seriously, but I like you, Elya. I want to know you. Everything about you."

Face heating, she glanced at his hand, and Finn prepared himself for her to slap it away, but when she instead placed her own on top of it, his pulse quickened.

She hesitated for a moment, but then resolve filled her eyes, and her voice was strong when she spoke.

"It's been a long time since I spent time with a man. My mate, Lios, was very sick when I met him. And we thought tying his life to mine would help. But it didn't. It was too late." She cleared her throat. "He came with us to Seigard, and we had two wonderful years together, but then he died. It nearly killed me as well. I guess it perhaps did kill a part of me, the part that was happy and careless and free. But Else needed me, and I think I clawed my way back to life because of her. I couldn't leave her all alone."

Tears burned behind Finn's eyes at the sorrow that lined Elya's beautiful face, the vulnerability in her eyes. His heart broke for the Valkyrie—no wonder she wrapped herself in a shell of ice and pushed everyone away.

"I'm so sorry, Elya. I had no idea." Finn wrapped his arm around her shoulders, blowing out a soft breath when she leaned into him, resting her head on his shoulder and her sweet scent enveloping him.

"I know you didn't. I don't speak of Lios. I don't think I've mentioned him in the past seventeen years. But perhaps it's time I do."

Finn squeezed her shoulder. "I'm here whenever you want to talk."

They remained quiet, but it was a comfortable silence as they watched more snow fall, and Finn couldn't wipe the smile that spread across his face when Elya nestled in closer.

36

Kian

When morning came, dark clouds rolled in across the sky, and it was almost impossible to see when the day broke. The snow had turned into an icy storm, and they all shivered as they glanced out over the dark landscape, barely able to distinguish the mountain range before them.

Lillian landed outside the cave and approached him, her hair plastered against her head and wings glistening. When Lillian's eyes found his, and her scowl turned into a smile, Kian couldn't stop himself from pulling her into his arms.

He couldn't believe she was truly his, that he was finally allowed to touch her, be with her.

Nestling his face into her wet neck, he kissed away the drops of water running down it. Goosebumps raced across his skin when she let out a soft sigh, her arms around him tightening when he gently nipped the sensitive skin above her collarbone.

"*Kian*," she moaned quietly.

Swirling shadows danced behind her eyes when he pulled back to look at her, and her cheeks stained with color as she met his eyes.

"Lillian," he grinned.

She brushed her lips against his, a jolt of electricity passing between them. "If you haven't found that place by tonight, the mountainside might have to do."

Kian laughed. "If it's an order, my queen, you know I can't refuse."

Not that he'd refuse her anything, regardless of whether she was queen or not. Now that he had her, he'd do whatever she needed—whatever she wanted.

She swatted at him. "I won't order you to do anything."

Kian wiggled his brows, "But I think I should like that."

Her eyes darkened, but she shook her head, her eyes darting behind him into the cave. "We need to focus. I flew over the Skandi and some of the neighboring mountains, but I didn't see anything. Not a whisper of the army the spy spoke of. It's almost eerily quiet. It's making me anxious."

Kian nodded. "There must be a cave or something where they're hiding. This awful weather might be a blessing, though. Even if it might make it more difficult for us to find them, it'll also be harder for them to stumble across our group. I can rift to the ground to check it out. See if I can find something you couldn't see from the sky?"

Lillian grabbed his hand. "I'll go with you. I don't want you to go alone."

He raised his brows. She'd just come back from scouting alone. But he didn't bring it up. He had seen the fear in her eyes as they looked to her for orders yesterday, and he was not about to instill any more doubt in her.

She needed to grow into this role, although he was pretty sure she'd be a natural. But when she shivered so hard her teeth chattered, Kian shook his head, "Lillian, you need to get warm first. You freezing to death is not going to help anyone."

Finn strolled out of the cave, wincing at the strong wind that whipped his golden hair around his face. "I'll go with you. You can rift us down, and I can help if we find something we'd need to fly to."

Kian nodded, "Thank you, brother."

Lillian's gaze flitted between them, and Kian sensed she was about to argue, but then it seemed she thought better of it. "Please, be careful. Do not risk anything, and do not engage. We need to have a plan first. Even if the spy didn't see Alek here, we don't know what we're facing."

They inclined their heads, and then Kian gripped Finn's arm, casting a final glance at his beautiful mate before rifting them down to the east side of the Skandi.

It was quiet when they appeared at the bottom. Thankfully, it was a bit warmer, the wind not as strong, and there was no ice filling the relentless snow. It was still dark down here, though, and Kian squinted as he stared at the rocky base of the mountain.

Narrowing his eyes, he turned his head from side to side while listening closely.

Lillian was right—he didn't like this either. Not one bit. "It's too quiet. If there is a whole army somewhere close, we should hear them. I think we should check the other side."

Finn held up his hand. "Give me a second."

He flicked his head in all directions, scanning the mountain and listening with his sensitive ears, but after a moment, he shook his head. "You're right. I don't hear anything either."

Kian trailed his eyes up the mountain, not able to see anything but swirling snow. "Let's head to the north side."

As he grabbed Finn's arm, Finn tensed. "Wait." Finn snapped his eyes to him and opened his mouth.

Then, the world went dark.

37

Lillian

Lillian fell to her knees on the cold ground in the cave as the bonds went taut and then snapped, a sharp crack echoing through her body. She screamed, a chilling, desperate scream as her body filled with black emptiness, pain forcing her eyes shut as her soul fractured.

Finn!

No!

There was nothing there. No golden swirls, no wildfire burning under her skin.

Elya sprinted to her, dropping down to search her for injuries. "What's happening, Your Majesty?"

Lillian couldn't breathe.

"The bonds— Th… they're gone," she got out.

The rest of the group came running as Lillian bit back another scream.

They couldn't be dead. She wouldn't allow it, couldn't even think about it.

She cleared her throat, shakily squashing another cry. "Something went wrong. We need to get down and find them. Now."

Elya nodded. "Where are they? Did you feel them before…"

Lillian narrowed her eyes, and Elya snapped her lips shut. "They were on the east side. Finn was listening to the mountainside. I'll take Sam. You both follow me."

Else spoke quietly, although her tone was urgent. "Your Majesty, we need to be careful. If they got both of them that quickly, they might be using the vessel or something else that could overpower us."

"I don't care," Lillian growled. "I will kill the vessel or anyone else if I have to."

She ignored the small voice inside her that had condemned Eli for doing the same thing, that still hadn't truly forgiven him for murdering all those children.

This was Kian and Finn.

She'd do anything for them.

"We leave now." Lillian didn't wait for a response before she dragged Sam to the ledge and gripped his torso tight, ready to step off.

"Are you sure about this? I can stay behind." Sam's voice shook as he stared out over the steep fall before them, the ground invisible in the snowstorm.

Lillian snarled before she could stop herself. "I'm sorry, Sam. But if they're hurt, we will need you to heal them. I can't leave you behind."

He nodded slowly. "Just… Please don't crash."

Lillian didn't respond as she pushed herself off the mountain.

It was heavier flying with Sam, but fear gave her an extra burst of energy.

Else and Elya flew closely beside her, the wind from their wings keeping her own beatings steady. Lillian didn't even feel the chill from the wind and snow as panic bubbled inside her.

They couldn't be dead. They couldn't. She repeated the words to herself until they neared the east side.

"Keep to the mountainside," Lillian whispered, the words barely distinguishable over the roaring wind.

They remained quiet as they scanned the mountain and the snow-covered ground, searching every crevice and outcropping.

"There!" Elya hissed quietly. "Do you see the light?"

Lillian followed her gaze and spotted the opening at the bottom of the mountain, the flickering light streaming out of it.

A whisper of hope brushed her skin. They had to be alive. There was no other possibility.

Lillian forced her voice to remain steady, the beatings of her wings strong. "Let's land over there, behind those trees."

She steered toward a small copse of trees, its branches weighed down by snow, with the two Valkyries following closely behind her.

38

Kian

Light flickered before his closed eyes, dancing over his eyelids, and Kian pried them open, shaking his head to rid himself of the fog filling his mind. His eyes widened when he realized he was in a massive, empty cave, its arched walls shimmering from two dozen or so lanterns placed a few feet apart.

The heaviness in his head lingered, and when he glanced down, iron bracelets encased both his arms, suppressing his magic. He groaned at the stifling sensation, blinding rage crashing through him when he couldn't feel the bond with Lillian.

He shook his head. She was safe. It must be the bracelets blocking it. It had been the same when she'd worn them during the trials.

But he clenched his fists as he realized she must be feeling the same thing. She wouldn't stop to think; she'd just follow them. He needed to make sure they got out of there before Lillian put herself in danger because they'd been stupid enough to get caught.

Finn moaned by his side, blood trickling down his temple, staining his golden hair red.

"Finn," he whispered.

When Finn didn't respond, he nudged the shifter. "Finn!"

One of Finn's eyes opened. "So much for super hearing. Where did they come from?"

"They used me."

They both tensed at the voice, flipping around as much as the chains they were bound in would allow. A girl with flaming red hair and blue eyes stared at them. She was also chained to the cave wall, but no iron bracelets encased her wrists.

Finn gasped, "You look so much like someone."

The girl offered him a small smile. "Maybe you know my sister Astrid? She's a rebel, which I'm guessing you are as well, based on the chains they put you in."

Kian went cold when he met Finn's sad eyes. When Finn opened his mouth to speak, he shook his head imperceptibly.

Kian cleared his throat. "What's your name? And what did you mean by 'they used you'?"

The girl glanced at her pale, chained hands. "My name is Josephine. And I can channel magic between people, to anyone but myself. There is a guard here who can turn himself invisible, so the king has me keep his army and guards hidden by channeling his magic into them."

"*You're* the vessel," Finn whispered.

Kian snapped his head up and glanced around the empty cave. "Are they here now?"

"Indeed, we are." A familiar voice rang before them. "Josephine, the king will kill these two when he arrives in a few moments, so you can stop channeling for now."

The chains clinked as Josephine scrambled back against the wall, and her face blanched as she stared into the empty space. When she closed her eyes and blew out a deep breath, sounds rang all around them in the cave.

Kian sucked in a breath when hundreds of children appeared before them, all standing in formation, filling the entire cave. Their eyes were glassy from fear, and they stood unnaturally still facing the entrance of the cave. All were clad in the black uniforms his father preferred, with their hands on the swords at their sides, and he gritted his teeth as he caught a few scared glances, some of which belonged to children no older than twelve or thirteen.

"What's wrong with them?" Finn breathed as the children remained frozen, only their eyes darting their way then immediately back ahead again.

"They're perfect." The guard, Commander Jon, Kian realized with a sinking stomach, stalked up to them. "They've been thoroughly trained and are well aware of what happens should they get out of line. We've used some techniques you should be very familiar with, *Prince Kian.*"

Kian shook his head, meeting the cold eyes of his old commander.

He'd considered Jon a friend once. When they'd gone through guard training together, Jon's sarcastic imitations of their captains had brightened even the darkest of days. But there was nothing left of that person now; his time as a commander had erased everything good about him.

"Jon, you know this is wrong. You don't think my father would spare your son, do you? How old is he now, five? And with two parents who can wield magic, I'm sure he'll be very gifted."

His nose crunched when Jon punched him in the face.

With warm blood dripping down his face, Kian sneered. "Punching someone chained, Jon. You're really outdoing yourself over here."

Jon lifted his hand again. "My king wants you alive, but he didn't say anything about roughing you up a little bit."

Kian's ears rang when Jon landed another blow to the side of his face.

"That was the last thing you'll ever do. *Commander.*"

Warmth and cold tangled within Kian upon hearing Lillian's voice, the icy rage in it as she snarled at Jon. Kian shook his head, trying to focus his vision after the last strike.

When he lifted his eyes, darkness surrounded Jon, and his eyes widened for a second before the light in them went out.

Dust swirled as Jon's lifeless body fell to the ground, face ashen and eyes unseeing.

In the back of the cave, guards began screaming orders that echoed between the walls as they started running toward the group.

Lillian, Sam, and the twins sprinted toward them from the entrance while Lillian raised a wall of darkness to hold off the approaching guards.

And despite everything, he couldn't help but stare in awe as Lillian's hair blew around her face where she ran, her eyes blazing with darkness, flickering like the wall of shadows separating them from the rest of the cave.

Panting, she fell to her knees before him. "I can't hold them off for long; there are too many."

A smile spread across his face when pure, undiluted happiness filled him upon seeing her face, and Lillian's lips curled into a small smile as well. Kissing him quickly, she whispered, "Let's get these stupid chains off and get out of here."

Kian nodded and began pulling at the thick chains, adrenaline thrumming in his ears but not enough to break the shackles tethered to the wall behind him.

"I'll help you." Else dropped to her knees beside him, her quiet voice barely carrying over the guards yelling orders to each other as they tried to find a way through the wall of night Lillian had put up. "I'm no sky wielder, but I am blessed with extra strength."

They all stared with wide eyes as she easily ripped the chains off Kian and Finn.

Lillian waved her hand impatiently. "Let's get the hell out of here before they get through."

Chains rattled behind them when Josephine crept forward, her face impossibly white as she eyed them pleadingly. "Please, don't leave me here. I can't do this anymore. You can kill me if you like, but don't leave me here."

Lillian sucked in a breath beside him, and he grabbed her hand. "It's Astrid's sister," he whispered.

Jerking her head to Else, she ordered, "Get those chains off her as well. She's coming with us."

Else inclined her head and started toward the young girl when a wave of warmth washed over them, and a sea of fire roared through the wall of darkness.

His father had arrived.

39

Lillian

Her magic was running out.

She'd used every last bit of it to hold off the guards—had carelessly wielded it to kill Jon when a red haze filled her vision upon seeing him strike Kian, and only a whisper of darkness lingered around her wrists when she turned to face the king. A chill snaked down her spine despite the warmth radiating from the fire at the cold smile gracing Alek's face.

Still, Lillian took a step forward, placing herself between the king and her friends.

Kian followed, gripping her hand tight as he took up the spot next to her, his back straight even as blood still trickled down his face from his broken nose.

Finn stepped up to her other side, with Sam and the two Valkyries hovering behind them, low growls vibrating in the Valkyries' throats. And even with fear reverberating inside her as she met Alek's eyes, when she shot a look at her friends, love settled within her as well—light joining the darkness.

She wasn't alone.

Alek glanced at her and Kian's joined hands while straightening the fur coat he donned. "If it isn't my traitor son and the half-breed he chose over his own blood."

Lillian tensed as the king's sharp gaze trailed over her friends.

"And you've gathered a little court. How sweet. But only two Valkyries? Let me guess, the old aunt wasn't too keen on you coming home?"

Lillian snarled, baring her teeth at the king, praying for her magic to refill so she could wipe that smug look off King Alek's face.

"She seems more wild than tame, Kian. Is that what you're looking for?" Alek laughed quietly. "I guess she's the opposite of your mother, so frail and sickly."

When Kian took a step forward, Lillian dragged him back. "Not yet," she whispered.

The king laughed louder, the cold sound bouncing off the arched walls. "Such control she has over you, son. Although, you were always a disappointment. No real bloodthirst in that one, young Valkyrie. You might want to reconsider taking him for a mate."

A growl left her throat, but she forced herself to stand still. Attacking now would leave them all dead in seconds, burned to crisps.

Lillian glanced at Kian's wrist, noting the iron bracelet still surrounding it. She clenched her jaw, trailing her eyes over the cave. Twenty or so guards stood behind the king, their swords readied. The children still faced the cave's entrance, but a few of them cast scared glances in their direction.

Alek followed her gaze. "They won't do anything until I tell them to. But should you make one move against me, it's them you will face. Will you kill hundreds of children for my son, Lillian?" He cocked his head. "I guess your parents did. I wonder if the same neglect runs in your blood."

Lillian bit her cheek until it bled, but pressure began building inside her, her magic refilling.

She angled her head to Kian, "Keep him talking. I just need a little more time," she breathed.

He squeezed her hand in understanding, and when Kian

took a step forward, Lillian had to fight every instinct inside her not to pull him back, pull him behind her.

"Father, is it not time to stop this madness? You are already king of Orios; what more can you want?"

Alek sliced his cold eyes to his son. "You never had much imagination, son. I have Adeon on my side. With his support, I shall take this whole realm. Every island in the eastern sea shall submit to me, and perhaps I will go even further. Take on new worlds. Time will tell."

Lillian nudged Kian again—just a little bit more.

"Well, let us leave you to it then. If you let me and my friends go, we'll let you carry on with your world domination."

The king's laugh boomed through the cave. "You've never been much of a liar, son. And your woman can't hide her feelings for the life of her. That one will die trying to take the throne from under me. But I do have a proposal for you both. Join me, and I shall convince Adeon to support you both. I'll even allow you to marry, be my heirs."

Lillian shuddered when the king winked at her, and she glanced at her friends, her eyes widening ever so slightly.

They inclined their heads.

"Now!"

Lillian

Lillian threw out her darkness with everything in her. The dark wall blocked Alek and the guards from view, casting their side of the cave in near-complete darkness.

Finn instantly shared his night sight, and for a second, Lillian wondered if she should try sharing her magic. But when Alek retaliated, his fire licking her night, she didn't dare, gritting her teeth as she drew up more magic to meet his flames.

The force of it ripped Kian's hand from hers, and when he lingered by her side, she screamed at him and the rest of their friends, "Run!"

She willed the darkness to make a path to the opening and blew out a soft breath when the group began sprinting toward the storming outside.

Hands shaking, she tried to hold on, but when Alek's fire burned through her magic, a whimper escaped her. Her insides burned with the darkness as the orange flames ripped dark, bleeding holes, and when guards pushed through one of the closest ones, drawing their swords as they approached her friends, she took a stumbling step forward to follow them.

"No! Please, don't leave me!"

Whipping her head around at the desperate cry, Lillian hesitated, but when Astrid's face flashed before her eyes, she steeled her jaw.

She owed Astrid her life.

"Lillian! Don't!" Kian's scream rang behind her as Lillian spun around, sprinting back to the girl.

A guard blocked her path, and Lillian sent a plume of smoke down his throat, his eyes bulging as he fell to the ground. She jumped over him, not allowing herself to think about yet another life she'd claimed, and reached the girl.

Panting, Lillian ignored the pain when she searched the girl's face—so similar to her friend's. "We need to get these chains off you."

The girl's eyes widened when she peered over her shoulder. "Watch out!"

Lillian whirled around and her darkness quivered as Alek took a step through a gaping hole his fire ripped. Behind him, her friends fought for their lives, guards surrounding them and blocking their path.

Kian screamed her name again, the panic in it fueling her own.

She swallowed hard when Alek leisurely strolled toward her, her magic sputtering as she tried to hold on to the wall of night, shielding her friends from more waiting guards.

"You look tired, Lillian. I wonder how long you can hold on?" The king winked and sent a wall of flame that towered over her.

Growling, she forced another dark wall to meet it, the night enveloping the fire before they both extinguished.

But the wall behind them broke apart, only whispers of smoke trailing around the cave, no longer keeping the guards away from her friends. Lillian tried to will her magic out again, but she was drained.

Shaking, she drew her sword instead.

Alek chuckled and sent another wall of flame that immediately engulfed the sword. Dropping it as the flames caressed her hands, the sword melted into the stone beneath her.

"You know, I meant it when I told you I'd allow you to be with Kian. Adeon was the one who suggested it—as long as you submitted under our rule. He's coming for you, Lillian. Might be closer than you think." Alek offered her a chilling smirk. "But perhaps you're not as similar to your parents as we thought. You just lost your one chance to be with your mate."

Lillian stared behind the king when he readied another wave of flames, the heat zinging her face and embers burning through her leathers.

She met Kian's eyes as he plunged his sword into the chest of a guard and kicked another off to get to her. Tears filled hers at the desperation in them, the raw fear seeping into the green as he watched the flames dance toward her.

I love you.

She hadn't even told him.

Hadn't told him she wanted everything with him.

The beach he'd spoken of filled her mind, and when a wall of flame rushed toward her, she whispered, "In the next life."

She didn't hear Kian's scream over the beating of wings that filled the air, and a shadow blocked him as it dove in between her and the king.

41

Lillian

"No!"

Lillian screamed as she fell to her knees by Elya's burned body.

The tears spilling down her face sizzled into steam as they fell onto the lifeless Valkyrie, and Lillian burned her arms when she threw herself over the flames still licking the Valkyrie's wings. Whimpering, she stared at the scorched feathers, the red blisters covering Elya's too-still body.

A blood-curdling cry echoed through the cave when Else flew to them, tumbling onto the ground as she landed by her sister.

"Sister! No!" Else shook her twin, but her blue eyes were vacant, her body limp in Else's arms.

Alek grinned at them, not a trace of emotion in his cold eyes. "Well, that was fortunate. I worried your friends would get away. But now I get to kill three half-breeds. Adeon will be very pleased with me."

Else snarled and rose to her feet, but Lillian grabbed her arm, pulling the blond behind her.

She stared at the king, her lips curling to show off her

sharp teeth. "You don't need to hurt her. You want me. You have me, so go ahead."

"You will not touch my mate."

The king doubled over as Kian's dagger lodged into his back, the flames flickering over his palms extinguishing.

But a cold laugh left Alek's lips as he braced himself against the cave wall. "You missed my heart, boy."

Kian ducked as the king sent a wall of fire toward him. Sprinting, he reached Lillian's side.

"We have to go now." Kian lifted the lifeless Elya into his arms. "Get Else."

Lillian turned to the twin, standing frozen in place. "We need to go."

Else blankly stared back at her.

"Else, please! We'll die if we stay here."

"Don't leave me! Please, I'll do whatever you want!"

Lillian stared at Astrid's sister, still chained to the wall, and the resemblance to her friend broke her heart as she realized she couldn't bring her—wouldn't be able to get to her and get her friends out in time.

"We'll come back for you. I swear we will come back for you." Lillian sobbed as she tore her eyes away from the desperate girl, from the tears that streamed down her dusty face.

Dragging Else toward the entrance, she fixed her eyes on Sam and Finn, who were fighting an impossible number of guards, their swords slashing again and again.

She met Finn's wide eyes as he screamed at them, "Get down!"

Lillian threw herself on the ground, pulling Else with her as another spark of heat flared above their heads. Risking a glance over her shoulder, she watched the king ready his flames once more, even as blood dripped from his mouth down onto his white fur coat.

"Come on," she hissed, stumbling to her feet.

Yet again, heat surged behind their backs, but Lillian froze when a roar echoed through the cave.

A silver dragon stalked through the entrance, rubble falling down the walls of the cave as it let out another screech.

Its icy-blue eyes fixed on her. *Run, young queen.*

She didn't need to hear it twice.

With a tight grip on Else's hand, Lillian ran toward Kian and the rest while the dragon stalked toward them, the guards dispersing in panic upon seeing the massive creature.

Lillian ran straight beneath the dragon's open maw, gasping as silver flames met the king's orange ones. The whole cave sparkled as the silver and orange fire exploded upon colliding.

Finn reached her side, lifting Else into his arms. "Let's get the hell out of here."

Too exhausted to even nod, she followed closely behind Finn as he raced out as fast as his legs would carry him.

42

Finn

Else was unresponsive, a dead weight in his arms as he sprinted from the cave. Finn glanced at the lifeless Valkyrie in Kian's arms ahead of him, tears burning behind his eyes upon seeing the charred wings, the black feathers falling off and trailing Kian's steps, stark against the white snow covering the ground. Shaking his head, Finn focused on getting away from the cave—one step at a time.

Lillian ran beside him, her face ashen and hands shaking as she tried not to fall behind. His chest tightened; she'd used so much magic in there to save them, and still, it hadn't been enough. Scanning the mountainside, he prayed for another cave or somewhere they could hide. Prayed today wasn't the end for all of them.

When a shadow flew above them, the silver dragon diving to land, Finn nearly stumbled over rocks hidden beneath the snow.

They all skidded to a stop, panting from the fast run. As Finn set Else down, she slid to the ground but at least stayed upright as she stared blankly ahead. Sam backed up behind him, his friend's hands trembling as they twitched toward his sword, his eyes flicking between the dragon ahead and the cave they'd left behind.

As Lillian took a shaky step toward the dragon, Finn held his breath. He'd recognized it in the cave; it was the one from the gilded cage that the king had in the courtyard, the one his insane friend had set free, but it was still a *dragon*. And Lillian looked so small beside it.

Kian stiffened beside him when their queen reached out a hand and placed it between the long black spikes lining its head. A purr vibrated in the dragon's throat as they stared into each other's eyes.

Finn frowned. "Are they talking?"

"It would seem so." Kian's eyes shone from pride and so much love that it made Finn's heart ache.

Turning to his friend, his voice shook as he quietly asked, "Is she alive?"

Kian's eyes filled with sorrow, and a strangled noise escaped Finn when he slowly shook his head. Deep in his heart, Finn already knew what the answer would be, but having Kian confirm it…

Pain, like he'd never felt before, filled him, overtook him, his vision going black, and Finn let his body tumble down next to Else.

The blonde turned to him, and he pulled her into his arms, holding on as tight as he dared. They stayed there, Finn's mind blank with agony, both silently weeping as their queen finished the silent conversation.

A small hand gripped his shoulder, and he looked up to tear-filled gray eyes.

"I'm so sorry. It's all my fault. She died because of me. Because I wasn't strong enough." Lillian's lips quivered as she stared at them, defeat lining her every feature.

Another wave of anguish surged within him, and Finn cleared his throat, trying to swallow the lump of despair. "It wasn't your fault."

He wanted to tell her that he'd seen the Valkyrie make her

decision as soon as Kian screamed Lillian's name. How she'd stopped everything, didn't hesitate as she flew, then dove in front of the wall of fire.

But no words left his mouth.

Lillian choked back a sob and gestured toward the dragon. "Nida knows of a place where we can hide for the night. We should go before they come after us."

Finn nodded and pulled Else with him as he rose to his feet, his vision still blurry from tears.

"We should lay her to rest here on Echo." Else wiped at her cheeks. "She hated Seigard, and her mate was from Echo anyway. I'm sure she would have preferred it."

Finn glanced at Lillian, who nodded with tears spilling down her pale face. "We'll do it tonight."

43

Kian

After Else helped remove the bracelets, Kian rifted himself, Sam, and Finn to the mountain the dragon had told Lillian of, while still holding onto Elya's burned body.

Else and Lillian flew with the dragon, even though Kian had tried to convince them not to. Lillian looked half-dead, and Else was in no shape to fly. But they'd both refused, needing some time to themselves in their grief.

Kian had nearly dragged Lillian down when she let out a small yelp of pain as she took to the skies, but after sensing the pure despair inside her, he let her go. He hadn't missed the shame and guilt that filled her eyes upon seeing Elya in his arms, seeing Finn and Else on the ground.

It wasn't her fault, but he knew there was no reasoning with her.

Not now.

When they landed on the snow-covered ledge, Sam stumbled upon a small cave, and Kian gently set down Elya's body onto the hard ground. He could barely breathe as Finn brushed the burned hair out of her face and shifted the Valkyrie's broken wings so they spread out beneath her before turning around and leaving the cave, his shoulders hunched and sobs racking his frame.

They remained quiet as they scanned the mountain, thankfully finding no guards hiding in any of the other small caves that littered the mountainside. After checking the entire area twice, Kian walked up to his friends, both sitting on a ledge looking out over the vast mountain chain, ignoring the snow that soaked them.

Kian lowered himself next to Finn and placed a hand on his shoulder. "I'm so sorry, Finn. I know you were becoming close."

Sam clasped his hand on Finn's other shoulder, meeting Kian's eyes over their friend's bent head.

Finn didn't hide the tears that fell down his face, dripping onto his bloodied leathers. "She did it for you, you know. You and Lillian. She lost her mate, and she couldn't bear for either of you to do so as well."

A lump formed in Kian's throat. He hadn't known Elya had a mate—he hadn't known the Valkyrie very well at all. He wished he'd spent more time with her, had tried to get to know her more.

She'd stood up for Lillian when no one else of the Valkyries had and had blindly followed her out of loyalty.

Kian met Finn's tear-filled eyes. "I will honor her sacrifice for the rest of my life. Lillian is my world. I wouldn't survive in one where she doesn't exist."

Finn clasped his hand over his, and Kian sensed no anger in him, no blame at what had driven Elya's decision. "I know, brother."

They remained quiet until the beatings of wings echoed between the mountaintops, the silver dragon leading the two Valkyries to the ledge.

Rising to his feet, Kian caught Lillian as she stumbled onto it, her legs collapsing from exhaustion, her body shaking —from exhaustion or grief, he didn't know.

Perhaps both.

He pulled his mate close, holding onto her as if she could disappear at any moment, and breathed in her night sky scent.

Yet again, he'd been so close to losing her.

Shaking, he let her small body, pressed against his, ground him—willing his mind to realize that she was there. That she was alive.

Sam mumbled something about building a fire, but neither of them responded as they pulled back, staring into each other's eyes.

"We should see if Finn and Else are okay," Lillian whispered after a while.

Kian nodded and grabbed her hand as they made their way to the cave they'd decided to stay in for the night.

When she leaned into him, he let out a soft breath and wrapped his arm around her shoulders. "Are *you* okay," he whispered.

When she glanced up at him, a tear trickled down her cheek, and she shook her head. He squeezed her shoulders, knowing there were no words that could make this night better. But even so, he would try.

Wrapping her body against his, he gently led her into the cave.

44

Lillian

It wasn't just one cave Nida guided them into to get away from the howling wind—it was an entire cave system.

Nervously eyeing the many dark openings snaking further into the mountain, she remembered very well what had happened the last time she'd stayed in a similar one. She sniffed the air but could only smell wet stone and the smoke from the fire Sam had lit.

Nida, who'd curled up in a corner, snapped her head up as they approached, fixing her eyes on Lillian.

Thousands of caves link together under this mountain, young queen. I advise you to stay close to this one, not venturing too far in. But the king shall not find you here. It's rumored to be cursed, the water in the pools filled with spirits who will drown you if you step into it. I believe it's only a rumor, though; your ancestors used these caves for their rituals, and none of them died, according to your mother.

"That's comforting. Thank you, Nida." The quip sounded hollow even to Lillian's ears, but the small dragon snorted and curled back up against the wall.

Lillian studied her, how the dim light shimmered off the silver scales and how the black spikes moved with every rumbling breath, not yet over the astonishment as Nida spoke to her and advised Lillian she could help keep her friends safe.

I am tired, young queen. When I learned where you'd gone, I flew fast and hard to get to you in time. I'd hoped you would come by us before you took on the king, but apparently, I was wrong.

"I'm sorry, I didn't think we had the time."

And it's not like she knew where the dragons dwelled, either. There wasn't exactly a ship route to wherever they resided.

Nida huffed, small sparks of silver fire bursting from her snout.

No time… I watched your power run out in that cave, Lillian. You shall come with me back to Narok, and we will teach you how to handle it, how to become stronger. We will stay here tonight, but tomorrow we leave. You will have to prepare; not all dragons are as friendly as I am.

Lillian rolled her eyes—more unfriendly creatures to win over. But when Nida opened a steel-blue eye and threw her a questioning look, she waved her hand dismissively.

Kian glanced at her, worry simmering in his eyes as he squeezed her hand.

Squeezing back, she said quietly, "Come, I'll tell all of you at the same time."

She dragged him to the fire, where Finn and Else sat in silence, staring into the dancing flames. Their faces were dusty and hollow, and their leathers tattered, burned, and ripped where the guards' swords had found their marks. Lillian motioned for Sam, who was sitting alone on the other side of the cave, staring out into the darkening night, to join them. He slowly made his way over, one eye fixed on the resting dragon.

Letting go of Kian's hand, she slumped down next to her best friend while Kian and Sam sat down on either side of Else.

When they looked at her, Lillian swallowed. "I'm so sorry. I don't know what to say. I don't know how to make this better, how to make it right."

"Don't apologize, Your Majesty." Else's voice was raspy, hoarse from crying.

She reached out a shaking hand to Lillian, and Lillian gripped it, surprised over the strength in Else's grip.

"Elya has been a ghost since her mate, Lios, died. I was sure she would die back then as well, but I think she forced herself to stay because of me. Twin bonds are strong, perhaps as strong as mating bonds, still, she never became herself again. But in the past few weeks, some of that fire within her was back. Since she met all of you."

A whimper escaped Finn, and tears filled all of their eyes as they stared at each other. Lillian couldn't bear to look at Finn, his body convulsing from quiet sobs next to her, but put her hand on his knee, trying to send any support she could muster through their bond.

Else sniffed as she continued, "She died for something she believed in, and I choose to think she was happy for it. But I can't stand thinking of her body… her body out there in the cold. All—"

Else's voice broke and she closed her eyes, her breathing shallow, as if each breath pained her to draw.

Lillian bent her head, her hair covering her face as she tried to regain her composure, not dissolve into tears.

She couldn't help but feel like this was her fault. She was the one who'd told them all to go here, who'd decided on the mission, who'd refused to stop to think when the bonds snapped. But she knew she couldn't break down; she needed to be strong now—needed to be the leader they all believed they followed.

Even if she didn't believe it herself.

When she could finally form words again, Lillian said quietly, "We'll lay her to rest here. Tonight. Else, I… I am not familiar with the Valkyrie traditions for burials. Aaron never taught me. What would you like us to do for her, and for you?"

Else glanced down at her hands resting on her crossed legs. "We are typically laid to rest at sea to give our spirit an easy journey as it floats to Vaelia, but since we're in the mountains, I think a grave should be sufficient. I don't think Elya would have cared too much anyway."

Nida opened an eye. *Young queen, if I may offer a suggestion. I'd be honored to drop the courageous Valkyrie who gave her life for our queen at sea.*

Lillian inclined her head. "Else, Nida would bring her to the water if you'd like. We could perhaps do a small ceremony here first to say goodbye?"

Else offered them a small smile through her tears. "Yes, I think she'd like that. Elya always wanted to bond with a dragon of her own. So to be laid to rest by one would surely have made her smile."

Rising on shaky legs, Lillian nodded again. But as she thought of the brave Valkyrie, who'd stood up against the Elders for her, who'd helped bring her back to life, she clenched her fists until they whitened, and the smell of iron filled the air from her nails piercing skin.

Elya deserved more than being laid to rest by one of the dragons she'd been so eager to meet. She didn't understand, couldn't understand how yet another brave soul was dead, but Alek still walked this realm.

He wouldn't be much longer.

As she slowly walked out of the cave, needing to feel the chill air on her skin, she promised herself that if it were the last thing she'd ever do, even at the cost of her own life, she'd take Alek with her.

————————————————————

45

Lillian

————————————————————

A sharp ache throbbed in her chest when Finn carefully lifted Elya's small body out of the cave and laid her on the frozen ground. Snowflakes fell upon her cold body, covering the burns and the broken wings, making it seem as if the Valkyrie was merely resting in the snow.

Else stepped forward, sinking to her knees by her sister and whispering words too quiet for Lillian's ears to pick up. The twins' blond hair mingled together when Else draped herself over her sister's chest, covering her body with her own and let out a cry—a raw, primal sound of despair.

When Else finally rose, her eyes cast down and face swollen from tears, Kian stepped forward.

"Elya," he bent a knee to stroke her face gently. "I am forever in your debt. There are no words to describe the gratitude I feel for you saving my mate's life. We would both be dead if it wasn't for your bravery. And while there are no words I can offer, I can promise you this: I will spend every day for the rest of my life trying to find a way to repay your sacrifice."

Tears streamed down Lillian's face when Kian backed up

and pulled her into his arms. She sobbed into his chest as he stroked her back, tears dripping onto her hair as Kian's tears flowed freely as well.

Sam's eyes were cast down as he approached Elya's body and kneeled before her. "Rest gently, winged warrior," he mumbled as he laid a small feather on her brow.

Finn was quiet as he took a shaky step toward Elya, his body trembling when he sank to the ground next to her.

Lillian, I can't do this.

The sorrow that flowed through their bond almost made her sick. Pulling out of Kian's arms, she walked up to her friend.

We'll do it together, Finn.

Lowering herself down next to him, she wrapped her arm around his waist. His body shuddered with more sobs as he rested his head on top of Lillian's, and she braced herself on the ground when her body mirrored his shivers.

"Elya," a sob lodged in her throat, but she forced herself to continue. "Elya, I have no words for what you did. I never wanted this. I never wanted any of this. I am so scared. But you had fears, too; even after a century, you were afraid. And you didn't let it stop you. So I won't stop either. Rest easy, beautiful warrior, loving sister, and loyal friend. I will see you in the afterlife."

Finn and Lillian held on to each other as if the world would break apart if they let go, watching more fresh snow dust the beautiful Valkyrie. Else, Sam and Kian stepped up behind them, and their friends pulled them into their broken tangle, each one of them quiet in their grief.

The ground shook as Nida walked out of the cave. *I think it's time, young queen.*

Lillian inclined her head and glanced at Else. "Are you ready?"

The Valkyrie nodded with tears spilling down her cheeks.

Finn and Sam backed up as Nida stalked over, her silver

scales mirroring the moonlight that broke through the dark clouds.

When she gently wrapped the Valkyrie in her front claws, they all stepped back, allowing the dragon to unfurl her wings.

Nida took to the sky, roaring her sorrow over the mountaintops.

46

Lillian

The others held onto each other as they returned to the cave, but Lillian lingered, her eyes following Nida until she disappeared over the snow-capped mountain range before them, her strong wings beating toward the eastern sea.

"Do you want to go inside?" Kian gently wrapped his arms around her, his warm breaths blowing through her hair and his scent enveloping her, layering over her like a blanket of safety.

Lillian stared out over the darkening sky and the gray clouds that once again shrouded the moon as it began its ascent. She was exhausted and cold, but she shook her head when Kian eyed her questioningly.

"I need to do something." She glanced at the Skandi, the wild mountain where she'd now lost so many.

"Do you want company?" Kian followed her gaze, realization settling over his features.

She turned to him, her eyes pleading with him to understand. "I think I need to do this alone."

Kian nodded slowly, his eyes full of love as he kissed her cheek. "Be careful. Even if my father seems to keep most of the guards in that cave, I believe there is another way up to the top. Too many guards flooded the area too quickly during the trial for them to have been hiding somewhere close to the plateau."

"I promise." Lillian offered Kian a small smile before she took a deep breath, drawing up the last of her energy reserves and spreading her wings. Throwing herself off the mountain-side, she let the chill wind carry her toward the Skandi.

The snow and wind had picked up again, but she didn't mind as thoughts swirled in her mind. Alek said that Adeon was coming for her. Not that it was much of a surprise, but she'd held a small kernel of hope that he might not, at least not yet.

She hadn't told the others yet, and she wouldn't tonight, not when today had been such a miserable failure. They were already scared, overwhelmed, and full of grief. How could she add more to the burden already weighing heavy upon them?

Lillian swallowed a sob as she steered toward the plateau where her whole life changed, where she'd lost the first boy she loved, where she'd *killed* the first boy she'd loved.

She felt it then, a ripple in the air as she scanned the horrid mountain.

She wouldn't make it out of this alive.

Not with both Alek and Adeon against her. She wasn't strong enough, didn't have time to become strong enough. But she could make sure the rest of her friends did—that they didn't face the same fate as Elya.

Lillian stumbled as she landed on the flat mountaintop. It was covered in fresh snow, the unlit lanterns the only remnant of the final trial that had taken place here. Slowly, she walked toward the eastern side of the mountain, cautiously making her way to the large rock formation where Eli drew his last breath.

No body lay under the white snow, perhaps consumed by the animals the mountain was home to, or it had been moved with the rest of the rebels and guards as there had been no bodies on the plateau either.

Lillian sank to her knees in the crunching snow, speaking softly to avoid attracting anything with claws or fangs. "Hi, Eli."

She clasped at her chest at the ache searing through her heart when his ocean-blue eyes flashed in her mind, the flick of his auburn hair when she frustrated him.

"I'm so sorry. I'm sorry that your life ended because of me, that you had to spend your whole life preparing to die for me to live. It wasn't fair, not on you and not on me. You deserved so much more, Eli."

The wind picked up, and Lillian stared with wide eyes as the snow twirled around her, a sparkling plume of snow gently caressing her cheek. She could nearly hear him then, how he would have told her to stop apologizing, that sacrifice was part of their responsibilities. That he died for what he believed in.

Lillian cleared her throat when emotion clogged it. "I loved you so much. I still love you, Eli. Thank you for letting me live, for letting me find Kian and the others, even if I might only experience it for a little while. I will always remember you, remember how brave and selfless you were, and I'll make sure the world knows it as well. Until the next life, Eli."

She let herself cry for a moment, thinking of the brave people who'd sacrificed their lives to take down Alek.

When her tears dried, only resolve remained.

She would not be scared to follow them—they'd all made sure she'd gotten more precious time, and she would make the most of it, even if she wouldn't live to see the world change.

When a low howl sounded in the distance, Lillian rose and pushed off the mountainside, heading back to her friends, to Kian's waiting arms.

47

Lillian

The wind had picked up further, and her friends had moved to a cavern further into the mountain to escape it. Thankfully, Kian had thought to rift back to the other mountain to pick up the things they'd left behind in their hurry, her satchel and beddings neatly laid out by the northern wall.

Finn and Else already lay in their beddings, quiet with their backs to the fire, when Lillian entered, while Kian and Sam sat by the fire, both seemingly lost in their own thoughts. Joining them, she leaned into Kian's chest and closed her eyes, allowing herself to seek comfort in his embrace, pretending for a moment he could protect her from the outside world.

Exhaustion spread through her bones, weakening her limbs, but Lillian wasn't ready to sleep, her mind still replaying the day and everything she needed to do.

Guilt also lay like a stone in her stomach—Josephine was still in the cave, in Alek's claws. Her brows drew together as scared, blue eyes etched themselves into her mind.

When she couldn't stand the silence a moment longer, she nudged Kian, who played absentmindedly with a strand of her hair as they both gazed into the crackling flames.

"Nida mentioned that there might be pools in the caves

further in. I don't know when we'll find time for another bath," she whispered.

Kian's eyes flitted between hers, the same understanding as when she'd left for the Skandi sparking in them, and he nodded. Lillian glanced at Sam with raised brows, but he shook his head.

"I'm going to sleep," he whispered and made his way to a spot in the back of the cave.

Finn stirred as they rose, and she stared at his broad back, gripping Kian for support when a wave of agony rolled down the bond.

Do you want to come with us, golden boy? I know how much you like to swim.

No, silver girl. Spend some time with your man. I don't think he's recovered from nearly losing you today. He needs you, and I need some time alone.

Lillian was about to argue; Finn never wanted to be alone, but she bit her tongue when Kian shook his head slowly.

If you need me, I'll be right inside those caves. I'm here for you, Finn. Always.

I'm all right, Lillian. Just try to keep it down, will you? The small flicker of amusement that rolled down the bond warmed her chest, but Finn cut off their connection before she could respond.

"You all right?" Kian studied her intently.

She nodded, "Let's see if Nida was right."

Kian took her hand and held on tight as they walked deeper into the mountain, his sharp eyes surveying every curve and tunnel.

The mountain quieted the further they walked, only the wind howling softly in the distance, and as they walked, Lillian marked a few rock formations around them so they would find their way back.

Soon the sound of water dripping reverberated between the stone walls, a soft, steady melody, and when the tunnel opened to a large chamber, Lillian sucked in a breath.

Two clear pools glittered in the darkness before them, a hole in the cave ceiling between them letting the dim moonlight in as the clouds parted, illuminating the entire circular space.

"This gives me the same feeling as the lake back in the capital," Kian whispered.

Heat pooled inside Lillian as she remembered the day at the lake, the first time she'd seen Kian's swirling tattoos, the mirror of her own darkness.

Her cheeks flushed when Kian eyed her, green fire blazing bright in his eyes.

"Lillian, you can go in alone. I'll stand watch outside if you prefer," he said gently.

She slowly approached him, even as she struggled to get her legs to cooperate, shaking her head. Lifting her hands to his face, she softly caressed his high cheekbones, down over his full lips, and finally reaching the tattoos that peeked over the neckline of his jacket.

He shuddered under her featherlight touch, his eyes trailing her fingers as she continued to trace the swirling black.

"No," she whispered. "I want everything with you, Kian. Perhaps tonight isn't ideal, but after what happened today, after Elya…"

Kian pressed a finger to her mouth. "Let's not go down that road, my dark queen. We're alive. And we're together. We don't have to rush anything; we will have time."

When uncertainty filled her, her gaze wavering, he tipped up her chin. "I'm not rejecting you. In no world would I ever reject you, Lillian. If you tell me you want to do this now, don't expect me to tell you no because that will not happen. I just want you sure," he whispered and cupped her face, kissing her softly until she wrapped her arms around his neck, pulling him closer.

Kian deepened their kiss, lifting her so her legs wrapped around his waist, and her heart began hammering against her chest. When his hands roamed over her shoulders, over her back, and further down, her breathing became shallow, and a soft growl escaped Kian as he held her closer, molding their bodies into one.

Backing up to the damp wall, they kissed—hungry, desperate kisses—that left them both out of breath until Lillian's lips were swollen, and Kian's hair was tangled from her hands pulling at it.

He laughed softly, shaking his head as he spoke against her lips, "I think I have some self-control until those lips of yours are on mine. Do you want to clean up?"

Lillian frowned, and Kian laughed again, quiet and filled with promise. "Tell me you want me, and you'll have me. Dirt and all. You just say the word, Lillian," he rasped.

He trailed his mouth down her neck, nipping at her sensitive skin and blowing his warm breath over her until her skin lit on fire. She leaned her head back, giving him more access, smiling when another growl left him as he explored her neck.

But as she sucked in a breath, the smell from her—from the both of them—filled her nostrils, and she wrinkled her nose at the smoke and iron and sweat. "Maybe we should have a bath after all."

He winked at her, smoothed out the wrinkle over her nose, and gently set her down. Reaching out a hand, he pulled her with him.

"The water does look nice."

48

Kian

It took everything in his willpower not to jump out of the pool and take her against the wall when Lillian slipped off her dirty leathers, exposing silky, tan skin shimmering in the soft light.

She was perfect.

Everything about her was perfect.

He couldn't tear his eyes away from her strong limbs, the dark hair that fell down straight down her back, and those gray eyes full of shadows that seemed to dance in the moonlight. Her cheeks were slightly red, mirroring her swollen lips as she slipped into the water.

"It's hot," she gasped.

Swimming to her, he pulled her body to his, and breathed in her scent. When her skin met his, her chest rising and falling rapidly, still out of breath from their kiss, his skin ignited, every nerve hypersensitive to where Lillian's body touched his. He gripped her tighter, wondering how he could ever let go.

"It is. We could stay here all night," he whispered into her hair.

She wrinkled her nose again, and Orios, if it wasn't one of his new favorite expressions on her.

"We'd be two prunes by then."

Kian couldn't stop himself. He gently flicked her nose, and she swatted at him.

"At least we'd be clean prunes," he grinned, his smile widening as the corners of her lips curled.

Kian let his fingers trail down her body, touching her shoulders, stomach, and back, noting every curve and scar—like he'd ached to do since the first time he saw her. He still couldn't believe she was his, that he was allowed to touch her like this.

"Kian…" Her voice was hoarse as she glanced at him, a sheen of sweat layering over her face.

"I'm just familiarizing myself," Kian winked, knowing every inch of her would be etched into his mind forever. "Come on, I'll get you clean."

Kian thought his heart might beat out of his chest when Lillian floated on her back, her wings spread around her like a dark shadow and the silhouette of her body glistening in the moonlight. He trailed his hands over her arms, slowly down her back, lingering above her wings.

"Can I touch them?"

Lillian nodded, and he gently let his fingers sweep across the glittering black. They were so soft, the feathers slipping between his fingers like water itself. Lillian jerked when he trailed his fingers further down the wings.

"Is this all right?"

"Yes," she whispered, so he continued.

Lillian actually purred when he brushed the top of her wings, softly massaging where they connected to her back. They were so beautiful. So perfect for her that he couldn't believe he hadn't seen a ghost of them before she broke the curse.

He couldn't imagine her without them.

After a while, she flopped onto her stomach. "I think it's my turn."

He nodded, and she swam to the brink of the pool, lifting herself up to sit on the edge, water dripping down her body.

Kian swallowed as he followed drops of water running down her curves, glistening over her soft skin.

He'd never seen anything so beautiful.

He blew out a shaky breath, telling himself to get it together, when Lillian waved him over. Slowly, he swam toward her, repeating to himself to wait until she was ready with every stroke. When he reached her, she placed him between her legs, and Kian had to take another deep breath not to pull her back in and wrap those silky legs around him.

His breath hitched when her fingers trailed over his tattooed back. "Why do you have these?"

When Kian tensed, Lillian slipped into the water behind him, wrapping her arms around his neck, and quietly repeated, her breath brushing his ear, "Kian, why do you have these?"

He shifted her so she straddled him, a smile pulling at his lips when her eyes widened at the proof of what she did to him. How she drove him to the brink of crazy—as if he was a mere teenager again.

"For as long as I can remember, there was only darkness and despair because of my father. But as I got older, I realized I didn't have to be like him. I don't have to spread evil and fear and misery. I got these as a reminder that while his darkness lives in me, I decide what I do with it."

He'd needed something to remind him every day, to make him choose light every day, not follow the path his father expected him to.

Lillian brushed her lips against his, her fingers trailing his neck, wrapping in his hair. "You're wrong, you know. His darkness doesn't live within you. You're pure light, Kian. I've known it since I met you. You're good."

He wasn't so sure of that, but when she continued to trail her lips against his lazily, he claimed her mouth instead of arguing with her. But he couldn't stop himself from whispering, "So when you threw that dagger at me, I was pure light?"

Lillian giggled, the airy sound sending waves of pleasure down his spine. "Perhaps it took a little while for me to figure it out."

He held her tighter for a few more beats before carrying her out of the pool. He was very glad she had—even if she might be wrong.

The air felt lighter as they dressed and slowly made their way out of the cave, and Kian couldn't stop himself from pushing her up against the stone every few feet to kiss her, so getting back to the others took a lot longer than when they'd left.

When they finally stepped into the firelight, soft snoring echoed through the cave—Nida had returned. The silver dragon was curled up by the entrance, blocking the strong wind and making the cave quite temperate.

No one stirred, so Kian pulled Lillian down onto his bedding, wrapping her tightly in his arms, and listened to her strong heartbeat as she drifted to sleep.

49

Lillian

She woke early the next morning, carefully untangling herself from Kian's arms, and slipped out of the cave. The skies were finally clear, and a thin layer of snow dusted the ledge. Lillian looked out over the mountain chain before her, the high peaks resting against the blue sky and the snow covering it sparkling beautifully in the early morning light.

She drew a deep breath of crisp mountain air. Her goodbye to Eli yesterday had brought some peace and relieved some of the guilt, but she still hated these mountains—nothing good had come from them, only death. Orios, sometimes she thought she might hate all of Echo. As if King Alek had tainted the whole island.

"Good morning."

She glanced at Sam as he joined her on the ledge.

"Morning. How are you feeling?"

She had barely talked to Sam since they danced together at the ball, and a knot formed in her stomach at the hard lines lining his usually soft face, at the heaviness in his posture. He had a sick brother she'd ripped him from. Even if she'd given him a choice, Sam was loyal, and she doubted he believed he had a choice himself.

"I'm all right. Don't worry about me." He placed a hand on her shoulder, looking out over the landscape. "What will we do next?"

Lillian followed his gaze, squinting against the early morning sun. "Nida wants me to go to the dragons. And after yesterday, I think she is right. I am not strong enough to take on Alek, not right now."

Sam shuddered next to her. "Are you sure? Can we trust them, Lillian?"

She shook her head, "I don't know what else to do. I know Nida was able to challenge Alek's flames yesterday. And if I can get them on our side, convince them to take on Alek with us, it could change everything."

Sam was quiet for a moment but then squeezed her shoulder. "I don't like it, but if it's what you want to do. I'll come."

She placed her hand on his, shifting her eyes to his knowing ones, once again reminded how similar they were to her father's; they had the same soulful depth to them as Atli's had.

"I don't know if I like it either. And I'm not sure what we'll face when we get there, Sam. But if you want to leave at any point, I hope you know I would never fault you. No one would."

Sam nodded slowly, "Thank you."

He followed her as she turned to walk back into the cave, where the rest of the group was waking up. Finn sat with his back against the wall, his legs drawn up, and stared blankly into the fire while Else and Kian quietly packed up their things.

Lillian tried to catch Finn's eyes, but he kept his gaze on the fire, not a muscle moving as she and Sam stepped inside. When she tried to reach him through the bond, it was shut off, and her stomach sank.

But she'd done the same, and Finn had respected her need to be alone, to grieve, so she would allow him the same space.

She offered Kian a small smile when she met his eyes, then cleared her throat.

"I'll be heading to Narok, the dragons' island. If anyone wants to stay back or return home, I'll understand—no reasons needed. I am not sure what will happen once we get there, how dangerous it will be, or if they'll even help us, but after yesterday, I think we all know that I'm not strong enough to take on Alek and his army. Not alone."

A knot twisted in her gut when the cave remained silent for a few moments.

"I've told you I will follow you anywhere, so if you're going to the fire-breathing monster lands, I will be right at your side." Kian wrapped his arm around her shoulders, and she smiled gratefully at him.

Nida huffed loudly. *Fire-breathing monsters. That one will have to watch his mouth when we get to Narok.*

"She doesn't like to be called a monster," she nudged Kian. "I think she prefers to be called an all-mighty fire-breathing dragon."

You need to watch your mouth as well, young queen.

Lillian rolled her eyes.

"I will come as well," Else spoke softly. "It's what Elya would have done."

Nodding, Lillian tried to smile at the Valkyrie, but her smile fell at the haunted look on her face and the emptiness in her blue eyes.

"I don't like it," Sam said, hovering by the cave's arched entrance. "I think we'd be better off trying to convince the Valkyries again. But I will come if this is your wish."

I don't like that one. Nida glared at Lillian.

Lillian grimaced. *Well, he doesn't like you either, but he is one of my friends, so you two are going to have to make do.*

Finn still stared into the writhing flames when he finally spoke. "I will join as well. If the dragons can help avoid more of us dying, I think it's the right thing to do."

Lillian walked up to crouch down before him, resting her

hands on his knees. Her heart ached when there was no whisper of his usual grin and twinkling eyes as he looked back at her.

You don't have to do this, Finn. I understand if it's too much to ask. You'll still be my favorite person, my best friend.

Finn stared at her for a moment, then the corners of his lips curled ever so slightly, his eyes shining with a little more life. *What about your most handsome friend? Am I prettier than your swimming prince?*

Despite everything, Lillian couldn't stop a small giggle from escaping. *The prettiest of them all, golden boy.*

Finn gave her a slow wink. *Then it's settled. I can't leave you alone with all of these lesser people.*

Shaking her head, she offered Finn her hand as she stood. Warmth settled in her chest when he took it, and his shoulders were a little less hunched when he straightened. Not letting go of Finn's hand, she took her time to look at each one in the group.

"I promise you all, I'll do *whatever* it takes to make them help us. I will make sure what happened yesterday isn't repeated."

At whatever cost, even if it meant giving up her own life.

50

Lillian

"How do we get to Narok?"

As the rest of the group finished packing up, the mood in the cave a little lighter and the air a little easier to breathe, Lillian sidled up to the silver dragon, stopping a few feet away when Nida rose and unfurled her wings to avoid getting knocked over.

We should fly so we arrive together. I don't think it's wise for you to get there without me.

Lillian frowned. "Why not?"

Nida's frosty eyes bore into hers. *I might not exactly have been allowed to come here and help you, and Tyr will be upset with me. And, by extension, you. So it's probably in your best interest to have someone speak for you.*

"Perfect." Lillian shook her head, not able to hide the annoyance sliding across her features. "Could you carry one of the men?"

Nida whipped her head up so fast Lillian barely had time to back away to avoid getting impaled by the razor-sharp spikes on her head.

We do not carry humans. Or Valkyries, for that matter. Tyr would have had your head just for asking. We're not your pets, young queen.

When smoke blew out of Nida's nostrils, her eyes narrowed to slits, Lillian threw her hands in the air. "I didn't know. I thought with Elya—"

That was an exception, as it was when you let me out, one we'll never speak of again if you care for your own life. Nida nudged her with her large head, the spikes nearly ripping through Lillian's jacket. *But you're in luck, it seems. Your other winged friends are finally arriving.*

Lillian glanced out of the cave. Nida was right. Hanin and Munion flew toward the cave, the black feathers on their large wings reflecting the early sun peeking over the mountains.

Lillian walked out of the cave to greet them, the rest of her friends and Nida following closely behind, the ground rumbling under the dragon's heavy steps.

Your Majesty. Munion inclined his head. *I apologize for our tardiness. The Valkyries are in turmoil. The Elders found out what Grete did, and many of them don't know what to think, some regretting they didn't listen to you.*

Lillian quickly translated for the rest.

"What do you want to do?" Kian brushed his hand against hers.

She drew a deep breath. "I think we should still go with Nida. I can't risk the Elders telling me no again, even if more of them support us. We need the dragons, and I won't waste any more time."

Kian nodded. "Then we shall go there now."

"I could go back, Your Majesty." Else eyed the two ravens. "If you wish, I could speak on your behalf, get them to see what happened, and tell them of Elya. Try to get them to join us, rally them while you rally the dragons."

Lillian nodded slowly. They would need all the help they could get, and it would also ensure that more of them were safe—at least for now.

"I don't think you should go alone." She glanced at Finn and Sam.

Finn stepped forward, his movements still not the assured

ones she was used to, but his eyes were clear and jaw set as he fixed his gaze on hers. "I'll join her. We'll get them on our side, Lillian. Be ready for when you've convinced the dragons."

As Lillian began to shake her head, Kian whispered in her ear, "I think you need to let him go. He needs this."

When tears welled in Lillian's eyes, a stray one snaking down her cheek, Finn pulled her into his arms, gripping her tight as a sob shook her.

We'll be okay, Lillian. It would only be for a little while, and we need more allies. You need more allies. I said I wanted you to consider me for your court—let me shoulder this responsibility for you. Let me help.

Lillian glanced up at him, his face blurry from the tears that lined her eyes. *I don't know if I can do this without you, Finn.*

She nearly choked at the thought of being away from him, of something happening to him when she wasn't there to protect him.

As if he read her carefully closed mind, Finn offered her a crooked smile. *We will always protect each other, silver girl. But you once told me you were fighting for something better, and what did I tell you?*

Lillian tried to smile back, but her lips wouldn't cooperate. *You said I'm in.*

Exactly. And this is what it means to be in. So you be strong now, take care of that man of yours, and get those dragons on our side. Also, Finn winked, *you and I are the only ones awesome enough to speak from a distance, so we'll be able to gossip whenever we want.*

Lillian snorted, but she bore her eyes into his one final time. *Promise me you'll get out of there immediately if anything goes wrong. Promise me?*

Finn pulled back, a ghost of a smile grazing his lips. *I promise. But you know me, I'll charm them into helping us with my amazingly good looks and even more incredible personality.*

Shaking her head, she wiped at her cheeks when more tears escaped. *You better, golden boy.*

They decided the ravens would also go back to Seigard to

mobilize the other guardians and get as many as possible behind them.

Kian gripped her hand tight as Finn shifted, and soon, the three birds and the Valkyrie took to the skies, flying swiftly over the mountaintops.

51

Kian

"I think we need to rift there, Lillian." He glanced at Sam, leaning against the outside of the cave, his head tilted to the sun and eyes closed. "You won't be able to carry both of us."

Lillian turned to Nida. "He's right. I don't want to stay here a moment longer than we need to. And we don't have time to find a ship that could take us."

The dragon huffed impatiently, blowing Lillian's black hair around her face, the heat from it flushing her cheeks.

"You're a faster flier than me, Nida. You'll have to meet us there."

Nida inclined her head, and with a loud roar that had Sam stumbling backward, the dragon beat her wings and took off, heading north. Kian followed her sparkling silhouette until she blended into the clear sky, only a glint of her scales betraying her.

His beautiful mate looked at them, her eyes still glassy from saying goodbye to Finn and Else and worry etched into her features.

It was all he could do not to pull her into his arms, rift her somewhere far away, somewhere he could hide her from the world. Where she could be safe, and her bottom lip wouldn't quiver from the fear he sensed from her.

"Nida wants us to land on the beach of Narok. Try to stay there if we can, avoiding the rest of the dragons, until she arrives tomorrow."

Kian nodded, trying to visualize the beach, the dragon island. "I'll do my best. Are you ready?"

Lillian nodded, and he pulled her tight to his chest, praying they weren't heading into another death trap.

"Sam?" His friend gripped his shoulder, and Kian let his magic envelop them, the tight air squeezing them through time and space.

When they landed, thankfully on the sandy shores he'd aimed for, he held on to Lillian as her body shook, and she drew deep breaths against the nausea. Gently stroking her hair, he waited for it to subside.

It had taken him years to get used to rifting himself—he'd cursed the gods many times for his magic before he mastered it.

Humans on our island. That's something I never thought I'd see again.

Kian jerked at the voice, and Lillian stiffened beside him.

"Shit," Sam whispered behind them. "Get down."

Kian threw himself over Lillian as a pillar of silver fire erupted above their heads, the heat from it pricking his scalp.

"Stay down," Kian hissed as another rush of air and a new jet of flames burst above them.

"You have to let me get up," Lillian whispered. "I need to tell them who I am."

Kian had to fight every instinct inside him to let his queen, his mate, to her feet. Rising with her, he stepped a half-step in front of her, placing himself between her and the dragon, even as she glared at him.

He only grinned back.

He'd take that glare any day to have her safe.

A current ran over his skin as he kept his magic ready, his

blood thrumming with adrenaline when Lillian spoke.

"Enough!" Her voice was commanding, with no fear in it, as she stared at the massive black dragon. "You know who I am, and you will not hurt me."

Young queen, you should not have come here. The dragon tilted its head. *And you brought humans with you. Are they perhaps an offering, a snack?*

Lillian snarled, "They're with me. You shall not hurt them either."

When she took a step toward the dragon, Kian gripped her hand and pulled her behind him, his body buzzing with raw energy as he glared at the dragon.

The dragon turned its icy-blue gaze to him, and a shiver snaked down Kian's spine at the intensity in it.

Your mate is a brave one. Or dumb if he thinks he could do anything to protect you here.

"I won't let you anywhere near her, fire-breather." Kian refused to break the dragon's gaze, ignoring the unease that raced across his skin as it straightened, showing off its full height and the inch-long spikes covering its entire body.

The dragon's twenty or so feet frame towered over them, hiding the sun behind it. Sam gasped as the dragon opened its mouth. But no fire left its mouth, only a loud rumbling that made its chest vibrate.

You can hear me, human?

"I think anyone on this damn island can hear you." Kian narrowed his eyes as the dragon took a step closer, the rocky ground beneath it shifting. "Not another step, dragon."

The rumbling in the dragon's throat sounded again. *A human who can speak to me, now that's something I've never seen before. I will not kill you; this is too curious. You shall all come with me.*

When the dragon began turning, Lillian cast a quick but curious glance at Kian before she spoke again.

"I know you. You were in my meadow. And you're the one who brought Hanin and Munion to help me. Who are you?"

I am Tyr, of course, young queen.

52

Lillian

Kian refused to let her take the lead, keeping her behind him, his hand locked on hers, as they followed Tyr off the beach. She rolled her eyes at his protectiveness but let him have his way when his tight shoulders told her there was no point in arguing. Sam was quiet, his body stiff as he walked beside her, whipping his head at the slightest sound rumbling between the boulders lining the edge of the shore.

"Did you hear him as well, Sam?" Lillian whispered.

He shook his head, "All I heard was growling. I was sure we were about to become a pile of ash."

She patted his arm. "It seems Kian intrigues him, so hopefully, we'll stay alive until Nida arrives."

Kian snorted. "I have no idea how I heard him, but I don't trust that fire-breather for the life of me. You both keep close, and I'll rift us to Seigard should they make one move."

When Kian gripped her hand again, Lillian glanced around the island. There was no forest here, only large boulders and gray stone as far as she could see. The ground was barren, with no grass or other vegetation on it.

Tyr led them down a wide stone path into what Lillian could only describe as a massive bowl made out of polished brown stone. They all froze when Tyr lifted his large head to the skies and let out a roar that shook the ground and the walls around them.

The air filled with the beatings of wings.

Dozens of dragons, in all sizes and colors, landed along the curved walls of the bowl, their eyes fixed on herself, Kian, and Sam. But one dragon made Lillian's eyes widen, a large silver dragon that walked up to Tyr's side with identical black spikes to Nida.

Brothers and sisters, we have company. Tyr flicked his head in their direction. *The Valkyrie queen is here, I presume, to ask for our support. And she brought two humans with her. But apparently, they're not food, so hold off for now.*

Low rumblings sounded in the chests of several of the dragons as they tilted their heads and studied them, tendrils of smoke from their nostrils floating up toward the sky.

Tyr turned his massive head over his shoulder. *Young queen, the floor is yours.*

A chill spread throughout Lillian's body when she felt every single pair of eyes in the bowl snap to her, and she was surprised her heart didn't beat out of her chest when the rumblings grew louder. She threw Kian a grateful glance when he squeezed her hand and stepped forward with her.

Lillian cleared her throat. "I have come to seek your aid. I know you supported my mother, and I ask you to do the same for me. I am planning to take down King Alek, but I cannot do it alone. I'm asking you to help me so that we all can live freely and peacefully in Orios."

The silver dragon turned to approach them slowly, her head lowered and eyes kind as they swept over her.

You look so much like her. Tears filled the dragon's eyes. *I am sorry we couldn't protect your mother. There is a piece of my heart that will always be missing in her absence.*

Lillian nodded, a lump forming in her throat. "I know why you couldn't," she said quietly. "But I was the one who freed Nida, and I ask that you help me in return."

And we are forever grateful for that. I was afraid we'd never see our daughter again. The silver dragon huffed softly. *I am Fafri, Queen of Dragons, and your mother's bonded.*

"Will you help me then? Nida was the one who brought us here, and she promised you would."

Lillian jerked when Tyr roared. *She did no such thing. Young queen, you cannot lie to our kind. Nida went against my orders to save your skin. It's the second time we've helped you and saved your life. I should think the debt is paid.*

Kian snarled next to her. "She saved your daughter from Alek's claws, but you did nothing to save her parents. The debt is nowhere near paid fire-breather."

Kian pushed her behind him when the dragons around them screeched, stomping their large feet, and while Lillian wanted to be annoyed at him for being so protective, she had to hold back a small smile at the defiance on Kian's face.

Fire-breather. She shook her head, allowing strands of hair to fall forward to hide her smile.

Silence!

Tyr studied them intently. *So curious. You are King Alek's son, are you not?*

Kian nodded once.

And you wish to go against your father, your own blood?

"He may be my blood, but I will be the one to spill his." Kian didn't back down as Tyr's warm breath blew through his hair, glaring right into his steely eyes.

Tyr stared at them for a moment longer, then sliced his gaze to the dragons once more. *We shall confer. You will wait over there.* He flipped his vicious head toward a large stone formation. *We'll get you when we're finished.*

53

Lillian

The formation functioned like a small house, with four walls and a roof that protected them from the strong winds from the sea, and Lillian gratefully sat down on a small boulder with her back against the smooth wall. Kian sat down next to her, wrapping his arm around her shoulder, and she leaned into his large chest, breathing in his scent as Sam took a spot opposite them.

Kian let his fingers whisper across her skin as they quietly waited for the dragons to make their decision. They slowly trailed her neck, her shoulder, anywhere he could find a bit of skin, and a shiver ran down her spine when he tickled her collarbone.

"What do you think they will decide to do?" she whispered, trying to distract herself from the tingling sensation radiating from her core.

Kian shrugged, "I'm not sure. From what I could tell, the dragon queen seemed to be on your side, so hopefully, she can convince them if Nida doesn't get here in time."

When another shiver went through her as his fingers moved to her neck, she snapped her eyes to his, frowning when his eyes glinted, and a small chuckle left his lips. She offered him a crooked smile in return—she loved this playful side to him, even if he were only doing it to distract her.

Sam shuddered, thankfully keeping an eye over his shoulder and not on Kian. "I almost wish they'd tell us to leave. They scare me to death, and I can't even understand them."

Lillian offered her friend a half-smile. "Me too. But we need them, Sam. I just hope they make the decision quickly."

Kian pulled her closer, nestling his face into her hair and blowing soft breaths across her neck that made her own breathing uneven, every nerve within her sparking with anticipation.

"Me too. I'm ready for this all to be over." He lowered his voice, his lips against her skin as he whispered, "Then you're mine, dark queen. I think we deserve a long, long vacation."

When Sam snorted, Lillian's face heated, but she nodded and met Kian's eyes, her skin blazing at the promise in them.

While they waited, the sun started its descent over the sea, and the day darkened, casting long shadows inside the stone formation. Lillian shivered from the sudden chill as an evening wind picked up, and Kian pulled her onto his lap, his arms shielding her from the cold.

"I'm starving," Sam moaned. "It's been hours. How long can this take?"

Humans… Always so impatient.

They whipped their heads up when Tyr's shadow cast the stone house in darkness. *That's the problem with their kind: They can't wait for things to happen naturally. Instead, they complain, start wars, and cheat.*

Lillian shook her head. "Not everyone lives forever, Tyr. Did you make your decision?"

The dragon jerked his head. *Come.*

As they made their way out of the house, Kian held her back for a moment. "If anything happens, we'll get out of here immediately. It's not worth risking your life if they say no."

Lillian nodded, all the while praying it wouldn't come to that.

The dragons were still in the bowl, in the same positions as they had been when they'd left them.

Tyr led them into the middle as he grumbled, *We've decided to help you.*

A smile spread across Lillian's face.

But you shall do what your mother did to prove you're worthy of our help.

Her smile fell immediately.

Few times have we bonded with Valkyries. And never has one of us bonded with a human.

Lillian's frown deepened, and she stared at Kian, who raised his brows and shrugged.

You and your mate will prove that we can trust you, prove the strength and bravery that lie within your soul. And should you succeed, we will help you both.

"Prove ourselves? Do you not think she has proven herself enough? She helped one of your kind before she even knew what she was, who she was."

Kian stalked toward the dragon, and Lillian's body went cold when Tyr narrowed his eyes as he stared down at Kian's hard face, the hand that rested upon the sword at his side.

Young human, never has one of your kind spoken to one of us. You and your mate will both prove your worth, and we shall allow both of you to bond if you live. As is our way.

Lillian swallowed. "What will you have us do?"

You will have to find your way to our most sacred island, where we hide our greatest treasures. You will face many challenges, as your mother did, young queen. But if you make it there, you will find it'll be worth it. Great power lies at the end, power that will let you take on Alek, even Adeon, should you wish.

54

Kian

He stared at Lillian as she stalked up to the massive dragon, her black hair flying behind her in the breeze and her eyes nearly as black as the dragon's scales. And while his muscles locked, the need to protect her nearly overwhelming, he couldn't help but smile when she wagged her finger at the dragon King.

"We don't have time for your games, Tyr. We need to make our move now."

The dragon growled. *This is our way. Either we kill you here, or you do as we say and win our favor.*

Kian stepped up to his mate's side. "She's right, Tyr. How long will this take?"

As long as it takes. When Kian snarled at him, the dragon actually rolled its eyes. *Humans... It took her mother four days, and she wasn't the fastest of the ones who succeeded.*

Kian gripped Lillian's hand when she started to argue. "We'll do it. But if we succeed, you will follow our queen's orders. No delaying your support and no finding a loophole out of it."

Tyr huffed. *I almost hope you make it, human. I think I shall like to bond with you.*

Kian's eyes widened, but he ignored the comment. Whatever Tyr saw in him or thought of him didn't matter right now.

"Where do we go? And what about Sam?"

Sam's face blanched when Kian gestured toward him.

The other human stays here, or he can leave. I don't particularly care. Only you and your mate may go; we don't bond with sniffling, braveless souls. Sam jerked when Tyr glared at him. *We won't harm him. He probably wouldn't be very tasty anyway. He can stay in one of the caves, and I'll even ask Nida to provide him with food.*

Fafri stepped up next to Tyr, but all Kian heard was growling from the silver dragon—not the clear voice booming through his head when Tyr spoke.

He glanced at Lillian as she translated for them. "He is speaking the truth. We won't harm him should he choose to stay. You will have to find the end. You'll feel its pull now that it's been decided. You will pass several isles on your way there, but you'll know when you're near. A part of your soul now rests upon it."

Kian nodded, a strange sensation already filling him as if a piece of him was missing, needing to be put back together.

But Lillian stiffened after she finished translating. "A part of our souls?"

Tyr inclined his head. *That's why you better find it, young queen. You can't live forever with a fractured soul.*

Kian swallowed the rage roiling inside him at the convenient detail they'd forgotten to mention and pulled Lillian close. "We'll find it," he whispered.

Turning to Sam, he clasped his friend's shoulder. "Are you all right?" Sam nodded. "We'll be back as soon as we can. Don't let these fire-breathers mess you around."

When a half-smile overtook his friend's face, Kian grabbed Lillian's hand and pulled her to the south part of the island, where something was softly calling for him, where an invisible rope dragged him.

He didn't bother saying goodbye to the dragons, even as he heard Tyr growl, *Humans*.

55

Kian

Lillian squeezed his hand, and he didn't miss the slight tremble in her voice as she spoke. "What do you think we'll face out there?"

They reached the shoreline, the dark sea before them wild with waves, crashing onto the small islands perched in the dark water ahead. The moon hung high in the sky, its reflection broken in the fierce water.

Kian turned to her and, upon seeing her white face, immediately wished he could whisk her away from yet another dangerous situation.

He needed her to be safe. Or at least to be able to get a full night's rest. But she would never agree, and he would not be the one to hold her back.

"I don't know, but I'm pretty sure it won't be pleasant." Warmth filled his chest when a smile pulled at her lips.

"I don't think I'd know pleasant if it smacked me in the face. What is it again?" Lillian winked at him. "Also, are we going to talk about how *Tyr* offered to bond with you?"

Kian shook his head. "I have no idea why or how I could hear him, so I'm not sure there is much to talk about. But once we've finished whatever challenges they've prepared for us, I guess it could be good to have the King of Dragons on our side."

"That it would be." Lillian smiled at him, and the sight of it hit him straight in the heart like an arrow.

What he'd do to see that genuine smile on her every day.

"Should we rest here? I'm being pulled to one of the islands, I think."

Kian stared out over the sea again. "So am I, the southern one?"

She nodded, her eyes tired.

He wished for nothing more but to allow Lillian to rest then, but a nagging feeling told him there was urgency, so despite his feelings, he gestured to the small island, only a dot in the vast sea.

"Maybe we should head over. I have this strange feeling that we need to hurry. But if you prefer to stay here, we'll find someplace to sleep."

She hesitated, glancing at the rocky beach behind them, then shook her head. "No, you're right. I'm anxious to be done with this—there is no point in dragging it out. I just hope there is nothing with fangs that is preparing to eat us for dinner."

Kian pulled her to him, his lips whispering over her cheek. "I won't let anything get its fangs into you, Lillian. I'm the only one who gets to bite this soft skin of yours," he winked, trying to relieve the tension in her body.

But when she wrapped her arms around him, he forgot everything else, especially as her lips brushed against his neck. He shuddered when she gently nipped the sensitive skin right above his collarbone.

"I know you won't," she whispered against his skin, her warm breath fanning over his neck.

"Lillian," he started, but when she did it again, he groaned and lifted her up so her legs wrapped around him.

If this were what she needed to distract herself from what was to come, he'd give it to her, like he'd give her anything she wanted. He let his fingers gently trail down her sensitive wings, grinning when she moaned softly in his ear.

When she glanced up at him, he softly pressed his lips against hers, his grin widening as she wrapped her hands in his hair, pulling him closer. The heat radiating from her body, together with the strong grip of her legs, made him shake from desire.

Lillian's breathing became uneven as she roamed her hands over his back and chest, pulling at his jacket, and Kian pulled back to look at her, at her flushed cheeks and clear eyes.

When Lillian frowned at the distance, he grinned at her, "You drive me crazy. We're supposed to go off to find a piece of our souls, and the only thing on my mind is this silky skin of yours," he kissed her again, "and these soft lips."

She winked at him, "And here I thought commanders received extensive training never to lose focus during a mission."

Kian growled and gently set her down. He may have gotten a little carried away in distracting her, but when her eyes were filled with heat like that...

Lillian laughed when he exasperatedly dragged his hands through his hair and frowned. "We do, but somehow, I seem to forget everything I've been taught when you're around."

He truly did, and he couldn't even be mad about it when she smiled at him, when a little of that weight she carried around seemed to lift.

56

Lillian

Heat still flared in her veins when Kian gently led her to the shoreline to rift them to the island. He wasn't the only one who forgot everything around them when her skin touched his.

She knew it wasn't the best timing, but when would it ever be? There was so much death around them, and even if they survived the next few days, they'd have to face Alek again.

She shuddered from the chill that spread through her body at the thought of his father, the hair on the back of her neck rising as fear pricked her skin. Forcing a small smile when Kian glanced at her, she tried to shake the feeling of dread.

Kian held out his hand. "Are you ready?"

Pushing away the last bit of fear, she took it and nodded.

They landed on a small island filled with tall pine trees, its ground littered with dried pine needles that crunched as they took a hesitant step inland. Kian held on tight to her as she recovered from the nausea, but thankfully she got to keep the contents of her stomach this time.

When the nausea subsided, she swept her gaze over the island, glimpsing the other side through the thick trees, and

Lillian blew out a breath of release after they'd walked around the entire shoreline without finding anyone or anything on it.

"Do you feel the pull anymore?"

Kian furrowed his brow when she shook her head.

"At least nothing on here seems to want to eat us." She tried to smile at him, but unease filled her stomach at the eerily quiet island. "I'm guessing we're supposed to stay here tonight."

Kian pulled her against his hard body, his arms protectively clasped over her chest as they scanned the small island. "It looks like there is a small opening in the trees over there."

She followed his gaze, noticing the small clearing, and nodded. "Let's rest here tonight."

They didn't make a fire—didn't want to risk waking anyone or anything that could be slumbering around them. Instead, they sat close together against a large tree, arms wrapped around each other to keep warm in the chilling breeze from the sea.

When Kian's breathing grew even, and his head fell back to lean on the trunk, Lillian leaned into his chest, scanning the area one last time before letting her own eyes fall shut.

"Lillian?"

She pried her eyes open and peered into the darkness, nudging Kian's hard chest. When he didn't stir, she turned her head, and her heart stopped.

She was leaning against the trunk. Jumping to her feet, she called out for him, and when he didn't answer, she frantically stumbled through the trees, calling out for him again.

"Lillian?"

She froze when a woman's soft voice drifted between the trees. There was something familiar about it, and when it called out again, she cautiously made her way toward the sound. When she reached the shoreline, a young woman with identical glittering black wings to her own sat on a rock a few yards out, her long black hair blowing in the wind.

"Join me, Lillian. I've been waiting for you for so long."

The pull she'd felt earlier returned with full force, nudging her toward the woman, and she stepped into the water, barely feeling the fall-chilled waves that washed over her legs.

She was so familiar.

Lillian squinted in the moonlight to make out the woman's features as she ventured closer. When she was right behind her, the woman patted the spot next to her and Lillian couldn't stop herself from sitting down.

As she glanced to the side and met gray eyes, she gasped, "Mother?"

Her mother gave her a sad smile. "I'm so proud of you, Lillian. My wonderful daughter." She reached out a hand and touched her cheek, and Lillian swallowed against the lump that formed in her throat. "You are so beautiful," her mother whispered.

"How are you here?" Lillian stared at her mother's face while tears burned behind her eyes.

She looked exactly like she had in that painting—looked so much like Lillian herself. The same slightly upturned nose, same gray eyes, and raven-black hair.

Liv smiled at her. "A piece of my soul will always be here, as shall yours. It's the price we pay for bonding with the drag-ons, but I am glad for it. It allowed me to see you and speak to you. I prayed you would come, my beautiful daughter."

Lillian drew a shaky breath. "Is my father here too?"

Liv caressed her cheek. "No. Your father's soul is intact, and he won't return to this realm. But we're together, Lillian. And it's peaceful where we are. The only thing that pains us is you. I wish your life weren't so full of struggle, and I'm sorry for the part we played in that."

Lillian gripped her mother's hand, holding on tight as if she would disappear if she blinked. "It's not all bad. I have friends who love me, and I've found my mate." She tensed, casting a glance behind her shoulder toward the small, quiet island. "Do you know where he is? I couldn't find him when I came here."

"He's asleep, Lillian. But he is safe." Liv lovingly trailed her eyes over her face. "We don't have much time, my daughter. I want to hear everything about you, what you're planning."

"Am I asleep as well?" Lillian pinched her arm.

She felt wide awake.

"In some ways, in some ways not." Liv took her hand again. "Tell me, what do you plan to do?"

Lillian frowned but responded. "We'll get the dragons on our side, and I'm hoping your sister's betrayal will have convinced the Valkyries to help. Then we'll take on Alek and try to free Orios." Her voice shook at the end, the dread she'd been pushing away filling her chest.

Her mother squeezed her hand. "Lillian. I knew you'd grow up to be brave and strong. But the fate of the world doesn't rest upon your shoulders alone, as it didn't on mine and Ivar's. You do not have to do this."

Lillian's lip trembled. "But who will if not me? I can't leave them all to suffer. Too many died for me to finish this."

Liv smiled a warm, big smile—a mother's smile—that made her heart ache. "There will always be someone else, my beautiful daughter. Come. Come with me. Let your father and I take care of you like we've always longed to do. You will be safe and loved. You're so loved, Lillian."

A sob lodged in her throat when her mother rose, pulling Lillian to her feet. "We only have to go out in the water. It's not so bad, is it?"

Lillian shook her head, but a feeling of safety, of peace filled her as the waves swept over her legs.

"I love you so much, my daughter. You will find peace."

She was not afraid as she followed her mother into the depths of the sea.

57

Finn

When they arrived back at Volantis, Finn realized the ravens might have been holding back. It was utter mayhem around the castle. Valkyries stood or flew in groups, urgently whispering to each other, while their human mates ran in and out of the castle, loading the balconies with satchels and other goods.

"What's happening?" Finn stared at Else, who shrugged, leaning over the railing and staring with wide eyes at the activity below them.

Hanin and Munion left them upon arriving at Seigard, flying directly to the guardians' towers to hear—and share—the latest news.

"You're back."

Finn scowled as Aaron joined them on the balcony, muscles tensing with apprehension and eyes snapping to the sword leaning against the castle wall.

Aaron followed his gaze, a wrinkle forming across his brow. "I know you don't like me, Finn. But I had no idea Grete knew. I promise I've only wanted the best for our queen."

When Finn only glared at him, Aaron shrugged, "The

Valkyries are talking about fleeing. Some of the ravens have picked up whispers that Alek is planning an attack."

Fear pricked Finn's scalp, and he pushed away the ember of guilt that threatened to settle in his stomach.

It wasn't their fault. If the Valkyries had stood by Lillian they wouldn't be in this position.

"Do you know when?"

Aaron shook his head slowly. "In a few days, maybe. We have spies out now to confirm." He glanced behind him. "Where are the others?"

"They're on Narok, trying to get the dragons to do what your people would not."

Aaron jerked. "Our queen is on Narok? And you're not there with her?"

Finn narrowed his eyes at the accusatory tone. "My queen asked me to come here so Else wouldn't be alone. And I, at least, will do what my queen asks me to," he said quietly.

"And where is the angry one?" Aaron raised his brows, looking pointedly at Else.

When she only shook her head, eyes cast down, Finn cleared his throat, swallowing against the emotion swimming inside him. "She didn't make it. Alek found us, and Elya sacrificed her life for Lillian."

He braced himself against the railing at the knife that twisted in his heart when he spoke Elya's name.

But he would never not speak it, wouldn't let the Valkyrie be forgotten, would make sure everyone knew of her bravery.

A shadow crossed Aaron's face. "I'm sorry to hear that. Elya was brave, perhaps the bravest of us all. I wish I had come with you. I won't stay back again, and I won't flee this time. What can I do?"

Else stared at her feet, but Finn bore his eyes into the male Valkyrie's. "We should start by convincing the Valkyries to stay and fight. Lillian is trying to bond the dragons, which I am sure she will succeed with, and she'll be coming here with them after. We can take Alek down once and for all."

Aaron paused for a moment, a flicker of uncertainty in his eyes before resolve overtook his features, and he dragged a hand through his blond mane. "Follow me."

Finn shifted when Aaron took to the skies, following the male Valkyrie as he steered toward the east tower. No sense of excitement filled Finn as the wind brushed his wings or when he passed several Valkyries, staring after the large owl as he let out a soft hoot.

He let the wind bring him up—tried to focus on the cool air blowing through his feathers.

He would be all right.

Elya was with her mate now, finally in peace. And he'd hopefully find peace as well.

Not today.

But one day.

When they landed on the eastern tower balcony, a small piece of the weight resting heavily on his chest lifted, and he blew out a deep breath as he shifted back into his human form.

There would be a time for grief, but right now, they needed to help their queen—help all of Orios. This is what he had prepared for, what his guard training was meant for.

Even better, it wasn't under Alek but for his best friend, for the group of people that had become his family.

Else carried the purple robe he'd worn that first night with her and threw it to him, offering him a half-smile when he winked at her.

Maybe they'd both be all right.

58

Kian

He woke with a gasp, his mind sluggish and thoughts clouded. Shaking his head, Kian grasped for Lillian, who'd been resting atop his chest.

But only air filled his hands as the sun sifted through the pine trees. Kian scrambled to his feet, scanning the dimly lit forest, but there wasn't a whisper of her, no shiny long hair, no tattered leathers, no black wings.

He started running, calling her name as cold dread gripped his insides. But the bond was still there, flickering, burning under his skin.

She was alive.

Kian repeated the words to himself as he sprinted around the island, scanning every inch for his mate. When he didn't find her anywhere, he paused, leaning his hand against a tree, and closed his eyes, trying to quiet his racing heart.

No danger rolled inside him, but something was off. A feeling he'd never sensed from Lillian vibrated along their bond.

His stomach dropped when he realized it was resignation.

His strong, beautiful, unyielding mate wasn't sending out the usual waves of determination or even fear but soft peace.

As if she'd given up.

Kian choked on a breath but willed himself to calm.

She was alive.

He could rift to her—their bond would know where to go. His magic vibrated across his skin as he focused on the love he had for her, the bond that tethered them.

When saltwater stung his nose, pure, undiluted terror flushed his veins. He broke the surface, finding the island far away. Desperately scanning the calm water around him, he screamed her name again. But there was no sign of her, no rings on the water. Kian forced his pounding heart to calm, drew a deep breath, and dove down into the dark, cold water.

The salt burned his eyes as he dove deeper and deeper, but he ignored the pain and the pressure on his lungs as he scanned the dark ocean, dismissing the dark silhouettes, too large to be his queen. When he thought his lungs would burst, he went up for a breath of air and immediately dove down again.

His hammering heart felt as if it was breaking when the bond began straining, and he forced himself to dive deeper, pushing aside thick seaweed that hindered his descent. Kian sucked in what must have been a gallon of seawater when bubbles rose below him, and he kicked with everything in him as black hair came into view.

Lillian's lifeless body floated right above the bottom of the ocean, tied down with large strands of algae. Her face was pale, in stark contrast to the dark hair gently floating around her and her black wings resting on the sandy bottom.

She looked serene, as if she were only sleeping through a pleasant dream. But it was too similar to how Elya's body had looked so peaceful on the mountain as the snow gently clung to her. Although his lungs screamed, he kicked harder and unsheathed one of his daggers to slash at the seaweed.

Black spots danced in front of Kian's eyes when he cut the final algae off, and with the last of his strength, he pushed off the bottom of the sea, pulling Lillian with him. Kian coughed up seawater when he finally broke the surface, willing himself to rift to the shore, but there was no energy left inside him, and he only rifted a few feet forward.

"Lillian, wake up!"

He dragged her behind him as he swam toward the shore, his heart breaking at her blanched face and blue lips.

"Lillian!" Panic flowed freely within him when he dragged her onto the rocky beach, falling to his knees to listen for her heartbeat.

A primal roar left his throat when her chest remained quiet, and the bond between them snapped, ice-cold darkness and despair replacing it. Kian placed his hands over her chest, pushing down, pausing only to breathe air into her lifeless body.

"Lillian, this is not how you die. You hear me?" He continued pushing, desperately screaming at his mate when her chest didn't move. "Lillian, no!"

Tears streamed down his face as he blew more air into her lungs while slamming his hand down on her chest, praying he wasn't breaking her ribs.

When a gurgle rose from her throat, he held his breath, only letting it out when his mate violently vomited seawater onto the pine-filled ground, and the bond snapped back in place.

He shifted her to the side, stroking her back as gallons of water, mixed with seaweed and whatever else she'd ingested in the depths of the sea, spilled out of her. When she finally stopped, he laid her on her back, his chest cracking wide open as her gray eyes met his.

"Lillian?" He could barely see her through the tears that clouded his eyes.

She reached out a hand and touched his cheek. "Is this the afterlife?" Her voice was hoarse, but a small smile broke across her face.

Kian shook his head. "No. Why would you ask me that?"

Heart pounding, he scanned every inch of her body and

searched for other injuries, but there were none—no physical ones, at least.

The smile fell from her face, and she closed her eyes, her brows pinching together. "I saw my mother. She promised she'd make it all go away. She promised she'd take all the pain away." Her voice broke when she whimpered softly.

A wave of cold swept through Kian at the sorrow lining her face, and he pulled her into his arms, brushing the wet hair from her face. When she whimpered again, he steeled himself against the pain in his heart.

"Lillian, the pain will go away. I promise you. I will make it go away. You will smile and laugh again. And we'll have a future, whatever type of future you want. We'll get married and have loads of little ones. Or it'll just be you and me if that's what you prefer. But we *will* have that. You will have whatever you want."

He held her until she stopped shaking, until color returned to her pale cheeks and lips, whispering every wish he had for the future—their future.

Every place he'd take her, every dream he'd ever had. When she finally stilled, her eyes still closed but features softening, he carried her back into the forest, keeping her on his lap until the sun hung high in the sky, drying both of their clothes.

Lillian's breaths became even, and when the sadness slipped from her face to make way for sleep, Kian gently settled her down onto the ground.

59

Lillian

Her throat was raw from saltwater when she finally pried her eyes open. Kian's worried face hovered over her, the pain shining in his eyes breaking her heart.

She glanced around, realizing they were back to where they'd gone to sleep last night, pine trees surrounding the small clearing, the fall sun dancing across the grassy ground.

Lillian went cold when the memories of her mother washed over her, her promise of taking away the pain ringing in her mind.

She'd felt so safe. Happy to let someone else take over, to let someone else decide. To let someone else carry the burden.

"Do you want to sit up?"

She nodded, and Kian gently guided her against the tree trunk.

"You should drink some water. All that salt will have dried you out."

She nodded again, and when Kian lifted the waterskin to her mouth, Lillian greedily drank more of the half-full waterskin than she should have, dreading the questions she knew he would have.

Steeling herself, she spoke before Kian could ask.

"I saw my mother." She winced at her cracked voice, clearing her throat before she tried again. "She told me she and my father were at peace. And they missed me, wanted me to come to them. She was proud of me, Kian. Even with everything I've done."

Tears stung her eyes as she continued. "I don't know what happened, but she promised it would all be better. They were going to make it better."

Kian's voice was soft when he responded. "Lillian, I'm not sure that was truly your mother."

A chill snaked down her spine, and she blinked furiously at the tears threatening to spill over.

But as she began shaking her head, she realized he might be right.

"Who was it then? Or what was it?"

Kian held her tighter, leaning down to brush his lips against her temple as if he couldn't stand another second keeping them off her.

"Was she out at sea?" he asked against her hair.

She nodded slowly.

"I'm thinking maybe it was a siren. They can take on different shapes, and they're quite convincing. They find your innermost wishes and use them against you."

Lillian sniffed, wiping at her cheeks with her sticky sleeve. "It was so real, Kian. I thought it was finally over."

He nestled his head into her neck and nodded. "Lillian, my beautiful queen," he whispered. "I thought I lost you, that I failed you. I'm so sorry I wasn't there."

Her heart shattered at his words, and she wrapped her arms around him.

"I think I was the one who failed you," she whispered.

Kian crushed her against his chest, using his hand to lift her chin.

"You have never failed me, nor will you ever, Lillian. You are the strongest person I've ever met. That you still stand, still smile, still care about your friends... It's more than anyone could ever ask of you. You are everything. And I promise you, even if it's with my very last breath in this realm, I will make that pain go away. You will be happy again."

When he kissed her, she pulled him closer, desperately crushing her lips to his.

As he tried to pull back, she whispered, "I just want to forget, Kian. Please make me forget."

His eyes hesitantly trailed her face, reading her, and when a soft growl left his throat, she knew she'd won.

Kian pulled her into his lap, heat pooling in her core and warming her ice-cold insides as his body hardened beneath her. He wrapped his hands in her hair, pulled her head back, and gently scraped his teeth against her neck.

A moan escaped her, and he ripped off her damp jacket while she pulled at his. Kian paused for a moment and then slipped out of his own jacket before gently shifting her onto the ground.

"Let me make you forget, my queen."

Lillian shuddered at the thickness of his voice, the desire blazing in his eyes. Kian slowly removed her vest, and started to unbuckle her leathers.

"Is this all right?"

His voice was hoarse, and she nodded—didn't trust her voice, the desire coursing through her the only thing she could focus on. Slipping off her trousers, his breathing became labored, and she quickly removed her silky undergarments.

Kian's eyes widened as he took in her bare body, fully exposed on the grassy ground, and slowly trailed his fingers down her chest, over her stomach, until she squirmed beneath him.

"You're the most exquisite creature that has ever walked this earth," he rasped.

Her face heated at the raw emotions filling his eyes—fire and love and possession—as he continued to stare at her, his hands gently, too gently, roaming over her burning skin.

"You're mine," he breathed.

When she didn't respond, he tipped her head up, forcing her eyes to his. "You're mine."

And even if it wasn't a question, she nodded.

When Kian's eyes roved over her skin, a flush crept up her neck. Tipping her chin down, she let her hair fall forward to cover her burning cheeks, but Kian gently brushed the stray strands behind her ears.

"Please, never hide, Lillian. Not from me. I love every inch of your face and your body, and I want to see it all."

When his hands trailed down her shoulders, down her stomach, and then further, she bit her lip to stop herself from crying out.

Kian kept his promise.

Lillian didn't even remember her own name as his fingers made stars explode inside her mind.

60

Kian

He covered Lillian with one of the thin blankets they'd packed but couldn't make himself shift her off him, so he stayed on the ground with her head resting on his chest, her hair spilling out across his stomach, and her wings tucked in tight, the feathers on top tickling his neck.

Slowly stroking her back, Kian replayed the sounds she'd made as his fingers had played with her until he thought he would burst. Shifting, he tried to think about something else— anything else—otherwise, he'd have to wake her and continue what they'd begun.

When she stirred, he was deep in thought of what the dragons might eat on the barren island, and he jerked as she whispered, "Is it still daytime?"

Kian cleared his throat, emotions brimming under his skin as her stormy eyes met his. "It is. How are you feeling?"

When a sleepy, content smile graced her face, he thought he might combust with pride.

"Much better."

His breath hitched when she winked at him. Actually, *winked* at him, after everything.

Shaking his head, he tried to lift her, but his mate jumped

to her feet, the blanket dangerously close to falling off as she stretched her wings behind her.

"Enough self-pity. I'm sorry I scared you, Kian. But I think we're all allowed a moment of weakness."

He smiled at his queen. "That we are."

She grinned back at him as she began slipping on her destroyed leathers, wincing at the still-damp material.

"Since I almost failed the first test, I suggest we get on with it. I won't be as easily fooled next time." She rose on her toes and kissed him softly, playfully nipping at his bottom lip. "Although I'm not going to complain about what it led to."

Kian snorted but pulled her to him, kissing her with more passion than he originally had meant to. "You only need to give me an order, my queen, and I'll comply every time."

He laughed when Lillian stuck her tongue out at him but didn't miss her face tensing for a moment, something he couldn't read flashing across her face as she stared out over the sea behind him.

"I'm just going to clean up quickly," Lillian kissed his cheek as she stepped away. "Will you pack up?"

He could sense she needed to be alone, that something bothered her, so he nodded but kept all senses on high alert, his movements jerky as he gathered their things. When she returned, Kian managed to convince her to eat a little bit before she dragged him to the shoreline.

"You sure you're ready to move on to whatever else we might face?"

He searched her face for any hesitation, but when Lillian only shrugged, a half-smile gracing her face, he pulled her into his arms and followed the tugging sensation in his gut to the next island.

When they landed on the beach, Kian sucked in a breath.

Lillian stood with her hands on her knees, but thankfully, she got to keep the food he'd convinced her to eat. He stroked her back as she took deep breaths to overcome the nausea.

"Lillian, look up," he whispered.

She gasped as she took in the beautiful island. "What is this place?"

Kian shook his head, "I have no idea."

It was the most beautiful place he'd ever seen. They were standing on a long white beach with pure white cliffs towering over them and a forest with silvery trees spread out behind it. The forest seemed to sparkle in the afternoon sun, and the bird song that rose from it made them both smile as they glanced at each other.

It was exactly the place Kian had imagined when he thought he would leave his queen behind.

"I can't imagine anything cruel living here," Lillian whispered. "It's too gentle."

Kian pulled her to him. "It might look gentle, but there is definitely a challenge here, and we need to be on our guard."

Lillian nodded, "Come on, let's see what this island has in store for us."

She dragged him with her up from the beach.

61

Finn

Aaron gathered the Elders in the dim ballroom, the rounded space completely transformed with no golden tapestries lining the walls and no fire flickering in the chandeliers, only thick tension possible to cut with a knife.

The Elders were spread out in small groups, hissing at each other with their large wings flaring when Finn and Else entered. He studied the Valkyries closely, noting who met his eyes and who still refused.

"Where is Grete," he whispered to Aaron when he didn't find the blonde anywhere.

Aaron cast his eyes down, his eyes fixed on his reflection on the polished marble floor. "She is in a cell beneath the castle. They haven't decided whether she'll be executed or not, but she's being kept there for now."

Finn nodded; even if he didn't necessarily agree with execution, Grete deserved to be in a cell for what she'd done to Lillian. "Should I speak?"

"I think this is as good a moment as any." Aaron clapped his hands and gestured for Finn to take the floor. "Elders, part of our queen's court has returned with news."

Clearing his throat, Finn strode into the middle of the

239

room in his robe, ignoring the strange looks some of the Elders shot him. No nerves sparked in his stomach, only pure resolve and the wish to do right by Lillian.

To do right by Elya.

"I know many of you voted against our queen." He glared around the room, a few Valkyries meeting his eyes, but many staring straight ahead with tight faces.

"We tried to go after the vessel when Alek showed up. Lillian held him off for as long as possible, but he was too strong. She nearly died. She would have died if it hadn't been for one of your own." Finn swallowed. "Elya sacrificed her life for her queen, for what she believed in."

Gasps sounded around the room, and the two younger Valkyries wrapped their arms around each other, their eyes shooting daggers at some of the other Elders.

"Our queen has gone to Narok. She will come back to us with the dragons' support. But we came here to ask you to support her as well, not to let Elya's sacrifice be in vain. We've seen what Alek can do firsthand, and he still has the vessel and so many others."

When Else placed a small hand on his shoulder, he inclined his head. The blond Valkyrie stepped forward, her hands shaking by her side, but her voice surprisingly strong as she spoke.

"I know most of you didn't agree with us going, and perhaps you think Elya has herself to blame. But she did it—we did it—because we remember what it was like under Liv and Ivar's rule. We were so close to peace like Orios had never seen. And I believe Lillian, *our rightful queen*, could succeed in finishing what her parents started. A peaceful Orios, with Hindra and Echo working together and the smaller isles joining under their rule—every creature allowed to live freely. I will stand with her, but we cannot stand alone. You've heard Alek's threat of coming here. Let's rise, like the warrior women we are, against the evil that threatens our world."

A few murmurs and nods spread across the room, the tension easing slightly.

Valeria and Breit stepped forward, speaking as one. "We shall fight for our queen. We are warriors, and we do not run. Our mates will fight as well."

Tild offered them a sad smile. "I shall fight. I've fought in many wars, but this is perhaps the most important. There is a chance for peace. Peace, like I haven't experienced in the past five hundred years. I should like to do so again before I move on to the afterlife."

"What about Adeon?" Anick interrupted, her mate hovering behind her, casting a nervous glance at Finn. When Finn glared at the flower monger, he cast his eyes down. "He will surely come after all of us. If not for standing with Lillian, for bringing the dragons here again."

Tild sighed. "We've already stood by when he killed one of our queens. He may be our father, but perhaps it's time to break away from his hold over us. I don't think he'll let us live in peace regardless—not this time."

The flower monger whispered something in Anick's ear, too low for even Finn to hear. She nodded slowly and gripped her mate's hand tight. "We shall fight then. We've already let our queen down once. We will not do it again."

Three other Valkyries spoke. "We shall fight as well. Alek has been threatening our people for too long. We are tired of hiding."

They all stared at the last three, who finally nodded, albeit a bit hesitantly. "We will fight with you."

Finn bowed his head, warmth spreading in his chest as they all looked at him.

"Then we will prepare. Can you send a spy to confirm when Alek will arrive? Then we can plan. I might have fighting skills, but I've never fought in a war. I would like to hear from the more experienced of you."

Tild nodded, and the Valkyries flew into action. A few left

the room while others began quietly discussing what to do next.

As Tild started to walk out of the room, she glanced at him. "I'll need most of the Valkyries to aid me. Could you help us with the mates? I'm afraid they're not as prepared as they should be, and I believe your skills will be of use."

Finn inclined his head, and she squeezed his shoulder before storming out of the double doors.

When a small hand slipped into his and Else offered him a grim smile, he blew out a deep breath.

There might be a chance yet.

62

Lillian

The forest was intoxicating. The scent of the colorful flowers made her want to lie down and just breathe it all in, and the trees seemed to whisper the kindest words as they slowly strolled through them. Lillian trailed her fingers across the silvery bark of a tall tree with blue leaves, smiling as the tree let one of its branches caress her cheek.

Welcome, Valkyrie.

She stared at it, but the tree spoke no other words, only gently nudged her forward with its silver branch.

"This place is magical," she whispered.

Kian squeezed her hand but narrowed his eyes as he glanced through the forest. Straightening, she followed his gaze.

"It's almost too quiet."

She nodded.

"We wanted you to have time to experience our beautiful island."

They both jerked when the melodic voice echoed between the trees, branches all around them lifting in the air, almost as if to wave hello. Lillian whipped her head around, but there was no one there, only the sparkling trees with their leaves blowing softly in the warm wind.

"Who are you? And where are you?"

"I am Selia. Queen of the elves."

They both snapped their heads up when a woman jumped out of one of the taller trees, gracefully flying down to the ground with her translucent, glittering wings.

When she landed on the soft ground before them, Lillian sucked in a breath.

She'd never seen anyone as beautiful.

Flowing silver hair down to her waist framed an oval face with dainty features and glittering blue eyes, and with her graceful, long limbs, the queen was almost as tall as Kian. Her translucent wings gleamed in the sunlight filtering through the leaves, floating behind the elf queen as she approached them.

Lillian had heard of the beautiful elves, guardians of the forest and nature, and some of the gentlest creatures of Orios, but she'd never thought she'd see one. Even before Alek, when they were free to roam Orios, they mostly kept to themselves, avoiding interaction with other species.

"You're beautiful, young queen. And so is your mate."

Selia walked up to them, cupping Lillian's cheeks and kissing her on both sides. Then she turned to Kian and did the same.

"We're so grateful you decided to come by our island. We rarely get guests, even though those who do come tend not to leave."

Lillian frowned. "We will need to leave, Your Majesty. We're only passing through."

Selia smiled, a blinding smile that made her entire being sparkle. "And so you shall. We are not savages; we do not make anyone stay who doesn't want to. But please, come with me. We will organize a feast in your honor."

Lillian glanced at Kian, who shrugged, "She seems nice enough, and I don't feel the pull anymore. I'm guessing we're to join her."

Selia winked at her, her dark eyelashes dancing across her tinted cheeks. "I promise you will not regret it, young queen and beautiful consort. Our feasts are legendary."

Lillian nodded and Selia grabbed her other hand, pulling her and Kian behind her as she sang to the trees around them, only letting go of Lillian's hand as she twirled to caress the flowers and bushes around them gently.

Selia led them through the forest into a clearing, where a massive sparkling cave spread out, its entrance over a hundred yards wide.

Its walls were covered in shimmering gemstones, and Lillian stared with wide eyes at the impossibly beautiful elves dancing out of the cave, smiling as they welcomed them.

"My elves, we have new company at last." Selia's voice was like a birdsong as she addressed her people. "Please welcome the Queen of Valkyries and her consort, the King of Humans."

When Kian cleared his throat, Lillian shook her head subtly.

Many of the elves kissed their cheeks, whispering how beautiful they were and how glad they were to have them come. Lillian raised her brows when humans, dressed in the same ethereal clothing as the elves, almost translucent in the descending sun, walked up to them.

When a human man gently cupped her chin and kissed Lillian's lips, Kian snarled, eliciting giggles from the elves around.

"Consort, don't fret. We are friendly people. Your queen is too beautiful not to kiss."

Lillian snorted when Kian possessively pulled her to him, his eyes challenging anyone else to try to approach her.

The thrilling giggles turned into laughter, and Selia gently wrapped her arms around them both. "Elves and humans, they are new. Please allow them some time to settle in."

When Kian grumbled behind her, his chest shaking, and

tightened his arms around her, Lillian couldn't stop a giggle from escaping.

"Come, queen, we will get you a bath and new clothing. Consort, please follow King Periso. He will get you settled as well."

A silver-haired elf approached Kian, smiling while he bowed to the both of them.

Lillian stared at Kian, unwilling to leave him out of her sight. And she wouldn't mind bathing with him again. Her cheeks burned when memories from earlier flooded her mind.

Kian lifted a brow, but she didn't miss the heat seeping into his own eyes as he huskily asked, "Could we go together?"

Selia laughed again, the sound relaxing the final apprehension within Lillian.

"We will meet soon, but it's tradition we get ready separately. It makes for such a joyous reunion, and I'm sure your mate will be taken with you when we are finished dressing you."

Lillian finally inclined her head, even as Kian didn't seem convinced. "I'll see you soon."

63

Kian

King Periso waved for him to follow him, and Kian glanced around in wonder as they entered the massive cave. The walls and ceiling sparkled in every color he could imagine, even some Kian had never seen before, and the back of the cave was divided into small halls by frosted glass walls.

He glimpsed large, white beddings on the floor and crackling fireplaces as some of the elves slipped into the rooms. Thrilling singing echoed between the tall ceiling and the polished white floor, so soft he couldn't make out the words, but all the same, the song filled him, delighting his every sense.

"Come, young king."

Periso led him through a long hallway covered by frosted glass that arched over them and seemed to hum as Kian took a first hesitant step into it. Several male elves and humans passed them on the way through, smiling brightly as they met Kian's eyes.

Kian drew a deep breath of the strong flowery scent filling the hall. "Where are you taking me?"

Periso hummed a soft tune and almost sang, "To our bathing chambers, of course. And after that, I shall lend you some new clothing. I think it is much needed."

Kian glanced down at the Valkyrie leathers he wore, ripped and sticky from saltwater.

Periso laughed softly. "You still look handsome, but we shall make your mate drool when she sees you next."

Kian snorted. Lillian definitely wasn't the drooling type, but he didn't want to offend the king, who stared at him so expectantly, so he only nodded.

"Here we are!" The elf king threw out his arms, and Kian sucked in a breath.

Before him the cave opened up to a huge waterfall, several glittering streams rippling down the sparkling walls and the ceiling open to let in the afternoon sun. When Periso began to undress, his eyes still fixed on Kian, he knitted his brows.

"Young Kian, let's not waste time on modesty. Elves do not worry about nudity, and neither should you. We're a free people—we do not let mere things like clothes hold us back from socializing."

Kian couldn't stop himself from laughing when Periso quickly slipped off his clothing and skipped to the streams of water, waving for Kian to join him.

Shaking his head, he followed. He could only imagine what his poor mate was going through with the queen.

After removing his clothes, Kian went to the streams, sighing happily as the warm water enveloped him. He scrubbed his entire body and rinsed out his salty hair while listening to Periso sing a beautiful song, in some of elf language that Kian wasn't familiar with. But he could still enjoy Periso's clear voice, reverberating through the streams of water.

When Kian finally stepped out, two human men approached him and wrapped him in a thick white fur blanket. As they made to wipe him down, Kian glared at them, and they backed away, smiling.

Periso was wiped down next to him, still singing the strange tune that layered across Kian's mind as a blanket.

When Kian glanced at him, the king winked, "Now you can get dressed."

The human men returned, carrying a bundle of clothes that shimmered in the same way as the cave walls, as if the clothing had been made out of the rainbow itself.

Sighing, Kian allowed them to help him into the flowy trousers and tunic, both made from the softest fabric Kian had ever felt. It was like the wind wrapping its soft arms around him.

"What is this material?" Kian studied it closely as it shifted around his body, whispering between his fingers as he pulled at it.

"It's tree-silk, made from the silvery pines on this island. We take care of the trees, and they give us gifts in return." Periso gripped his shoulders, a broad smile on his face as he offered him a flute filled with sparkling liquor.

When Kian hesitated Periso sipped from his own, then broke out into that song again, the melody filling Kian's entire being, vibrating softly across his skin. He couldn't stop his hand from lifting to his mouth, nearly groaning as the liquor slipped down his throat.

Smiling, Periso waved for him. "Now we shall feast and dance and get to know the new king and queen. It shall be magical."

64

Lillian

After baring her teeth at the elves who tried to help her shower and only getting laughter in return, Lillian finally allowed them to help her get dressed.

Two silver-haired elves worked on her hair, weaving her black strands into an elaborate hairdo and adding dainty golden chains to it, while two others slipped her into a flowy dress, carefully avoiding her wings. The fabric shifted in every color she could imagine and caressed her clean skin as it clung to her shoulders, leaving her entire back exposed.

"You are a dream." Selia squealed, pulling Lillian's hand to make her spin. "Your mate will never leave your side."

Lillian shook her head and smiled at the elf queen. "I don't think he would, regardless of how I look."

Selia's laughter echoed in the rippling waterfall. "Of course he wouldn't. You're exquisite, my dear Valkyrie. And those wings! So strong and proud. Come, come. Let's go to the feast! I can't wait a moment longer."

When Selia dragged Lillian by the hand, Lillian shook her head again at the silver-haired beauty who hadn't stopped smiling since they arrived. She'd never met anyone so carefree and happy.

She even rivaled Finn.

Lillian clasped at her chest when emptiness filled her at her best friend's absence. She missed him already, missed his crooked smiles and teasing. Reaching out through the bond, she tried to tell him, but only a soft echo of her own voice vibrated along the golden and silver twirls.

Frowning, Lillian tried again, but with the same result. She could feel him, though, a ghost of his feelings whispering along her mind.

Perhaps they were too far apart?

Lillian tried to shake the feeling of apprehension that gnawed at her, focusing her eyes on the other elves, all with the same pearly hair and translucent wings, who joined them in leaving the waterfall, their singing and whistling bouncing off the glass walls surrounding them.

When they walked out of the cave, the meadow before it had been transformed. Several long tables were placed across the soft grass, and the dark sky was filled with fireflies that buzzed softly, millions of tiny embers floating over the tables.

The evening sky was clear, and even the stars seemed to shine brighter on this magical island, winking at Lillian when she tilted her head up. As she drew a deep breath, she realized the air smelled like Kian, only stronger and more potent, and a sense of calm settled over her.

Selia giggled next to her. "Look at your mate, young queen. He is so handsome."

Lillian followed her gaze until it settled on Kian. The elf queen was right; Kian was dazzling. His black hair and tan skin seemed to gleam as he approached her with a golden flute in his hands, and the smile grazing his face took her breath away.

She'd never seen him smile like this before, not even when she asked him to kiss her.

Kian stopped a few steps away, trailing his eyes in awe over her body, before pulling her into his arms. "You are the most incredible creature that's ever walked this realm, or any other," he whispered into her hair, making her skin prickle with goosebumps.

Lillian laughed softly when he peppered her neck with kisses and lifted her up to spin her around. "So happy. Did that bath completely change you?"

Kian set her down and offered her that blinding smile again. "I'm just glad we came here. It's perfect. I think we should stay for a while."

When she met his eyes, they sparkled in a lighter green than she'd ever seen, like two glittering emeralds below his dark brows.

Lillian frowned, but before she could ask Kian what he meant, Selia dragged them both to a long table. After settling them into two golden chairs, Lillian's already accommodated for her wings, the elf king and queen sat down opposite them.

Periso snapped his fingers, and the glass table filled with dishes. Lillian stared with wide eyes as all her favorite dishes appeared before her. A soft gasp escaped her when she picked up a piece of bread and recognized it as the same bread Astrid had shared with her that day in the forest.

"How?" She stared at Periso and Selia.

They grinned at her, their perfect white teeth shining in the light from the millions of fireflies above their heads.

"We call our island the island of dreams. We can make every dream you have come true. Isn't it wonderful?" Selia winked at her and started filling her golden flute with sparkling liquor.

"A toast! To the new Valkyrie Queen and the Human King." Selia's melodic voice amplified and carried over the meadow, quieting all the elves and humans as they lifted their flutes.

"To the new Valkyrie Queen and Human King," they all repeated.

Lillian's face heated when hundreds of eyes settled on her, but only friendly smiles graced the faces at the tables. She curiously studied the many elves and humans, all dressed in the same beautiful clothing as her and Kian, as they sipped the liquor. Beside her, Kian took a big drink of wine.

"Drink." Periso clinked his flute against hers. "I promise it will be the best wine you've ever tasted. We make it ourselves."

Lillian nodded slowly and lifted the flute to her mouth, but when Periso and Selia both eyed her closely, she stiffened and snapped her eyes to Kian. He smiled wide and hummed along to a song that the elf next to him was singing.

Her stomach churned; although he was beautiful like this, with no hardness lining his face, there was something off about him.

"Kian," Lillian nudged him with her arm, and when he turned to her, she inhaled sharply as the eyes that met hers were impossibly light, the green almost translucent. "Kian, what's wrong?"

He laughed and pulled her to him, cupping her face with both of his hands and kissing her. "Nothing is wrong, my dear queen. It's perfect here—don't you see?" Kian threw out his arms and gestured to the beautiful meadow. "Look, even the fireflies love us."

Lillian stared above them, where the fireflies had gathered to form a crown over each of their heads.

Selia reached over the table to squeeze her wrist. "Lillian, put your mind at ease. We're gentle people. Drink, eat, and relax. You deserve it."

Biting her cheek, Lillian lifted the flute to her mouth again, discreetly sniffing its contents. When the pungent smell of magic filled her nostrils, she recoiled and set the flute down.

She glared at the king and queen. "Are you drugging us?"

Selia laughed her trilling laugh again, but this time, the beautiful sound sent a shiver down Lillian's spine. "It's not drugs, dear Lillian. It's a dream in a cup. You'll love it, I promise."

Shaking her head violently, Lillian pulled the flute out of Kian's hands. "Don't drink or eat anything else."

He only stared back at her, his expression vacant.

Periso leaned forward, his long fingers spread out over the table. "You don't have to worry. It won't harm you. It will just make your time here better. You'll never want to leave."

Heat flared on Lillian's neck. "I've told you—we are not staying here. And I will not drink or eat anything. I think it's time for us to go, actually."

She gripped Kian's hand and made to rise when Periso hissed.

Snapping her head to the king, Lillian froze.

Before her eyes, Periso and Selia's beautiful faces contorted into vile, skeletal masks, darkness seeping into their silvery features, their wings frayed and broken. And all around them, other elves shifted as well, turning into dark, bony figures as they snarled at her.

The soft singing and gentle atmosphere evaporated, replaced by hoarse snarls and damp coldness that seemed to seep into Lillian's bones.

She shot up from her seat, baring her teeth and willing her darkness out, wrapping both herself and Kian into the protection of her night.

Selia let out a cold laugh as she sent a swarm of fireflies against the darkness, the fire within them burrowing small holes in her shield.

"Let us leave, or I will kill you all," Lillian snarled.

"I don't think so, Valkyrie." Periso snapped his fingers, and the beautiful meadow turned into barren ground.

The cave behind them was no longer lined with gemstones, but crumbling walls of whitened stone, and the trees around them weren't sparkling silver anymore but charred, burned stumps.

Lillian's eyes widened when she could see all the way to the wild sea, as the forest no longer obstructed her view.

"See, we need an influx of magic to keep our island the island of dreams. If we don't, it turns into this—and we transform into the worst version of ourselves. You and your half-human mate arriving was the first time in a decade this island was restored to its former glory. You will not leave."

Cold sweat broke out over her skin, from the damp air or from struggling to fill the holes the fireflies burned into her magic, Lillian didn't know, but she forced her voice to remain steady as she snarled at the elf king. "Oh, I promise you we will."

She pulled at Kian, who still smiled softly, his eyes distant as he turned to her.

"Kian, snap out of it," she hissed while wrapping the darkness closer around them.

When Periso and Selia approached them, Lillian lashed out with two dark whips, leaving red gashes on the elves' fraying skin. The elf monarchs snarled at her, their white teeth shifting into sharpened points, and conjured long blades with black hilts into their hands as they backed up to avoid the darkness still reaching for them.

"Kian, rift us away now!" She pulled at him again, but Kian only swayed on his feet, staring blankly ahead, unfazed by what was happening around them.

Periso laughed, a hollow, empty laugh that chilled her veins.

"His magic is drained, young queen. The wine subdues him, and he will be of no help to you. I wish you hadn't made it this difficult, we truly did mean you no harm. But alas..." Periso gestured to the elves behind him. "Get them."

Lillian growled when dozens of elves stormed them, all with various variations of sharp blades and daggers that glinted in the moonlight. Gritting her teeth, she unleashed her darkness upon them, forcing the switch in her mind to turn them deadly.

The first elves that reached her yelped as her magic surrounded them before they fell lifeless to the ground.

Shaking, Lillian sent out another plume for the next onslaught, biting her cheek as more of them died, as more of their lights went out in the darkness.

But her magic was already draining, and when a fresh wave approached her, the dark wall surrounding her and Kian only slowed them down, and she screamed when several of them pushed through and gripped Kian, forcing him down on the ground.

65

Finn

The human mates were not good fighters.

Finn sighed as yet another man flinched and dropped his wooden sword when Else charged him. That they hadn't spent the past years training with the Valkyries, but rather by themselves was truly evident. They'd become too reliant on their Valkyrie mates protecting them—too docile the past eighteen years.

And they were afraid; fear shone bright in their eyes as they glanced at each other.

He prayed that the Valkyries and Elders were better equipped, that they would actually have a plan for surviving Alek's attack, that they would live up to their warrior reputation.

When Else shook her head and jumped off the training platform to join him where he leaned against the railing of the large balcony, Finn called out to the men. "All right, everyone gather over here."

Finn dragged a hand through his hair as the men slowly made their way over, catching Else's eyes. The Valkyrie grimaced before turning back to the men approaching them.

"Alek is coming here in three days. I hope our queen will

have returned with the dragons by then, but if she hasn't, we will need to protect this castle until she does. I know most of you aren't trained fighters, but I'm guessing many of you have magic. Can you please share what abilities you have with us?"

Finn studied the men facing him, his stomach sinking at the tension lining their features.

Most didn't have offensive abilities, but one man was able to wield water, turn it into ice, and master the sea surrounding the island, and another could make people see visions—make them believe they were somewhere they weren't.

The flower monger, hovering in the back with guilt still lining his tanned face, mumbled that he could wield plants and trees.

Finn nodded and asked them to step aside. There were also a few shifters, one massive golden-haired lion shifter and another who could shift into a large bear. Finn pointed to the magic wielders and asked the shifters to join them.

"You'll train with me. We'll have to be strategic with where we place you, and you'll need to defend yourselves against Alek's soldiers, as they'll try to take you out first. Start by practicing with each other, and please try not to kill anyone. We need every man we can get."

The men stalked off to a corner of the balcony, and Finn gestured to Aaron, who'd just flown in, landing gracefully on the ground beside him. "The rest of you will train with Aaron."

When Aaron furrowed his brows, Finn raised his in challenge.

The winged man sighed as his eyes flitted between his, but he didn't argue, only waved for the other men to join him in the training ring.

"Have you been able to reach Lillian?" Else slipped up to his side, her quiet voice laced with worry.

Finn shook his head, "It's strange. I can feel her, but for some reason, it's like calling down an empty void. I only hear my own voice echoing when I try to reach her."

Fear gripped his heart—it had been like this ever since he'd left her on Echo.

He tried to reach out again, but there was nothing, only gulping darkness where the usual golden and silver twirls should be. He could sense that she was alive, but no emotion flowed through the bond.

"She's okay, Finn." Else placed her hand on his shoulder. "She has Kian and Sam with her. I'm sure they're all okay. I don't think that dragon would allow any harm to come to her either."

Finn nodded slowly. "I'm wondering if we should go to Narok if we haven't heard anything by tomorrow. I don't like this; perhaps they need aid."

He would never forgive himself if he remained here while something happened to Lillian, Kian, or Sam.

Else stared pointedly at the training ring, and when Finn followed her gaze, he winced at the poor swordplay from the men, the slow strikes, and clumsy footwork. "I think we might be needed here."

Finn sighed, "I think you might be right."

Approaching the men, Finn watched them as they showed off their abilities and buried his worry for Lillian deep down. He would ensure they did everything they could to hold off Alek's forces until she returned.

That his queen would have *anything* to come back to.

66

Lillian

"Kian!" Lillian growled as she pushed and kicked the elves that tried to grab her, shakily enforcing the wall around them to get the elves off Kian. "Please, snap the hell out of it. I need you."

Kian only smiled at her. "Just let go, my beautiful mate. They are wonderful, are they not? They're so friendly."

"Kian—"

A blade slashed through her shield of night, and she pulled up more magic, whimpering as her hands shook from the effort, and a metallic taste filled her mouth.

If she could only get the elves to back up, she might have a chance to grab Kian and fly off, but even though she'd flown with Sam before she wasn't sure she'd be quick enough.

The elves had wings too.

She tried to reach Finn and call for help, but her stomach sank as her desperate cry echoed back, only an empty abyss where their bond should be.

Lillian hissed when yet another elf reached for Kian and sent a plume of darkness down his throat, his eyes going vacant as she took his breath.

"They are not. Look around you! Truly look, Kian!"

When he still only smiled and tried to approach the elves attacking them, she sucked in a breath and smacked him hard across the cheek. Kian whipped his head up, and she released a breath as the dark green in his eyes slowly returned.

"What is happening?" He stared at her with wide eyes.

"We're getting attacked by these insane creatures. And I can't hold them off. Can you rift us out of here?"

Kian gripped her arm, his eyes wild, but they didn't move an inch.

Shit. Shit. *Shit*. Lillian would have welcomed the nausea a thousandfold if it could get them away from the elves.

Selia and Periso stalked up to them, cold smiles gracing their dark features and with those long daggers in their hands, and Kian pushed her behind him.

"Kian," she hissed. "Neither of us have any weapons. Step aside."

When he refused, she pulled at him, but her mate didn't budge. Peering over his shoulder, she watched Selia and Periso slow to a stop.

"Why did you have to make this so difficult, young monarchs? We would have treated you so well if you only had partaken in the festivities we organized on your behalf. You would have never wanted to leave."

Kian snarled in warning when Periso made to step around him, but the elf king snarled right back, his silver eyes pits of black, so dead they made Lillian shiver.

"I guess we're doing this the hard way then." Periso raised his shiny dagger, but as he was about to let it fall, a screech echoed through the meadow, and the night around them became impossibly darker as Nida's shadow cast the barren ground in darkness.

Get your filthy hands off my bonded, you stupid elves.

Nida opened her mouth, and a blast of silver flame erupted.

Panic ensued, and the elves scattered, running toward the sea as the dragon beat her strong wings to hunt them down.

Periso and Selia growled at the dragon. "You're not supposed to interfere. They haven't finished our challenge, and we have a right to them until they do. It's the deal we made."

Nida beat her large wings and turned to them, slowly flying closer while narrowing her eyes. *I don't think so, elf scum.*

And while Lillian wanted nothing more than to see charred ground where the terrifying elf king and queen now stood, something stirred within her, making the hair on her arms rise, and she screamed, "Wait!"

Nida quickly closed her mouth, but both she and Kian stared at her as if she'd gone mad.

Perhaps she had.

Shakily, Lillian turned to Periso and Selia, both stiff and ready to leap at them, while keeping a sharp eye on the dragon hovering above. "Leave. Leave now, and we will spare your lives. But remember the grace I showed you today—the grace the Queen of Valkyries, Queen of Orios, showed you."

The elves snarled, but with a glance at each other, they took off, sprinting across the barren ground until their broken wings lifted them into the air, quickly disappearing over the dark sea.

Nida gracefully landed before them, her eyes narrowed to slits as she stalked closer. *What are you two doing? How do you not know not to drink or eat anything the elves provide? You just had to say no, and you could have been on your merry way.*

Lillian rolled her eyes as she translated for Kian. "These tests didn't actually come with instructions. We're doing the best we can out here."

Nida growled. *It's not good enough! Come on, you need to follow me. You need weapons. And real clothing.* The dragon shook her head and huffed a deep breath that blew through the billowing clothes the elves had gifted them. *This elf stuff is like a beacon for danger.*

"My magic is depleted, and I don't know if I can carry

Kian." She glanced at him, slipping her hand into his when guilt overtook his face. "Can you rift us out of here?"

Kian shook his head. "Not yet. I knew it was too good to be true. I didn't think! I should have understood what they were up to when Periso kept pushing me to drink. I'm sorry, Lillian. I let you down."

She gave him a quick peck. "One for one."

But Kian's features didn't soften, and he barely met her eyes as she searched his face.

Nida huffed. *You'll have to fly with me then.*

Lillian stared at her. "I thought you didn't carry anyone on your back—that it was beneath you."

Well, I can't have my bonded to-be die on me. Now, get on before I change my mind.

Nida lowered her leg, and Lillian gently stroked her spike-lined face before jumping on. The scales were slippery, and she had to squeeze her legs hard not to fall off on the other side.

When Nida turned her head and glared at her, Lillian whispered, "Sorry."

Kian gracefully pulled himself up behind her, wrapping her tight in his arms, and she leaned back into his broad chest as Nida whipped her wings and took to the sky.

67

Finn

Finn rolled his neck. He was exhausted, every single muscle in his body aching, and his mind filling with a cloying fog as he said goodnight to the humans and shifters.

By the time Finn and Else were finished with them, the mates had all looked ready to drop dead. Wincing, Finn realized he probably didn't look much better.

There was no way the mates would be ready for combat in three days, but they at least had a good grasp on their magic, so as long as they could stay away from the midst of fighting, they'd be useful. The shifters were thankfully slightly better fighters in their animal forms, and they should be able to withstand an attack if they were prepared.

At least for a little while.

The lion was especially terrifying. His battle roar had even the seasoned Valkyries stumble backward as he threw himself into the fights, maw open and vicious claws out. As long as he could control his impulses, he'd be deadly. But he'd nipped Finn a bit too hard when his instincts took over, and they'd had to take a break as Finn wrapped his arm.

He'd missed Sam then, realizing how convenient it was to have a healer at hand at all times. But mostly because Sam would have loved to watch the lion take down the warrior women.

Lillian had been surprised when she'd seen Sam in battle, how skilled he was, and how strong his fighting instincts were, but it didn't surprise Finn in the slightest.

It was always the quiet ones you needed to watch out for.

Even with exhaustion sweeping through him, Finn debated whether to shift and take to the skies—to fly around the tall castle, out over the dense forest surrounding it, perhaps even out to the sea—to clear his clouded mind.

But upon glancing down at his bandaged arm, he thought better of it. He should probably rest so he'd have no issue shifting if it was urgently needed. Instead, he walked the long halls in the tower, sporadically trying to reach out to Lillian, wishing for nothing more than her voice softly speaking into his mind. But all he was met with was a soft echo.

"May I join you?" Aaron fell in step with him.

Finn stopped himself before he rolled his eyes. "It seems you've already done so."

Aaron shrugged, a crooked smile on his lips. "I know you don't trust me, but I'm trying, Finn. I should have stood by Lillian. But I…" He cleared his throat. "I was angry she turned me down and perhaps a bit jealous. Not that it excuses my behavior. But I will do better. I spoke to the Elders, and we're meeting tomorrow morning to plan for the attack. They asked that you join."

Finn nodded, "I'll be there."

And even though he knew this was real battle, with real lives at stake, a tiny flame of excitement burned in his chest at the chance to learn from the fiercest warriors in Orios.

They continued walking quietly down the dark halls, but when Aaron kept stealing glances at him, Finn broke the silence.

"Out with it." Finn glared at the male Valkyrie.

"I just… Do you think we have a chance? The humans I trained with should not be in battle. They will all die within minutes with a real enemy." Aaron's voice was barely a whisper as he fixed his eyes on the white carpet lining the hall.

Finn eyed him, noting the fear that lined his wide blue eyes, the stiff shoulders, and the slight tremble of his hand as he brushed it over the embellished sword at his side. For a moment, he thought about lying to him to try to instill hope, but when Elya's face flashed in his mind, he decided to be truthful. There was too much at stake.

"I don't know," Finn shook his head. "If Lillian comes back in time and brings the dragons, we should win. If she doesn't… I guess it's up to us."

Every fiber of his being prayed it wouldn't come to that, that he'd be fighting alongside Lillian like they were destined to—like they were bonded to. Even if they'd had little time training together, he knew they'd be formidable, the strongest familiar and magic wielder Orios had ever seen.

Aaron inclined his head, his usually perfectly combed hair falling into his eyes. "Then we shall go down fighting. I'm the only one of the Valkyries who hasn't seen war. And everyone here is my family. I just—I don't want to see them die."

Finn glanced at his feet when a new emotion, an unwelcome emotion, settled in his stomach.

Self-doubt.

Blowing out a breath, he tried to shake it off, tried to find the fearlessness, the recklessness he and Lillian shared. When Aaron eyed him questioningly, he realized he'd been staring out of the window in the hallway, his eyes fixed on the dark horizon.

"I haven't been in battle either. I only know what my parents taught me and the little training we got with King Alek's guard. But I studied them there. The men in Alek's guard are scared, Aaron. They're only loyal to him because they have no one else to follow. They won't last long in war."

"But they're not the problem, are they? It's the magic wielders—the children. Will we kill children?" Aaron clenched his jaw so hard Finn heard his teeth grinding together. "We're

Valkyries; we're ruthless and sometimes cruel, but we have never harmed a child. It's vile."

Finn balled his fists. Only the biggest coward hid behind children, but that was exactly what Alek would do. He was sure of it.

"We'll have to devise a plan to avoid it. I don't condone harming children, either. And I know Lillian would never approve. She'd probably kill us for it, if anything."

Finn scratched his cheek, the stumble he hadn't had time to shave brushing against his rough palms.

They'd failed last time, but was there any other option?

Slicing his eyes to Aaron's again, he said, "We'll need to free the vessel before they arrive. That way, they're at least not all able to channel whatever magic Alek intends for them, and we might be able to leave them be."

Aaron nervously brushed his hand over his sword again. "Why don't we just kill her? One life is better than hundreds."

Finn lowered his voice, and there was a sharp edge to it as he responded. "Because we owe a life debt to her sister. Lillian will not allow it. And neither will we."

When he closed his eyes, Josephine's blue ones stared back at him. There had been so much fear in them, fear lining her every feature, but he'd also seen the defiance in her face, the anger lurking under her skin—so similar to her sister's.

Setting his jaw, he realized they had to get her out.

There was no other way.

68

Lillian

She would never tell Nida, but Lillian definitely preferred flying by herself. The dragon's scales were slippery, and every time Nida banked, Lillian held her breath, praying they wouldn't fall off and tumble down into the dark water beneath.

Kian remained quiet behind her, his arms strong where they lay across her stomach, but when she squeezed his hand, he didn't shift, nor did he respond when she tried to speak to him over the strong wind.

A knot formed in her stomach. Kian was so protective, and he'd already felt like he had failed her on the first island.

Hold on. I need to land.

Even with Nida's warning, Lillian and Kian slipped when the dragon dipped forward, and Lillian warily gripped the long spikes lining the dragon's neck to keep them from sliding off. She winced when the spikes cut into her hands as Nida angled further down, aiming for a small, barren island.

When they finally landed, Kian quickly jumped off, offering Lillian his hand to help her down. She smiled at him as she slid off, her legs shaking from the exertion of squeezing Nida's body.

But Kian didn't smile back, only met her eyes briefly before he stalked off to scan the island for any danger. Still, she didn't miss the anger simmering behind the blazing green, and Lillian sighed as she stared at his broad back before turning back to Nida.

"Where are we? I think I'm being pulled somewhere else. This doesn't seem like the next test." Lillian stared out over the dark water, at the moon reflecting on the calm surface, toward another island, larger than the one they stood upon, and gestured toward it. "I think that's where we need to go."

Nida huffed. *Yes, but you don't have any weapons or proper clothing, impatient queen, so I brought you here to take care of that before you continue the journey. You'll be safe on this island, so I'd suggest you rest here tonight.*

Kian returned, his posture a little more relaxed but eyes still wary as he swept them across the rocky island.

"There's no one here. When my magic is refilled, maybe we should try to rift to Seigard to get weapons. Perhaps you can ask Finn to gather some for us?"

Lillian shook her head, dread settling in her stomach. "I can't reach him. I don't know why, but something is blocking our connection. It has since we started this."

Kian's eyes snapped to hers, his face hardening again, but as he opened his mouth to speak, Nida interrupted, and Lillian held up a hand to listen.

Humans… only see what's right in front of their noses. Like all the other islands out here, this one has magic. When Alek drove all magical creatures from Hindra and Echo, they spread out, taking over small islands for themselves. This island belongs to Nailus. He is a water sprite, closely related to the siren you already encountered. But he doesn't show you a different face, and he lures you out with his music. But you can bind him and ask him for gifts if you find the way.

Lillian tilted her head. "Let me guess, you're not going to tell us how to bind him?"

Nida rolled her eyes. *I don't know how to bind him, young queen. But I suggest you listen—like you should have been doing so far but have failed to do. Listen to what these creatures are saying and to what they're not saying. And you shall find the answer.*

She was getting really tired of these cryptic answers, but Lillian bit her cheek from snarkily responding with something that would surely anger the dragon and nodded. As she explained what Nida told her, Kian offered her his hand, and she took it, warmth filling her when he pulled her close.

"I'm guessing he'll be somewhere in the water then."

Gently tugging her with him, he held her nearly pressed against his side as he approached the rocky beach, glancing out over the water. "Let's walk around and see what we find?"

Lillian squeezed his hand, and they slowly made their way around the rocky beach, taking cautious steps over the damp boulders lining the edge of the water. When soft singing rang over the calm sea, Kian halted.

"There."

He pointed out over the water, where a small boy sat on a rock in the still, dark water, his back toward them, playing a gilded harp and singing a soft tune.

It was the most beautiful sound Lillian had ever heard, the melody like seeping water. Even more beautiful than the elf songs, although that sound might forever be tainted for her now.

Kian wrapped his arm around her shoulder, and they both stilled and listened, their breaths the only sounds mingling with the alluring song.

Come join me in the singing waves. Where the water is calm, your soul will get what it desires. Where the water is fierce, your soul shall heed to its depths. Come join me. Come join me in the singing waves.

"Do you think that's the clue?" Lillian whispered.

Kian shrugged, holding her closer. "I'm not sure. Let's wait a moment longer."

Come join me in the singing waves. Interrupt my song, and your soul will heed. Let it ring over the waves, and your soul will get what it desires.

Kian furrowed his brow, his grip on her tightening. "I

think we need to get in the water. But we can't make a sound. Or a splash, I suppose."

Lillian violently shook her head, dread from when she'd last been in the water filling her. "No. I don't think it's worth it. We'll find another way."

Kian let go of her hand, his hands lifting to cup her cheeks. "You will not go in that water, Lillian. I will."

When she was about to argue, she met his eyes, seeing the raw pain and guilt in them. His set jaw. His drawn-down brows.

Lillian wanted to tell him he didn't have anything to prove, that he'd never failed her—could never fail her—but the resolve in his face made her think better of it.

Kian needed to do this.

Not for her but for himself.

She finally nodded, "Please, just—be careful."

Offering her a half-smile, he warily stepped over the rocks and onto the small beach. Lillian held her breath when he dipped one foot, then the other, into the water, careful not to let a single ring, a single ripple disturb the blank surface.

Hello, human.

Both Lillian and Kian remained quiet as the young boy turned to them, spinning in one fluid motion on top of the water. He didn't look a day older than fifteen, with unruly black hair and equally dark eyes fixed on Kian.

I see your soul, Kian. There is much love there—oh, so much love. But there is also sorrow, anger, and guilt—so much guilt. Mm, I can taste it. It's delicious.

The boy let out a soft laugh, a smile playing on his lips, as he shifted his gaze to Lillian on the beach. Despite his young appearance, fear pricked her scalp when she met his eyes; there was nothing young about them.

Ah! You don't think you're worthy of the young queen. That you failed to protect her like you failed your mother. The boy laughed again. *I can't tell if you're worthy, human. Only you may know.*

"Stop with the mind games," Kian said quietly. "We need weapons, clothes, and food. Can you help us?"

Can I help you? I see your soul, your needs, your innermost wants, and you dared enter my waters. What you seek is already with the queen.

Lillian glanced down, her eyes widening as bundles of neatly folded clothes and shining weapons—Valkyrie weapons —appeared at her feet.

Now we shall see if you can return to her. Perhaps you don't want to. All that guilt. Mm. I could take it away, you know. You'd never feel again, never have to worry if the darkness that resides in you will win.

The boy floated over the water like he was part of it—as if he was made of water himself. When he neared Kian, Lillian tensed, and her hand twitched toward the weapons on the ground.

But Kian held his ground, the water around him still, and his eyes fixed on the young water sprite.

Brave he is.

The boy circled Kian, floating on top of the sea with his legs crossed. Small ringlets formed on the dark water when he swept his pale fingers through it.

You have so many questions, human. I might answer them if you ask. The boy stilled and sniffed the air. *Curious. You're not entirely human, are you?*

Lillian took a stumbling step forward, a frown lining her forehead, but Kian remained still. His eyes stayed fixed before him, ignoring the water sprite's movements. "What do you mean?"

Hm. So curious. Old blood flows through your veins. The winged beast king already noticed. But you don't know. Oh, this is so curious. Come with me, Kian, and I will give you all the answers you seek.

"I will do no such thing." Kian carefully turned, slowly moving through the water so as not to upset the calm sea, and Lillian held her breath as he made his way to the rocky beach. But when he was about to step onto land, the water sprite spoke again, causing him to still.

Do you not want to find out what your soul is made of, young Kian? Or who your real parents are?

Her heart began pounding in her chest, but Kian only shook his head slowly. "I know what you're doing. I won't fall for your tricks or let you drag me into the depths of the sea. I have no interest in your answers."

Lillian bit her cheek. She wasn't sure if it was purely a trick to make Kian hesitate and trip. The water sprite knew that Kian could hear Tyr. Perhaps there was something they didn't know.

The boy floated closer, his young face tilted and black eyes sparkling with curiosity as he studied Kian. Heart thundering, Lillian slowly reached down for one of the daggers that glinted on top of the bundle of clothes.

Both Lillian and Kian jerked when a growl sounded behind them, and Nida inched closer to the beach. A strangled cry escaped Lillian's lips when it caused Kian to stir the water, the small splash seemingly echoing across the quiet island as he steadied himself.

When the waves washed onto the shore the water sprite didn't hesitate—he launched himself at Kian as he scrambled to get out of the dark water.

"No!"

Lillian sprinted toward them, but she couldn't get a clear shot to let the dagger fly as Kian and the water sprite tangled with each other. Reaching for her magic instead, she readied the darkness and surrounded them both in it.

But she wasn't sure how to separate the deadly plumes without risking Kian's life, so she held back, even as her magic screamed at her to protect, burning in her veins to protect what was hers.

When she met Kian's eyes as he struggled against the sprite's impossibly strong grip, he glanced at the dagger she gripped and reached out his hand. Lillian didn't hesitate; she let the dagger fly, praying she wouldn't embed it in the man she loved.

She blew out a breath when Kian caught the hilt and plunged into the neck of the water sprite. With a sharp hiss, the water around them went wild, waves crashing around them and onto the shore, and when Kian scrambled onto the beach, Lillian gripped his wet tunic to pull him further up.

"Run!"

Kian pushed her ahead of him, and nearly tripping, he grabbed the bundle of clothes and weapons, sprinting behind her to get away.

With a racing heart, Lillian reached Nida, only an inch from slamming into the dragon when she lazily stretched her wings as she glared at them.

That's one way to do it, I guess.

Lillian snarled at the silver dragon before pulling Kian into her arms, burrowing her face in his neck.

69

Kian

He held her until her heart no longer hammered against her ribcage, goosebumps rippling across his skin where her hot breath fanned across it. When Nida huffed loud enough that plumes of smoke blew over their heads, Kian finally pulled back, and Lillian offered him a small smile, her steely eyes flitting between his.

But even as love filled him, warmth lining his chest as he watched those beautiful lips turn up, he couldn't bring himself to return it.

He'd let her down.

They'd nearly died at the hands of the elves, and it was entirely his fault.

Kian clenched his jaw at his own stupidity. How could he have fallen for Perio's gentle demeanor? He was a trained soldier, for Orios' sake, and had been taught over and over how an enemy would try to get to you, regardless of whether it was torture or pretty words. He closed his eyes when Lillian narrowed hers, clearly reading too much in his gaze.

He didn't deserve her—didn't understand why he was her mate when he couldn't even protect her from his own foolishness.

Kian's eyes flew open when Nida snarled behind her, and he eyed the dragon as Lillian translated her words for him.

"I shall leave you now. The final test is with the giants. You can eat their food and drink their ale but do remember they want entertainment, and you will serve as it. And until my father has deemed that you've succeeded, listen to what is said and what is not said. Not all that is said is spoken."

When Kian nodded at the cryptic message, the dragon started to turn but as she stretched her wings, she whipped her head back and glared at him, and he nearly stumbled when Nida's voice rumbled in his mind for the first time.

Young one, there is a reason you were chosen as her mate. Trust in your bond and in your love. With that, the dragon took to the dark sky, scales shining like the moon she headed for.

Kian stared with wide eyes at Lillian. "I heard her."

"So did I, Kian." Lillian grabbed his hand, and his skin tingled under her intense gaze. "You're wrong. You are perfect for me. We are perfect. I knew it even when I stayed away from you, even when I didn't know you were my mate."

Kian exasperatedly dragged a hand through his hair. "Lillian, I let you down. I'm supposed to protect you. Make sure you are safe, always, above everything else. You're not just my mate, but my queen and I almost let them..." He clenched his jaw, rage rolling through his veins, thinking about what could have happened.

"Kian," Lillian lowered her voice and gently cupped his face with both her hands, forcing his eyes to hers. Nervously chewing her bottom lip, she searched his eyes, letting her thumbs gently smooth out the hard lines between his brows.

"I love you," she whispered.

Her full lips curled, breaking into a blinding smile. It was one of those rare genuine smiles that lit up her entire face, one of the smiles he'd promised himself to see more often, and he sucked in a breath at how it affected him, how her smile slammed right into his heart.

"I loved you even before I broke the curse, even if I didn't want to admit it to myself." Lillian shook her head, "And perhaps that makes me a bad person. A horrible, selfish, disloyal person who fell in love with you when I did. But I'd rather be that horrible person than stay away from you."

Lillian leaned in closer, darkness dancing behind her gray eyes. "You've saved my life more times than I can count. And not just from enemies or creatures trying to kill me, but because you didn't give up. Even when I turned you down, when I pushed you away, you pulled me out of the darkness. So, I love you, Kian, with all that you are. In this life and the next."

Kian froze, his pounding heart the only thing moving, a frantic pulse throbbing in his ears as he stared at her.

She'd never told him she loved him.

Even if he'd felt it, could see it in her eyes, he knew how much it meant for her to say it. She'd only ever told Eli she loved him, and with the way that ended…

Kian drew a trembling breath. He couldn't pull away from her.

Not now.

Not ever.

He'd promised to stay by her side and make her happy. And if he truly made her happy…

He forced the guilt away—shoved it deep inside him. He'd promised himself he'd do anything to be worthy of her love, and he wouldn't let pride or guilt come in the way. He would not be the reason the light in her eyes went out.

When silver filled Lillian's eyes, a tight pressure built around his heart, and he quickly responded. "I love you, too." Crushing her to him, he leaned his head on hers. "In this life, in the next, and whatever comes after that, I'll love you. There is nothing that can tear me from your side. Nothing."

Lillian's arms tightened around his waist, and when she looked up at him, a tear slipped down her rosy cheek. Bending down, he kissed it away, lingering with his forehead to hers.

When she stared at him expectantly, he slid his hands into

her hair and kissed her softly, deepening the kiss when a sigh left her lips. Fire burned under his skin as she dragged her hands down his back, roughly pulling him closer.

Flames that spread like wildfire at the breathy sounds she let out, at the way she nipped his lip, at the growl she let out when she tried to rid them both of the layers separating them. Everything about this wild creature consumed him, mesmerized him, captivated him. He could never get enough. No lifetime with her would be enough.

A hiss escaped her when he trailed his hands over her wings, and she scraped her teeth across his neck before jumping up and wrapping her legs around him so forcefully they tumbled to the ground.

Pouting, Lillian pulled back, and Kian couldn't stop himself from laughing. He nipped her bottom lip until she joined him, a small giggle making its way up her throat, her full lips curving into another heartbreaking smile.

She'd never been more beautiful.

Chest heaving, lips swollen, black hair tangled around her face, and eyes filled with smoke, she was every bit the wild queen he loved.

Kian couldn't help leaning in to claim her lips again, dragging his hands over those black feathers until she moaned into his mouth. Panting, she finally pulled back, resting her head against his shoulder as she caught her breath.

"Maybe we should set up a fire and eat something. Nida said we were safe here, so we should probably rest before we join the giants tomorrow," she whispered.

When he nodded, she slipped out of his arms and began going through the clothing and weapons the water sprite had somehow conjured. Kian stared at her for a moment, unable to think straight as she bent down to pick something off the ground before him, then swallowed and followed her.

70

Finn

The sun barely peeked over the dark mountain the castle was nestled into when Finn dragged himself out of bed and quickly got dressed. But even so, Aaron already waited outside his room, leaning against the wall opposite the door.

The otherwise so put-together Valkyrie was disheveled, his long hair limp and unkept, and his tunic rumpled. And the way his leathers hung off his hips… Finn held back a snort when he realized Aaron wore them backward.

"Did you not get any sleep?" Finn greeted him.

Aaron shook his head. "I know I probably should have, but with Alek coming in only days, I spent the night training and reading up on old war tactics. I will not let our people down by being unprepared."

Finn nodded. He'd only been able to sleep because of the exhaustion from the training, which, for a moment, silenced the thoughts swirling through his mind as he tried to imagine how they would take on Alek, especially if Lillian didn't return in time.

But they'd returned with full force as soon as his eyes snapped open, joined by gnawing worry for Lillian. The bond between them was still broken, the darkness where gold and silver should shine becoming worryingly familiar as he tried to reach her.

"Are the Elders gathering this morning?" Finn began walking, grateful for the silver flames as the fall sun did little to light the dim hallway.

"They're already waiting for us." Aaron's hands shook as he fell into step with Finn, and a small ember of sympathy clawed its way into Finn's chest at the shadows of apprehension that sparked in the male's eyes.

Halting, he gripped Aaron's shoulders and the Valkyrie's eyes sliced to his. "You're allowed to be scared, Aaron. Even if you're a warrior, being scared means you have something to lose. And that's what will give us an upper hand. We're not fighting for a king who rules with fear. We're fighting for something better. A better world."

Aaron offered him a grateful smile, even as his eyes remained wary. "I just hope we'll live to see it."

Finn hoped so as well, but he didn't respond, only squeezed Aaron's shoulder quickly before they continued walking in silence to the meeting room.

Finn's pulse hammered a frantic rhythm against his bones when they reached the white doors, the Valkyrie wings adorning them softly gleaming in the firelight from the lanterns lining the walls on each side of it.

Madick and another Valkyrie stood guard outside, but there was no spark of recognition in her vigilant eyes when she opened one of the doors.

Taking a deep breath, Finn prayed that the Elders would agree to the plan he'd formulated last night—even if it was risky—before he stepped into the room.

The Valkyries at the large oval table were quiet as they entered, the air crackling with unspoken tension. Aaron slipped into a chair by the end, and Finn took the seat next to him, an ordinary chair already in place for him.

Tild rose when they were seated, her eyes sharp in her age-lined face.

"We have much to discuss today, Elders. Finn has an idea for how to avoid harming the children Alek is using in this war, but we should also discuss how to maximize the protection of Volantis. And then there is the matter of Grete. We need to decide what to do with her; if we let her out to help us, or if she's to be further punished, and if so, what that punishment should be. I urge you to take a step back and think about what would be most helpful for us in the next few days. We need all the help we can get, but as we've come to learn Grete also betrayed our queen, betrayed all of us. So I suggest we put it to a vote."

Murmurs drifted across the table as the Valkyries whispered to each other, too low for even Finn's ears to pick up.

He wasn't sure what he'd vote for—if they even allowed him a vote.

Grete had known about Lillian and had forgone the opportunity to help her queen. But Tild was right. Grete was a powerful Valkyrie who'd already fought in many wars. They could use her experience.

Tild tilted her head as she studied Finn, noting the emotions he was sure raced across his face. "I would like to call the vote for Grete first. I don't condone what she has done, but she is one of our best fighters and we could use her help in strategizing as well. I vote in favor of letting her go."

Valeria and Breit glanced at each other, and after a moment, Valeria spoke quietly but with steel edging her hushed words. "She should be punished for what she did. She betrayed all of us. We vote no."

Tild nodded slowly as a few other Valkyries offered their opinions. The vote was even: half of the Valkyries sided with Tild, while the others wanted Grete punished. Soon, only Finn and Aaron remained.

Aaron cleared his throat. "I vote to have Grete help us. While it won't redeem her for what she's done, she will fight to the death to protect us, to protect Volantis."

Tild inclined her head and looked to Finn. "Since you are part of our queen's court, we will allow you a vote, Finn."

He brushed a hand through his hair, staring at the wooden table. He wished he could reach out to Lillian, hear what she wanted. It didn't feel right for him to make this decision for her.

But a small part of him knew that Lillian would vote in her favor. She hadn't outed Grete when she'd found out, and she'd want as much support and resources as possible to help her people.

"I vote to release her, as I think that's what Lillian would want."

Tild clasped her hands together, her gray hair falling over one shoulder as she swept her gaze over the table. "Then it's decided. Madick, please get Grete and bring her here immediately."

Madick nodded, and swiftly exited the room.

"While we wait, would you like to share what you were hoping to do, Finn?"

Finn's gaze flickered over the Valkyries around the table, and he received a few encouraging smiles as he met their eyes.

"I know we're all in agreement that we don't want to harm the children. So, we need to get the vessel out of Alek's hands. Without her, the children will not be able to channel fire or any other magic Alek prefers to unleash upon us. Though they'll still have magic themselves, it won't be as devastating. I propose that I, together with Else and Aaron, leave as soon as possible to get her free."

When doubt filled the Valkyries' eyes, he glanced between Aaron and Else, quietly sitting beside him. He'd spoken with them last night, and while he didn't have much to offer in terms of a solid plan, they'd both agreed they needed to try again. And since they'd do it without the people King Alek wanted the most, perhaps there was a chance they'd succeed.

Finn steeled his gaze, meeting every pair of eyes he could. "We were taken by surprise last time, but we won't let that happen again. And regardless, we have to try. We'll lose this war before it's even started if we have to face those children."

A murmur of assent rippled across the room, fueling Finn's resolve. "Once your spy is back and can confirm where Alek is, we'll fly there and get her out. I doubt he'd leave her out of his sight. Then we'll come back here as quickly as possible."

"That sounds like a *great* plan." Grete's drawl was raspy, and Finn almost didn't recognize the Valkyrie as she and Madick strode through the door.

Dressed in a gray tunic and breeches, with dust covering her face, there was nothing of the proud blonde, always dressed in black.

"I heard it went so well last time. Are you that eager to walk through death's doors?"

Finn narrowed his eyes. "Do you have a better plan? Or do you prefer us to kill innocent children, perhaps? I guess you didn't mind when it was your own queen so what's a few hundred children."

Grete rolled her eyes, her back straight as she strode into the room. "If I would have brought Lillian here when I found her, she wouldn't have broken the curse. Our queen would be *dead*. Her father trusted Atli with his life—with Lillian's life. And I trusted him to figure it out."

Else snarled softly beside him, "It nearly broke her. Lillian will have to live with what she did for the rest of her life. You condemned her to that fate when you didn't allow her a choice, didn't allow her to make an informed decision."

"We all have to live with the choices we make," Grete said quietly. "At least she is alive to do so." She brushed some dust off her tunic before leaning her hands on the table and snapping her eyes to Finn's. "I will join you in finding the vessel. I can veil us from Alek with my magic. Give you an actual chance."

Finn started to shake his head, but Aaron interrupted him,

placing a hand on his shoulder. "She's right, Finn. She can hide us while we find her."

Finn sighed. His mind and heart screamed at him that Grete couldn't be trusted. But the memory of Elya's burned body flashed before his eyes, and he pursed his lips as he glared at Grete.

She raised her brows in challenge, but Finn refused to give in to her, refused even to nod, and only continued looking into those ruthless blue eyes.

A cold smile slipped over Grete's lips. "Excellent. Then it is decided. We saw the spy return when Madick dragged me out of the gods-forsaken cellar, so he'll be here shortly. Once he is, I'll tell you how to protect Volantis."

71

Finn

The spy—an eagle shifter and Valeria's mate—informed them that the King was still on Echo, residing in the castle with a company of his soldiers. When the spy told them he'd spotted several warships braving the eastern sea, each loaded with hundreds of undead soldiers, already heading toward Seigard, Finn shuddered.

If he never saw another undead again, that would be too soon.

The ships would likely arrive in three days' time, but the spy wasn't sure how the king would transport the rest of his army, still waiting under the Skandi.

"He has someone who can open portals," Finn suggested, forcing his voice to remain steady as memories of that final night in the trials haunted his thoughts. "I'm guessing he'll be utilizing him to get the rest of them there."

Grete nodded, her brows pinched as what looked like a million thoughts crossed her face. "Breit, I believe your mate can wield water?"

"He can." Breit rose from the table and glanced at Valeria. "I will inform him of the ships. We will guard the beach, hold them off for as long as possible." The brunette spun on her heel, her black wings flaring as she rushed out of the room.

Tild tapped her fingers on the table. "I haven't encountered a necromancer in many years, but my fire has killed the undead before. I shall join them and greet our guests warmly."

Finn couldn't stop the shocked smile that spread across his face at the wickedness flashing in the old Valkyrie's eyes and the embers of silver fire flickering over her palms. Even if she was old, older than he could imagine, it was clear this was not a woman to mess with.

"Good." Grete stared at each remaining Valkyrie in the room. "The rest of you know where your places should be and what you need to do. We've done this before, and we'll do it again. It's just another enemy, Valkyries."

A low murmur of agreement echoed around the table, and a fragile ember of hope sparked inside Finn when shoulders and backs straightened, and sharp teeth flashed as low snarls vibrated in their throats.

The air shifted, electricity and thrumming power filling it.

Finn's grin widened. Perhaps these warrior women would be enough to veer off Alek's forces until Lillian returned.

Grete settled her piercing gaze on him. "Do you think Alek will be able to transport the rest of his army all at once, or will they be arriving in waves? If it's the latter, we should station some of our fighters around the island to intercept them when they arrive. Smaller groups will be easier to break apart. And if we can get the vessel out of his hands, we can try to convince the children not to fight against us but join us. Or at least take them out with as little harm as possible."

Finn shrugged, "I'm not sure. We were only transported one and one, but I doubt the portal wielder can transport hundreds at a time. It would be too much of a strain on his magic. I'd like to think we can assume they will be coming in waves."

Tild paced around the room, the deadly fire still flickering over her palms. As his eyes tracked her, Finn wondered if she wasn't doing it on purpose to rally the Valkyries. Regardless, it was working—more snarls and vibrations of lethal magic tingling the air.

"So we'll station fighters around the island. Perhaps some of the mates so they can reach out once we know where the soldiers intend to appear?"

Each Valkyrie offered sharp nods, even as worry for their mates fluttered in many eyes around the table. But the worry quickly turned into fury, eyes all around the table blazing with protectiveness and rage at the threat against their partners, their people.

Finn stared with wide eyes as masks of rage shadowed every female's features.

These were the warrior women he'd been warned about as a child, and he was very glad he was fighting on the same side as them.

Grete opened the doors to the large balcony connected to the room. Pausing for a moment to tilt her head up, she closed her eyes against the bright sun and breathed in the crisp fall air.

"Valkyries and the rest of the mates will be stationed on different levels, and we'll close off the lowest balconies. Destroy them if we have to. We'll use the height of this castle to our advantage. Liv built Volantis to ensure not even siege towers would pose a threat, and I doubt many outside the winged shifters will be able to get to the top. Then we station a few groups in the forest, hidden so that they can push from behind while we attack from the top."

Finn nodded, and even though he would never forgive Grete, he was glad the experienced Valkyrie was there.

72

Lillian

They remained quiet as they changed into the Valkyrie fighting leathers and the cloaks the water sprite had conjured, leaving the many swords and daggers piled on the ground.

Kian collected whatever firewood he could with the ground mostly littered with wet branches and proceeded to light a smoky fire. Huddled together, they sat in the opposite direction of the wind to avoid breathing in the coiling tendrils of gray smoke.

Hypnotized by the wisps of smoke trailing toward the sky, Lillian leaned her head on Kian's shoulder, and he wrapped an arm around her.

"What do you think the water sprite meant with you not being entirely human?"

"I don't know. He might only have been trying to unsettle me." Kian pulled her closer, his warm breath tickling her scalp, once again igniting those flames in her veins.

Clearing her throat, she glanced up at him. "The elves said something too, Kian. They called you half-human, I think."

"I don't think it matters right now. We need to get through the final test tomorrow—preferably alive—and get back to

Finn and the others." He pulled back to look at her. "You still haven't been able to reach him?"

Lillian shook her head, unease gnawing at her. "It's still a black void. It's so strange, but perhaps it has something to do with a part of my soul being gone. Maybe it interrupted the bond somehow. I can sense him being alive, a flicker of his life force out there somewhere. And the past few days, there have been moments where I've felt a glimmer of urgency. I can't put my finger on it but I have a feeling we need to get back as soon as we can."

Kian hummed absentmindedly while trailing his finger down her arms, goosebumps rising where his fingers brushed her skin.

"Talking about bonds…" Her stomach churned, and she snapped her mouth shut.

But when he eyed her curiously, she forced herself to follow through.

Kian was the last person she should be afraid of. Still, it felt easier to take on Alek again than to have this conversation.

"I want you to know that I want to accept the mate bond, Kian. More than anything I've ever wanted before. But Aaron told me that if we do, your life will be tied to mine. So if I die —" She couldn't continue, couldn't even speak the words.

As she averted her eyes, Kian placed a finger under her chin and tilted it up again, a smile spreading across his face.

"Lillian, I need you to hear me. *You* are my life. I might care about our friends; I might care about the fate of Orios… But if you die, there is nothing left for me here. I'd rather have one day bonded with you than spend years without you." Kian brushed his lips against hers, sending currents of electricity through her body. "I don't think I'd survive it either way. So, if you're ready, I am as well. I've been ready since I saw you that day in the market. You just have to say the words."

Lillian shook her head, an ache settling in her heart. She couldn't be responsible for another man she loved dying.

Kian gently cupped her face. "I know what you're thinking, and it's not your fault, Lillian. He made the decision himself, like I am making my own decision now."

Sighing, she forced herself to look into his eyes. There was nothing but love and determination in them, not an ounce of uncertainty in his smile.

Emotions wrestled within her, and she didn't know what to say. So she settled for crawling up into his lap, wrapping her legs around him and kissing him while the heat from the fire burned on her back.

But even though she lost herself in him, it didn't ease the haunting sense of urgency preying on her mind. It was like the gods themselves were telling her to do it, to give in before it was too late.

And she wasn't sure if it was the sense of her own mortality or if it was Kian's.

73

Kian

When they woke, limbs tangled in each other, Kian savored the early morning breeze and the clear sky before kissing Lillian awake. As she rose, so beautiful in the early daylight, the sunlight reflected in her black hair and made her black wings sparkle.

He almost pulled her back down then to try to do anything in his power to convince her to accept the bond. But he knew she had to come to terms with it herself, so instead, he stayed on the ground, drinking in the sight of her while she stretched out her wings and squinted against the fall sun.

When Lillian raised a brow, Kian laughed softly before getting up and collecting the weapons.

They strapped as many swords and daggers as possible to their backs and thighs but still had to leave several blades scattered on the ground.

"I guess I should have thought to ask for a satchel," Kian winked.

She snorted, "Next time, we'll know better. Although I hope we don't have to encounter these creatures again—at least not anytime soon. I am almost starting to understand why Alek drove them from Hindra and Echo."

Kian nodded, but somehow, he had a feeling it wasn't the last time they encountered any of them. The look in Lillian's eyes told him she mirrored the feeling.

He followed her as she cautiously walked south toward a large rock jutting out over the dark, calm sea.

"Well, it's definitely that island." She pointed to an island far in the distance, filled with large trees and surrounded by tall, steep cliffs towering over the water. The waves crashing against them barely reached one-tenth of their height.

"It seems like it. Are you ready? My magic is refilled again." Kian reached out for her and wrapped one of her small hands in his.

"As ready as I can be. How many ways do you think they'll try to kill us this time?" Lillian grinned at him. "I thought I was creative with the ways I wanted to kill some of the novices during the trials, but apparently, I have little imagination."

Fear gripped his heart, but when Lillian rolled her eyes at him, he made himself grin back. "I'm sure they'll find a way. No one has tried to stomp us to death yet."

Lillian still giggled while he rifted them to the island.

Kian aimed for the small part of the cliff that didn't seem overgrown by trees, holding on to Lillian, ready to steady her if she was going to be sick, but relaxed his grip when she gave him a tight smile.

"It's definitely getting easier. I don't want to spew my guts all over you anymore." She squeezed his hand.

"Who dares come onto our island?"

Kian whipped his head up at the deep voice, gripping Lillian's hand tight upon spotting the massive men and women towering over them. Apprehension snaked down his spine when he realized the trees they'd spotted were, in fact, the giants, moss, and greenery covering their skin and clothing, like they'd somehow grown part of the island itself.

Lillian sighed next to him. "I'm so over these dramatic greetings."

Before Kian could react, his queen growled back, "You

know why we're here. We know why we're here. Let's get on with it. How do you plan to kill us?"

The genuine laugh that rumbled from one of the giants in the middle made Kian jerk, and he gripped one of the swords tight in his hand, keeping the other hand locked with Lillian's in case they needed to rift away.

"I've missed the Valkyrie tempers, I have. And the half-human you brought with you seems feisty as well. Look at the way he grips his sword and his mate. A fighter, that one."

Kian stared into the emerald eyes of the giant who spoke, straining his neck as he had well over five feet on him.

The giants were all dressed in various shades of green, the fabric seemingly a mixture of moss and leaves. But the one who laughed, the only one who'd spoken, also bore a crown of branches woven together over his wide forehead, his wild dark hair tangled in it.

Kian cleared his throat. "Are you the leader?"

"That I am. My name is Lokas, and this is my mate, Angrod. The rest of the brutes are our people." Lokas threw out his arms, and the other giants waved their large hands, hands the size of serving trays, as Kian and Lillian stared at them. "And what are you, pray tell? You are a strange one. I don't think I've met your kind before."

"We're not sure," Lillian spoke again before Kian could respond. "But that's not why we're here. Give us the challenge so we can move on. I don't want to have to ask again."

Kian's eyes widened when Lillian let her night swirl around them like a dark shadow, and he almost laughed when the giants backed up, eyeing her cautiously.

Seeing Lillian glare at these huge creatures, her nostrils flaring as they warily studied her and stepped behind Lokas, was truly the embodiment of her spirit being back, of her being the dark queen he knew she was.

"I told you not to make me ask again," she growled when Lokas tilted his head, his eyes raking over the darkness surrounding them.

"I heard you the first time, queen." Lokas scratched his long brown beard. "A sky wielder. We haven't seen one of you since your father. And what a mighty magic wielder he was. Your mother, too—such a strong earth power. Not an offensive power, of course, but powerful in her own way. Making Hindra flourish in a way that Echo could never match."

"Yes, I know all about my parents' mighty powers already. We're in a rush, Lokas. Let's get on with it." When Lillian squeezed Kian's hand, he sensed the urgency in her and caught her eyes darting east toward Seigard for a moment.

"You're so much like your mother. The same fire burns in both of you," the giantess behind Lokas said, her voice gentle in contrast to her frightening appearance as she examined his mate.

She was taller than Lokas, with long, wavy, black hair falling down to her waist and a smaller wooden crown gracing her head.

The giantess smiled at them, her large teeth glinting in the sunlight. "Liv was my friend. We will get on with the challenge, as you ask, but if you'd visit with us for a little, we can tell you about her. I'd like to know her daughter, especially since you seem hellbent on risking your life taking on Alek. And Adeon, I presume."

When Lillian began to argue, Kian whispered, "We can sacrifice a little time, Lillian. I'm sure Nida would have warned us if Finn was in danger."

Lillian stared at him for a moment but finally inclined her head before she pinned the giants under her gray stare. "A little time then. But we must get going today."

74

Finn

When they wrapped up the meeting, the castle bustled with activity, and Finn watched in fascination as the Valkyries leaped into action, instructing everyone in their way about Alek's arrival and how the Valkyries planned to counterattack.

In every room he passed, Valkyries began pulling out weapon after weapon from cabinets and hidden storage rooms —bows, swords, daggers, harpoons, and crossbows were dealt out and carried to the various balconies they were to strike from.

"I guess it's a good thing there are no children around. At least we don't have to think about where to hide them." Aaron fell into step with Finn as they hurried back to his room to lay out a plan for getting Josephine out of the king's claws.

"I wouldn't go that far. You are still a child in our eyes, Aaron. Perhaps we should find you a hiding spot instead of bringing you with us?"

Aaron gaped when Else offered them both a crooked smile.

A smile pulled at Finn's lips. "Was that a joke?"

The Valkyrie laughed quietly. "Perhaps. It's what Elya

would have said if she was here, so I thought I should give it a try."

Even as his heart clenched, Finn offered Else a genuine smile, his grin widening when she winked at him.

"Well, I'm the same age as our queen, and I don't think anyone would ask her to hide. So I won't either. I shall fight alongside the rest of you." Aaron frowned as he nervously gripped the hilt of the decorated sword hanging at his waist.

Finn glanced at Else, and he couldn't stop the laughter that bubbled up as she rolled her eyes. When she snickered, he threw his head back and howled with amusement, embers of warmth sparking in his chest. And he couldn't stop laughing when Else's laugh rang louder, both of them gasping for breath when Aaron kept asking what was so amusing.

Finn still couldn't look at Else when they reached his room, his shoulders shaking from trying to quench the laughter. Walking up to the balcony, he opened the double doors to get some air but stopped in his tracks upon finding Lillian's two ravens perched on the railing. Hanin let out a low caw when a snort escaped Finn, tilting her head to glare at him.

"Lillian's right, you are really judgy." Finn grinned at the massive bird.

When Hanin made to approach him, Munion smacked her with his wing. Munion whipped his head toward the clear sky behind them, and Finn's jaw dropped at the hundreds upon hundreds of ravens that circled the tower, their large shapes stark against the blue.

"You've rallied all the guardians?"

"They've rallied more than that, it seems." Else offered the ravens a deep bow. "It looks like every raven in Orios is here to support us."

When Hanin shook her head, Else added, "Well, except the nestlings, I assume."

Hanin inclined her head.

Finn nodded, "Thank you. Have you already been informed of the plans?"

The ravens nodded.

"So you know we're taking off? We're planning on leaving tomorrow; intercept the king and his army before they leave Echo."

Munion cawed softly, waving his wing toward himself and Hanin while flicking his head east toward Echo.

"It seems they want to come." Else studied the ravens.

Hanin nodded vigorously, the feathers lining her head flipping with the force of it.

"I won't say no to more help." Finn brushed his hair out of his face. "But what if Lillian comes back here? Will you not wait for her?"

The ravens glared at him, unwavering.

"All right, I guess that means you're coming. We should bring as many weapons as we can. I guess you can help carry."

When the ravens continued studying him, their intelligent black eyes fixed on the group as they began discussing how to handle the king, a chill brushed his skin—and not from the fall breeze that blew through the open doors.

But from wondering if Lillian's guardians sensed something that they didn't, that they knew where their queen was.

75

Lillian

The ground beneath them shook as they followed the giants through the dense forest. Tall trees formed a tunnel over their heads, shielding the bright sun and casting thick shadows across the ground. Lillian shuddered and pulled her black cloak tighter as the cool breeze blew straight through her leathers.

When the forest opened up to a clearing, her hand flew up to shield her eyes against the bright sunlight. Blinking until her eyes adjusted, she realized massive gray stone houses, all linked together, lined half the circular enclosure, with smoke twirling out of the many chimneys attached to the long chain of homes.

In the middle of the chain, an impossible tall house stood, and the massive black door creaked when Lokas pushed it open and gestured for them to enter. Lillian stretched out her arms but couldn't reach either side as she passed through it.

Warmth washed over her from the fireplace in the heart of the room, and she had to jump to climb onto one of the wooden benches surrounding it. The bench was covered in some type of white fur, the texture impossibly soft as Lillian skimmed her hands over it.

"Giant wolf," the giantess next to her whispered.

When Lillian only stared at her, the giantess smiled and flicked her red hair. "It's what our tribe hunts. Giant white wolf. We're called the Wolf tribe. The wolves destroy our forests and disrupt the order of nature. They're not real wolves, part demon they are, and so we keep this realm free of them. But they have nice fur," she winked.

Nodding, Lillian glanced at the massive piece of fur while a shiver rolled down her spine. If the giantess called *the wolves* giants, she had no wish to ever stumble across them. She'd had enough of wolf-like creatures after the Garms in the trials.

She brushed her fingers over her stomach, over the scars she now carried because of the Garms, but quickly stopped when Kian pulled himself up next to her and questioningly eyed her hand.

"Welcome to our home."

Lokas smiled at them, a seemingly genuine smile, but Lillian still kept a watchful eye on the giants around them while Kian firmly gripped her hand in his and let his other rest on the hilt of the sword at his side.

"I won't tell you to relax. I know you've visited with some of the others on our neighboring islands, and I'm assuming they weren't too welcoming."

"Or they were too welcoming if I know those snotty elves," a giant on Lokas's side snickered.

Lokas rolled his brown eyes. "We heard they might have lost some lives when you passed through."

When Lillian and Kian both stiffened, and Lillian cast an eye on the open door, Lokas smiled at them again.

"They surely deserved it. We put no blame on you, Valkyrie. It saddens me what they've turned into, how they abuse magic to live as they used to. You might not believe it, but they truly did use to be some of the gentlest creatures in Orios. Care for nature, for all creatures roaming this realm. But since your parents died," Lokas threw Lillian a sympathetic look, "and we had to flee Echo and Hindra, nature hasn't been balanced. I've seen good turn evil, animals and creatures die out, and I believe your kind are having trouble reproducing if we are not misinformed."

Lillian nodded. "No Valkyries have been born in the past eighteen years. Someone told me they suspected Adeon had something to do with it."

A wrinkle formed between her brows. She hadn't thought too much about the challenges the Valkyries faced—had been too focused on her mission. But what if it was bigger than Adeon punishing the Valkyries? What if something was disrupting the order of the entire realm?

Lokas shook his head slowly, "Adeon is not the god of earth and nurture. That's Fray, his brother."

When Lillian's brows pinched further, and Kian tilted his head, Lokas continued, "I know for many species, especially for the short-lived humans, the gods are nearly forgotten. And why wouldn't they be, with the way they treated most creatures? But I was born when the gods still roamed on Orios— before the War of Gods, before they left for Vaelia."

Lillian stared at the giant, at the firelight dancing across his long beard. "But that would make you…"

"Very, very old, yes. I don't keep count anymore; too many centuries have passed. But my memory is intact, even in my old age." Lokas wrapped his arm around Angrod. "This one keeps me young."

The two giants grinned at each other, and Lillian couldn't help but smile at the love that shone in their eyes.

Lokas turned to them again. "I remember the gods very well. Fought beside Fray himself in the war."

Lillian frowned; she knew the humans and shifters had sided with Fray. Fray, who'd led the war against his own brother, who'd convinced Thoras, the shifter goddess, and the rest of the gods to join him. But she hadn't known other creatures had fought as well. When she glanced at Kian, he shrugged—apparently, it was news to him as well.

Lokas caught their shared look, offering them a crooked

smile. "Humans forget quickly, as they always have. Perhaps that's true for half-humans as well." He stared pointedly at Kian. "But the Valkyries should remember. They fought in the war. I believe your aunt led one of the flanks."

Lillian's eyes narrowed at the thought of her treacherous aunt, and her magic opened an eye inside her, the constant shadows licking her veins burning hotter.

Rolling her neck, she took a deep breath, reigning in the swirling emotions. "I haven't been Valkyrie for long. I grew up human. And we were too busy fighting King Alek to focus much on history lessons. I was getting lessons on Seigard, but King Alek is still a threat, so they ended. At least for now. I don't really see what this has to do with me or my parents, though."

Angrod waved to two giants sitting in the back of the room. "Please, get some food and ale for these two. And don't fret; it's not enchanted. Giants don't have magic," she winked at Lillian and Kian. "But this has very much to do with you, dear Lillian. Adeon killed your parents, even if he had Alek carry out the despicable task. And he will come after you if he hasn't already. Understanding the gods is crucial if you plan on taking him on."

Lillian shuddered but shook her head. "He hasn't. Could he be gone too, like the rest of the gods?"

A whisper of hope sparked in her chest. No one had seen or heard from Adeon, and she'd broken the curse months ago. Perhaps her luck had turned.

"I very much doubt that," Lokas said quietly, instantly squashing the small ember of hope. "We believe he has been quite busy the past eighteen years. As I was saying, Fray is the god of life—of prosperity. Adeon is his dark reflection, the god of war and magic, and, of course, the god of death. That nature's balance has been disrupted, that babes are stillborn or not born at all, that magical creatures are losing their magic, must have to do with Fray. We suspect Adeon might have a hand in it, that he might have harmed his brother or at least interfered with him."

"But the gods have all gone to Vaelia," Kian interrupted. "I thought Adeon couldn't enter. How could he have harmed Fray if he is in Vaelia?"

Lokas eyed him, his eyes trailing thoughtfully over his face, and Lillian instinctively moved closer, readying her magic at her hands.

Lokas grinned at her. "So protective. I'm just curious—whatever your mate is, he's not entirely human, that one. But you knew that already." He bore his eyes into hers. "Although you don't know what he is, and neither does he. Please do let us know when you find out. I should like to have that knowledge."

"A Valkyrie queen will only be mated to someone equal in strength and power," Angrod mused. "You must be of a powerful bloodline."

"He's King Alek's son," Lillian waited for disgust to overtake the giants' faces, but there was only mild curiosity as they waited for her to continue.

"Adeon gave Alek some of his powers, so could he somehow have affected Kian too?"

When Kian stiffened beside her, she whispered, "Sorry, I just thought of it now."

"Perhaps, but it seems unlikely. So very interesting," Lokas said softly.

They were interrupted when two giants returned with food, offering Lillian and Kian a bowl of steaming soup each and a goblet of ale. The stem was so large that Lillian had to hold it with both hands while balancing the bowl on her lap.

"We don't get to host guests that often; I apologize for the unfortunate sizes." Angrod stalked up to them and relieved Lillian of the goblet while some of the giants laughed.

Waving aside the giantess who sat next to Lillian, Angrod took her spot, her gaze sweeping over Lillian's face. "You look so much like her."

Lillian smiled at the friendly giant. "So I've heard. I wish I had met her."

"I'm sure you will," Angrod smiled back. "Well, I know we've taken much of your time already, and our challenge can be performed while eating. Would you like to begin?"

Lillian glanced at Kian, who straightened his back before she inclined her head.

76

Kian

"Our challenge is simple. We'll present you with a riddle, and if you solve it, you will be free to leave." Lokas rose from his seat, towering over them as he spoke, his large frame blocking the light from the flickering fireplace.

"And if we don't?" Kian narrowed his eyes at the giant as a hum of unease thrummed over his skin.

"Let's not speak of that now. You both seem clever enough. I'm confident you will figure it out quickly." Lokas smiled encouragingly at him. "But don't fret; no harm shall come to you or your mate. Even if I wasn't aware of what your dragon did to those elves," he grinned at Lillian, "we won't hurt you."

Kian glared at him, unable to hold back the edged tone in his voice. "That's what they all say. I'd prefer to——"

But when Lillian elbowed him in the side, he clamped his mouth shut. Kian glanced at her, shaking his head when she winked and whispered, "If it comes to that, I'd say we could take them, even if they're three times our size."

Angrod threw her head back and laughed beside her, the bench they sat upon shaking with each rumble. "You have your mother's spirit as well. I should think we'll become great friends, little Lillian."

Lokas clasped his hands together. "Giants are known for our knowledge and curiosity, and we thrive on friendly challenges like riddles and games. As I said, we've prepared a riddle for you. There is only one answer, so please take your time and don't answer hastily."

Clearing his throat, Lokas began to speak quietly, but his deep voice still echoed through the room.

"I am the beginning and the end,
No one knows me, yet many will for me send,
In times of need you're all my friend,
But not all of you can on me depend,
For there are those that won't me defend,
I am the beginning and the end."

Kian stared at Lillian as she furrowed her brows.

It can't be that easy, he thought.

"It must refer to the gods?" Lillian whispered.

Kian nodded slowly, but worry made his muscles coil and he kept darting his eyes around the room, ready if the gentle giants changed their minds about harming them.

"Remember, there is only one answer."

Smiling encouragingly, Angrod rose to clear away the bowls and goblets. Kian studied her frame as she walked through the room, his gaze flitting over a few other giants, all of whom offered him friendly grins.

Sweat formed over Lillian's brow from the fire, and Kian gently wiped off a drop that snaked down her temple as he whispered, "Could it be that easy?"

Lillian tilted her head and eyed Lokas and the rest of the giants sitting on the circular benches around the fire, all watching him and Lillian closely.

"It must be Adeon," Lillian mused. "He is the god of death, and he created most of this realm."

"But why would you make it this easy for us?" Kian frowned while addressing Lokas.

The giant said nothing, only stared back at him while pulling Angrod onto his lap. When Kian searched the giantess's face, she smiled again.

"The answer is Adeon," Lillian said, pinning the giant leaders with her steely eyes.

Kian froze when the giants remained silent for a moment, but no heaviness or sudden movements filled the room upon her answer.

Angrod's eyes sparkled. "We knew you were clever. And so you are free to leave."

"But why?" Kian shook his head in disbelief.

"Because we believe in a free world. We should like to come back to Echo and Hindra when you've finished your mission. We would like to live freely again. And unlike some of the other magical creatures you've encountered, we haven't let hate fill our hearts. They blame your parents for being forced to retreat to these islands, young queen. Before they were driven from Hindra and Echo, they were gentle creatures, albeit a bit fickle. But rarely did they try to kill as they've now begun," Lokas said, the other giants rumbling their agreement.

Lillian smiled at them, one of those genuine smiles that made Kian's heart race. "I will make sure you are free to return as soon as we take down Alek."

Lokas and Angrod smiled back at his queen, but Kian didn't miss the fleeting shadow of worry that crossed their faces as Angrod whispered, "Let's hope you succeed, Valkyrie Queen."

Lillian

———————————————

Angrod offered to show her the library while Lokas brought Kian to the kitchen to gather some food for the rest of their trip. Lillian's eyes widened at the massive room, books four times the size of normal ones covering every surface—every inch of the long wooden shelves lining the walls and the many tables spread out across it.

"Young queen, I sense there is something that's bothering you." Angrod tilted her head. "There is a sense of urgency in you, yes worry for your friends, but there is something else."

Lillian studied the gentle giantess, surprised at herself when she answered, "I have this strange feeling. I don't know why, but my instincts are telling me something is about to happen. And that it won't be pretty."

Angrod nodded. "I suggest you trust those instincts. But you should also trust those around you to share the burden, Lillian."

Lillian's stomach churned as Angrod shot a glance at the door toward the kitchen. "I do trust him. I just…" She walked up to one of the tables, letting her fingers trail over the dusty books.

"I just don't know what he'll be able to do if—or when—

Adeon comes after me. And even if we haven't seen a whisper of him, I have this sense of being watched, of someone tracking my every move. I thought it might just have been apprehension after Alek, but perhaps it's Adeon after all."

She'd held on to the small hope that Adeon might leave her be, that he hadn't shown his hand because he'd moved on. But after hearing what giants told her today, that hope had been crushed into swirling dust.

"You'd be surprised what love can accomplish," Angrod said gently.

"Look at my parents. Love killed them. I don't want him to die for me. And I know he would. Every day, he risks his life for me, and I can't bear for him to worry more." Lillian swallowed hard at the lump that formed in her throat.

"I worry more when you hide things from me."

Her stomach dropped, and she spun around to find Kian leaning against the doorframe, his face soft as he looked at her.

"I…" she started, but Angrod interrupted her by walking up and giving her a hug, lifting her off her feet and enveloping her in her earthy smell.

"The giants will stand with you. We'll be ready when you need us. I will see you again, Lillian. Trust your instincts; they'll lead you onto the right path." With that, Angrod walked out of the room, leaving Lillian and Kian to stare at each other.

"Will you share this feeling you spoke of?" Kian slowly approached her, stopping a few feet away, offering her the choice to step into his arms and trust him with this.

Lillian blew out a soft breath and bridged the gap between them, letting Kian's strong arms ground her.

"It began a few days ago. At first, I thought it was only that I couldn't hear or feel Finn, and I was worried for him, Sam, and Else. But it's something more. It's like a feeling of doom, like something or someone is just waiting to get me. I know it probably sounds dumb, but I can't shake it."

Kian held her tighter. "It doesn't sound dumb. We'll be even more careful, keep our eyes on anything that seems amiss." His breath tickled her neck as he burrowed his face into her hair. "Is this why you don't want to accept the bond?"

Lillian nodded. "I know you don't want to think about it, but there is a real chance I might die," she swallowed, "and then you perish as well. I can't stand the thought of it."

"Lillian. I will find you in all worlds. Nothing can stop me from finding you, wherever we might be." Kian pulled back to look at her. "I will always let you make your own decisions, but you should also trust me to make mine."

That feeling roiled within her again, the urgency to accept it, to accept him.

She threw her head back and stared at the wooden ceiling. Angrod told her to trust her instincts. But what if they led her astray?

"They won't."

She snapped her eyes back to his, narrowing them.

Kian brushed his lips against hers. "No, I can't read your mind, but I know you, Lillian. And your instincts are telling you to do this. I, for one, vote for you to listen," he winked.

Trailing her eyes over his face, his forest-green eyes, dark brows, and messy black hair, the corners of her mouth lifted. He was so certain of them—had been since the trials.

Perhaps it was time for her to trust in it, too.

"All right," she whispered.

Kian's eyes widened. "All right?"

When she nodded, he lifted her up, spinning her around with the broadest grin she'd ever seen grace his face. Broader yet than the one he'd sported on the elves' island.

"All right."

78

Kian

They each carried two satchels filled with food that the giants pressed into their hands as they left. Kian tried to explain that they'd been told this was the final challenge and should be able to return to Seigard—hopefully with the dragons by their side—but the giants refused to hear it.

Lillian remained quiet as they walked to the edge of the water, but the air between them crackled with electricity, and Kian smiled at the faint blush on her cheeks from their earlier conversation. He'd hoped they could find somewhere nice, even if it were the Valkyrie castle, or at least somewhere safe, for them to have that first night together.

But when she'd whispered 'all right,' he'd been ready to do it right there and then, not caring one bit about the giants in the next room. He wanted everything with her, and if it would have to be on a damn island in the middle of the eastern sea, then so be it.

A current rolled down his spine when she glanced at him. Seeing her every day and holding her every night had his insides burning with desire, and the need to make her his was becoming overwhelming. And now…

He had to use every bit of restraint inside to keep himself from dragging her to him and sealing it this very moment.

When they stopped at the edge of the water, Kian tugged at her hand to get her to turn around from the crashing waves. Pulling her flush against him, her body molded into his so perfectly that he let out a soft groan. He couldn't wait to get those leathers off her, roam every inch of her soft skin, and see that flush deepen with pleasure.

When Lillian tilted her head up and her gray eyes searched his face, he bent down to kiss her. And when she opened for him, her lips urgently crashing against his, he deepened the kiss, kissing her with more passion than he'd intended.

They were both out of breath by the time she pulled back, and Kian smiled at the rosiness in her cheeks, the tangled black hair that tumbled down her back, and her wide eyes as she stared at him.

"What was that for?" she whispered.

He kissed her again, lingering with his forehead against hers. "Because I love you. And because I'm so grateful I found you. For so long, my life was an empty, dark void. And then you tumbled into it, with your wicked temper, your daggers, your beauty and loyalty, and your own darkness." Kian smiled at her. "You showed me that darkness can be beautiful. That even within shadows and death and all-consuming night, there is beauty. I shall always treasure it. As I shall always treasure you."

Lillian blinked rapidly as silver filled her eyes, her voice thick as she responded. "I should have guessed from that night in the tavern when you sang for me that you were a sappy bastard."

Kian threw his head back and laughed, unable to stop when Lillian snorted as she joined him. They held on to each other until the laughter ebbed away, although a smile lingered on Lillian's face as he bent down and kissed her nose.

If I could vomit, I would. But I'd probably burn you into little wisps of ash if I tried. Nida approached them, sparkling against the dimming sky. *Come on, you passed the trials, and you shall be reunited with your souls. Although I have to say the giants really didn't give you much of a challenge, did they? I thought they might at least make you fight one of their giant wolves.*

"Hello to you, too." Kian waved at her. "How come I hear you now? I didn't used to."

I didn't know you would be able to hear me, so I didn't speak to you, Nida said simply. *What are you waiting for? Take your mate to our sacred island so you can finish this. You'll feel the pull of your soul, let it guide you there.*

Kian rolled his eyes and turned to Lillian. "Ready?"

As Nida took to the skies again, she turned back to glare at them, her icy-blue eyes narrowed. *Try to get there in one piece. I can't be saving your asses all the time.*

79

Lillian

When they landed on a white beach, Lillian sucked in a sharp breath. She'd thought they'd return to the barren island where they'd first met the dragons, but instead, they stood upon the whitest beach Lillian had ever seen, surrounded by crystal clear water, not the murky waters of the eastern sea.

White cliffs, as tall as the mountain range in Echo, rose behind them, lining the entire island. The gentle breeze carried a lingering flowery scent, tangling with something wild and untamed Lillian had never smelled before.

Her eyes sliced to Kian when he drew deep breaths beside her, his hands on his knees as he swayed slightly.

"Are you hurt?" Lillian worriedly searched his face, pushing his black hair out of his sticky forehead as he caught his breath.

Her magic stirred within her, ready to protect him and fight whatever came their way, and she had to squash the snarl wanting to make its way up her throat at something harming him.

Kian drew a few more shaky breaths before he finally shook his head, "I rifted to where my soul pulled me, but it required more effort than I've ever had to use. I think we've left Orios, or at least that we're somewhere far away from the forgotten isles and Echo."

When Kian straightened his back, his face no longer so pale, Lillian's shoulders lowered, the tension from her magic easing. She tilted her head toward the sun warming her face—its rays were not those of the chill fall sun back in Orios but warm, like the midsummer sun.

You made it, young ones. I heard rumors of a narrow escape, but apparently, luck smiles upon you. Or perhaps my daughter went against my orders and intervened.

Tyr glared at them from where he perched on a ledge above them, tendrils of smoke wafting from his nostrils. Lillian began to argue, but a loud roar from Tyr had her shut her mouth quickly.

The waters whisper to me. And I've told you before, you cannot lie to me, young queen. I can always tell. But I've promised my daughter not to punish you, so I shall not. You may enter our island, but stay clear of the dragons. While Nida has decided to bond with you, I am still torn about your mate. I shall give it one more night to ponder, but we will ensure your comfort in the meantime.

Lillian ground her teeth, but when Tyr narrowed his frosty eyes, she decided against arguing with him. They'd come this far—she was not letting her temper get in the way.

One more night, then she'd see Finn and the rest again.

Clearing her throat, she responded quietly, "Thank you, Tyr. We appreciate the graciousness."

The black dragon inclined his head. *Follow me. We will take you to the quarters where you may stay the night.* Tyr jerked his head to Kian. *You may use your gift to get to the top, but you won't be able to rift into or out of the valley. One of the previously bonded Valkyries enforced it with wards against traveling magic to ensure no one could get in unseen, so you'll have to walk down.*

Kian nodded, offering Lillian his hand, and the world whirled before her eyes once more as he rifted them to the top of the cliffs Tyr had indicated.

They both froze as they stared out over the massive valley.

Waterfalls lined every wall of the circular dale, and the sunlight danced on the water's surface like a million tiny crystals as it cascaded down the bright white cliffs. The valley itself was filled with copse of the greenest trees Lillian had ever seen, with large fields of yellow and green grass in between them.

But it was the hundreds of dragons that flew over the trees or lay in the sunlight that made her pulse thrum in her ears. The twenty or so that they'd encountered on the barren island had been intimidating enough. Here, there were dragons of every size and color, many gleaming in the same silver as Nida and Fafri but also green, blue, black, and orange, with different types of spikes lining their backs.

Silver glinted in the corner of her eye, and as she locked her gaze with Nida's, the dragon's eyes sparkled with amusement. *It's beautiful, isn't it?*

Lillian nodded.

There were no words to describe what this place was.

Frowning, she eyed the dragon. "How did you get here so fast?"

Nida tilted her head. "Some secrets we don't even share with our bonded."

"So this is your home then. What of the other island?" Kian's lips parted in awe as he glanced between Nida and the valley below.

The dragon huffed. *Do you think we're dumb enough to tell anyone where we actually live? With even the gods fearing us, we've kept this a secret for millennia. Only our bonded may ever know of this place, and you'll be sworn to secrecy when you leave. But let's not dwell here. We have a comfortable place for you to rest. It was built for our bonded, and it shall have everything you need. I'm sure you're tired of sleeping on the ground.*

She winked before spreading her wings and heading for one of the massive fields.

80

Finn

Finn rested his elbows on the railing while he glanced out over the large balcony toward the eastern sea, where King Alek's ships would soon appear over the horizon. The sea was quiet right now, the stars flickering in the sky reflecting on the dark surface.

Despite the quiet night, a shiver of apprehension danced its way down his spine. Tomorrow, they'd leave for Echo to try to get Josephine out of the king's hands.

And he had no idea if they'd succeed.

Or if they'd even make it out alive.

They'd spent the day training—with weapons for himself, Aaron, and Else while Grete shielded them from each other with her magic. And even though he had not forgiven the Elder for what she'd done to Lillian, he did appreciate her coming along. He didn't fully understand what her magic did, but it allowed them to melt into the surroundings, only a flicker of their movements shining through the veil she placed over them.

Hanin and Munion had also partaken, and while Finn couldn't speak to them, the ravens were trained fighters. The way they were able to take them down, even with Grete's magic, had instilled a flicker of hope in him—that there was actually a small chance for them to carry out the mission they'd soon embark upon, that there was a chance none of them would end up dead.

A soft knock interrupted his thoughts, and Finn walked back into his room, grateful for the flickering fire that filled the room with heat.

He couldn't hide his surprise when Grete stood outside his door, once again dressed in the black uniform, two golden raven wings stitched across the chest of the jacket. There was no sign of the dust and grime that had marred her skin as they trained, her long blond hair clean, sparkling like the golden band over her brow.

"May I come in?" Grete glanced behind him, raising a brow at the many weapons he'd laid out on the unmade bed and the bundles of clothes on the floor.

Finn rolled his eyes, "Make yourself at home."

Grete strolled right through the room, out onto the stone balcony, and tilted her head toward the evening sky. "I can barely stand being inside after having been kept in that basement," she said quietly.

"It's not like you didn't deserve it," Finn muttered. "Why are you here?"

Grete leaned against the railing, her eyes trailing his face. "You know it's quite rare for a Valkyrie to have a familiar. I've only seen it once or twice before. Is that why you are doing this? Risking your life for Lillian? For a people that is not your own?"

Finn narrowed his eyes. "My people are also at risk. It's not like life on Echo and Hindra is enjoyable. We all live in fear of what Alek will do next, fear of not being able to pay the taxes he imposes on us. Fear of what he will do to our families, our neighbors, our friends. So no, I'm not doing it because of the bond. It might have started with the bond—I followed Lillian because of it. But I believe in her, in what she wants to do. Even if she has faults I think she'll make an amazing queen, and I want to be part of helping her take the throne."

"So noble," Grete mused. "I will say I was unsure of her intentions at first. She is volatile, that one. But perhaps I was too quick to judge. The same fire that burned in her mother, that burns in me, fills her. Even if her magic might be dark, there is light there."

Finn nodded. "So, is that what you came here to say? That you've had a change of heart? That cellar must have really messed with your head."

Grete laughed, a quiet, hollow laugh. "I guess I deserved that. But no. I came to ask you for a favor."

Finn stared at her, his mouth drawn into a thin line and anger swirling in his stomach. As if Grete was in a position to ask him for a favor. If it weren't for her, Lillian would be here right now.

"I know I have no business asking anything from you. But I cannot shake the unease clouding my mind. It started already during my imprisonment, and I attributed it to the dungeons," Grete shuddered.

"But it still lingers—it consumes me. I've said Adeon will come after Lillian, and I think it might happen sooner than we think. Something is brewing in Orios—something evil."

A knot of apprehension tightened in Finn's gut, twisting with nameless foreboding at the worry that lined the Valkyrie's features. "And what favor of mine will help with this?"

Grete glanced down at her hands, knuckles white from her clenching them. "I don't think anyone can stop Adeon coming after her at this point. The favor I came to ask is purely selfish. Help me keep Aaron safe tomorrow. Male Valkyries are rare, and there is a reason for it. They're not as strong, but Aaron won't hear it." She desperately met Finn's eyes. "I love him like a son, Finn. I never carried any children, nor will I ever, and I cannot lose him."

Finn stared at her, at the real fear lining her blue eyes, and swallowed against the fear clawing at his throat.

Grete didn't believe they'd all make it out alive.

Perhaps didn't believe any of them would make it out.

Closing his eyes, he blew out a deep breath. They needed to have hope because if they didn't…

They wouldn't have anything. And if this vow would give the powerful Valkyrie hope, he'd promise it.

Finn opened his eyes, watching a single tear make its way down Grete's pale cheek. "I will do what I can to keep him safe."

Grete nodded once, and with a final glance at him, she strode out of the room.

81

Kian

Nida guided them to a cottage nestled in a small clearing, surrounded by tall trees. The white wood was stark against the green valley, and its straw roof shimmered like gold—as if the rays of sun that shone through the greenery had solidified.

They'd passed dozens of dragons as they walked through the dale, and even though Lillian and Kian kept their heads down, he felt sharp eyes trailing him until Nida snarled viciously, and the dragons continued whatever they were doing.

Even so, the strong beatings of wings and the whisper of scales against the tall grass still filled the air around them. Kian hoisted the satchels the giants had given them onto his shoulder and flexed his hands, keeping them ready to grip the swords on his back at a moment's notice.

Even if he knew they would do little against the dragons' fire.

As soon as they'd started down the wide path, lined with thick green bushes, into the valley, his magic had dried up, the feeling eerily similar to the iron bracelets his father favored, and he prayed there would be no need for him to rift them out of there—that the luck they'd had with the giants would stick.

There is food and water inside, and you can clean up in the stream behind the house. Nida jerked her head toward a trickling creek snaking behind the house and into the rich forest by its side.

Lillian's eyes flew wide, and Kian gripped her elbow as she stumbled to a stop. "Wait. Where is Sam? Did you not bring him here?"

Nida snarled. *He was not offered to bond with one of us. He will never see this island, and he shall never hear of it either. Regardless, he left soon after you. We heard whispers of Alek rounding up men on Echo and Hindra, and he worried for his brother.*

When Lillian's eyes dropped to the ground, Kian's stomach churned, and he gently cupped her cheek, lifting her face to his.

"It's not your fault, Lillian. It would have happened regardless of what we're doing." His heart ached for her, for Sam, and the rest of the people on Echo and Hindra. While he might not have anyone left on the islands he cared about, his friends did.

The same pain filled Lillian's eyes as she whispered, "Finn's whole family is still on Hindra, Kian. What if he doesn't know?"

Kian shook his head, "Finn decided long ago, before you even bonded, that he'd follow you, Lillian. Do not take on the guilt of another's decision."

Nida nudged Lillian with her snout, her eyes soft. *He is right. I am being summoned, so I will leave you now. No one will disturb you here. The dragons have been told not to enter this meadow. My father is making his decision tonight, so be ready by dawn.*

As the dragon spread her wings, she turned her head to Lillian and winked, *Enjoy.*

Kian held back a snicker at Lillian's blood-red face as she stomped up to the house and opened the squeaking door, revealing a small but cozy wooden kitchen and sitting room with a wooden table and plush couch in front of the stone fireplace.

He cast a cautious glance over his shoulder before entering

the house, but no dragons lurked between the trees or in the small meadow before it, so after drawing a deep breath of flowery air, Kian walked through the door.

Lillian rummaged through the kitchen cabinets, her back toward him. "I'm starving. Are you starving? I think we should eat, and then maybe clean up. What do you think?"

Kian suppressed a smile at her rambling, sensing the nerves coursing through her body.

"That sounds great." He stepped up behind her and gently let his fingers trail down her wings, savoring the shaky sigh she let out as her wings twitched in response to his touch. But when she didn't turn around, he kissed the back of her head and stepped back.

"I'll go check out the rest of the house. Let me know if you need any help with the food?"

Lillian nodded, still with her back toward him, as she took out some dried meat and bread.

Kian had to force himself to turn around and walk through the sitting room to the closed wooden door on the other side. He wanted to tell her that there was no pressure, that they could wait, but he sensed it wasn't what she needed to hear.

She needed some space to think through what tonight would entail if he knew his mate, the thoughts that often consumed her and made her withdraw.

She'd let him know if she wasn't ready.

Kian curiously opened the door to the small bedroom, smiling at the large bed placed in the middle of the room and the second fireplace, smaller than the one in the sitting room but with a large fur rug laid out in front of it.

The pink and orange light from the imminent sunset cast its soft glow over the wooden floor, and he lit the two lanterns over the bed to prepare for the darkness that would soon follow.

"All right, with the food in here, and what we got from the

giants, I think I've gathered enough for a small army, so we should eat."

Warmth filled him upon hearing Lillian's voice, the steadiness of her tone, and smiling, he left the bedroom.

82

Lillian

Her hands shook as she tried to force herself to eat a piece of chicken. She bit her cheek, willing her racing heart to calm.

Why was she so nervous? It was Kian. The man she loved, who she knew she wanted to spend the rest of however long she'd have in this realm with.

She wanted this. Although Lillian knew one word from her, and Kian would happily wait, she didn't want to—she didn't want to wait another day. She was ready, but all the same, butterflies filled her stomach when she met his green eyes.

He was so handsome. Even with dirt and grime sticking to him from their travels and his midnight hair windswept, he was still the most gorgeous man she'd ever seen. She trailed her eyes over his leathers, lingering on the swell of his muscles playing beneath as he quietly ate the food she'd laid out. When he sensed her stare, he offered her one of his blinding smiles and a grin spread across her own face, even as heat crept up her neck and her blood roared in her ears.

Kian pushed the plate away. "Are you finished?"

His voice was gentle, quiet, as he started to clear out the

dishes and put the food—hers mostly untouched—back into the cabinets.

Nodding, she wiped her sweaty hands on her leathers, and a shiver skittered down her spine when Kian approached her.

"Do you want to clean up? The waterfall behind the house looked amazing. And this time, we won't have to worry about the elves trying to kill us," he winked.

Lillian nodded again, feeling as if she'd forgotten how to speak.

"Do you want to go together, or do you want some space?" Kian searched her face, a twinge of worry filling his eyes.

She cleared her throat, her voice barely a whisper, "No, I want to go with you."

Lillian took the hand he offered to help her up, and when he pulled her to him, she relaxed against his chest, breathing in his comforting scent. Her heartbeat became steadier, her breathing more even as Kian's strong arms enveloped her.

When her heart didn't feel as if it would beat out of her chest, Kian led her out of the house into the early night. As she walked next to him, heading for the silvery stream behind the small cottage, Lillian tilted her head to the sky, watching the bright stars wink at her and the large moon rising over the white cliffs surrounding them.

The valley was quiet. There were no sounds of wings or heavy stomps, only the trickling of water falling onto the smooth rocks beneath the waterfall, and a sense of calm settled over her as they quietly began removing their dirty clothing.

Kian stood with his back to her, offering her privacy should she want it, and she couldn't help but steal a glance at his broad back, the black swirls that tangled across his shoulder blades, weaving their way up toward his neck.

Closing her eyes, she removed her undergarments, and when she opened them again, she slowly approached him.

The silvery moonlight shimmered across his tan skin, and

the tattoos covering his entire torso seemed to dance over his muscles when they tensed upon hearing her approach.

Lillian trailed them with her fingers, her lips curling into a small smile when Kian shuddered under her touch.

Slowly, she wrapped her arms around him, replacing her fingers with her mouth as she kissed his shoulders, his back, his neck.

When a low growl vibrated in Kian's throat, she nipped his shoulder, and his body tensed before he spun around and lifted her up so that her legs wrapped around him.

They stared at each other for a moment, Lillian's breathing becoming heavy at the desire burning in his eyes, the awe in his gaze.

"You are so beautiful," he breathed, then carried her over to the waterfall, only setting her down once they were under the warm, trickling water.

"May I?" Kian rasped as he pointed to her wings.

Lillian nodded, a moan escaping her when Kian tenderly washed them, the warm water and the gentle touch of his hands nearly too much already.

Heat flared inside her as he glanced at her for permission and let his hands move to her shoulders, to her breasts, further down her stomach: his touch still so delicate she thought she might combust.

Her eyes trailed his fingers, and she nearly squirmed at the wonder on his face as he slowly swept his gaze over her. It was as if he needed to know every inch, leaving no part of her skin untouched.

When he shifted his eyes to hers, a jolt shot through her at the love and adoration shining bright in the green, and her last remaining nerves washed away with the water running down their bodies.

She let her own hands explore his body, his hard shoulders, his muscled stomach, her skin igniting as her touch left goosebumps in its wake.

When his fingers lingered right above her most sensitive

area, softly stroking in small circles, her muscles went taut, core clenching, and she wrapped her hands in his hair, pulling him to her and kissing him so hard she thought she might draw blood.

A low growl built inside her, and she hissed against his lips, "If you don't bring me inside right this second—"

She didn't have time to finish the sentence before Kian scooped her up into his arms and sprinted into the house, his mouth not once leaving hers.

83

Kian

He was glad they hadn't closed the door to the cottage when they left to get cleaned up, or he might have broken it down in the rush to get Lillian inside.

A searing heat scorched his skin, his entire body sizzling as he kissed her while trying to stay on his feet long enough to bring them into the bedroom.

As he kicked the door open, Lillian nipped at his neck, and he groaned as his body responded.

They didn't make it to the bed.

The fur in front of the fireplace was closer, and he gently laid her down on it, her black hair and wings stark and beautiful against the white. Her arms wrapped around his neck, and she dragged him with her, pulling him on top of her.

He continued exploring every inch of her silky skin as he kissed her, grinning into her mouth when she arched into his touch.

The low, breathy moans she released almost had Kian lose control completely, but he forced himself to push up onto his elbows, staring into her eyes—nearly black from the shadows that danced behind them as she stared back at him.

"Why are you stopping?" she whispered, her voice quivering as she tried to catch her breath.

Kian bent down and kissed her softly, growling against her mouth when she dragged her nails down his back, trying to force him closer.

"Are you sure," he whispered into her full lips.

He jerked when Lillian's hand confidently slipped between them, wrapping around his length. Kian gritted his teeth as desire crashed through him, his mind going entirely. Muscles vibrating from holding back, he met her glazed-over eyes, and a pang shot through his heart.

This woman would be his undoing.

And when she whispered, "Yes," and began to stroke him, not the shy, unsure way he'd expected, but hungrily, possessively, he lost all control.

Lillian whimpered when he gently removed her hands, pinning them above her head and slowly slid down her body. He gently nudged her legs apart, letting his tongue and mouth explore her inner thighs, kissing and nipping until she snarled at him, writhing beneath him.

He wasn't gentle when he finally tasted her, his tongue firmly exploring every fold, his teeth nipping at the sensitive bud. As he added a finger, growling at the warmth of her, darkness exploded out of Lillian, surrounding them, fully blocking out the flickering fire.

"Kian," she moaned as she wrapped her hands in his hair and tried to pull him on top of her. When he resisted, she snarled at him again, the darkness around them thickening and tendrils of night wrapping around his arms to support her grip on his hair.

"Kian, please," she begged.

He laughed hoarsely as he teasingly let his finger move inside her. "I told you I should like for you to give me orders. Is that perhaps an order, my queen?"

Lillian snarled again, her voice thick as she responded, "Yes, it's an order. Get up here, now."

"As you wish, my dark queen," he purred and slowly dragged himself on top of her. When he opened his mouth to ask her if she was sure again, she narrowed her eyes and crashed her lips into his, her nails digging into his back.

Nearly every last ounce of self-control left Kian when she shifted her hips, guiding him to her entrance. Holding his breath, he gently nudged inside her, but when she raked her nails down his back once more and breathed his name into his ear, begging him for more, he growled and thrust deep into her with one strong stroke.

Their bodies molded together perfectly, stars exploding within the darkness surrounding them, dark and light flashing as he filled her entirely.

She might have called his name, he might have called out for the long-lost gods—but as she sank her teeth into his neck, he lost all sense of space and time. Could only think of the warm heat enveloping him, of Lillian's burning skin against his as he buried himself in her.

The bond between them burned and sparkled, darkness and light binding them to each other until their minds—their souls—intertwined, and the very threads of their beings wove together.

Their bodies were one, the love and desire pouring out of them tangled as they held onto each other, the night sky around them quivering as they both came undone, over and over.

84

Lillian

Kian lazily kissed her where he lay on his back; her naked body half-draped over him as they enjoyed the warmth of the sparkling fire. Warm, pure satisfaction graced his face as she gazed up at him, the mirror to the expression she was sure lined her own features.

That was something else.

The strength of the bond between them made her breathless—only Kian's even breathing kept the air flowing into her own lungs as if his breaths could replace her own.

It really was.

Kian's deep voice caressed her mind, the love inside him filling her, yet again threatening to take her breath. She let that love consume her, pushing away the worry, fear, and darkness that lurked within her, feeling as if she was made of light, as if the world itself had brightened by their love.

She grinned at him, "I didn't realize you'd be that into me bossing you around."

He playfully nipped at her ear, grinning back at her when she let out a soft breath. Her heart rate increased yet again, and electricity ran over her skin like blasts of lightning, heating her core.

"I could definitely get used to it," Kian winked, pulling her fully on top of him, nestling his face into her hair.

"I didn't think it would be possible to be this happy," he whispered, and she didn't miss the vibration of worry inside him, the fear of someone or something tearing them apart. But just as quickly, he sent another wave of love through her, forcing her lips to curl.

"Especially with everything that is happening outside the walls of this house." Kian pulled back to look at her, his eyes darkening. "You are my life, my dark queen. Before I met you I was barely living—an empty shell walking this realm. But now, I live with every fiber of my being, and every single one of those fibers lives for you. I want you to boss me around forever."

Lillian's throat constricted. "I didn't think I'd ever be this happy either," she mumbled, her voice thick. "Even with everything we still have to face, I think this is the happiest I've ever been."

More love and happiness crashed through her—consumed her—the might of the emotions rushing down the bond bringing tears to her eyes. She felt every thread of the pure, undiluted love he had for her, like his love was a tangible force that enveloped her.

When Lillian let her own emotions flow freely between them, Kian's arms tightened around her, and a deep sense of home settled over her. Wherever Kian was was her home now —a home she'd never want to escape, that she'd never want to leave.

"When was the last happy day you had before this?" Kian whispered as he wiped a stray tear from her cheek.

She pondered his question for a moment.

She wasn't sure. It felt as if her life had been filled with so much horror and death lately that she couldn't remember when she'd last felt happy. She'd had moments of happiness, despite everything, during the trials, especially after meeting Finn and the rest of her friends. Still, her father's death and her mission had loomed over her, never allowing her to give herself over to happiness fully.

"I think perhaps the summer solstice last year."

Kian nodded, his eyes asking her to continue, so she drew a deep breath.

"It was a beautiful summer day, warm but not humid. The hunting party in our village had immense luck and brought down several summer-fattened deer, so we all gathered in one of the meadows to eat and dance. Even my father—Atli—joined, which was rare since he never saw the point in socializing unless it benefited the rebels. I wasn't as sick then, and I spent the whole night dancing until my feet almost bled. The sun never set, so when we walked home, there was this light in the forest, like the sun smiled at us. I was happy then."

Her heart ached for Atli and Eli, the two people she'd spent most of that night with, who had smiled and danced. Who had been alive.

"That does sound wonderful."

Kian searched her eyes. "You can talk about him, you know. You loved him, Lillian. And I owe Eli everything. Without him, you wouldn't be alive; you wouldn't be here with me."

He shuddered. "I can't even think about it. He was an honorable man, even if he forced you into an impossible choice. But if it had been me in his position… I can't say I wouldn't have done the same thing, Lillian."

Lillian nodded, burrowing her face in Kian's neck. "I know."

If the roles had been reversed between her and Eli, she would have made the same decision.

She just hoped she could live up to his sacrifice.

85

Finn

The sky was dark, and white froth covered the wild sea as if the weather mirrored the storm brewing inside him when the group gathered on the highest balcony of Volantis.

Grete and Else wore identical expressions of resolve, the matching golden bands over their brows gleaming like the twin swords they had strapped to their backs. Aaron's face was pale, with deep circles of purple under his eyes and his blond hair stringy, and he fidgeted nervously with the sharp dagger hanging at his waist.

The Valkyries were all dressed in fighting leathers, thicker than the ones Finn had been given for training, enforced over the heart and trailing higher up the neck to provide more protection. Finn hadn't bothered wearing his, instead packing them into the travel pouches the Valkyries would carry. He felt a bit out of place standing in a robe as the Elders came to bid them goodbye but shook it off quickly.

Vanity had no place here.

Tild inclined her head to Finn when they locked eyes. "Thank you for your bravery. I speak for all the Valkyries when I say we're proud to fight beside the humans and shifters that protect and follow our queen."

A large raven with graying feathers landed on the railing next to Tild, and she tilted her head as she studied him. "The ravens are proud of you as well." The old Valkyrie smiled at Hanin and Munion, the younger raven puffing out her chest as she cawed back.

Tild gestured to the raven. "Kain expects the ships to arrive in two days' time, perhaps even one and a half depending on if there are any storms. You won't have much time when you arrive." She eyed Grete. "And if Adeon is there, do not engage. It's not worth the risk, even if I know you were close once."

Grete offered the Elder a cold smile, not an ounce of the uncertainty her gaze had held yesterday shining in her sharp eyes. "You're giving me orders now? How the tides have turned. But I shall not engage. We will be back here tomorrow morning with the vessel. Perhaps we can even use her against Alek," Grete mused.

Finn ground his teeth, remembering the terror in Josephine's eyes. "She will not be used as a weapon. We need to show that we are better than Alek. It's the only way we'll be able to convince any of the children to switch sides. If they see us using the same methods, what's the point of all of this? We need to be better, do better."

Grete scoffed, "You have much to learn, young shifter. There is nothing noble about war. War is about death and power, and no one is innocent." She shook her head, shooting a look at the rest of the Elders. "We've fought in many. And there is no winner, no better side. Both sides lose, regardless of what happens."

Finn glared at her. "She will be offered the choice at least. It's what Lillian would want."

Grete fixed her fierce stare on him. "Our queen isn't here to make these decisions. If she returns successfully from the dragon isle, she will be consulted, but in the meantime, we will decide."

When Finn snapped his eyes to Tild, to Valeria and Breit, they cast their eyes down.

Tild sighed when she finally looked up. "She's right, Finn. In times like these we need to make unfortunate decisions, horrible decisions. But if there is another way, we'll give the girl a choice. I swear it."

Finn didn't bother responding as he shifted, taking to the skies to try to squash the anger building in the pit of his stomach at the disregard for Josephine's life, for her choice.

He didn't turn around, but the beatings of wings behind him confirmed that the rest followed, the screech from the ravens flanking him echoing over the sea.

86

Lillian

Lillian yawned as she stepped out of the small cottage, squinting against the orange sun rising above the white cliffs before her. Smiling, she listened to the melodic birdsong drifting from the lush trees, and even if her body ached slightly and she was exhausted, happiness flowed through her like the soft summer waves that rippled across the lakes on Echo.

They'd made love several more times, slower and less urgent, taking their time getting to know each other's bodies until light began seeping in through the large window in the bedroom.

Perhaps staying up all night hadn't been the wisest decision, but Lillian hadn't wanted to fall asleep, hadn't wanted to leave the small bubble of love and peace they'd created.

Sighing, she wished for a little bit more time, selfishly hoping that Tyr might need another day to make his decision. But when beatings of wings interrupted her thoughts, and Nida gracefully circled the small meadow in front of the cottage before landing, she knew the bubble was bursting even before Nida spoke.

My father has made his decision.

Lillian eyed the small dragon, but no emotion crossed Nida's face, and she only narrowed her eyes when Lillian arched a brow. Rolling her eyes, she realized there was no point in trying to ask for more information. Nida wasn't speaking, and she couldn't tell if that was a good or bad sign.

When Kian exited the house and closed the distance between them with long strides to give her a lingering kiss on the cheek, a whispered promise of more to come, Lillian prayed that the night of peace wouldn't be the final one they'd have.

Dread opened an eye in the pit of her stomach, and only when Kian squeezed her hand, sending a wave of love through her that had her lean into him, could she draw a shaky breath again.

This way. Nida jerked her head toward the forest behind her. *You're to meet my father and the others in the meadow just over there.*

They remained quiet as they followed Nida through the trees, and as Lillian let her hands sift through the soft grass, high enough to tickle her wings, every scenario she could think of ran through her mind.

What if they said no?

Bile burned in her throat. They had technically not passed the test of the elves—had needed Nida to help them get out.

We'll be all right. If they say no we will find another way, I promise. We'll do this together.

When Kian smiled at her, another wave of warmth washed over her, nearly igniting her skin, and a deep blush crept up her neck at the devotion filling his eyes, at the soft curl of his lips.

Blowing out a deep breath, she tore her eyes away and fixed her gaze on the thinning tree line ahead, where a glimpse of black and silver sparkled.

Tyr and Fafri stood in the middle of a meadow, much larger than the one by the cottage, with gushing waterfalls behind them. On either side of the dragon royalty, ten dragons perched quietly as their sharp eyes watched Lillian and Kian approach, two with the same ebony scales as Tyr and the rest in various shades of orange and green. Nida took up the spot between Tyr and Fafri, fixing her gaze on Lillian as she slowed to a stop.

At the small twitch of Nida's eyes, Lillian cleared her throat. "We've understood that you've made your decision."

She turned to Tyr, brushing her hand over daggers for comfort as the large black dragon stared back at her with an unreadable expression.

Tyr inclined his head. *I have. You made it to our island alive, but the only way your soul shall be whole again is through bonding with one of us. After consideration I have decided to help you. But you'll do well to remember that bonding is for life.*

Tyr fixed his eyes on Kian as wispy hazes of smoke dissipated in the wind from his large snout. *I will personally bond with the half-human. I am too curious to find out what blood flows in your veins.*

And I have claimed you, Lillian. Nida winked at her. *We shall be bonded forever, and I shall like to help you tap into your full power.*

Without breaking their stare, Nida began stalking toward her, lowering her head.

Not so hasty, daughter, Tyr growled.

But Nida didn't listen. With her eyes fixed on Lillian, she approached until she stood before her.

Nida, we have a ceremony for this, and there are precautions, steps, that need to be taken. You will step down now. It's an order.

More thick smoke curled up toward the sky as Tyr took a step toward them, and the ground shook as several of the other dragons began stomping their feet at Nida's insubordination.

Nida!

A shiver snaked down Lillian's spine as a plume of silver fire zinged over their heads, small embers falling upon the yellow and green grass.

No, father! We've waited long enough. I'm sorry, Lillian. This will hurt.

Nida didn't spare her father a glance as she bent her head, the longest black spike on her head tearing through Lillian's jacket before Nida thrust it into her shoulder.

Lillian couldn't hold back a cry as fiery pain sliced through her.

Kian's hand was ripped from hers when they both doubled over from the blazing fire that tore through her. Panting, she fell to her knees, gripping her shoulder to ease the pain.

Crawling to her, Kian held onto her as she tilted her head to the sky and screamed. Her wings whipped the air but did nothing to soothe the invisible flames licking her body from the inside out.

Black spots still flickered before her eyes when the pain numbed, fewer and fewer waves of hot coal crashing through her until it finally faded, then vanished. Still, Lillian's hands shook as Kian helped her to her feet.

She glared at Nida. "That did more than just hurt."

But it feels better now, doesn't it?

Lillian swore the dragon smirked.

Flexing her fingers, she almost doubled over again as raw power pulsated through her, and she couldn't stop the thick threads of smoke that left her hands, the pressure of her magic overwhelming her.

The exhaustion from the sleepless night faded, replaced by bursts of energy that made Lillian tremble as she tried to remain standing. Kian had to hold on to her as she drew deep breaths, trying to gain control over her magic and body.

This is exactly why we have a ceremony. She wasn't prepared, Nida. Tyr narrowed his eyes as he stared between Lillian and Nida.

What is done is done. You made me wait too long, father. Nida defiantly glared back at Tyr. *She is a quick learner; she'll figure it out.*

I guess I understand why she chose you. You are both equally rebellious. Kian winked at her, but his playful expression fell when a whimper escaped her, and her magic ripped out once again, filling the meadow and blocking the forest surrounding them from view.

87

Finn

It was quiet when they arrived in the capital; the slanted stone town and the dark castle looming over it eerily silent under the cloud-filled fall sky. Little light shone out of the windows in the slums, the crumbling homes in seemingly worse condition than when Finn had first seen them all those months ago.

He sighed; it felt like a lifetime ago he'd excitedly strolled into the capital of Echo, eager to take his place in the guard and even more eager to find Lillian.

None of his brothers had ever found their familiar, and he had been so excited to finally have something that set him apart from them. Being the youngest had been tough growing up, especially as his brothers lived up to everything his parents hoped for. They were both content supporting the family business and had quickly found a wife to settle down with.

His parents had never understood Finn's wish to explore the world, the restlessness he felt working in the weaponry shop. They'd been relieved when he told them he would join the King's Guard, hoping that he'd finally find purpose in life.

He winced as he wondered if they knew what he'd done, how he'd betrayed the reigning crown. They must have heard what happened at the trials—unless Alek had somehow found a way to keep it quiet. But he doubted it. The guards were known gossips, and so many of them had seen Lillian transform, had stared with wide eyes as she openly challenged their king.

"Come on, we should get going." Else nudged him with her elbow, offering him a gray cloak to wear over the Valkyrie leathers he'd slipped on.

It was too short for him, barely reaching his knees, but he guessed the leather breeches, although in pristine condition, would draw less attention than the entire uniform. At least his boots were his own—worn and dusty from many years of use. There had been no boots his size in Seigard to switch to.

Else's cheeks reddened from following his gaze, clearly remembering his 'you know what they say about big boots' quip.

Grinning to himself, he pulled the cloak over his head and glanced at the rest of the group. The ravens had separated from them when they reached the southern harbor of Echo, flying straight for the castle as they were able to soar over the clouds, remaining hidden from sight.

He and the Valkyries had kept to the coast, using the forest covering wide parts of Echo as cover and avoiding the towns not to risk detection.

The Valkyries donned their own tattered, gray cloaks, but unease swirled in his stomach as the outline of their wings still glimpsed through. They were too large for the cloaks to cover fully, and if someone looked close enough, they'd definitely get suspicious. It would have been better if Grete could shield them, but she wanted to save her energy and magic for the castle, not risk running out before they'd even entered the courtyard.

"You can't, like, tie them down, somehow?" Finn whispered as Aaron struggled with his cloak. Taller than Else and Grete, the cloak didn't fit him very well either, and he was the most at risk of exposing the black wings on his back.

"And risk not being able to get away quickly?" Grete

snarled. "No. We'll just have to keep to the darker alleyways and smaller roads. As you shall learn, *shifter*, the wings are our pride. We would never sully them by tying them down."

Finn rolled his eyes. These damn proud Valkyries would be the death of him. Quite literally, if their pride had them discovered. But when Grete didn't waver, and even Else's mouth was set in a thin line, he shrugged, "Shall we get going then?"

"You lead the way." Grete waved her hand impatiently for him to walk through the eroding stone wall to take them up to the dark castle presiding over the stone town.

They weren't the only ones traveling on the narrow cobblestone roads. Others, most dressed in similar cloaks to their own to shield them from the chill wind that whistled through the streets, walked with their heads down beside them. A few groups were gathered outside the taverns Finn had come to know intimately during his stay here, but there was none of the bustling activity or singing there had been in the summer.

The people here spoke quietly, their postures tense and movements jerky.

Finn picked up a few words here and there—whispers of war and Alek finding the Valkyries reaching his sensitive ears. He was so focused on keeping his head down and trying to overhear anything helpful that when a hand grasped his shoulder in one of the dark alleys, he jumped three feet into the air, biting back a gasp.

Heart pounding, he spun around, but joy replaced the fear as he met Sam's brown eyes. Finn pulled his friend into a hug, and Sam laughed in his ear as he hugged him back.

"I cannot say how happy I am to see your face! Are Lillian and Kian with you?" Finn glanced over his shoulder but Sam was alone, no sign of their other friends.

Sam shook his head. "They will be soon, though. I heard they passed the dragons' challenges. I was heading to Hindra to see my brother, but when I heard of Alek's plans, I realized you'd likely come back to try to find the vessel, so I decided to come and help."

Finn grinned at him. "I am forever grateful. We could use someone else who has knowledge of this wretched town."

Sam winked at him. "I can do you one better. I know of a secret way into the castle."

88

Kian

Lillian seemed to vibrate beside him, her head tilted back as she tried to draw air into her lungs. Nausea rolled through him when Lillian's power surged through the bond—uncontrollable, wild, immortal power slamming into him.

He could taste her magic, the chill of night whispering over his skin as she struggled for control, the electricity and power soaring in the air. He had felt her power yesterday, had felt himself become stronger, something within him shifting as Lillian bit him, as their bond snapped into place.

But this was different.

He held onto her as she spasmed, ignoring Tyr roaring at Nida for being so careless. Kian forced himself to remain calm, even as pressure laced his chest, his nerves firing, and whispered soothing words in Lillian's ear, trying to send calming energy through her.

Her darkness surrounded the meadow, shifting in the breeze, but thicker, darker, than he'd ever seen before. Thunder rolled in the distance, and a bolt of lightning flashed for a second before the impossibly thick darkness drowned it.

The air itself sizzled from magic, and Lillian tried to pull away from him, willingly or not; he did not know.

"Get out of here," she got out, her wide eyes purely black from shadows covering the gray, her face paling with every moment passing. "I can't handle it; I don't know what is happening."

Kian pushed away the mounting dread at the panic in Lillian's eyes. "No. Your darkness doesn't scare me, Lillian. It never has." He made sure to let the truth of his words flow down the bond, praying she wasn't too far gone to feel it.

Lillian snarled at him, her lips curling back to show off her teeth. "It scares *me*, Kian. Get. Away."

He only shook his head, turning to Tyr and Nida. "Do something! She's losing control."

Kian held onto his own control with everything in him, not allowing the rage roiling in his stomach to take over.

She needed him, and damn if he was going to let her down.

Tyr let out another roar when Nida tried to step closer to Lillian, the authority in his booming voice causing the silver dragon to cower beside him.

You've done enough, Nida. Leave. Now! Fafri, you stay with me. The rest of you get out of here, spread out, and if it comes to it, you will unleash your fire upon her.

The dragons swiftly took to the skies, whipping Lillian's darkness into funnels of swirling black, winding toward the clear sky above.

Nida cast him a regretful glance before she also took off, her silver scales mirroring the dark magic around them. Kian tried to step in front of Lillian, tried to catch her eye, but when her magic whipped at him, heat sparking within it and burning holes in his leathers, he was forced to step back again.

"You will not touch her. I don't care what you threaten with. If you so much as leave a scratch on her, I will kill you. And then I'll find you and kill you again in the afterlife."

He glared at the dragons while firmly holding onto Lillian. As he tried to rally his own magic and nothing happened, he swore loudly, remembering Tyr's warning about the wards against his type of magic.

Fafri spoke to Kian for the first time, her voice gentle as it filled his mind. *We will do everything in our power not to let it come to that. She needs to stop being scared of her own power. She needs to remain calm.*

Kian narrowed his eyes but bit his tongue when Tyr spoke again.

Lillian. Look at me! Tyr lowered his voice, but the same authority filled it, forcing Lillian's eyes up. *You're untrained. And Nida is young. It's a lethal combination. Your bonding unlocked the restraint on your magic, but you are still in control. Your emotions are getting the better of you now. Breathe and trust in your own strength. It rivals the gods now, but you are in control of it—you're always in control of it.*

"Very helpful," Lillian got out through gritted teeth, her body and wings convulsing from the little restraint she managed to grab hold of.

The darkness surrounding them began to dissipate slowly, but when Lillian sucked in a shaky breath, it returned, black, dense walls surrounding them in all directions, shielding every tall tree from view. More thunder boomed in the distance, but the wall of magic was so thick Kian couldn't tell if lightning followed the storm that was rolling in.

A sob escaped Lillian—a sob that split his chest wide open—and the darkness began to spread. Dark clouds traveled across the ground, further and further out from the meadow and further and further up toward the sky. Screeches rose in the distance, mingling with distant rumbles of thunder.

"I'm…" Lillian's voice cracked. "I'm going to kill you all. I can't hold on."

Fury filled him at the fear lacing her voice, and Kian urgently spoke in her ear, unable to move with the darkness now surrounding them in all directions, heating the air and making drops of sweat form across his forehead.

"You won't. Remember what I told you: you could destroy this entire wretched world if you wanted, but you won't."

The darkness seemed to still, the air around them holding its breath for a moment, and an ember of hope filled Kian.

But it quickly diminished when Lillian spoke again. "You said I'd give my life for it," she whispered, her voice hoarse. "You'll have to kill me, Kian. I can't, I can't—"

Sobs wracked her body, her magic convulsing with each one, darkness pulsating in the air around them.

Kian's heart broke, and he'd have fallen to his knees if he could move an inch.

He hadn't thought of how he'd ended that sentence. He was such an idiot. Of course, that's what she'd remember. Of course, that's what she'd cling onto.

"Lillian…" he started, but Fafri interrupted him, the ground rumbling as she made her way toward them.

You can, Lillian. You might have a different magic than your mother, but you have the same strong mind. Do not let fear consume you. Allow the magic to fill you; give yourself over to it, but don't let it scare you. You are one with it.

Fafri lowered her head, inching closer to Lillian, blowing small plumes of silvery fire to disperse the thick darkness and create a path. Tyr snarled next to her, a warning to stay back that the dragon queen ignored.

When nothing happened, and the darkness remained thick and impenetrable, Fafri turned her icy gaze to Tyr.

Bond with her mate. The dragon queen flashed her teeth when Tyr narrowed his eyes. *I can't tell you it will work, but they are one soul. There is a reason he is her mate. Perhaps he can help her.*

"Do it. Do it now!" Kian growled at Tyr as Lillian's weight fell upon him, her legs giving out, the darkness blinding him as it pushed closer. He could feel she was about to fully submit to the magic, only a small thread of control still lingering within her.

As you wish.

When Tyr stomped up to him, the black spikes lining his head nearly invisible in the darkness surrounding them, Kian closed his eyes, praying to whoever was listening to help him save his mate.

89

Finn

Sam led them through the winding roads, keeping to the less crowded streets and slipping through narrow alleyways where possible. Finn was glad the storm brewing above them cast the stone town in gray, dim light as they inched closer to the castle on top, concealing their identities from the people and guards that strolled through the streets.

A heavy weight settled upon his chest when they passed the inn where he'd first encountered Lillian—where his life had changed forever.

But even if the path it had led him down were cast in darkness and death, Finn would never regret approaching the silver girl in the window. Would never regret bonding with her, his queen and familiar. He'd never had a purpose before, had only aimlessly wandered around Hindra, from bed to bed, from tavern to tavern, until that night he'd heard whispers of the trials and a tug, perhaps from the gods themselves, had urged him to travel to Echo.

An ache spread within him at the emptiness in his mind without Lillian's snarky comments filling it. She'd surely find a way to tell him he was being sappy, that she wasn't anyone to follow—even though she was wrong. He even missed the despair and sorrow that had filled him those first weeks on Seigard, the depth of the feelings too intense for Lillian to block completely.

At least then, he'd known were she was—had known that she was safe.

"We're almost there," Sam whispered, and Finn pushed the thoughts aside.

Lillian had to be safe.

He very much doubted they wouldn't have heard otherwise. And Kian would fight until his last breath before he let something happen to her. Fixing his eyes on his friend's broad back, he followed Sam up a familiar slanted road, the tall and proud homes lining it dark in the dimming afternoon light.

Frowning, he clasped Sam's shoulder. "This is where Astrid lived."

He'd never forget the night in the library, how worried he'd been for Lillian, the doubt that threatened to seep into his bones at not being able to break the curse. Finn shuddered and forced the thoughts deep down. He'd hidden them then, and he'd hide the worry now as well.

Sam glanced at him from over his shoulder and nodded, "Astrid harbored more secrets than purely being a rebel. There won't be anyone home. We should hurry before anyone sees us."

Finn opened his mouth to respond but two guards strolled past them at that moment, and he quickly shut it, angling his head to the pebbled street.

When Sam opened the metal gates to Astrid's family home, Finn winced at the creaking sound that broke through the silent streets. But no one approached as the group hesitantly walked up to the dark house, Sam in the front, the three Valkyries following him closely, with Finn last.

Else lingered when Sam burst the double doors open without faltering. Hovering beneath the stairs leading up to the entrance, she fell into step with Finn.

"You trust him?" She flicked her eyes to Sam, waving for them to join him in the house.

Finn inclined his head, not breaking her narrowed blue gaze. "With my life. I've known him since before the trials started. He's saved both mine and Lillian's lives before."

Else glanced at the pathway behind them, where evening shadows now rippled, and nodded. "Good. Let's hope he'll bring the luck we surely need." With that, the Valkyrie strode into the dark house.

Taking a deep breath, Finn made to follow but gasped when a surge of power shot through him, desperation and fear coursing through his veins as Lillian's emotions filled him, filled his core.

The force of it was so strong that he nearly fell to his knees —would have if Else hadn't rushed to his side, her arm wrapping around his waist to keep him upright.

"What's happening?" She worriedly eyed him as she dragged him over the doorstep, quickly kicking the door shut behind them.

"Finn? Finn!" Else shook him, her small hand digging into his upper arm.

Finn shook his head, unable to speak as magic vibrated across his skin, burning and chilling him at the same time.

He'd never felt anything like it.

He had never shared Lillian's powers before. Even if he'd been curious, there had never been the right time.

But now....

Darkness seeped from him, filling the entire hallway. The magic pulsated as if the darkness itself was alive, and he jerked when a loud rumble crackled in the sky as if answering to the night quickly making its way through Astrid's home.

Finn forced himself to take deep breaths. He'd seen what it had done to Lillian before, how she'd lost control, and he needed to remain calm. But Lillian's panic crashed through him like a wild sea, unleashed, raw power brimming under its surface.

"Shit!" Finn swore quietly as the darkness thickened. "Something is wrong with Lillian. I don't think this is normal!"

Else squeezed his arm hard enough to bruise. "Block the connection, Finn. You might kill us all."

Finn shook his head, but then Sam popped up before him, a hardness Finn had never seen before gracing his face, and snarled, "Finn. Get it together. Do you realize what it'll do to Lillian if she kills us through you?"

Finn swore again. But Sam was right. Drawing shaky breaths, he ignored the heaviness in his chest, focusing on breathing in through his nose and out through his mouth.

The dark magic quivered, lightning slightly, until Finn was able to reign it in completely, severing the connection with Lillian. Still, the shadows licked his veins and seeped through his body, making him tremble as he tried to keep them from surfacing again.

Finn bit his cheek until the taste of iron filled his mouth.

Was this what Lillian had to go through?

Sam's eyes trailed over his face as Finn struggled against the pressure building inside him, only held back by sheer will. "You've got this, Finn. Think about Lillian. Your friend. Your queen."

Finn nodded, but when another wave of power surged through him and lightning flashed through the windows, he flinched, unable to stop the darkness that ripped from his hands, from his body, surrounding them all in thick, daunting, dark silence.

90

Lillian

Lillian tried to reach for the daggers at her thighs, panting as she willed her muscles to obey. She'd stab herself in the heart before she let anything happen to Kian and Nida. Or the rest of the dragons.

But fear and shame rippled through her soul, and she couldn't move an inch as the magic Nida unleashed surged yet again, whipping and flooding her body and the island around her.

She barely heard Kian scream as her knees buckled, darkness now pulsating all around her. Lillian could taste it—could taste the night tinged by icy, burning fire as it consumed her, as it threatened to take down the world around her.

I'm so sorry. I love you.

She flung the thought out to Kian, letting go completely as she sensed the pain crashing through him. The pain she was causing as she killed him. Lillian sucked in a breath, breathing in the darkness, choking on the heavy air.

She was killing her mate.

She was killing Kian.

Screaming, she tried to rein in the darkness.

One final time.

But her magic did little more than quiver, sputtering silvery flames sparking through it like winking stars. She fixed her eyes on those small sparks of light, watching as millions more appeared in dancing darkness.

Was she about to obliterate this entire island? The entire world?

Please! Make it stop! You have to kill me! Fear slithered along her spine, fear of what she had done, fear of what she was doing, fear of what she would do.

You don't have to be afraid, Lillian.

Kian's voice boomed through her head. Strong, no pain lacing it, no fear making it quiver. Lillian's eyes widened when bright light, twin to the glimmering stars in her magic, broke through the darkness behind her. But she couldn't move, her knees glued to the ground as magic continued pouring out of her.

Lillian, breathe. Breathe.

A warm hand clasped her shoulder as more light circled her, driving her darkness away.

No. The light fused with it, light and dark entwining, twirling within each other. The pressure inside her lessened, no more icy fire brimming under her skin, the sense that she was about to explode out of her own skin vanishing.

Instead light filled her, filled the area around them, until silver and darkness sparkled like the clearest night sky. Her eyes widened at the beauty, at the pulsating power, how the rawness of it tinged the air. And when the air filled with Kian's scent, so potent—as if his being had merged with the world itself, her breath hitched.

Breathe. Kian's hand gently squeezed her shoulder until she drew a breath. *You are the master of your power, Lillian. You are in control. We are in control together. Look.*

She drew another breath. The meadow lightened, the blue sky breaking through. Then the forest came into view. Then the dragons.

Breathe, my beautiful mate.

Finally, Lillian could feel her body again, her muscles obeying.

It started in her fingers, every limb tingling until she could feel the soft grass beneath her hands. Then, in her legs, gentle spasms bringing the muscles back to life. As she drew another breath, she straightened one leg, then the other, until she stood on shaky legs, Kian's warm hand still grasping her shoulder.

When Lillian turned to face him, she gasped.

Light—bright silvery light—poured out of Kian.

His green eyes flickered with silvery embers, his tan skin glowing, and his hair flowing around his face in a phantom breeze. She stared at the meadow around them, her darkness finally evaporating, the light absorbing the last few tendrils of the night sky.

Starlight.

Kian and Lillian turned as one to Tyr. Tyr's icy-blue eyes were fixed on Kian, and Fafri's face was lined with wonder as she also stared at Lillian's mate.

"Starlight? Is that what this is?" Kian lifted his palms where bright light playfully sparkled in the sun. The light slowly made its way back to Kian, gently caressing Lillian's face as it passed her, small wisps of it dancing across her skin before vanishing.

No wonder you're mates. Fafri shook her large head, her silver scales sparkling like the light that lingered over Kian's skin. *Starlight and night sky.*

Lillian remained frozen, no words leaving her lips. Guilt and shame tore through her as she shakily looked at Kian. He didn't respond, only pulled her into his arms, holding on to her so tight she thought he might never again let go.

Kian spoke softly into her hair, sending waves of love through Lillian as he tried to overpower the guilt that threatened to tear her apart.

"How is this possible, Tyr? How do I have magic I've never accessed?"

Tyr's voice rumbled behind her.
You are no human, son. God's blood flows through your veins.

Kian

Kian still held on tight to Lillian, breathing in her scent to calm himself and trying to soothe the turmoil roiling inside her. The naked fear that had filled her, had nearly broken him, and he could only have felt a fraction of what she did through their bond.

He hadn't realized she'd been afraid of her own magic.

But he should have guessed. She'd killed so easily with it, and while Lillian had a temper, she valued life—-didn't want to kill and destroy. Hell, he'd nearly yelled at her when she freed Nida from his father's claws for not aiming to kill the guards coming after her. When he'd seen the arrow in the guard's *shoulder,* he almost lost it.

When she stopped shaking, her body relaxing against his, he finally drank in Tyr's words. Reluctantly pulling back from her, Kian stared up at the black dragon.

"What do you mean god's blood?"

I knew you were different. Your soul called to mine like no human soul has ever called to a dragon. I should have guessed it, then. But it's been so long since one of you walked this earth.

"So I am a god?"

Kian nearly huffed a laugh, but Lillian's unnatural stillness beside him, the complete silence across the bond, and her vacant eyes stopped the chuckle from bubbling up. He squeezed her quickly, but while she didn't inch away, she made no move to squeeze him back.

Tyr shook his head. *Demi-god, I should think. We don't bond with full-blooded gods—they don't share their powers, nor can we unlock more for them. There must be human in you as well. I wonder who your sire is. I very much doubt it's Alek.*

Unease rippled through Kian. If Alek wasn't his father, who was? And how had he ended up with Alek?

"Could it be Adeon?" Lillian's voice faded to a mere breath as she finally focused her eyes on him, a shudder going through her, making her wings shiver.

Perhaps. But I wonder why he wouldn't have raised Kian himself, why your powers were bound?

Kian's confusion must have flitted across his face because Tyr continued. *Yes, your powers were bound. I am not sure if the starlight is the full extent of your powers or if our bond only unlocked part of them. Very intriguing, I must say.*

Kian didn't feel like this was intriguing at all. What if Alek wasn't the worst sire of them all? What if it was Adeon? The monster who had started all of this.

Finally, Lillian's small hand wrapped around his, her gray eyes searching his face. "It doesn't matter if Adeon is your father. You are good, Kian. You're light."

The light to my darkness.

You're good as well, Lillian. Your darkness doesn't make you evil. Like killing our enemies doesn't make you evil.

Lillian's lips twitched, a tiny ember of shadow flickering behind her eyes, making Kian's heart clench. She was trying to push the fear away. He could sense the struggle inside her, sense how she tried to be strong for him, for what lay ahead.

Two demi-gods going up against Adeon. Now, that will be something for the books.

Lillian sucked in a breath, but not at Tyr's words.

No. Fear once again filled her eyes as she stared at Kian. Fear that mirrored in his own eyes at the swell of dread that rolled down another bond, golden twirls of fear rushing through him. He stiffened as he stared back at his mate.

"Something happened to Finn," she whispered.

92

Finn

It was all Finn could do to hold onto Else as Lillian's magic unleashed upon them. But even if it filled the entire house, not a glimpse of light breaking through, the night never turned deadly. He could hear his friends' labored breathing in the dark room, sense Sam before him, the hand still clasping his shoulder.

Finn tried to send soothing thoughts down the bond—tried to reach Lillian, but her emotions were too strong, blocking his efforts. He inhaled sharply when another presence, another sensation, whispered down the bond. Bright light filled his mind, a familiar yet unfamiliar mind connected to it.

Kian and Lillian must have bonded.

Light replaced the pressure within his veins, the darkness flitting across his skin vanishing, and Finn sighed shakily when the night lifted, and he could finally see Sam, see Else beside him again.

Grete stood in front of Aaron; had pushed the male up against the wall, a wild look on the older Valkyries face as she snarled at the lingering dark shadows. Had Finn not been so frightened himself, he might have smirked. He'd seen what

Lillian had done to Grete, the darkness she'd shoved down her throat in Lillian's mind.

"Well, that was new," Else said quietly.

Finn nodded. "I sense them both now—Lillian and Kian. Something must have happened. I don't think that power was any ordinary magic. It felt ancient and wild—like Lillian couldn't control it. And there was something else within it, something light."

Lillian.

Finn tried to reach out to her, but the soft echo that he'd become so accustomed to still lingered. He frowned as he slipped his hood off. Why could he sense Lillian, sense her simmering emotions—even sense Kian's emotions—something like surprise vibrating along the silvery and golden twirls, now gleaming slightly in his mind with Kian's presence, but not reach her?

"Are they coming here?" Sam searched his face.

Finn chewed his lip. "I can't reach her. But at least we know they're alive. We can't count on it, though, and we don't have much time. We need to get to Josephine tonight."

When Finn glanced outside the window, he realized evening had already fallen, the darkness outside twin to what had just filled the room.

Urgency coursed through him; they needed to get back to Seigard by dawn.

Dipping his chin, Sam gestured for them. "Follow me."

He led them down below the house, a familiar route to Finn from the last time he'd been here.

Stopping outside the painting of the raven, Sam turned to them. "Astrid's family didn't own this house. She was allowed to stay here by someone who knew she needed easy access to the castle, that she needed to be able to sneak in and out undetected."

"How do you know all this?" Finn stared at his friend.

Sadness flashed in Sam's eyes. "We became close. She

might not have shared everything with me, but she did share this."

"What is it that this Astrid shared?" Grete impatiently clicked her tongue as she strode up to study the painting. "And why is there a painting from our castle hanging here?"

Finn's eyes widened as he stared at the large painting, the majestic bird gracing it. He'd known there was something strange about it when he first saw it but hadn't thought much of it since.

"Because this house belonged to an old friend of the Valkyries. They were gifted this painting by none other than your mother." Sam offered Grete a one-sided smile. "There might be a vast library behind this door, but there is also a secret tunnel, a way into the castle that even Alek doesn't know about. Apparently, Ivar didn't know of it either. All Valkyrie Queens had to swear not to breathe a word about the passage, and Liv was no exception."

Finn tilted his head and studied his friend, impressed by the knowledge he'd harbored. He knew Sam was a dark horse —he kept quiet until he had something brilliant to say—but Finn couldn't believe he hadn't mentioned this before now. Although, since it would be extremely useful tonight he wasn't complaining.

Aaron cleared his throat. "I guess we should get going. We're really pushing it."

While the male Valkyries voice was strong, Finn didn't miss the slight tremble rippling through his wings. The Valkyries had all removed their cloaks for now, gripping them tight in their hands while allowing their wings to stretch out behind them.

After a quick glance at the group, Sam cautiously pushed the door open. They quietly followed him as he walked up to one of the curved walls and gently pressed his hand against a dusty leather-bound book.

The walls seemed to fold into themselves, moving to reveal

a dark tunnel, and pure, undiluted dread shot through Finn at the stench of undead that washed over them.

But when Sam unsheathed his sword and without hesitation took a step into the thick darkness, Finn followed him, the Valkyries unstrapping their own swords before falling into step behind him.

93

Lillian

Lillian clenched her fists as the fear for her friend yet again threatened to overwhelm her, dark wisps of night flickering over her skin in response.

She couldn't lose control again—wouldn't lose control again.

Drawing a deep breath, she forced the emotions deep down, locking them up tight in a box inside her.

When little rays of light danced across her skin and met her magic, softly tangling with it, she nearly smiled as the magic in her veins hummed in response. She flicked her eyes to Kian—Kian, who watched in wonder as the rays leaving his hands merged with her darkness.

We do this together. Kian's green eyes blazed, silver flecks reflecting in the green as he fixed them on hers. *You and me.*

She inclined her head. With Kian by her side—with her mate and match by her side—she would not be afraid. Whatever happened would happen to them both. They'd be together, even if they failed. She bit her cheek at the pain of the thought. A world without Kian—she couldn't bear to think about it.

In this life and the next, my dark queen. Kian smiled at her, and she made herself smile back. Made herself absorb the light that tickled her skin, illuminating her before disappearing.

In this life and the next. Lillian pulled him to her and brushed her lips against his, soft at first, then harder, desperate, until Tyr cleared his throat, smoke leaving the dragon's maw as he stared at them.

"We need to go. Our friends are in danger." Lillian forced her voice to remain strong. "Will you come with us?"

She glared at the dragon king when he took his time responding, when even Fafri remained quiet. Her magic roiled again, anger at the hesitation in Tyr's eyes as he flicked his gaze to his queen.

"You swore," Kian growled. "If we did what you asked, you swore you would help us without delays. It's time to fulfill that promise."

Tyr lifted his head to the sky for a moment. *I did. And I will keep my promise. The dragons fly to Seigard tonight.*

The dragon fixed his stare on Lillian. *Nida is young by our standards, Lillian. She has never fought a war, and she is unwilling to listen, cannot follow orders. Her recklessness had her caught eighteen years ago. I will not risk that again.*

Lillian nodded. She didn't want to risk Nida either and didn't want to worry about the wild dragon on the battlefield. "Leave her behind."

I can't believe you.

Nida stomped into the meadow, and her blue eyes narrowed with puffs of white leaving her snout. *You are my bonded. Where you go, I go. You cannot leave me here.*

The silver dragon's voice shook at the end, what sounded like a sob causing her glittering body to shake.

"I'm sorry."

Lillian didn't know what else to say. She felt the dragon's despair as if it were her own, and perhaps it was, but she had risked everyone's life bonding with Lillian so carelessly. It wasn't the time to risk more surprises.

Don't do this. Nida pleaded with her, her voice soft and

begging. *Please, Lillian. I promise I will behave. I will do as you and my father say.* Nida glanced at Tyr, but only hard resolve lined his face.

You will stay behind. That is an order. Tyr flicked his head, and a large orange dragon stomped into the meadow, silver streaks gleaming around the dragon's eyes as it trailed its eyes over Lillian and Kian.

Take her with you.

Lillian couldn't watch as Nida screamed in fury when the orange dragon sent out tendrils of silver smoke, wrapping around Nida like a leash, and dragged her out of the meadow toward another part of the island.

The screech ripping from Nida broke her heart.

It reminded her so much of the screech she'd let out in that courtyard, inside the gilded cage. Clenching her jaw, she tried to block out the sound. She wouldn't risk Nida being imprisoned again.

This was for the better.

Kian glanced at her, sorrow filling his eyes as well. "We should go. I will rift us to Finn." Kian glared at Tyr. "You will follow us to Seigard as fast as possible."

We'll be there by dawn. Tyr and Fafri stomped off before they had time to respond.

Lillian turned to Kian when he reached out a hand, holding on tight as they walked the pathway to the top of the white cliffs. With the green valley behind them and the clear ocean before them, he turned to her, his strong jaw set and eyes filled with resolve.

"I love you, Lillian," he said quietly.

She didn't know why, but her chest caved at his tone, at the worry that laced his words. But she remained quiet as she gripped his warm hand and only allowed herself to lean into his strong chest as he rifted them to Finn.

94

Finn

Dread thrummed through him, in rhythm with the drops of water that dripped from the stone walls, as they walked through the dark tunnel. The air was heavy and wet, each breath becoming heavier to draw the further they walked.

Finn led the way, his night sight allowing him to see every brick lining the arched tunnel, the mice scuttering around their feet, and the pools of water lining the walls.

Else and Sam kept a hand on his arms, with Aaron and Grete following close behind. To distract himself Finn counted the group's uneven breathing, the shallow breaths coming from Aaron the most noticeable. But he kept a watchful eye on the tunnel ahead, grateful that no alcoves lined its path, that there was nowhere for an enemy to hide.

When the air turned thick with the stench of the undead, Finn had been prepared to fight his way to the castle. But they must not have been in these tunnels, must not have found their way here, only the putrid scent of them somehow traveling underground, as the tunnel was eerily quiet. Not one sound apart from their breathing, water dripping, and their soft steps echoed through the darkness.

Finn's breaths quickened when light appeared ahead,

breaking through the misty darkness and illuminating the stonewalls surrounding them. Sam's grip on his arm tightened, and Finn slowed his strides, eyeing his friend questioningly.

"We will enter through the dungeons. I don't know where the king keeps the vessel, but we'll likely have to fight from here," Sam whispered as he pointed to the stone door before them, at the sliver of light that trickled through it.

"I will shield you as we step over that threshold. But let's put on the cloaks. If we're separated, it will buy us a few seconds before the guards recognize us for what we are." Grete's voice echoed through the tunnel, even if it was barely more than a whisper.

Else released her grip on his arm, and while she flung her cloak over her wings, Finn pulled up his hood to cover his face. When Else was finished, she glanced at him, and Finn didn't know why, but he pulled the Valkyrie into a hug, wrapping his arms carefully around her to avoid touching her wings. Else stiffened at first but then relaxed into him, letting out a soft breath as her arms circled his waist.

When Finn pulled back, Else winked at him. "Back to your usual ways, are you?"

Finn couldn't help the snort that escaped his lips. "I guess I am. Now, let's take on this stupid king."

When Else giggled, the others stared at them with wide eyes.

"You might want to take this seriously." Grete glared at them both, Sam mirroring her disapproving expression. "This is not a trial. This is war. And war is serious."

A shocked giggle escaped Aaron.

And that was that.

Finn and Else burst into laughter—nervous, hysterical, wheezing laughter, bringing Aaron with them until even Grete and Sam's lips curled.

"Please tell me you're not my rescue committee."

A hoarse, raspy voice sounded on the other side of the

door, and they quieted immediately, holding their breaths as Sam kicked the door open, sword raised.

Flaming red hair and piercing blue eyes stared back at them.

Josephine glared at them all before fixing her gaze on Finn, a flicker of recognition shining in the sky blue.

He offered her a small bow. "Rescue committee at your service."

Josephine only continued staring at him, the cellar quiet, only the chains binding her feet and hands rattling.

Finn stared right back, noting the similarities to her sister and the beauty they shared. But where Astrid had been timid and soft, Josephine was all hard lines and a lifted chin. Even dusty and bound, she kept her shoulders back, her gaze clear.

Steps rumbled above them, and they all jerked, Josephine paling and scrambling back against the wall she was chained to. Finn glanced at his friends as they straightened their backs and tightened their grips on their weapons.

But as he was about to speak, Sam interrupted him. "Get her out." He nodded at Josephine. "I will hold them off."

Finn began shaking his head when Sam continued. "They're coming for Seigard, are they not? You are needed there. Don't worry about me. It's time I did something, too."

When Finn met his eyes again, he knew there was no point in arguing. Only unwavering resolve filled Sam's brown eyes, something determined burning in them. So he nodded and reached out a hand to his friend.

"Be safe, Sam. And come back to us."

Sam inclined his head and sprinted up the stone stairway toward the steps that rang louder and louder.

95

Kian

Shock rippled through him when no sea breeze met him and Lillian as he rifted them to Finn. Shock that turned into unease as the smells of the capital, of people and food and horses and stone, washed over them.

Kian whipped his head around, narrowing his eyes as he stared at the dark castle of Echo. They'd landed behind the castle—where Nida's gilded cage had been, where he'd ripped those guards to death for threatening Lillian. Lillian, who now stood by his side, shadows twirling behind her eyes as she surveyed the empty courtyard and the dark windows of the castle.

"How did we end up here?" His mate stared at him questioningly.

Kian shook his head. "I feel Finn through our—your—bond, so I just let the bond take me to him. Apparently, he's left Seigard. Unless the two bonds got me confused."

Kian swore quietly, praying his senses hadn't led him astray. But there was little doubt in him that Finn was somewhere on Echo, somewhere in the castle. He could feel him, couldn't explain how, but he could sense his friend, the golden, pure kindness that was Finn's bond with Lillian somewhere on the island, somewhere in the capital.

The bond between Finn and Lillian was so different from his own bond with her. There was nothing soothing about the mating bond—it was pure wildfire, bristling, burning between them. Need that didn't fade even as they faced the danger ahead, that didn't fade even as fear licked their skin and apprehension shivered down their backs.

Kian couldn't stop himself from pulling Lillian close, from dragging his mouth across her neck, from letting his hands roam over her body as she let out a low sigh. Undiluted heat filled Lillian's eyes when she looked up at him, and without breaking their gaze, she softly brushed her lips against his. When his breath caught in his throat she offered him a small smile that nearly had his heart stopping.

"We need to get to Finn," she whispered, even as her hands wrapped in his hair, tugging him closer and sending shockwaves of pleasure through his body.

They definitely needed to, but it still took all of Kian's strength to pull away and gently remove Lillian's hands.

"I know. But now we have something to look forward to later," Kian winked.

Lillian rolled her eyes, but a smile pulled at her lips as she straightened her black jacket. When her gaze once again flitted across the empty courtyard, Kian prayed that there *would* be a later time for them to explore each other's bodies once more. That there be a later for him to love her, to be with her, to just *live* with her.

With a heavy heart, Kian gripped Lillian's hand in his. They slowly made their way around the castle, to the courtyard where he'd nearly died from shock upon finding Lillian standing amongst the novices for the trials, the sun reflecting in her bright white hair and her gray eyes sharp as they met his for the first time.

Already then, he would have done anything for her.

Would have burned the world to the ground for the

woman before him. But he'd done his best to push her away, to get her to leave and be safe.

Not that he'd been able to do it for long.

As soon as those lowlifes had hurt her… Kian snarled softly, remembering how he'd cut their throats, the fear in their eyes as he watched them die in that shady tavern. But he snapped out of it when worry slithered down the bond, and Lillian eyed him questioningly.

The silence in the courtyard was stifling. No guards were stationed outside the gates or along the dark walls, and his ears didn't pick up a sound as they made their way into the castle. Lillian's hand trembled when they walked through the double doors into the softly lit hallways.

"Do you feel him?" Kian whispered, wanting to ensure he wasn't the only one who felt the tug toward the cellar down into that musty, dark, wretched place.

Lillian looked back at him, her dark hair shimmering in the firelight and eyes steeled as she shifted her gaze toward the stone staircase.

I do. He's down there.

Kian didn't hide the shudder that danced along his spine as they descended the spiraling stairway.

96

Lillian

A scream that chilled her to her very bones broke through the darkness when they descended. And when it cut off after only a second, Lillian's heart nearly beat out of her chest. Kian also tensed beside her, releasing her hand to draw his sword. With a glance at him, Lillian unsheathed two daggers at her thighs, her wings twitching as they walked further and further down the spiraling staircase.

As Lillian was about to take the next step, Kian's arm slammed into her chest, and she stilled, barely breathing.

Soft steps approached them. There wasn't a hurry to the gait, no indication the person knew she and Kian were mere seconds away. Glancing at Kian, she gripped her daggers tightly, a jolt of pain rippling through her heart as she thought of Eli, the look he'd given her when she'd last been in this stairway.

But as her mate's green eyes fell on hers, the love and resolve in them steadied her. She smiled at him before fixing her eyes on the dark stairs below, the flickering firelight shining its soft light on the next four steps.

Blonde hair came into view, and then a tall, muscular man

dressed in black leathers, gripping a sword tightly in his fist, stared at them.

"Sam," Lillian breathed before jumping two steps down and wrapping her arms around her friend.

"Sam," she whispered again as his arms tightened around her, his body softly shaking from the chuckle he let out.

"I, too, am glad to see you here," Sam whispered.

Lillian snickered, remembering the first embrace she'd offered him. When she pulled back, Kian replaced her, pulling Sam into a tight hug as well—words she couldn't pick up passing between the two men.

When they pulled apart, Sam offered them a small smile. "You arrived just in time. We freed Josephine—and were just about to get out of here. I'll take you to the others so we can get the hell off this island."

They followed him down to the cellar levels, into the suffocating darkness that ripped the air from their lungs. Still, a small ember of warmth filled Lillian as she followed her friend with her mate behind her.

Perhaps it would all work out. If they were all together, there was a small chance that they'd be all right, that they'd be able to take on the king and his army.

Even win.

Light flooded the stairway as they descended, so different from when Lillian had last visited the cellars, when only one lantern had shone its light onto the children there.

The children who were no longer.

Lillian swallowed hard against the guilt and shame that ate at her at the thought of Emile, of the young boy who hadn't been able to rise but whose cries were etched into her mind.

This time, she'd get everyone out.

"So we meet again."

Kian pulled her behind him so fast that her wings scratched against the hard stone lining the stairway, and she hissed softly when he pressed her against the wall, his body shielding her from view.

Sam frantically spun around, his eyes wide as he met Lillian's.

But the King's Guard was too fast.

Two guards instantly appeared, dragging Sam into the brightly lit cellar. The light, Lillian realized, came from the king himself, from the fire burning around him like an angry flickering shadow, floating embers from it sparking in the wet air of the circular cellar floor.

Kian turned as if to drag them both up—as if to rift them out of there, but Lillian snarled at him when his magic filled the air.

"We will not leave him." She stared Kian down, let her gray eyes burn with the same intensity his green eyes usually did.

We can take him on, Kian. Together, remember?

A low laugh rumbled behind them.

"She has so much power over you, son. Such a disappointment. You are no Crown Prince of mine. You're a mere follower."

Lillian's lip curled back over her sharp teeth, a rumble filling her chest as she stared over Kian's shoulder at the king.

But Kian didn't tear his eyes from hers, begging, pleading with her. *Lillian, leave. I will get Sam out. Please, do this for me.*

She slowly shook her head, even as she could feel the desperation within him flowing freely between them. *I'm not running anymore. We are taking him down now. Together.*

She smiled at him then, a genuine smile, but she also let a hint of her power shine through, a lick of darkness curling at her lips, and her smile widened as she embraced it— welcomed it.

She was in control, and she would use her damned power to take out the evil of this world. To wipe that smug smile off the king's face.

When starlight flickered behind Kian's green eyes in response, Lillian playfully wrinkled her nose. *It's almost too cute how our magics complement each other.*

Kian snorted—a beautiful, sincere sound. A sound she'd savor forever.

Let's kill this bastard.

Kian rolled his eyes, but finally, he offered Lillian his hand.

And together, they stepped into the firelight.

97

Kian

King Alek. His father, or not father, smiled coldly at them as they took the final step into the cellar room. Several guards were posted around the room, a few whom Kian recognized. Commander Eirik's eyes widened slightly when Kian met them, but the way he gripped Sam tightly told him Eirik would be no friend tonight.

Eirik had been stationed on Hindra—he and Kian had basically grown up together—and he knew deep down that Eirik was a good man. He'd grown up poor, an orphan roaming the streets, before one of the guard's wives took mercy on him and took him in. Kian and Eirik had explored their teens and early adulthood together—had learned how to fight and drunk their first ale with one another.

But none of that mattered tonight.

No. Eirik's blue eyes remained cast down as Kian and Lillian strode into the circular space, holding onto each other tightly while darkness and light vibrated around them, the air heavy from magic.

"If it isn't the son that stabbed me in the back. Literally." Alek raised his brows at the magic swirling around them. "And his half-breed mate who has all of Orios squealing."

Alek cast a lazy glance at Lillian. "I don't see it. You're supposed to be the almighty queen, the heir, fulfilling the long-lost prophecy. But you're just average, aren't you? A scared girl who hides behind others to do her bidding, like you did in the trials?"

Lillian's body vibrated from the snarl that escaped her throat. Holding onto her hand was all Kian could do when she lunged for the king, darkness whipping out to meet the flames flickering over Alek's palms.

Alek laughed softly, eyeing Lillian once more. "Perhaps you've learned a thing or two. But we all know how this will end." He flicked his green eyes to Kian. "With you and my son dead. And me ruling over all of Orios."

Thrumming power surged through Kian, anger, or perhaps fear, indulging his magic, allowing it to brim to the surface, illuminating his skin, and brightening his eyes.

King Alek blinked, the only emotion he would ever show.

But it was enough for Kian. He let the starlight shine bright, replacing the orange glow of the cellar with a silvery one, and gripped Lillian's hand tighter, awe filling him as her darkness met his light—as their magic fused to one.

Starlight and night tangled together, pulsating through the room and easily squashing the flames that Alek flared to meet it. Sam and the guards were pushed up against the walls, hiding them from view, only their screams as they were trapped behind them breaking through.

Kian couldn't hold back a grin when their magic filled the entire cellar, making it seem like the standoff was taking place in the night sky itself, winking stars the only thing lighting the room.

"I think you might be wrong about what will happen tonight." Lillian flashed her teeth at Alek. "Your useless son, and our average magic will kill you."

Kian turned his head to her and met those sparkling gray eyes. The intensity in them nearly made him stumble back, and he lost his breath as he realized how much he loved this female.

His woman.

His mate.

His Queen.

Her eyes asked him a question.

He inclined his head.

Together.

They both blew a breath, their hands still in a tight grip, letting their magic fuse into an ancient, wild power that had the guards outside it sprinting into the dark tunnels surrounding the room.

"Together, Kian," Lillian whispered.

They turned their gaze toward the king, their combined magic vibrating, surging through the room. Alek's eyes widened, fear lining his features as the wall of fire he put up evaporated.

Again.

And again.

Kian allowed himself a smug smile when Lillian squeezed his hand. *Let's end this now.*

And then Kian let go completely. Allowed himself to become one with the starlight as Lillian became one with her darkness, their magic roaring beneath the castle, rushing for the king—the night eager to turn into a new day.

He glanced at his mate, and Lillian grinned at him within the shadows, reaching out to pull him into her arms as she cast a final glance at the king. Their magic swept toward him, surrounding him, preparing to end him.

Kian could only make out Alek's bulging eyes as he realized what was happening, how his fire was useless against their combined force. The king fell to his knees, hissing when their magic closed in, the swirling funnel ready to obliterate Alek from this realm.

Not wishing to spend one more moment of his life looking

into those hateful eyes, Kian locked eyes with his mate again, letting his love for her shine through. They'd done it.

But then Lillian's eyes widened.

Not from fear or anger.

But from shock.

Pure, undiluted shock that rippled through him and shook him to his core as Sam lazily strolled in between them and the king.

With a wave of his hand, their magic evaporated into nothing.

98

Finn

They rushed through the dark tunnel, Finn dragging Josephine behind him, when a wave of shock and betrayal, followed by fear, crashed into his chest.

Not just from Lillian but from Kian, from them both.

Fear like Finn had only felt once before.

Fear he'd only felt when Eli held the knife to his throat, and Lillian's screams echoed between the mountaintops as she tried to reach him in time.

Finn stopped in his tracks, pulling Josephine with him. Dust and grime swirled around them as his boots dug into the soft ground, and he barely noticed when she slammed into his back, hissing at him.

"What's happening?" Else was instantly at his side, her blue eyes flitting between his, worry lining every feature of her face.

Finn tried to rein in the surging emotions inside him, panting as he responded, "Lillian and Kian are back there. And something is wrong. Very wrong."

He could barely stand it, couldn't stand the oily betrayal reverberating down the bond. He whipped his head around and stared down the dark tunnel they'd just escaped through, then back to the soft light from the open bookshelf in Astrid's old homestead. He could almost hear Lillian's anguish, the soft cry of despair escaping her lips.

Silver girl! Lillian!

Nothing.

Lillian, what's happening?

Nothing.

Desperately, he turned to Else, to Aaron and Grete, who hovered right behind the blond Valkyrie.

"I need to go back." Finn sucked in a breath as another wave of dread rolled through him. "I need to go back. Now!" he cried.

"I'll come with you," Aaron stepped around his aunt.

"No!" Grete snarled. "You're leaving. That's an order, Aaron."

"You're not my queen," Aaron said quietly. "If Lillian is in danger, I am going. You cannot stop me."

Finn shook his head, starting toward where they'd just left, barely able to get any air into his lungs from the weight pressing on his chest. "We don't have time for this. I am going alone."

He snapped his eyes to Else, jerking his head toward Josephine who leaned against the tunnel wall, her face pale as she whipped it back and forth. Nodding, Else quickly lifted a kicking Josephine into her arms, sprinting down the tunnel.

But when he began running back toward his queen, he wasn't alone.

Aaron's labored breaths brushed his shoulder, and Grete's quiet swearing joined him on the other side. And while cold dread thrummed with every step he took, he still managed to offer them each a grateful smile.

He had a feeling they'd need every single person they could spare.

99

Lillian

"Sam?" Her voice shook as she stared at her friend.

"Get up," Sam sneered as he ordered the still-kneeling king to stand.

"You're absolutely useless," he spat when Alek rose on shaky legs, his black uniform rumpled and dusty. There was nothing of the warmth she'd come to know in Sam's voice, only ice-cold authority filling it.

"Sam, what's going on?" Kian asked quietly, tightening his grip on her hand as he began pulling her toward the staircase.

"Ah, we can't have that."

With another wave of Sam's hand, Lillian was slung into the cellar wall, Kian's hand ripping from hers as he was hurled into the wall opposite her.

She locked eyes with him across the floor, realization dawning on his face at the same time as the thought speared through her.

No.

He couldn't be.

"Adeon?" Lillian whispered, her lips barely moving, unwilling to believe the name leaving her.

"You're not entirely stupid, then." The corners of Sam's

lips curled into a glacial smile. "Ah, to finally shed this unworthy body."

Lillian and Kian were once again pushed against the walls when bright light exploded through the room, blinding them both for a moment before it vanished just as quickly as it appeared.

In Sam's place stood a beautiful man, taller than Sam by a foot and a half, with raven hair, gleaming green eyes, and skin that glowed softly even in the dim light. His face was pure perfection, with chiseled features and unmarred skin apart from a small burn mark above his left eye, like a silver flame that licked the skin toward his temple.

Ancient power flowed from the man, more potent and untamed than even hers and Kian's magic combined. It filled the cellar, pounding against her skin and making every nerve inside flicker.

Adeon snapped his fingers, and the too-small Valkyrie leathers that stretched across his tall frame were replaced by a flowing green robe over a white tunic and breeches. The weapons he'd had strapped to his back and his waist fell, clattering to the floor, and Adeon pushed them aside without batting an eye.

Lillian snapped her gaze to Kian, his face frozen as he stared at Adeon, but when he felt her eyes on him, he turned his head. Despair, fear, and betrayal filled her; the same feelings mirrored in the eyes of the man she loved.

Her skin prickled with agony, tears burning behind her eyes as she realized how stupid they'd been to think it would be that easy, that they'd be able to walk out of this together. She'd known Adeon would come for her. But Sam... She choked on a silent sob.

I love you, Lillian. Don't give up yet.

Despite his words, she could feel the same despair inside Kian, the one drawback of their bond, and his eyes fell when he realized it. Despair that knew no bounds when they tried to draw on their magic, and there was nothing. Chills raced across her spine when she realized her veins were as empty as they had been before she'd broken the curse.

"Well, you must have many questions for me." Adeon picked at his nails, unbothered as he ripped Lillian from her thoughts. "Go ahead, I'll entertain you."

"How long," Kian demanded, his voice revealing nothing of the turmoil she could sense within him.

"Ah, great question, Kian!" Adeon clapped his hands excitedly, the echoes slamming against Lillian's ears, pulsating in rhythm with her terrified heart.

"I intercepted dear Sam in the port of Echo before the trials even began. It took some time to fully take over his mind, though. He fought hard; he must have been quite a brave young man."

When Adeon gestured to the floor behind him, where King Alek leaned against the wall with a smirk on his face, Lillian gasped. Sam's unmoving body lay crumpled on the floor, his limbs bent at unnatural angles as if he'd taken a great fall.

"Why?" Lillian couldn't keep the emotion out of her voice, her throat constricting as she shot a glance around the room, trying to find a way out.

Out of the corner of her eye she noticed Kian do the same, his blazing gaze flicking between the dark tunnels leading further into the cellar and her own eyes.

"Mm, another excellent question, my dear Lillian." Adeon offered her a blinding smile, emphasizing his unnatural beauty. "You didn't really think I didn't know you were alive, did you?"

He let out a cold, deep laugh that struck her like a cold fist through her gut.

"I've been watching you your entire life, Lillian. I saw you nearly succumb to the unfortunate side effects of my curse, and we couldn't have that, could we? You are one of my children, after all. So, I gave Atli and Alek a nudge to set it all in motion, to see if you'd succeed where your parents didn't."

Lillian could barely breathe; only Kian's unwavering eyes, locked on hers, kept her standing.

"What does Alek have to do with it?" Kian got out through gritted teeth, his body trembling from anger.

Lillian tried to let his anger fuel her own, and when Adeon tilted his head and offered Kian a cruel twist of his mouth, it wasn't hard. Raw energy crackled under her skin, threatening to erupt as Adeon took a step closer to him. When a warning growl left her throat, Adeon paused, his grin widening.

Pointing to Lillian, Adeon responded. "For that exact reason, dear Kian. Since you've managed to unlock some of your powers, I expect you know that you're not entirely human?"

Kian didn't answer, his nostrils flaring as he glared at the god.

"I'll take that as confirmation." Adeon nodded to himself. "Well, nephew…"

Kian and Lillian sliced their gazes at each other.

At least he's not my father.

Lillian couldn't force her lips to curl the slightest bit, her brows crashing together as pieces began falling together, even before Adeon continued.

"Yes, my stupid brother fell in love with your mother. A god and a mere human?" Adeon shuddered, his lips curling into a sneer. "And then she fell pregnant. Tsk tsk, we couldn't have that. Fray tried to hide you from me, but he's always been weak, and it didn't take me long to find you. And imagine my surprise when I realized what you were! The mate to the newly orphaned Valkyrie queen."

King Alek stirred behind Adeon, and the god spun around. "Did I say you could move? Stay where you are, human."

Alek's wide eyes flitted from Kian to Lillian, the information apparently news to him as well.

Adeon stretched his arms over his head, sighing. "So good to be back in my own skin. Where was I? Ah, yes! So, of course, I needed to ensure your paths would cross. I knew you would seek out Alek at some point, Lillian. If not for revenge for your own parents for the adorable little rebel cause Atli led. So I just needed to ensure Kian would be there when you did. And where better to place him than with the king himself? After I killed your mother, and I have to say she fought me hard, I bound your powers and took you to Alek making sure he believed you were his son."

Lillian didn't dare take her eyes off Adeon as he began strolling around the room, his hands casually clasped behind his back as he smugly eyed them both.

"And then I waited for you both to grow up. It was a few boring years, but I had Fray to entertain me when the day-to-day became too dreadful." He shot Kian a sideways look. "Yes, your father is still alive. It's certainly difficult to kill a god, although we bleed and scream like any other creature."

Wait Kian!

She felt him prepare to lunge, her words hurriedly tumbling down the bond, snapping him out of the blinding rage. Fury consumed her as well, a red haze overtaking her vision, her hands shaking by her side as she narrowed her eyes at the god.

Adeon lifted a perfectly manicured brow, but they both stayed planted, albeit shaking.

Adeon hummed to himself, winking when Lillian couldn't hold back another snarl. "When I couldn't bother to wait any longer, I got Atli to sacrifice himself—a beautiful plan if I do say so myself, although I thought your taste for revenge would be a bit stronger, Lillian. You forgave *Commander Atlas* so quickly for not managing to save your father. Not very Valkyrie of you."

He wagged his finger at her before he went on. "I wanted to stay close to make sure you didn't die another way, so I took Sam's body to keep tabs on you both. And I'll be honest. I did instigate a little bit: tipping Astrid off that you were the Valkyrie heir was easy, and giving Eli the idea to kill her, putting the blame on the commander so she didn't ruin his plan—even easier! I even tried to get Alek to pit you against each other in that final trial, making you choose between Finn and Kian. Brilliant, no? But my efforts kept failing, and what I didn't count on was that your feelings for Eli were real, Lillian. Imagine my surprise when *he* helped you break the curse."

Adeon sighed deeply. "I won't make that same mistake again. This time, your *mate* needs to die for either of you to get your powers back."

When Kian's eyes found hers again, they only stared at each other, grief already pooling inside them.

That's why their magic didn't work—Adeon had cursed them.

Again.

100

Finn

Grete and Aaron stared at him with rounded eyes from where they hovered behind the hidden door. Finn didn't know how to process the information, couldn't fathom that Sam had been Adeon all this time.

How could he have missed it? There had been signs—Sam disappearing so often during the trials and at Volantis, his curiosity as he studied the Valkyries, his reluctance to find the dragons.

But why had he helped them get Josephine out?

Finn ground his teeth when he glimpsed Lillian through the door, the pure devastation on her face as she refused to let her eyes leave Kian's.

"What should we do?" he whispered, praying that Grete, the only one who'd dealt with Adeon before, would have an idea.

But when the Valkyrie's head fell forward, her shoulders slumping, the little hope he'd had vanished into nothing, and a dark pit of anguish opened in his gut.

"We have to do *something*," Aaron snarled, his face twisted with fear but there was also resolve in his blue eyes when Finn shifted his gaze to him. "We can't just stand here and watch him kill them."

Finn's heart flew into his throat when Adeon spoke again, his voice booming through the dark tunnel.

"Like I don't know you're standing there, young Valkyrie. And I shall not kill them. They will kill each other. At least one of them. Come on out. You're welcome to watch."

Grete tried to push Aaron to run, shielding him with her body as she hissed at him to go, to get out of there, but her back shot straight when Adeon laughed.

"If he runs, I will have the tunnel come down upon him, my dear Grete. Come on now. We used to be such good friends, you and I. I'd like to formally introduce myself to the Valkyrie you've taken as a son."

Fury flared in Grete's eyes when she slowly turned toward the small crack, where dim light sifted through, dancing over her black leathers. Her jaw clenched so hard Finn could hear her teeth clattering together as she slowly pushed the door open and stepped in first, her hand fisting Aaron's jacket as she pulled him behind her.

When Finn lifted his foot to step over the threshold, he sent a prayer to Thoras, to any of the gods, to please help them get out of this. But the world around them remained quiet as he strode into the room, his shoulders back and eyes fixed on Lillian's.

"Hello, Finn." A cold smile played on Adeon's lips when Finn turned in his direction.

"Hello, bastard," Finn nodded back to the god, swiftly making his way to Lillian and taking up the spot by her side.

Shifting his eyes to Kian's for a moment, he dipped his head imperceptibly at the gratitude that shone there as Finn hovered a half-step before her.

Adeon chuckled darkly. "I'm surprised you didn't figure it out, Finn. The familiar bonds were given by the gods, after all. Only a god could block your connection. Although, I have to say Thoras is clever. I couldn't sever it completely, only block you from communicating with each other."

Finn's eyes widened for a moment before he could lock down his features, and he cursed silently when Adeon laughed louder.

A small hand slipped into his and squeezed softly. "I missed you, Finn. I'm sorry for all of this."

When he turned his head over his shoulder and met his best friend's gray eyes, tears lined them, and a single heart-breaking one snaked its way down her dusty cheek, leaving a soft trail behind.

He squeezed her hand back and whispered, "Don't you dare apologize to me, silver girl. I told you once I'd be honored to die for you. That still stands."

He ripped his gaze from hers when a whimper left her throat, couldn't stand seeing her face crumble, or he'd start crying as well.

But he meant every word.

He would die for her if it came to that. Not just because of the familiar bond but because he loved her. He'd die for every single one of his friends in this room—even Grete. They were family now, and like his parents and brothers, he'd do anything for them.

As if she sensed his thoughts Grete's eyes flew to his, something in her gaze hardening as she stepped forward, slamming Aaron into the wall behind her as he tried to follow.

"Adeon, isn't it time to end this? Lillian didn't start this, and she shouldn't be paying a debt her parents owed." Grete glanced at Lillian, her eye twitching the only sign of the nerves Finn was sure filled her.

Adeon tilted his head, his black hair falling over his shoul-der. "But that's where you're wrong, Grete. She should be paying that debt. Isn't that what we all do in the end? Pay for our parents' mistakes? I mean, look at yourself: your parents named Liv heir, not you. The softer, kinder of the two of you. I think the world would be quite different had you ruled, don't you think? And look at Kian: his father was too weak to protect his own son, so now Kian will pay. Perhaps with his life."

Finn met Kian's gaze again across the room, narrowing his eyes when Kian tried to mouth something. But as Adeon spoke again, he jerked his head back to where the god inched closer to Grete.

The Valkyrie didn't cower when Adeon closed the final distance between them; she only angled her head to continue meeting his eyes with her defiant blue ones, her hands clenched into fists by her sides.

Finn's stomach flipped when Adeon lifted a hand and gently caressed her cheek with one of his long fingers. "You were always a true fighter," he mumbled. "Too bad…"

Screams filled the cellar when Adeon's hand gently wrapped around Grete's neck, the sharp snap of broken bones drowning in the desperate sounds.

Aaron's face contorted into a mask of pure pain and rage, and the Valkyrie lunged for Adeon, but the god only flicked his hand, and Aaron flew back into the wall, his lifeless body collapsing onto the stone floor.

When Adeon released Grete, her body fell into a heap by his feet, her eyes still filled with defiance, even in death.

"Rest gently, winged warrior," Adeon mumbled before brushing his hands over his robes and turning toward Lillian, his eyes cold as he announced, "And that's what will happen to every single one in this room until you stab your mate through the heart. Or he yours, although from the look in his eyes, I'd say that's unlikely."

Every ounce of warmth from Finn's body bled onto the cold stone floor when Adeon slowly turned his gaze to him, his green eyes drilling into his soul.

"But Lillian… The shifter is next."

101

Lillian

A storm of emotions raged in Kian's eyes, mirroring the turmoil inside her. She refused to look at Adeon. Wouldn't waste another second of her life on his worthless soul.

Without breaking their gaze, she tugged on Finn's hand, forcing him behind her. Kian's eyes flitted between her and Finn, then settled on her again, his gaze unwavering. When Lillian lifted her chin, Kian set his jaw.

I'm not letting him get away with this. She jerked her chin toward Finn. *He will not die for me. I won't allow it.*

Kian's eyes widened, and he started to shake his head, but she tore her eyes away before the pain in his face could change her mind.

"Do you know what the problem is with gods, Adeon?" Lillian squeezed Finn's hand, meeting his panicked stare for a brief moment over her shoulder before she released him and strode into the middle of the cellar floor.

"Lillian, don't." Kian's voice was soft, as if he knew that any urgency on his part would only speed up what she was planning to do. "Lillian, look at me. Don't. Please."

She couldn't look at him.

There was no way she could meet those loving eyes again

because then she might just choose to be selfish and sacrifice yet another friend for a few more moments alive with Kian, for a few more moments breathing the same air as him.

Realization dawned on her then. This was why Tyr had sent them through these challenges, why Nida had urged her to listen to what wasn't said. So she wouldn't be selfish and choose the path her parents had, leaving Orios and everyone in it vulnerable once more.

She and Kian were the only ones who could stop Adeon. And they could only do so if at least one of them had their magic.

Keeping her eyes on Adeon, she forced her voice to remain steady. "See, the problem with believing you are superior to everyone else is that you end up alone. And because you're a lonely, lonely being, you underestimate what we *less* superior beings are willing to sacrifice for those we love."

Lillian flicked the dagger in her hand, letting her finger drag across the sharp edge until a small drop of blood formed on her fingertip. The cellar was so quiet she swore the soft sound of it landing on the stone reverberated in the entire castle.

Adeon glared at her, "If you kill yourself, you're taking him with you."

"Ah, but not if I break the bond."

Lillian held up her hand when Adeon opened his mouth, blocking out the horrible sound leaving Kian.

Forcing her broken heart to stay together just a little while longer, she continued. "See, I didn't put it together until you told us who Kian's father was."

When Adeon's face blanched, Lillian offered him a small smile.

"Yes, that probably wasn't your best move, was it? I'd wondered why you targeted my parents when there had been so many strong Valkyries and mates before. But it was because my father was also a demi-god, wasn't it? He must have been, wielding the sun itself."

Adeon's mouth set into a thin line, and Lillian nodded. "And since Valkyries are demi-gods by birth, with a father that was also a demi-god, that would make me three-quarters of a god. And that's what scares you, isn't it? I am more god than anything else, which in turn means that I can break the bond."

Everything inside her screamed at her to stop, to wait, when she slowly turned to Kian, her gaze fixed on his boots. But even so, she couldn't escape the desperation flowing through him to her or her to him.

"I'm so sorry," she whispered, letting go of the self-imposed barrier she'd put up against her power, feeling it tear through her veins, roaring between her ears.

Then she was tackled to the floor, her face slamming into the hard stone as Finn's body covered her.

I can't let you do this. I love you, my dark queen.

"No! Let me go!" Lillian elbowed Finn and gouged her nails down his arms until the smell of iron filled the air around them.

"Kian! I will *never* forgive you. Do you hear me? Kian!"

Her sobs shook her body as Finn pressed her further into the cold floor. Wheezing, she managed to lift her bloodied face enough to meet Kian's eyes under Finn's outstretched arm.

Her mate smiled at her, even as silver filled his eyes.

I won't apologize for this. I promise I will find you again. But until then, keep fighting, Lillian. Let the world see that fire within you. Burn it down if you must. But then rebuild it. Make it a better place.

"No! Kian! No!" Her scream echoed between the stone walls, taunting her as Kian raised a dagger, its blade reflecting his green eyes.

With a final look at her, Kian drove it into his own heart.

102

Lillian

Lillian screamed, the chilling sound not once reverberating within the stone chamber.

As if the pain was too great.

As if the loss was too much to repeat.

The mating bond snapped.

A harsh, biting, bitter snap that should have shaken the world.

Her vision went black. Midnight black. No stars danced behind her eyelids. No light lit up the darkness. She barely registered Finn shifting off her, or the sobs that wracked his body, or the grunt of pain he let out as her pain slammed into him.

Her mouth snapped shut. Dragging herself across the floor, she made her way to Kian's lifeless body. Cradling his head into her lap, she stroked his beautiful onyx hair, down his cheeks, to the mouth she'd kissed only a few moments ago.

"You promised…" Her voice broke. "You… You promised never to leave me. You promised, Kian." She hiccupped as the pain became unbearable. "You lied to me! You lied—" Another scream escaped her lips at the darkness in his eyes.

She couldn't stand it.

Couldn't stand him lying there; his black hair fanned out over her leathers, his chest unmoving as blood pooled beneath him.

No, it was unacceptable.

She would fix this.

Panting, Lillian forced herself up, gently stroking Kian's cheek once more. The red haze that had clouded her vision since Adeon killed Grete turned crimson, pulsating as she fixed her eyes on the god.

Adeon leaned against the wall, his lips slightly curved as he eyed her. "Not exactly how I expected that to turn out, I must say. But I guess the outcome is the same. Now, you can stop your silly missions and take your rightful place by my side. I'll even let you kill the king, should you like."

Behind him, Alek stood frozen, his face pale as he stared at Adeon's back. Aaron moaned on the floor, pushing himself up with a hand, his eyes wide as he took in the scene before him.

"Aaron, Finn, get behind me. Now."

Lillian snarled when they didn't move fast enough. "I said now!"

She didn't meet either's eyes as they passed her, only gestured for them to back up when they hovered too close to her.

Adeon cocked his head. "And what will you do now, dear Lillian?"

"Now, I kill you."

Closing her eyes, she fully let go—didn't allow herself to worry if her magic killed everyone in Echo when she threw it out. Lillian let darkness fill the world, let every broken part of her, every moment of pain, of sorrow, of heartbreak fuel it. But she also let love embed itself in it, a cry leaving her lips as she let every moment with Kian, every moment with Eli, every moment with Atli, every moment with Astrid fill her mind, stoking the flames of darkness around her.

Thunder rumbled above them, and Lillian felt the sky

itself roar out her pain as lightning flashed and booms echoed all over Orios.

She felt it then, the control she hadn't believed she possessed.

She was one with the darkness, and it wasn't evil at all.

It wasn't anything but power to be molded.

And she would wield it.

Opening her eyes, her hair flowed around her, her wings beating in rhythm with her heart. Curling her lips, she stared straight into Adeon's eyes and took a step toward him.

The god staggered.

Her crazed smile widened as she took another step. Adeon waved his hands, but when he did little more than whirl the darkness around, Lillian let out a humorless laugh. "Another problem with gods? You overestimate your own ability."

Lillian lifted her hands, ready to crush him, when Adeon arched a brow. "Perhaps, but we have also had time to train our abilities far longer than you."

And with a snap of his fingers, Adeon disappeared.

"Come back, you coward!" Lillian sprinted to the spot where Adeon had stood, falling to her knees and slamming her hands against the floor when there wasn't a whisper of him.

Tilting her head to the sky, she screamed, "I will find you, Adeon. I will search every inch of this realm, and the next, and the next, and the next until I do. And when I do... You will wish you'd never even thought of creating us."

The sky boomed in response, a deafening crack of thunder echoing Lillian's primal roar, shaking the entire castle from its highest tower to the very foundation beneath their feet.

103

Finn

He couldn't move as the darkness seeped back into Lillian, could only watch as she yet again crawled to Kian's cold body, pulling his head into her lap and whispering words Finn didn't dare try to make out.

The castle rumbled around them, rubble and debris falling down as it kept shaking, the walls creaking as they shifted.

The castle was coming down.

Finn didn't allow the panic within him to fester as he dragged Aaron with him to Lillian's side.

"Lillian, we need to go." Finn gently gripped her shoulder.

When she shook her head, Finn gripped her bloodied chin, wincing when he realized the force in which he'd slammed into her had split open her brow and left a deep cut across her cheek, the blood still dripping down her neck.

"Silver girl, the castle is breaking. We'll die if we stay here. K—" Finn swallowed. "He wouldn't want you to die here."

Lillian's eyes were black, no trace of gray left, when she locked them on his, quietly studying him. It wasn't until a piece of rubble fell onto Kian's body that her chin dipped, and she rose, lifting Kian into her arms.

"I can carry him, my queen," Aaron said gently, his eyes darting between her and Finn.

"No." Lillian didn't look back as she walked toward the stairs.

"You forgot about me, half-breed."

As heat flared behind them, raw fear clawed at his throat, but Lillian didn't even turn her head as she responded, "No, I didn't. I think beheading is swift enough for a king, don't you?"

A lash of darkness surged over Finn's head, forming into a lethal blade and slashing across the king's neck. Alek's head fell onto the floor with a soft thump, his mouth still open in surprise.

And so the king was no more.

"Come."

Lillian placed her foot on the first step, and Finn choked on a sob at seeing her small frame carry Kian, at how his feet nearly dragged on the floor. But he didn't dare say anything when he and Aaron fell into step with her as she led them up the stairs, through the quaking castle, and out into the courtyard.

As soon as they'd taken the final step onto the pebbled ground, the castle bellowed, caving in on itself. Whirling around, Finn watched as the ground opened and swallowed the castle in its entirety, leaving a heap of broken stone and boulders where the proud castle had once stood, taking the bodies they'd left behind with it.

Turning back toward Lillian, a choked sound escaped his throat at the hundreds of dragons that lined the courtyard, some perched on top of the rooftops facing them, some on top of the stone wall.

And his eyes widened when dozens of giants stomped into view, marching through the metal gates and gathering to the left of the squared courtyard. Terrified human eyes filled the windows of the homes lining the road before them, and haunted whispers rose across the slanted town.

Lillian didn't falter. She walked right into the middle of the grounds and gently laid Kian down on the stone before she rose again, her back straight and face hard.

Come here, Finn.

When Lillian's voice finally rang in his mind again, it was all he could do to put one foot in front of the other. As he reached her side, he put a hand on her shoulder, and she cast him a quick glance before facing the town and the creatures before them.

"King Alek is dead."

Lillian waited for a beat before continuing, her eyes traveling over the dragons, giants, and the few humans who'd dared leave their homes.

"Orios has a new queen. As of this moment, I, Lillian Volantis, accept the throne and the duties of being queen. My first act as regent is to release all prisoners kept by Alek and allow all creatures who were banned from Echo and Hindra to return should they like to."

Lillian nudged Finn forward, but his eyes were still glued to her as she continued. "Finn here is my Hand. He will communicate the other changes that are to happen around here. Until then, spread the word."

Lillian waved her hand dismissively, dropping to her knees beside Kian's body once more, not even lifting her head when the giants first, then the dragons, and after a bit of hesitation, the humans bowed to her and spoke as one.

"All hail Queen Lillian."

Lillian

Lillian pulled the upper half of Kian's body into her lap, not caring that the giants wanted to speak to her, not giving one shit about Tyr's voice rumbling in her mind, and definitely not worrying about the humans who filled the streets.

Aaron took it upon himself to drive everyone away from the courtyard until she could only make out the beatings of wings in the air and the soft steps of giants and humans as they walked down the slanted road. How, she didn't care. Even if he killed someone for them to leave her alone, she wouldn't punish him.

For hours, she sat under the starless sky, her mind blank as she softly stroked Kian's hair. When the sun started rising, the orange light casting long shadows on the ground, Finn dropped down next to her and gently touched her cheek. She lifted her eyes to his, the amber in them burning like the sun behind him.

"You have to say goodbye, Lillian." Tears spilled down his golden cheeks, and she reached out to wipe one away with her thumb.

"No, Finn." Lillian brushed her fingers through Kian's hair again. "This isn't goodbye."

She felt the uncertainty, the worry that her mind had gone flowing from him as he whispered, "He's dead, Lillian. There is nothing you can do. There is nothing anyone can do."

"That's where you are wrong, too." Lillian let her divine magic fill her once more, and Finn nearly stumbled at whatever he saw flickering in her eyes. "I am a *god*. And I will bring him back."

She didn't wait for Finn's response as she pressed her lips to Kian's forehead.

"You told me once I wouldn't burn this world down, Kian. But I will rip this world apart, destroy it shred for shred until I find you. Until you are back in my arms."

An answering jagged bolt of lightning tore across the clear morning sky, its roar rippling through the realms and resounding across the land, shaking the very foundations of the world.

Acknowledgments

I have to start by thanking you, the reader. Thank you for supporting me, and for sharing the love for the Echo Series with me.

To my Beta readers, thank you for taking the time to help me bring Echo of Deceit to the next level. Your kindness and support has made this process more fun than I could ever imagine.

To Aimee, my editor. Thank you for always patiently answering my questions and providing guidance when I am stuck.

To Amanda, my friend and fellow lover of fantasy. Thank you for always brainstorming with me, and for being the kindest soul throughout this process.

To Michael, my husband. Thank you for letting me hole up in my writing den, and letting me obsess over my stories day in and day out.